About the Author

Mable Caldwell is a teenage American author who was raised in the states of Florida and Kansas. Growing up, Mable loved writing and creating stories of her own. At the age of fifteen, Mable decided to finally take her writing to the next level and write her first-ever novel, *The Dangers of Chemistry*. Now, thanks to tons of love and support, Mable's novel is out and ready to be read by all.

The Dangers of Chemistry

Mable Caldwell

The Dangers of Chemistry

Olympia Publishers
London

www.olympiapublishers.com
OLYMPIA PAPERBACK EDITION

A CIP catalogue record for this title is
available from the British Library.

ISBN: 978-1-80074-783-8

This is a work of fiction.
Names, characters, places and incidents originate from the writer's
imagination. Any resemblance to actual persons, living or dead, is
purely coincidental.

First Published in 2023

Olympia Publishers
Tallis House
2 Tallis Street
London
EC4Y 0AB

Printed in Great Britain

Dedication

I dedicate this book to Cookie, my dog.

Acknowledgements

Thanks to my mom and dad for their endless love and support. I know I couldn't have done this without them. Thanks to all my friends and other family who kept my hopes up and reassured me anytime I was down. Thanks to my mom and grandma for reading my manuscript and letting me know that it was truly something. Thanks to Ailecia for taking my amazing headshot; I couldn't have done any better. And finally, thank you to my pets for sitting by my side during the long and stressful writing and editing nights, I couldn't have done it without you.

Chapter 1

Emma Grace, the most beautiful girl at South Ray High. Everything about her is perfect, her long silky hair, her crystal blue eyes, and her flawless skin. She's amazing in every way; any guy would kill to be able to say that she is theirs. I would do almost anything for Emma Grace just to notice me, say my name, or just give me one of her angelic smiles.

"Maybe if you stare at her long enough, she'll duplicate."

"Ezra!" I said as I jumped back.

"Fifth scare of the week, I think it's a new record," Ezra said, sounding accomplished.

"You enjoy such stupid things in life," I said.

"Stupid things are simply the best things in life," She explained.

Ezra truly did enjoy some of the small stupid things in life. I've figured that out over the many years we've known each other. She is one of my best friends, even if it doesn't sound like it. We've known each other since we were in elementary school, which has made us extremely close. Honestly, she's one of the only people that tolerate me, and I thank her for that.

"So, how long was I staring at Emma Grace for?" I asked, hoping she'd say only a few seconds.

"Only for like two minutes that I saw," she said with a slight smirk on her face.

"That's not too bad," I said, trying to reassure myself.

"It's not bad if you're the one staring," she said.

"Shoot, you're right," I said nervously.

"You're fine," Ezra said. "Emma never even notices you."

"Yeah, you're the only one," I said back.

"Well, one of the only ones," Ezra said while pointing down the hall.

"Are you kidding me?" I said while looking down the hall. "Teagan Matthews?"

"The one and only," Ezra said jokingly.

Teagan Matthews was the one guy in South Ray High that no one messed with. He could end anyone in a matter of seconds, and I'm lucky enough to be one of his least favorite people in this whole school.

"Teagan looks mad," Ezra said.

"Well, no, duh!" I shouted at her.

"Here, I'll try to distract him so you can have time to make your grande getaway," Ezra said.

With all the times Teagan's tried to attack me, Ezra always tries to help me out, even if she's not that successful. See, Ezra has one advantage when it comes to Teagan, her brother. Ezra's brother graduated a year ago, but for some reason, he was really good friends with Teagan, which makes him never want to hurt Ezra.

"He's still going to get me," I complained.

"Well, if you wanted to avoid this, you wouldn't have been staring at his girlfriend," Ezra said with little remorse.

I wish Ezra was lying, but it's sadly true. Emma Grace, the most perfect girl at South Ray High, dates the worst guy possible, Teagan.

I don't want to sound rude, but Emma Grace could do so much better than him. Honestly, she'd even be better off with Alex King, and that's saying something.

12

"Do you think Teagan is coming over here?" I asked Ezra.

"Honestly, I have no idea," she answered me.

Right as I was starting to think Teagan wasn't going to come to kick my ass, he made eye contact with me and mouthed the words *you're dead*.

"Oh no," Me and Ezra said in sync.

"I'm not in the mood to start my day with a black eye," I complained to Ezra.

"Then start running, Aaron. The farther you get away from him, the better chance you have of making a proper getaway," Ezra said.

I knew she was right, and I knew I had no choice.

This was always a dread of my day; I hated being so weak and scrawny. I wish I could just stand a chance against Teagan, but until I nearly double in size, that'll never happen.

"I'm gonna go," I said to Ezra as I started to run down the halls.

"Good luck; meet me outside Mrs. Jones's room when you get away!" Ezra shouted down the hall.

I hoped I would actually make it to Mrs. Jones's class on time and make it there unharmed.

It's kinda funny how teachers never get mad at me for running in the halls any more. They're so used to it they'll even move out of my way. Honestly, most of the students also move out of my way, they know I'm the poor soul that has to deal with Teagan most of the time, so they don't hesitate.

Now I wish I could say all students, but sadly some don't, and by some, I mean the junior boys that think they're better than everyone else just because they play football, and of course, today they had to be right in my path.

"Excuse me!" I shouted down the hall, hoping they'd move

before I'd have to come to a stop.

But of course, they didn't, and I had to come to a full stop.

"Can I get through?" I asked them in a hurry, knowing it would only be a matter of seconds before Teagan caught up to me.

"Why should we let you through, little man?" one of them laughed.

I knew they wouldn't move for me, so I had to give them a good reason to move, fast.

"Look, I know you won't move for me, but I think you'll move for little Teagan back there," I said while pointing down the hall.

They looked back and saw the one thing they were scared of, Teagan Matthews.

"Let him through, Dave; I'm not repeating the incident," one of the taller Juniors said.

"Fine," Dave said as he moved out of my way.

"Thank you," I said as I quickly ran through them.

I was full-on sprinting. I was not going to be caught today.

I was starting to think of a way to easily escape when it came to me, a turn. I've seen Teagan run track and I know he's horrible at making quick turns. So I took the first turn I saw, almost whipping out myself.

I looked down at my watch to see how many minutes I had until the bell.

"Okay, it's only 8.01. I still have time to make it to class," I said to myself.

I turned around to see how far Teagan was from me when all of a sudden, I saw him stop in his tracks. I didn't understand why he stopped until I ran face-first into a locker. At that moment, I realized I had made one of the dumbest mistakes of my life. I had run down one of the only hallways in our school that was a dead-end.

"Looks like Aaron Cripple made his second dumb mistake of the day," Teagan said, trying to sound intimidating.

I turned around towards Teagan to see him standing there with a dumb smirk on his face.

I wanted to walk over to him so bad and just smack that smirk right off his dumb face.

"You just gonna stand there like a baby, or are you gonna come fight me like a man," Teagan said, still trying to scare me.

"You know, Teagan, we don't have to do this," I suggested. "We can just move on with our day and forget about this."

Teagan looked at me for a second and then started laughing hysterically.

"Oh, Aaron, your stupidity today has just been too perfect. I'd be a fool to pass up this amazing opportunity," Teagan said as he started slowly walking toward me.

I started to back up even though there was nowhere to go.

"Aww, does Aaron have somewhere better to be?" Teagan laughed.

"Yeah, I do. It's something called Algebra II," I said.

"Oh, come on, it's no fun in there," Teagan said.

"Of course, you'd know that. You've been in that class for three years," I said jokingly.

Teagan's eyes lit up with rage. I instantly regretted saying that.

I just never know when to shut up, and that's the reason so many people at this school hate me.

"Oh, you are so dead!" Teagan shouted at me.

Teagan started coming at me faster, and I just kept backing up until I backed up into a locker. I looked up at Teagan and saw the full rage in his eyes. I've seen Teagan mad, but I don't think I've ever seen him this mad, at least in a while.

At this point, I was full-on petrified.

"Look, I'm… I'm so, so sorry… I ah… said that," I said with a shaking voice. "It was a stupid thing to say; I'm sorry."

Teagan stood there silent for a little bit, probably deciding if he wanted to take pity on me or just snap my neck.

After a few moments of silence, Teagan took a breath and punched the locker right next to my head as hard as possible. I looked over to see a large dent left in the locker.

"Are you scared of me?" Teagan asked me as I turned back towards him.

"What?" I asked, kinda puzzled.

"Answer the question, Aaron!" he shouted at me.

"Um… um," I stuttered. I didn't know what to say.

Teagan was acting weird and just kept getting more mad with every second he continued to look at me. I just stood there mortified. I didn't know what to do.

At that moment, the 8.05 bell rang; I couldn't believe it had only been four minutes.

"Look, Teagan, we should get going to class," I said while slowly getting off the lockers.

Teagan said nothing and put his hand around my throat as he pushed me back against the lockers.

His grip wasn't strong enough to prevent me from breathing; it was just there to freak me out.

I tried pushing him off, but he only tightened his grip. Now I was officially alarmed.

"Teagan, it's okay, please just let go. I won't tell anyone about this," I said as calmly as possible

"I hate you so much," Teagan said angrily.

"I'm aware, and I don't blame you. I can be pretty annoying," I said while trying to relax him. "Please just calm down before someone gets hurt."

"You mean before you get hurt?" he said.

I wanted to yell at him, no, duh, but I was too scared. He could easily just stop my breathing, and I did not want that fear.

"I'll just take that as a yes," Teagan said as he slightly tightened his grip.

I was officially panicking, and I think Teagan could tell. He just smiled, it was sick how much he was enjoying this.

Usually, Teagan would just punch me a few times; he's only done this a few times before.

"Teagan, please," I said while trying to sound calm.

"Oh, don't you enjoy this?" he asked me happily, knowing I could barely respond.

I knew I had to get out of this, but I didn't know exactly how.

At that moment, I knew I had to use any guy's weakness. I looked him dead in the eyes and then kicked him right in the sweet spot.

His eyes widened. I knew I got him.

My plan quickly backfired, though. It didn't make him let go of me or drop down to the ground. All he did was tighten his grip.

At this point, I was struggling to breathe. I started tapping on his hand, letting him know this was no longer a joke but more of a life or death situation, but he did nothing.

I felt everything beginning to fade when all of a sudden, I heard a voice.

"Teagan, that's enough. Let go of him, now!" The voice yelled.

17

Teagan turned around to see who it was and instantly let go of me.

I instantly fell down to the ground while catching my breath.

I looked up to see Emma Grace.

"Teagan, you can't do this!" Emma Grace shouted. "Stuff like this isn't funny!"

"It was just a joke, Emma; I wasn't actually hurting him," Teagan said, trying to explain himself.

Luckily Emma Grace knew he was full of it.

"Go to class," Emma Grace demanded.

Teagan, feeling defeated, walked away. I was relieved.

"Are you okay?" Emma Grace asked.

I looked up at her.

"Aaron, right?" she said with a smile.

I couldn't believe she knew my name; Emma Grace knew who I was.

"Hello?" she said.

"Yeah, Aaron's right," I said as I quickly scrambled to my feet.

"Sorry about Teagan. I don't know why he loves to mess with you," she said.

"It's fine. It's not your fault," I reassured her.

She looked up at me with a smile.

I still couldn't get over the fact that Emma Grace was talking to me.

"Well, you better get to class; it's 8.09, and one of us doesn't have a pass," she said.

"Oh shoot, you're right," I said. "Thank you, Emma Grace."

"Please, just call me Emma," she said.

"Okay, Emma, see you around," I said while beginning to run away.

"See you!" she shouted back.

I ran as fast as I could to Mrs. Jones's room. When I finally made it, I saw Ezra standing outside the room waiting for me.

"Took you long enough," Ezra said as we walked into class.

Right as we walked in, the bell rang.

Mrs. Jones instantly looked at us with her are you kidding me look.

"Technically, we're not late," I reassured her.

"Just go sit down, you two and open up your books to page 56," Mrs. Jones said to us.

I walked to my seat and sat down.

I was honestly surprised I made it to class on time, and I still couldn't believe that Emma Grace saved me.

"Aaron, book," Mrs. Jones said, already tired of me.

"Sorry," I said as I opened my book up to page 56.

I still couldn't concentrate, this morning was so crazy. I wondered if Teagan would've actually killed me; I mean, he's crazy but is he that crazy?

"Okay, class, that's all the notes I have for you, your assignment is the five practice questions on the back of the page," Mrs. Jones said to us.

I looked down at my notebook and realized I hadn't written down a single thing. I started to panic. Mrs. Jones was going to kill me.

I think Mrs. Jones noticed me panicking because she walked up to me and looked down at my notebook.

"Where are all your notes?" she asked me, confused.

"I forgot," I said nervously.

"Really, Aaron, see me after class," she said in an annoyed

tone as she walked away.

I laid my head down on my desk. I was so ashamed of myself.

I usually wasn't that bad of a student, and now I was going to get my first detention of the year. This sucked, and I knew it would be even worse at home when Carl found out about this.

"You good?" Ezra asked.

"Why on earth are you over here?" I asked while lifting my head up.

"'Cause I'm done with my assignment and you seem upset," she said.

"I'm just about to get my first detention, nothing much," I said.

"Oh shoot, Carl's gonna kill you," she said while feeling sorry for me.

"I'm aware," I said.

"Aaron, can you come over here?" Mrs. Jones asked.

"Here goes nothing," I whispered to Ezra.

I stood up and walked over to Mrs. Jones's desk ready for the worst.

"Do you have a phone?" she asked.

"Yeah," I said nervously.

"Do you have it on you?" she asked.

"Yes," I answered her nervously once again.

I knew what she was going to do; she was going to make me call my mom and Carl and tell them I had detention and why I had it.

I pulled out my phone and sat it down on her desk.

"I don't need that," she said.

"Then why'd you ask for it?" I asked, confused.

"So you could take a photo of the notes and copy them

down tonight," she said.

I looked over at her, kinda puzzled.

"Wait, so am I in trouble?" I asked.

"Well, I'm not happy with you, but since you're normally a good student, I'm going to let this slide. Just don't let it happen again," she said.

"Okay," I said gratefully.

I quickly took photos of all the pages of notes and then looked back over at her.

"Thank you," I said to Mrs. Jones.

"You're welcome," she said. "Stay out of trouble now."

"I'll try," I said as I walked back to my seat.

"Detention?" Ezra asked.

"Surprisingly, no," I said.

"Well, that's good," she said.

"Ezra, seat!" Mrs. Jones shouted.

"Okay," Ezra said back. "See you at lunch, Aaron."

"See you," I said to Ezra as she walked back to her seat.

After the first hour, the rest of my morning went by pretty fast, and before I knew it, I was sitting at a lunch table with Ezra.

"So, are you gonna tell me what happened this morning with Teagan?" Ezra asked.

"Do you really wanna know?" I asked while opening a bag of baby carrots.

"Yes," she said.

"Do you, though?" I said while obviously annoying her.

Ezra just gave me a look while I started eating my baby carrots.

"Wait a minute, did he grab you by the throat again?" Ezra asked me, surprised.

"Yeah," I said while looking down.

Ezra sighed and looked down at her food.

"You gotta start standing up for yourself more," she said. "I know Teagan's bigger than you, but you gotta try more."

"I know," I said, annoyed. "It's just hard."

"I know," she said. "I mean, I don't know exactly, but I can certainly imagine."

I looked up at her and sighed.

"Does my throat look red?" I asked, worried about her response.

"Lift your head up a little," she said.

I did as she said and lifted my head while she looked at my neck.

Ezra was always pretty chill when it came to this kind of stuff. She knew how my parents were. She's been over enough to be able to guess how my parents would react to a red mark around my throat.

"I don't see anything," she said.

"Phew, didn't want to have to steal Jaelyn's foundation," I joked.

"Omg," she laughed.

Our lunch conversations are usually pretty weird like this, and that's simply because we're weird. We always have been and always will be.

The rest of the day was pretty boring until the passing period between seventh hour and advisory.

Ezra and I were walking together since our advisories were right next door to each other when all of a sudden we heard loud arguing coming from down the hall.

Since we were the really curious type, we went to see who it was and what was going on.

We soon discovered it was no other than Teagan and Emma

Grace.

"Em, you need to chill out; it's no big deal!" Teagan shouted at Emma.

"No big deal?" Emma screamed back. "I've seen you choke not one but two people today!"

"Emma, come on, they deserved it," Teagan said, trying to defend himself.

"Were they hurting you physically?" Emma shouted.

"Well, no, but come on, they're idiots," he said, trying to reason with her.

"The only idiot here is you," Emma said boldly.

Teagan froze; he probably had never heard Emma act this way. Honestly, none of us had.

"You're being overdramatic," he said while looking at her like she was crazy.

"Yeah, I'm the overdramatic person, not the guy who chokes people when they say mean things. That totally makes sense!" she shouted.

At this point, the bell had rung, but honestly, no one cared; this was too interesting. Some of the teachers were even outside their classrooms watching this take place.

"Okay, I admit maybe Alex didn't deserve it, but Aaron definitely did; that guy's been harassing me for so long," he said.

"What?" I whispered under my breath

"He's crazy," Ezra whispered back.

"Okay, I don't know Aaron that well, but from what I've heard, you're the only one harassing in that scenario," Emma said, annoyed.

"Are you kidding me? That little punk kicked me, you know where earlier!" Teagan shouted.

23

"He probably did that because you deserved it!" Emma shouted back.

"Unbelievable!" he shouted. "You're taking his side over mine."

"Yeah, I am, 'cause at this point, I would rather take anyone's side except yours!" she shouted.

Teagan was mad. I knew that look better than anyone else. He walked over to Emma with anger in his eyes.

"Do you think he's gonna hurt her?" I whispered to Ezra.

"I hope not," she whispered back.

Teagan and Emma were officially face to face. The crowd was silent.

"You don't wanna do this," he said.

Emma just stood there, she didn't respond. I could tell she was done with him and his crap.

"Are you breaking up with me?" he asked.

She just stood there, keeping silent.

"Are you!" he yelled at her.

I didn't know how she was remaining so calm; this seemed terrifying.

"Answer me!" Teagan yelled as he grabbed her shoulders.

Emma looked up at him so calmly. This was all happening so quickly but yet so slowly. It felt like a movie scene.

"Let go of my shoulders," Emma said quietly.

"Answer my question," Teagan said while squeezing her shoulders.

Emma looked him dead in the eyes as she kicked him right in his shin. Teagan instantly fell down in pain.

"What is wrong with you! I'm an athlete. I can't be injured for my seasons!" he screamed at her.

She bent down to his level making perfect eye contact.

"When a girl tells you to let go of them, you let go of them," she said in a stern tone.

He stood up and faced her, and right as he was about to say something, a loud smack echoed through the hallway. Emma had full-on smacked him across the face.

"Oh, and to answer your question, we're done," she said as she walked away.

Everyone just stood there stunned, including Teagan. No one knew Emma was able to act this way, but I think everyone loved it. Emma was one of the sweetest people in this whole school, and to see her break up with Teagan in such a badass way was amazing.

"Teama's officially over!" a random girl shouted.

That's when I realized Emma Grace was officially single, and Teagan was as sad and lonely as me.

Could this be one of the best things to ever happen to me?

Maybe things would actually start to turn around for me...

Chapter 2

"Rise and shine, Aaron," my mom called into my room.

"Morning already?" I groaned.

I looked out my window to meet eyes with the sun.

"Ow," I moaned as I pulled the blanket back over my face.

"Aaron, come on, we're running late," my mom said.

"Aren't we always?" I complained, still not wanting to get out of bed.

I looked at my bedroom doorway and saw her looking at me with the look.

I just slammed my head into my pillow. I did not want to get up.

"You can have five more minutes," my mom said. "But then I want you up, no complaining."

"Okay, thank you," I said as I sunk back into my bed.

It was always a great morning when I got extra time in bed. I felt that it always made me more energetic throughout the day.

I didn't know why my mom wouldn't let me do this every day. My grades would be through the roof.

"Aaron!" Carl shouted.

"What?" I said, already annoyed with him.

"Get up!" he yelled at me.

"Mom said I can have five more minutes," I said while beginning to doze off.

"Well, I'm not your mom, and I told you to get up!" he yelled at me.

I didn't respond; I wanted to have as much relaxation time as possible, and my responding to Carl would've only shortened it.

"You have no respect for me!" Carl yelled as he ripped off my blanket.

"'Cause all you do is yell at me!" I yelled back.

Carl was so mad at me.

I just got out of bed and walked out of my room.

"I wasn't done with you!" Carl yelled.

"Well, I was done with you!" I yelled back.

I knew he was mad at me, but I didn't care.

Carl was one of the worst people ever.

Take all the angry and mean people in the world and mix them together; that's Carl.

"Will you two stop fighting with each other!" my mom shouted at Carl and me.

"Tell that little shit to respect me, and then we won't fight!" Carl shouted back at her.

I just walked into the bathroom.

It was only seven a.m. and I was already done with today.

"Someone woke up on the wrong side of the bed," Jaelyn said as she came out of her room.

"Who, me or him?" I asked.

"Both," she said jokingly.

I rolled my eyes and shut the bathroom door. I still had to get ready.

"Aaron!" Jaelyn shouted at the door.

"What? I just got in here!" I shouted back.

"Effie wants you," she said.

"Tell her to wait; I'll be out soon," I said.

I still didn't know why Effie loved me so much, I was the

annoying older brother, and Jaelyn was the cool older sister.

I would assume being the only boy in the family would get me less attention from everyone, but it doesn't, and I don't know why.

I'm the middle and the least favorite, my grades suck, and I'm kind of a loser, the screwup, to be honest.

Effie is the baby of the family and is the neediest, Jaelyn, on the other hand, is the oldest and is always on the principal's honor roll at school. With all of that, they should get all the attention, not me.

"Aaron, come out here when you're done!" Mom shouted.

"Will do!" I shouted back.

I knew my mom was going to give me a lecture on respecting Carl, and I wasn't looking forward to it.

I finished getting ready as quickly as possible since we were running a little behind.

Once I was done in the bathroom, I ran to my room and got dressed.

After that, I knew I had to brave one of Mom's lectures.

"Morning, Mom," I said, trying to get on her good side. "So, anything good for breakfast?"

"Aaron," she said while giving me a look.

I knew that she was over me already and that there was no saving me, but I wanted to try and avoid this as much as possible.

"You need to be nicer to Carl," she said.

"Okay," I said, trying to wrap things up.

"Aaron, you need to; I'm not playing around any more," she said, getting frustrated

"I said okay!" I shouted at her.

"Don't give me lip!" she yelled at me.

I started to walk away when Mom grabbed my arm.

"Aaron, I don't want you to be mad at me, I just want you to be nicer to Carl, and if you won't for me, do it for Effie, she hates watching you two argue," she said.

"Maybe you can tell your lovely Carl to stop yelling at me for no reason, and I'll work on being nicer," I said as I pulled my arm out of my mom's grasp.

Mom just sat there in silence. I felt bad but what I had said was true. Every argument Carl and I have ever gotten into was started by him. I probably don't help, but I never start anything; it's always him.

"Aaron!" Effie shouted as she ran into the kitchen.

"Morning, Effie," I said with a smile.

"It took you like a million years to get out of your room," she said.

"Sure did," I laughed.

"I like your shirt," she said, pointing to my dumb white shirt with a cartoon dog on it.

"Well, thank you, I like your shirt too," I said with a smile.

"You like my shirt?" she said excitedly.

"Of course, you have the best fashion sense in the family," I said.

Effie smiled so big. I could tell how happy she was.

Effie was the sweetest thing, even though she was fifty percent, Carl.

"Aaron, come on, we're gonna be late," Jaelyn said as she grabbed her keys off the counter.

"Bye, Effie," I said as I ran out of the house.

"Dang getting in an argument with Mom and Carl. Is someone in a bad mood?" Jaelyn asked me as we walked to her car.

"Oh, come on, Jaelyn, it's Carl, and Mom was only defending him," I complained.

"I was joking, Aaron. I know how they are; I live with them too," Jaelyn said as she got into the car.

I quickly followed her lead and got into the car too.

Since Jaelyn was sixteen, she drove me to school every day, with herself, of course.

We'd probably ride with Effie, too, if her school weren't on the other side of town.

Our town was organized so dumb, having the high school be ten minutes east and the elementary ten minutes west.

"You think you're ever going to drive me to school?" Jaelyn asked as she started the car.

"Is that a serious question?" I asked.

"Kinda, I mean, you're fifteen, Aaron, you're not that far behind me," Jaelyn said while looking over at me.

"Maybe one day," I said while looking out the window.

I looked out the window with thoughts running through my head.

I thought about Emma and Teagan again and how they were officially over.

I hoped Teagan wouldn't be full of rage without Emma. Everyone always thought that Emma was the only thing that kept Teagan from killing someone, and for my sake, I hoped that was false.

"Does Teagan still mess with you?" Jaelyn asked.

"What?" I said, caught off guard.

"Teagan Matthews, the one that broke up with Emma?" Jaelyn said, trying to specify.

"No," I said, trying to avoid the topic.

I think Jaelyn knew I was full of it, but she wouldn't say

anything.

Thankfully for me, we arrived at school shortly after, which meant Jaelyn had no more time to ask me questions I didn't want to answer.

"Wanna get out here? I see Ezra over there," Jaelyn asked.

"Sure," I said as I unbuckled my seatbelt.

Jaelyn knew I liked walking in with Ezra, so she would let me anytime I could.

"Bye," I said as I got out of the car.

"Bye, Aaron, love you," Jaelyn said.

"Love you too," I said while running to Ezra.

It was kinda funny how some people thought Jaelyn and I were too close. If only they knew what we've been through, then they would understand why we were as close as we were.

"Ezra, wait up!" I shouted as I ran over.

Ezra turned around and looked at me with a smile. She also enjoyed it when we walked in together.

"Looks like we're both running late," she laughed.

"Are we running late?" I asked.

Right as she was about to answer me, the 8.00 bell rang.

"Guess that answer's your question," she said jokingly.

"Guess so," I laughed.

Ezra and I began to walk into school with a crowd of roughly fifty kids.

Our school always seemed especially huge when we were stuck in a crowd this big.

"I love you, Jaelyn," I heard some kid say behind me.

I turned around to see Teagan and his friends. They were obviously mocking me.

"Very funny," I said sarcastically.

I grabbed Ezra's hand and pulled her through the crowd. I

didn't want to hear those jerks go off about how Jaelyn and I care for each other and will tell each other stuff like, I love you.

"Those guys are idiots Aaron, don't let them get to you," Ezra said. "You and Jaelyn have a great relationship."

"I know," I said. "I'm just not in the mood for their stupidity today."

"Don't blame you," Ezra said as she went to her locker.

I followed in Ezra's footsteps and went to my locker.

It was always annoying how people laughed at me for telling my sister I love her. They just don't understand what it's like to lose someone close. You gain a fear that'll never leave you, a fear that your loved ones will just disappear. Jaelyn and I have this fear, the worst out of my whole family. I hate it, but there's nothing I can do. It'll be stuck with me until the day I die.

"Are you ready to go to first hour?" Ezra asked from behind me.

"Yeah, let's go," I said as I shut my locker.

We were about halfway there when I realized I had forgotten my notebook.

"Darn it," I said under my breath

"What's wrong?" Ezra asked.

"I forgot my notebook; it's in my locker," I said, frustrated.

"I'll go get it with you if you want," Ezra said.

"No, it's fine, just go to class," I said.

"Okay, I'll try to keep Mrs. Jones from giving you a tardy," she said as I started to walk away.

I speed-walked down the halls. I knew the 8.05 bell had already rung and that if I made it to class, it would be a close call.

I got to my locker as quickly as possible and got my

notebook out.

It was weird how almost no one was in the hallway. It made the school feel kinda like a ghost town.

After I got my notebook, I began to walk back to class.

As I walked down the hall, minding my own business, I managed to walk right into someone and drop all my stuff.

"Omg, I'm so sorry, Aaron," the person said.

I looked up to see Emma Grace.

"Oh, Emma, you're fine. I wasn't looking where I was going," I said quickly.

She smiled and went to help me pick up my things. She really was one of the kindest people.

"Guess things don't work well when two people aren't looking where they're going," Emma laughed.

"Guess you're right," I replied.

After we had picked up my stuff, the 8.10 bell had rung.

"Dang it," I said to myself. "I'm so getting a tardy."

"Who do you have first hour?" Emma asked.

"Mrs. Jones," I answered her.

"Sweet, Mrs. Jones loves me," she said. "Let me walk you to class. I can get you out of that tardy."

"Okay," I said, surprised.

I didn't know why Emma would want to help me, maybe she felt bad for bumping into me or for Teagan's outburst yesterday, or maybe she was just being the kind person she always was. I didn't know for sure.

"So why are you rarely in your first hour?" I asked, trying to start a little bit of conversation.

"Well, I'm ahead in my work, so Mr. Smith sends me off to do some tasks for him," she explained.

"That makes sense. I wish I was ahead in Mr. Smith's

class," I told her.

"You're not that far behind," Emma said.

"How do you know?" I asked.

"'Cause Mr. Smith made me look through your class's missing assignments, and you only had two, it's not that bad," she said.

"Makes sense," I said.

Before I knew it, our conversation was over, and we were at Mrs. Jones's room.

Emma and I looked at each other and quickly walked in.

"Hey, Mrs. Jones," Emma said as I walked to my desk.

"Hey, Emma, why are you here? I shouldn't be seeing you until seventh hour," Mrs. Jones said.

"I just came to let you know that I accidentally knocked Aaron's stuff out of his hands in the hallway, and that's why he was late; it wasn't his fault," Emma explained to Mrs. Jones.

"Well, okay then, thank you, Emma," Mrs. Jones said as Emma walked out. "Looks like you're off the hook, Aaron."

"Yeah," I said as I pulled out my book.

"All right, class, let's start right where we left off yesterday," Mrs. Jones said.

Before I knew it, Mrs. Jones's class was over, and I was off to Mr. Smith's class. When I walked in I saw Mr. Smith talking to Emma.

I waved at her as I went to my seat, she waved back.

"Bye, Mr. Smith," Emma said as she walked out.

I watched Emma walk out before I pulled my things out. She was so pretty. I didn't know how she wasn't a model.

The rest of my morning classes went by pretty quickly and were fairly normal. My whole school day was pretty normal until lunch.

"So, are you gonna tell me what you were doing with Emma earlier?" Ezra asked.

"What else do you need to know? I told you we bumped into each other, and she felt bad for me being late so she walked me to class," I explained to Ezra.

"I feel like there's more to it," Ezra said as she shoved a turkey sandwich in her mouth.

"There's really not," I said, annoyed.

We stopped talking and started to eat our lunch.

At school, they only gave us sixteen minutes to eat, which meant we had to rush. It was pretty annoying.

"Are you kidding me!" someone screamed from the other side of the cafeteria.

"Who do you think that was?" Ezra asked.

"I have no clue. Should we go see?" I asked.

"You really wanna go see?" she asked me, surprised.

"Well, it's either that or eating crappy school food," I said.

"Fair point," Ezra said. "Let's go before I finish this gross sandwich."

Ezra and I got up and started to walk towards the crowd of kids that had formed from the scream.

"Help!" I heard someone scream.

I tried to get a closer look, but I couldn't see over everyone.

"This will be less painful if you just stay still!" I heard someone else scream.

At that moment I figured out who was screaming earlier. It was Teagan.

I guess he was still in a bad mood from yesterday.

I squeezed through the crowd to get a better look. When I had made my way to the front, I saw Teagan trying to pulverize Alex King.

I figured that he had spilled something on Teagan, and now he was going to get his butt kicked.

I don't know why but I felt like I had to do something.

"Leave him alone, Teagan!" I shouted.

Teagan looked over at me and smirked.

"Or what?" he said, trying not to laugh.

"Teagan, this isn't any kind of bet. Just leave him alone," I said, getting aggravated.

"Whatever you say," he said while backing away from Alex.

"Wait, really?" I said, surprised.

"Yeah, I'll leave him alone, but you, on the other hand, aren't going to like what happens next," Teagan said.

Everyone turned their attention toward me.

I froze, I should've expected this, but I didn't.

Teagan stood there waiting like I was going to just come over to him; he was acting like he was a king.

I tried to go back through the crowd, but no one would move; I felt helpless.

"Come here, Aaron. I'll give you a lunch to remember," Teagan said, obviously trying to threaten me.

"I'm good. The bells are going to ring soon. I ate enough crappy food; we are all good to leave," I said, still trying to move through the crowd.

"Enough!" One of Teagan's friends shouted as he pushed me closer to Teagan.

I looked around and saw all eyes still watching me, including Teagan's.

"You know it's not nice to make people's girlfriends break up with them!" Teagan shouted.

"Is that what this is about? I did not make Emma break up

with you. She broke up with you because of your own stupid actions," I said angrily.

"Kick his ass, Teagan!" one of his friends shouted.

"Why? He has no reason to!" I shouted back.

More kids had officially gathered around. This was getting interesting for everyone watching.

"A nice size crowd," Teagan said as he began to walk over.

I ran back towards the crowd, trying to get through again, when all of a sudden Teagan grabbed me from behind. He locked his arms around me.

"What are you trying to do? Give me a backward hug?" I asked, trying to distract him.

All the kids laughed at my comment, which threw Teagan into a rage.

He lifted me up and threw me to the ground. I felt the impact of the hard lunch floor across my body; it did not feel good.

"You like being a clown at the wrong times!" Teagan shouted as he placed his foot on my throat.

"Get off of me, Teagan," I said while trying to push him off.

"You'd like that, wouldn't you," he said as he was thinking about what he wanted to do to me.

"Teagan, leave him alone!" I heard a familiar voice shout.

"Oh, it's a fellow Cripple, how sweet," Teagan said out loud.

I figured through Teagan's comment that the voice was Jaelyn.

She was so going to kill me later for lying about Teagan, but I didn't care. That was the least of my worries right now.

"Very funny, now take your foot off him," Jaelyn

demanded.

Jaelyn had made a risky move coming in the middle of this. I just hoped it would do more good for her than bad.

"Why would I do that? This is hilarious," Teagan said while looking down at me

"Don't do anything stupid!" Jaelyn shouted as she began to walk closer.

"Like this?" Teagan asked as he kicked me in the face.

Everyone gasped.

I looked up at Teagan again and then up at Jaelyn.

As I looked over at Jaelyn, I saw her eyes widen.

"Teagan, let him up now!" Jaelyn shouted, alarmed.

"Why would I?" Teagan said.

"Teagan, I'm not playing. Let go of him!" Jaelyn shouted in a worried tone.

Teagan looked down at me and then let me up. He looked just as alarmed as Jaelyn.

"Shit, I was never here," Teagan said as he ran away.

I sat up and felt something drip down my face. I wiped my hand across my face to see what it was. I looked down at my hand and saw it covered in blood. I started to freak out.

"Aaron, look at me," Jaelyn demanded.

I looked up at her and only started to panic more.

"Aaron, calm down. It's okay," Jaelyn said as she pulled me to my feet.

I knew so many people were staring at me, but I didn't care; I had a bigger problem right now. I was being faced with one of my biggest fears, blood.

"Someone get a teacher!" Jaelyn shouted.

My breathing became quicker by the second. I started to feel light-headed.

"Aaron, breathe; you're going to be okay," Jaelyn said while trying to calm me down.

"I... I... Don't feel... go... Good," I said as I blacked out into Jaelyn's arms.

I woke up to see Jaelyn looking down at me.

"You okay?" she asked.

I didn't answer; my head was still spinning, I couldn't concentrate.

"Is he up?" I heard someone ask.

"Yeah, he seems a bit loopy, though," Jaelyn answered.

I turned my head to see Mrs. Jones walking toward me.

"Hey, Aaron, can you hear me?" Mrs. Jones asked.

I nodded my head slightly.

"Did he hit his head?" Mrs. Jones asked Jaelyn.

"No, I caught him," Jaelyn said.

"Well, that's good," Mrs. Jones said. "I'm going to get him some water; you stay here."

"Okay," Jaelyn said as Mrs. Jones walked away.

Jaelyn looked at me. I could tell she was upset about what happened with Teagan and me.

"Aaron, please don't lie to me again; I'm your sister. I care about you," Jaelyn said.

"I know," I murmured.

She smiled. I think she was glad that I had responded to her with words.

"Wanna go sit down?" Jaelyn asked.

"Sure," I said as I began to sit up.

Jaelyn helped me to my feet and walked me over to a table.

"You gave everyone quite a fright," Jaelyn said as she sat by me.

"I know," I said. "What even happened?"

"You got kicked in the face; it wasn't pretty," Jaelyn said.

"Sounds great," I said sarcastically.

I looked over and saw Mrs. Jones walking back towards us.

"Here's some water, Aaron," Mrs. Jones said as she handed me a water bottle.

"Thanks," I said with a forced smile.

"Aaron, just wanted to let you know we called your parents, and they are on their way to pick you up," Mrs. Jones said.

"Okay," I said while taking a drink of water.

I honestly didn't want to see my parents, but I knew I had to get my nose looked at; it was throbbing.

"Let's go to the office and wait for your folks," Mrs. Jones said. "Jaelyn, you can head back to class."

"Okay," Jaelyn said. "See you later, Aaron."

"See you," I said as I began to walk to the office with Mrs. Jones.

I sat in the office for only about five minutes before Carl showed up.

I wished my mom would've been the one to pick me up, but I knew she was at work.

"Let's go, Aaron," Carl said as he began to walk out.

I followed behind.

"Why can't you just be a normal kid?" Carl asked.

"You can shut up, Carl," I said as I got into the car.

"I just don't get what went so wrong with you," he said, annoyed.

"What's that supposed to mean?" I asked, annoyed.

"I just don't see why you can't be like your sisters. They get good grades and don't start fights at school," Carl said, frustrated.

"I didn't start a fight!" I shouted. "Teagan attacked me."

"Well, either way, now I have to waste one of your mom's paychecks to make sure your face isn't broken," Carl said as we drove out of the parking lot.

"Well, sorry, that's a responsibility of being a parent," I said, annoyed.

"I didn't sign up to be your parent!" Carl shouted at me.

I didn't respond, I knew Carl hated me, but for some reason, that comment hurt.

Chapter 3

My doctor's visit didn't last very long. They just asked me a few questions and looked at my nose for a few seconds.

Thankfully, Teagan hadn't broken my nose, he had just popped some blood vessels.

Carl and I walked out of the doctor's office in silence. I couldn't tell if Carl was mad at me or if he just felt bad about what he said earlier. All I knew was that I was getting some kind of silent treatment from him.

"Waste of money," I heard Carl say under his breath.

I was going to respond to him, but I decided not to.

We got in the car and began to drive off. About ten minutes away from the house, I saw about five cop cars parked around an old building.

"What's going on over there?" I asked Carl.

"Why would I know?" Carl responded.

"I don't know," I said while continuing to look out the window.

"This town is really going downhill. Before we know it, the crime rate will be the worst in the state," Carl complained to himself.

"I haven't noticed anything, really," I said.

Carl just turned and looked at me like I had bugs crawling in my hair.

"Of course you haven't! You're a stupid kid! You don't know anything! You think the world is so simple!" he shouted at me.

I just looked at him. He always yelled for no reason, and Mom wondered why we didn't get along.

"I'm so done," I heard Carl whisper under his breath.

I just turned back over to the window. I was done too.

We pulled into the driveway a few minutes later. I got out of the car as soon as possible, and I was so done with Carl.

The second I walked in, my mom ran over to me.

"Aaron," Mom said as she hugged me. "Are you okay?"

"I'm fine, Mom," I said as I escaped her grasp.

"I was so worried," she said.

"I know," I said.

"Is your nose okay?" She asked.

"Yep, everything's fine," I said with a forced smile.

Everything was fine physically, but I was destroyed on the inside. Carl's words always found a way to hurt me.

I should be used to him, but I'm not...

"I'm gonna go to my room," I said as I walked past my mom.

"Love you," she said.

"Love you too," I said as I walked into my room.

I closed the door behind me. I didn't want anyone to come in.

My room was like my safe place; it was where I felt I didn't have to pretend. I sat on my bed and let my head fall into my hands. I wasn't crying, but I was pretty darn close.

Before I knew it, Jaelyn and Effie came home. I heard them talking to Mom and Carl. They all sounded so happy. I was starting to think maybe I was the problem, not Carl.

"Aaron?" Jaelyn said as she knocked on my door.

"What?" I said in response.

"Can I come in?" she asked.

"Sure," I said.

I didn't really wanna see anyone, but I knew Jaelyn was probably worried about me.

"You okay?" Jaelyn asked me as she walked in.

"Yeah," I said as I sat up.

"You sure?" she asked.

"Well, the doctors said I didn't break my face, so I think I'll be all right," I said with a slight chuckle.

"I already heard that," she said.

"Well, then why'd you ask if I was okay?" I asked, confused.

"'Cause today was crazy, and your eyes are a little red," she said while pointing at my face.

"What?" I said, surprised. "My eyes aren't red, and I'm fine; you can leave."

"Aaron, you can talk to me," she reassured me. "Please don't hide your emotions. I heard that ages people ten years."

"Really?" I said in surprise.

"Really," Jaelyn said. "So you going to tell me what's wrong, or are you just gonna die ten years earlier."

"Carl was just being rude, that's it," I said.

"What did he say?" Jaelyn asked.

"Stuff," I said.

"Aaron, come on," she said, annoyed.

"Why are you so nosey?" I asked as I fell back onto my bed.

"Because I'm your sister," she said as she fell back on the bed next to me. "I'll get it out of you."

"Oh really? I'd like to see you try," I said.

"Okay," Jaelyn said as she began to tickle me.

44

"Stop, stop!" I shouted as I laughed hysterically.

"I'll stop when you tell me," Jaelyn said, and she continued to tickle me.

"Fine!" I shouted, still laughing.

Jaelyn stopped tickling me and started laughing.

"That always works," she said proudly.

"I hate you," I said while smiling at her.

"So, what did Carl say that made you upset?" Jaelyn asked.

"He pretty much said how I was the screw up out of all of us and how he didn't want to be my parent. I know I shouldn't get upset, but I still do, and what sucks is I'm starting to see what he sees. I have the worst grades, I get into fights, and from what I've heard, you all are so much happier without me. Maybe everyone would be better off if I just disappeared." I ranted.

I looked up at Jaelyn and saw how bad she felt. I realized I had just changed the whole mood. I really do screw things up.

"I'm sorry," I said as my eyes filled up with tears.

She remained silent. I felt like the worst person in the world.

I stood up and began to walk out when all of a sudden, Jaelyn grabbed my arm. I looked back to see that she was also crying a little bit.

"Aaron, it's okay," she said as she hugged me. "I love you."

"I love you too," I said as I hugged her back.

Jaelyn always cared about me. I didn't know why; she just did.

After a few minutes, Jaelyn let go of me.

"Please ignore Carl, Aaron, he's an awful person, and the more you listen to him, the worse you're going to feel," Jaelyn said.

"I'll try," I said as I looked up at her.

"I'm gonna go do some homework now, don't hesitate to come into my room if you need anything," Jaelyn said as she began to walk out.

"Okay," I said as she walked out.

The rest of the night was pretty quiet. I was able to do some school work and watch some TV before it was time for bed.

I was sleeping so peacefully until I was disturbed by my favorite second-grader.

"Aaron? Are you awake?" Effie asked while tapping my shoulder.

"Well, I am now," I said as I sat up. "What time is it?"

"It's 2.53," Effie said.

"2.53? Why are you awake?" I asked, still half asleep.

"I had a nightmare, and I can't go back to sleep," Effie explained.

"Well, you can lay in my bed for now," I told her. "I'm gonna get some water."

"Thank you, Aaron!" Effie said as she jumped into my bed.

"No problem," I said as I walked out of my room.

It's a rare occasion when I'm out of my room in the middle of the night, and now that I am, I see why; it's creepy.

I walked over to the cabinet to get myself a glass for some water, it may have been dark, but this seemed easy enough.

I reached up to get a glass when all of a sudden I heard a loud crash.

"Crap!" I shouted.

I ran over to the light switch and turned it on so I could see what exactly had made that loud crash.

When I walked back over to the cabinet I noticed my mom's favorite mug was shattered on the floor.

"I'm so dead," I whispered to myself.

"What is going on down here!" I heard Carl shout.

"Nothing," I quickly replied.

I sped over to the closet and looked for the broom and dustpan, but they were nowhere to be found.

"Aaron!" Carl shouted.

"Yeah," I said back nervously.

"Get over here now!" he shouted again.

I walked over to the cabinet to see Carl standing over the shattered mug. He was furious.

"Carl, I can clean it up," I said, trying to calm him down. "I just need the broom and dustpan."

"What were you doing!" he shouted at me.

"I was getting a glass, and Mom's mug fell out. I'm sorry, just help me find the broom and dustpan so I can clean it up and get back to bed," I said.

"Why didn't you turn the light on!" he shouted at me again.

"I wasn't thinking; I'm sorry!" I shouted back.

"Don't give me lip! Now clean this up!" he shouted.

"I'm trying to," I said, annoyed.

Carl didn't say anything; he just stood there.

I quickly walked back over to the closet to try and find the broom and dustpan again.

"Have you guys seen Effie?" Mom asked as she turned on the second light.

"She's in my room," I said while digging through the closet.

"Why is she in your room?" Carl asked angrily.

"She had a bad dream and wanted my bed for some reason," I explained.

"What are you doing, Aaron?" Mom asked.

"Looking for the broom and dustpan," I said.

47

"He broke your mug being an idiot," Carl said.

"It was an accident," I said under my breath.

I was about to start looking deeper in the closet when all of a sudden, my mom pulled me back.

"What are you doing?" I asked, confused.

"You've done enough, sweetie; go back to bed. I can handle the rest," she said while yawning.

"Honey, let him clean this mess, it's his fault, and he has done nothing to help clean it up!" Carl shouted.

"Carl, it's three a.m., and he has school tomorrow. Leave him alone; it was an accident," she said in an annoyed tone.

"Thanks, Mom," I said as I walked back to my room.

I walked in to see Effie sound asleep.

It made me happy to think that Effie will always know I'll be there for her.

I laid down next to her and fell asleep in a matter of seconds.

The next day was a blur, I guess I was just too tired to remember much of it. I knew I told Ezra about my crazy night, but that was all I was able to comprehend. Nothing interesting had happened till the end of school that day.

"Hey, Aaron," I heard someone say.

I looked over to see Emma Grace standing next to me.

"Hi, Emma. What are you doing here?" I asked nervously.

"I'm just getting some fresh air before I go back inside. Why are you here?" she asked me with a smile.

"I'm just waiting for Jaelyn. She has to pick up my younger sister, Effie," I explained.

"Makes sense," she said.

"Why do you have to go back in the school?" I asked.

"I promised Mrs. Jones I'd help her hang some stuff up in

her classroom," she explained.

"That's nice of you," I said while looking into her beautiful blue eyes.

"Thanks, that's probably the nicest thing a boy's said to me all week," she joked.

I laughed with her. I had completely forgotten that she had gone through a breakup only a few days ago.

"So, if you don't mind me asking, are you and Teagan a hundred percent over?" I asked, scared for her response.

"Definitely, he was a massive jerk, and I can't believe I didn't see it sooner," she said while looking away from me.

"Sorry I asked; it's none of my business," I said while avoiding eye contact.

"You're fine," she said with a sigh.

"You can talk to me if you need to get something off your chest," I said while looking back at her.

"It's just hard going through a breakup. I know he's horrible, but I did love him and seeing him be such a monster just hurt me, and now I don't know if I'll ever be able to find anyone else. The only people who have crushes on me are jocks, and they're pretty much all jerks," Emma ranted.

"It's okay. I know I don't know how it feels to go through a breakup, but I can imagine how horrible it is, and please don't worry about finding someone else. You're amazing and beautiful. Any guy would be lucky to have you," I said, trying to comfort her.

She looked up at me with her gorgeous smile. I was in disbelief with what I had just said, but it seemed to do more good than bad.

"Thanks, Aaron, you're great at comforting, just like your Mom," she said. "I better get back inside soon. Wanna trade numbers?"

"Umm… Ahh… Sur… Sure!" I stuttered. I couldn't believe what was happening.

We both wrote our numbers on a piece of paper and gave them to each other.

"Have a good night, Aaron," Emma said as she walked back into the school.

"You too," I said, still in awe.

I was standing there in shock. I couldn't believe I was holding the phone number of the girl of my dreams.

"Aaron!" Jaelyn shouted as she honked the horn.

I jumped; I had no idea she was there.

"Really?" I shouted as I walked to the car.

"I was ready to leave, and you were too busy eyeing my childhood best friend," she said.

"Childhood best friend?" I said, confused.

"Do you not remember Emma coming over all the time?" she asked, surprised.

"I thought it was a different Emma," I said while getting in the car.

"Nope, it's the same Emma you used to call M&M," she said while laughing.

"Oh gosh," I said as I laid back in my seat.

"Aaron, it's not a big deal. You were six," Jaelyn said as she started to drive away.

"Do you think I have a chance with Emma?" I asked, just wondering what she would say.

"I don't see why not. You're nice to her and decently smart," she said.

I smiled at her. Jaelyn knew I had a thing for Emma. She's known for a while.

The rest of the night, I was on cloud nine. Emma always managed to brighten my days.

After dinner, I decided to text her.

Hey Emma, it's Aaron. I just wanted to say I enjoyed talking to you; feel free to talk to me anytime :)

"Sent," I whispered to myself.

It was only seven thirty, so I couldn't imagine her not responding. No one goes to bed this early, I thought to myself.

My thoughts were sadly proven wrong, though. I watched the hours fly by until eleven p.m., then I tried to fall asleep.

During the night I went over everything in my head. I was wondering what I did. If I accidentally made her hate me, it stressed me out.

Before I knew it, morning had come and still no response. She never even read it.

"You good?" Jaelyn asked me as I walked out of my room.

"Yeah," I said while walking to the bathroom.

I got ready and came back out to the kitchen.

"Morning, sweetie," Mom said.

"Morning, Mom," I sighed.

"Do you feel okay?" she asked.

"Yeah, just bummed," I said.

"Sorry to hear that. Rant to Jaelyn in the car; she's a great listener," Mom said as she started to get things ready for work.

"Will do," I said as I walked out to the car.

"Took you long enough," Jaelyn said as I got in the car. "So, what are you ranting to me about?"

"How'd you know I was going to rant?" I asked, confused.

"Mom sent me a warning text" she laughed.

"Omg," I laughed back.

During our fifteen-minute car ride to school, I told Jaelyn

51

about Emma and how she ignored my text; and how I thought I did something wrong.

"That's weird for Emma; she always responds to texts. She'll even respond to me, even though we don't talk much any more," Jaelyn said, puzzled.

"I'll just ask her at school, bye Jaelyn," I said as I got out.

"Bye," she said as she drove off to park her car.

I walked into school and went to try and find Emma or Ezra when all of a sudden, I noticed a lot of people were crying.

I ran over to my locker to see if Ezra was waiting for me, but she wasn't. I walked over to her locker to see her standing in silence, which was weird for her.

"Ezra, what's going on?" I asked, confused.

She looked up at me in confusion.

"You don't know?" she asked me, confused.

"No, what happened?" I asked again.

She stood in silence, probably deciding if she should tell me or not.

"Aaron Cripple," I heard a deep voice say behind me.

I turned around to see an officer standing behind me.

"Officer? Is everything okay?" I asked with a shaking voice.

"I need you to come with me," he said.

"Can I put my things away first?" I asked, still freaking out.

"Fine, I'll be back in five minutes. Don't you dare try anything. I know how you Cripples are," he said as he walked away.

I stood there shaking.

"Ezra, what is going on?" I said, officially freaking out.

"Aaron, Emma Grace went missing last night," she said.

"What?" I said in confusion. "She was perfectly fine

52

yesterday; how is that possible?"

"It's gonna be okay," she said calmly.

"Why do they need me?" I asked in a worried tone.

"I don't know," she said quietly.

Ezra hugged me; she knew I was panicking.

"Just stay calm. Everything will be fine," she said in a calming voice. "Now go put your things away before the officer comes back."

"Okay," I said while trying to calm myself. "Tell Mrs. Jones where I am."

"Will do. Good luck, Aaron," Ezra said while I walked away.

I put my things away, still in disbelief of the whole situation. I couldn't believe Emma was gone.

"Aaron Cripple, let's go," the officer said from behind me.

I just nodded my head and walked behind him.

This walk through the hallway was the definition of the walk of shame. Everyone was looking at me, thinking I had done something to Emma.

"Monster!" I heard one of Emma's friends shout at me.

I looked at her in confusion. I knew I wasn't a monster, but I sure felt like it. This was like a nightmare, the girl of my dreams vanishes and I'm the one who's left to blame…

Chapter 4

"Have a seat, Mr. Cripple," the officer said. "We will be with you in just a few minutes."

I sat down like he said.

I was starting to calm down a little bit. I knew I wasn't going to jail or anything, but I was still worried about what the police wanted from me. I had never talked to a police officer under such stressful conditions before. I just hoped I wouldn't mess anything up.

"Hey Aaron, you okay?" I heard Mrs. Wilson ask me as she walked into her office.

"Yeah, just worried," I answered her.

"You'll be okay. Just answer them honestly, and nothing will go wrong," she said as she handed me a bottle of water.

"Thanks," I said quietly.

She looked at me with a smile and walked out of her office.

While I waited for the police officer, I just tried to calm down even more by drinking water and taking deep breaths.

After a while, I calmed down and realized that this probably wouldn't be as scary as I thought it'd be.

"All right, Mr. Cripple, thank you for waiting," the officer said as he walked back into the office. "Let's get started."

"Okay," I said while mentally preparing myself.

"Okay, Aaron, when was the last time you saw Emma Grace?" the officer asked.

"I talked to her yesterday after school, sir," I said

surprisingly calmly.

"Okay," he said as he wrote something down. "And please, call me officer Miller. Sir is too formal for me."

"Will do," I said, trying to sound calm.

"All right, Aaron, when you were talking to Emma, did she state anything like where she was going or what she was doing?" Officer Miller asked.

"Emma told me she was going to go back into the school to help Mrs. Jones with something," I answered him.

"Did she say where she was going after helping Mrs. Jones?" He asked.

"She did not," I said while shaking my head.

Officer Miller wrote down a bunch of things while I sat there waiting.

I could tell that he hoped I would know more, I felt bad that I wasn't much of a help, but there was nothing I could do.

"So, Aaron, what did you and Ms. Emma Grace talk about yesterday?" Officer Miller asked.

"Umm… just teenager things," I said nervously.

I knew I wasn't a police officer, but I thought that was a weird question to ask, and I didn't really know how to answer.

"A little more specific, please," Officer Miller asked, obviously getting frustrated with me.

"I don't know. We were just talking about school and life, nothing important," I said while starting to sweat.

"Aaron, when someone is missing, anything can help lead us in the right direction," Officer Miller explained. "Now, tell me exactly what you guys were talking about before I lose my cool."

I tried to remember what we were talking about, but I honestly couldn't remember. The stress I was feeling must've temporarily cleared my head of anything useful.

"Officer Miller, I can't think of what we were talking about; I'm sorry, my mind's blank," I said while panicking.

"I know you're lying to me, Cripple. I've dealt with people in your family before; I'm used to the innocent card being played," he said sternly.

"I'm not lying, Officer Miller, I swear," I said, just trying to calm myself.

"Kid, don't make me force you to talk 'cause that won't be fun for either of us," he said, completely done with me.

"I'm sorry, I don't know. This is just so stressful for me; please don't do anything foolish," I said, still trying to appear calm.

Officer Miller looked at me and stood up. He walked over to me until he was pretty much breathing on top of me.

"I'll give you one more chance before I turn into the bad guy you think I am," he whispered in my ear.

"Look, I don't know, I really don't," I said while my eyes began to water.

"Get out," he said, pointing to the door.

"What?" I asked, surprised.

"Out!" he shouted. "Just know if this girl is found dead, it's on you."

I stood up and walked out of Mrs. Wilson's office. I was glad it was over, but it was way worse than I thought it would be.

My heart was still pounding in my chest. I was so scared officer Miller was going to do something to me.

I walked over to Mrs. Wilson to try and figure out what I should do since I had no idea.

"Mrs. Wilson, where should I go?" I asked, trying to sound

like I wasn't about to break down.

"Go to your first hour. The bell's not going to ring for another fifteen minutes," she said, obviously noticing I was a mess.

"Okay, thanks," I said as I walked away.

I walked down the halls trying to take deep breaths and be as calm as possible before I returned to class.

I decided to walk over to the water fountain to get a drink since I had left my water in Mrs. Wilson's office. I hoped that would help calm me down even more.

"Scary interrogation?" I heard someone ask me.

I looked up to see Mr. Smith standing over me.

"Yeah, I guess," I said as I started to walk away.

"It sucks what happened to Emma Grace," he said, trying to continue a conversation with me.

"Yeah," I said, continuing to walk away.

"I heard they have no leads; it's pretty crazy," he said, starting to walk behind me.

"Yeah, well, I gotta get to class. See you next hour," I said while speed walking away.

Mr. Smith wasn't a bad person or anything. I just didn't want to talk about the interrogation with anyone right now. I just wanted to forget about it.

I continued to walk until I got to Mrs. Jones's classroom. I walked in to see everyone just sitting at their desks in silence. Mrs. Jones saw me and walked over to me.

"We're all just having an easy day today, just sit down and relax; everything's okay," Mrs. Jones whispered.

"Okay," I whispered back.

I walked over to my desk and sat down.

Ezra was asleep at her desk across the room, so there was

no one to entertain me.

I decided to follow in Ezra's footsteps and try to fall asleep.

It was easier than expected, and before I knew it, I was sound asleep.

"Aaron, wake up," Mrs. Jones said while she gently shook my shoulder.

I sat up and rubbed my eyes. I felt like I had just slept for a whole day.

"What time is it?" I asked while still trying to wake myself up.

"It's time for you to go to lunch," she said.

"I slept through all my morning classes?" I said, surprised.

"Yeah, but all classes were taking an easy day, so I just told your teachers you were here. I didn't want to wake you, you seemed upset," Mrs. Jones explained.

"Thank you, the interrogation was stressful," I said.

"I know. I had to do one earlier; it wasn't fun," she said.

"Well, I'm gonna go; thanks again," I said as I started to walk out of the classroom.

"You're welcome," Mrs. Jones said.

As I walked down the halls, I kept just picturing Emma Grace. I saw her around every corner. I looked at the place where she broke up with Teagan, the place she saved me from him, and the place we bumped into each other and had a good laugh.

I hoped Emma would be found soon. I couldn't imagine never seeing her walk around these halls again, she made them brighter, and without her, they were just as boring as a black and white movie.

"Aaron!" I heard Ezra shout.

"Hey, Ezra," I said back.

"You wanna get in line, sleepyhead?" she asked.

"Line for what?" I asked, confused.

"Lunch," she said with a slight chuckle.

"Oh right, sorry, I'm still half asleep," I said.

"I can tell," she said jokingly. "Well, let's get in line. I'm hungry,"

Ezra and I quickly rushed to the back of the lunch line.

We waited for only a few minutes before we got our food and then sat down at our usual table.

I was still half asleep, which didn't help me at all.

"So, how long did you sleep for?" Ezra asked.

"Till the lunch bell," I answered her.

"So you just woke up?" Ezra said with a chuckle.

"Yep," I said while starting to eat my crappy school lunch.

"That interrogation must've really tired you out," she said.

"Yeah, it was awful," I said back.

"What happened?" she asked.

"I don't wanna talk about it," I said.

"Come on. I'm your best friend," she said.

"I know what happened," I heard someone say from behind me.

I turned around to see one of Emma Grace's friends standing behind me. The same one that called me a monster earlier.

"How would you know what happened, Jessica?" Ezra asked her.

"She doesn't know," I said to Ezra. "I haven't told anyone."

"You don't need to tell me anything. I already know what happened," Jessica said.

"Well, what happened?" I asked honestly, wanting to know what she would say.

"The police officer got mad at you because you wouldn't tell them where you're keeping Emma Grace," she said confidently.

"You're a little off," I said jokingly.

"Cut your bullshit. Where is she?" Jessica shouted at me.

"Wait a minute. You actually think I did something to her?" I asked, surprised.

"Why else would the police question you?" she asked, obviously frustrated.

"If you want to know Jessica, they questioned me because I was one of the last people to see Emma Grace, no other reason, I am not a suspect," I said, completely done with her.

"If you're innocent, then say it to my face!" she shouted at me.

"I just did!" I shouted back at her.

She was so mad at me. I couldn't believe she actually thought I would do something to Emma. Honestly, why would anyone? I'm one of the weakest people in the universe. Even if I wanted to do something to Emma, she could easily overpower me. I would be no match for her.

"I'm done with this!" Jessica shouted as she smacked me across the face.

"Ow!" I shouted at her. "Leave me alone. I didn't do anything!"

"I won't leave until you tell me the truth!" she shouted at me.

"Jessica, leave Aaron alone! He gave you his honest answer!" Ezra shouted at her.

Ezra usually stayed pretty chill. It was weird to see her act this way.

I guess she just wanted to eat her food in peace, and Jessica

60

was preventing that.

"You shut up!" Jessica screamed at her. "Your kind of people are the ones who started all these crimes in this town! I bet Emma is being guarded by a bunch of runaway slaves!"

The cafeteria went silent. Everyone knew Jessica wasn't the best person, but making a racist comment like that was a new kind of low for her.

"Leave!" I shouted while looking her in her eyes.

Jessica's eyes began to water. I guess she didn't know what it was like to be yelled at, especially by someone like me.

"Did I stutter?" I said without missing a beat.

"You've turned into a horrible person, Cripple," Jessica said while holding back tears.

"No, I haven't, but you have. Now leave before you say anything else you will regret," I said, completely done with her and her attitude.

She ran out of the cafeteria crying. I couldn't tell if people were mad at her or me, but I didn't care. I wasn't going to let her say stuff like that, especially to my best friend.

"Aaron over here making girls cry for me," Ezra said jokingly.

"Shut up," I said back.

We started laughing together. I always thought it was dumb how some people were treated differently just because of their skin.

Ezra was pretty lucky that it didn't happen to her often, but it still happened sometimes, and that's not okay.

"You okay?" I asked once we were done laughing.

"Yeah, stuff like that happens, and there's nothing I can do. It's not like I can become a privileged white male," she said, obviously joking a little bit.

I just rolled my eyes at her, even though she was sadly right in a way.

After lunch, the day flew by, and before I knew it, I was riding home in the car with Jaelyn.

"So, how was your day?" Jaelyn asked.

"Okay, I guess. I was questioned by the police and made a racist girl cry at lunch," I answered her.

"Wait, really?" she asked.

"Yeah, I was one of the last people to see Emma Grace before, you know, she disappeared, so the police asked me a few things, and then a girl was being racist towards Ezra, and I wasn't going to put up with it," I explained.

"Well, your day sounds interesting," she said.

"Yeah, how was your day?" I asked.

"Boring, the most exciting thing that happened to me was being butt-dialed by Mom," she said.

"Sounds about right," I laughed.

We got home pretty quickly after Jaelyn and I finished our mini conversation.

We walked inside to a surprisingly empty house.

"Where's Mom and Carl?" I asked Jaelyn.

"Mom's still at work, and Carl stopped to get Effie ice cream," she said.

"Of course he did, his favorite child," I said.

"It's okay; we're hated together," she said.

"True, but I'm hated more," I said. "I bet Carl's going to bring you ice cream and not me."

"If he brings ice cream, it's going to be for both of us," she said.

"Whatever you say," I said as I walked to my room.

I got to my room and opened up the messaging app on my

phone.

I opened up the message to Emma Grace to see if anything had changed, but nothing did.

I closed the messaging app and started to play games on my phone to get my mind off of Emma Grace.

It only took a few minutes of playing games on my phone before Carl and Effie got home.

"Jaelyn, Aaron, I made you guys things at school!" I heard Effie shout happily.

I set my phone down and walked into the living room to see Effie giving Jaelyn a picture she had painted.

"It's beautiful. What is it?" Jaelyn asked Effie.

"It's a butterfly," Effie said happily.

"Very nice, go give Aaron his picture now," Jaelyn said while pointing at me.

"Aaron, I worked hard on this!" Effie shouted as she ran over to me.

"Let me see it," I said, honestly excited to see what picture I would be able to add to my collection.

Effie handed me a photo of what appeared to be a bear holding a heart.

"It has a heart 'cause I love you," she said while pointing to the heart.

"It's very nice," I said.

"I'm gonna go get my ice cream," she said as she ran off.

Once Effie was outside, I made my way over to Jaelyn. I was wondering what her butterfly looked like.

"Show me the beautiful Effie butterfly," I said to Jaelyn.

She turned the page over to show me something that looked like a deformed chicken.

"That's a butterfly?" I said, questioning myself.

"Apparently," Jaelyn said. "You're lucky; your's actually looks like a bear."

"I know. I guess Effie just likes me better," I said jokingly.

"You just realized that?" she said.

"Jaelyn, I was joking. Effie loves us both," I said.

At that moment, Carl walked in with Effie, both with an ice cream in hand.

"See, none of us get ice cream," Jaelyn whispered.

"Guess so," I whispered back.

Right at that moment, Carl walked over to us and handed Jaelyn the ice cream cone he was holding.

"Thanks," Jaelyn said.

"Guess we share, Aaron," she said.

"No, you don't," Carl said sternly. "That's just for you."

"Do I get one?" I asked.

"You'll get ice cream when you get good grades like your sisters," he said.

"My grades aren't that bad," I said, annoyed.

"One word, chemistry," he said.

"Really?" I asked.

"Really," he said as he walked away.

"I told you this was going to happen," I said to Jaelyn.

"What is your science grade?" Jaelyn asked.

"Seventy-nine percent, a C+," I said.

"That's not that bad," she said.

"I know! He acts like I have an F," I said.

"He's an ass. Take my ice cream; you deserve it," she said.

"No, he gave it to you. He'll kill me if he sees me with it," I said.

"True," she said. "Just take a lick from it real quick; he'll never know."

"Fine," I said as I took a lick off the ice cream.

"Good?" Jaelyn asked.

"Yep, it's chocolate, a classic," I said.

Jaelyn smiled and took a lick for herself.

"It is good," she said with a mouthful of chocolate ice cream.

"Don't choke on it," I said jokingly.

She started laughing, then took a second to actually swallow the ice cream before she legitimately started choking.

"Don't make me laugh when I have food in my mouth," she said, starting to laugh again.

"I'll try," I said as I walked back to my room.

Jaelyn and I definitely both got Dad's love for chocolate as kids. I knew if he were still here, he'd be running off with Jaelyn's ice cream while we all laughed, chasing him around the house.

I looked over at my old family photo of me, Jaelyn, Mom, and Dad.

"Miss you, Dad," I said to myself.

"I miss him too," I heard Jaelyn say from behind me.

"He would've taken your ice cream," I said with a smile.

"I know. He would've taken both of ours," she said.

"Both?" I said, confused.

"If Dad were here, you'd have an ice cream cone too," she said. "If Carl was like Dad, he would've noticed that you did bring your chemistry grade up, and he'd be proud."

"I hope Dad's proud of us," I said while still holding the family photo.

"Me too," Jaelyn said as she looked at the family photo. "We were so little."

"I know, it's weird. I feel like Dad was in our lives longer than he actually was," I said.

"Me too," Jaelyn said.

Dad's death definitely hit Jaelyn and me hard.

I've always thought maybe it'd be easier to move on if Carl wasn't so bad compared to Dad, but there was nothing Carl did better than Dad. Dad was perfect, and I missed him.

"I'm gonna go start cleaning up my room; it's a disaster," Jaelyn said.

"Okay, see you later," I said as she walked out.

Once she left, I lay on my bed just thinking about everything.

It hurt me to think that I might lose Emma Grace just like I lost Dad. I lost him so soon and unexpectedly. I didn't want Emma Grace to turn out the same.

Out of curiosity, I pulled out my phone to look at Emma Grace's message again to see if anything had changed, even though I was pretty sure nothing had.

"What?" I shouted out, confused.

Emma Grace's message had been marked as read.

That meant she might still be alive.

I quickly sent her a text even though I knew the odds of her responding were very low.

Emma, are you okay?

Was she the one who opened the message? Or was it someone else? I had no idea. All I knew was someone was using Emma's phone.

This may seem like nothing but to me, it gave me hope, hope that the girl I cared so much about was still alive somewhere, and that's all I needed to keep me going.

Chapter 5

That night I couldn't sleep. Thoughts were just running through my head nonstop.

After a while of constant tossing and turning, I decided to pull out my phone and check the time.

"2.14?" I whispered to myself.

After I realized how late it was, I decided to get up and have another attempt at getting a glass of water.

I walked out of my room into the dark hallway. I tiptoed across the kitchen to the cupboard, and this time, I decided to get a plastic cup, so I couldn't break it.

Everything was going so smoothly; I didn't even need the light.

"Aaron?" I heard Jaelyn say as she turned on the light.

"What?" I said as I rubbed my eyes.

"Why are you awake?" she asked.

"I can't sleep," I answered.

"So you decided to get water? Even though last time you did this, you somehow managed to shatter Mom's favorite mug?" she said as she walked over to the counter.

"Yep, but I grabbed a plastic cup, so it's fine," I said.

"A Barbie plastic cup, nice," she said jokingly.

I looked down at the cup to see if Jaelyn was right, and sure enough, I saw Barbie staring right at me.

"I honestly forgot this cup existed," I said while still looking at it.

"Figured, you're not cool enough for Barbie," Jaelyn said jokingly. "So, what's keeping you up?"

"Well, something crazy happened, and I can't get it out of my mind," I explained.

"And what happened that's so crazy?" she asked.

I stood there for a second deciding if I should tell her or not. I didn't know if it meant anything, but if it did, I didn't want to risk hurting Jaelyn; she's the only good family member I have left that's over the age of ten.

"I don't think I should tell you," I said quietly.

"What?" she said, surprised. "Do you want me to tickle you again?"

"Fine, but you can't tell a soul," I said.

"Okay, mister mystery," she said while walking over to me. "So, what is it?"

"You know how I messaged Emma Grace?" I asked.

"Yeah?" she said, confused.

"She opened it," I said.

"What?" Jaelyn said, surprised. "Did she respond?"

"No, she just read it, and honestly, I don't even know if it was her," I explained to Jaelyn.

"Aaron, I don't even know what to say. I mean, should we tell the police?" she asked.

"I don't know; the police seem to hate me," I said.

"What do you mean?" she asked.

"During the interrogation, the police officer got so mad at me and said he dealt with people in our family before and he knew what I was doing, which confused the crap out of me," I explained.

"Well, we do come from a line of people that have learned to trick the police," she said.

"What?" I said, confused.

"Grandpa on Dad's side was crazy and killed someone, and Grandpa's mom was a complete psycho. She killed so many people, some of them even being children," Jaelyn explained.

"Well, I see why the cops don't like us," I said.

"Yeah, I'm pretty sure the last name Cripple just scares them at this point," she said while laughing to herself.

"So let's not tell the police," I said.

"Yeah, but I feel like we should do something,' Jaelyn said.

"Me too," I said back.

"Wait a minute, can't you track her phone?" Jaelyn asked me, knowing she had just struck gold.

"Maybe," I said, shocked. "I would need Ezra, though."

"Invite her over after school; it's Friday," Jaelyn said.

"That sounds like a plan," I said. "Wait, what if Mom and Carl say no?"

"Just don't ask them and tell Mom Carl said yes and tell Carl Mom said yes," she said.

"We're so getting grounded," I said.

"You're getting grounded. Ezra's your friend," Jaelyn said while starting to walk away.

"You're such a butt," I said, following her.

"I may be a butt, but just remember this was my idea. So I'm a smart butt," she said while beginning to walk into her room.

"You mean a smartass?" I said jokingly.

"Whatever you say," Jaelyn said as she rolled her eyes.

"Night, smartass," I said as I walked away.

I walked into my room and lay on my bed. I just hoped this plan wouldn't backfire on me, Jaelyn or Ezra. This plan honestly could be considered risky. But was it risky enough to actually work? Could we really save Emma Grace? My head was filled with questions, but right now they needed to be left unanswered. I just needed sleep.

The next morning I was exhausted. I could barely open my eyes, but I knew I had to. Today could be a big day, and I needed to be ready for it.

I walked out of my room to see Jaelyn in the kitchen stealing a sip of Mom's coffee.

"Tired?" I asked Jaelyn as I walked up to her.

"Of course, I live with you," Jaelyn said, still half asleep.

"Well, I'll see you in the car," I said as I walked toward the bathroom.

"Don't forget about what we talked about last night!" Jaelyn shouted.

"I won't!" I shouted back.

I got ready as quickly as possible. I was already running ten minutes behind, so I didn't need to slack any more.

The second I was done, I grabbed my bag and ran out to the car.

When I got there, I saw that Jaelyn was just sitting on her phone, waiting for me.

"How'd you get here so fast?" I asked while out of breath.

"That's my secret I'll never tell. Now get in; we have to go. We're running late," Jaelyn said while she started the car.

"So glad it's Friday," I said while getting in the car.

"Me too," Jaelyn said. "No more three a.m. chit chats on a school night."

"No promises," I joked.

The car ride seemed quicker than normal that morning. I couldn't tell if I was still half asleep or if Jaelyn had just gone over the speed limit a bunch. Either way, we somehow made it to school on time.

"Is time management another hidden talent of yours?" I asked Jaelyn as I got out of the car.

"Probably," She answered me. "Now go. I still have to park."

"Okay, I'll see you later," I said to Jaelyn as she drove off.

I ran up to the school and walked in through the main doors.

The hallway was crowded like normal, but as always, I still managed to find Ezra.

"Ezra!" I shouted while making my way over to her.

"Hey," she said as we started to walk to my locker.

"So, how long have you been waiting for me?" I asked as I opened up my locker.

"About ten minutes," she answered me.

"Dang, How early do you get here?" I asked.

"Earlier than you," she said with a smile.

Ezra always seemed the most joyful on Fridays, and I didn't blame her. The end of the week is always a time to look forward to.

"So got any fun plans over the weekend?" I asked while opening my locker.

"I get to go stay with my brother at his apartment," she said.

"That sounds nice," I said.

"Yeah, I'm looking forward to it," she said while we started to walk down the hallway.

"When are you leaving?" I asked.

"Not till Saturday morning, sadly," she said.

"You should just come chill with Jaelyn and me," I said.

"Sure, will your parents know about my arrival?" she asked.

"They'll figure it out," I said.

71

"You're weird," she said back.

"Yeah, but you are too, and that's why we're friends," I said while we walked into Mrs. Jones's room.

"True," she said. "So, are we gonna do anything fun?"

"We are gonna track a phone," I said.

"Who's?" Ezra asked.

"It'll be a surprise," I said.

"That sounds interesting," she said. "I'm gonna head to my seat; talk to you later."

"Okay," I said as Ezra walked away.

I sat down in my seat and just waited for class to start.

After a few minutes, the bell had rung, and everyone was there except Mrs. Jones.

After about ten more minutes of waiting, everyone started to get a little concerned.

"Is Mrs. Jones here?" Alex King asked me from behind.

"I don't know," I said. "I'll ask Ezra."

I stood up and walked over to Ezra's desk and sat down beside her.

"Is Mrs. Jones here?" I whispered to Ezra.

"I saw her this morning, so unless she left like five minutes ago, she should still be here," Ezra answered me.

"Do you think the teachers have a meeting or something?" I asked.

"That would be weird for teachers to just leave kids in a classroom, so I doubt it," she said.

"Guys, you might wanna come over here," Alex King said while looking out the window.

Everyone ran over to the window as quickly as possible. We were all curious.

I looked over to see police cars and an ambulance.

"Holy shit," I heard Ezra say from behind me.

"What is happening out there?" I asked.

"I have no clue," Alex answered me.

"Should we go ask someone?" I asked everyone.

"You can," Alex said.

"I'll go with you, Aaron," Morgan said.

Morgan was one of my classmates that rarely talked. She was one of the smartest people in my grade, even though I've never even heard her say a full sentence. So it was weird when she offered to come with me.

"Okay, let's go," I said as I moved away from the window. Morgan followed behind me.

We walked into the hallway to not see or hear anyone.

"All the doors are shut," Morgan whispered to herself.

"You think we're in a lockdown?" I asked.

She didn't answer.

Morgan started knocking on some classroom doors, but no one answered.

"This is so weird," I said out loud.

I tried knocking on a door myself but I got the same response as Morgan, nothing.

"Let's try the office," she said.

"Okay," I said.

At this point, Morgan was leading me around the school, which made sense. She was the smarter one, after all.

We walked up to the office only to find a familiar sight, nothing.

"I'm gonna try calling my sister," I said to Morgan as I pulled out my phone.

I dialed Jaelyn's number and waited for her to answer, but she never did.

At that point, we started to hear voices coming from the other side of the hallway.

"Let's go," Morgan said as she started to walk toward the voices.

"Okay," I said as I followed Morgan.

I didn't know if this was a good idea or not, but I was so scared to say no to Morgan for some reason, so I just followed along.

We walked to the end of the hallway to see some adults standing in the conference room.

"Ask them," Morgan whispered.

"Why me?" I asked.

"Because I said I would go, not figure this out," she said.

"Fair enough," I said.

I walked over to the doorway and knocked lightly on the open door.

"Hi, sorry to bother you, but what is going on?" I asked them hesitantly.

All the adults in the room just looked at me like I was diseased. I felt like I was about to be in so much trouble for absolutely no reason.

"What are you doing out of class, young man? We're in a lockdown," I heard a deep voice say to me.

"Sorry, sir, I had no idea," I said, starting to regret ever asking them.

It was weird. I didn't recognize anyone in this room. I would think that with South Ray's low staffing level, I would know almost everyone, but I guess not.

Before I got asked anything else, I looked around the room more closely. Everything seemed normal except for the guy standing in front of the closet door. He looked on edge. It looked like he was ready to kill someone. I didn't know what was going on, but I knew it wasn't good.

I looked more closely at the guy and noticed the glare of a sharp pocket knife coming out of his pocket.

"Where are you supposed to be, young man?" The guy asked me as he walked closer.

I looked up at him in fear before blurting out an answer.

"Mrs. Jones's classroom. We're from her first hour."

"I see," he said while looking at the other adults.

"I'll go back there if you want," I said, wanting to avoid any confrontation.

Right as he was about to answer me, we heard a high-pitched scream echo through the halls.

Before the guy could say anything else to me, I bolted out of the room.

As I ran out, I saw Morgan standing there like nothing was happening.

"We have to go!" I shouted.

"Do you know what's happening?" she asked.

"All I know is we need to go!" I shouted at her.

"I want answers!" she shouted back at me.

"And I want to live!" I shouted back. "We're going now!"

"Fine," she said.

We started running down the hall towards Mrs. Jones's room.

We got to the door only to find it locked.

"Shit," I said under my breath.

"Just knock," Morgan said, surprisingly calm.

I started knocking a bunch hoping someone would open the door, but it was quiet.

Right before I was about to start shouting for Ezra, I heard another scream.

"Open the door!" I shouted while continuing to knock.

"They probably think you're the killer at this point, Aaron," Morgan said, frustrated.

"Well, sorry, I don't want to die!" I shouted at her.

"You're not gonna die!" she shouted back at me, annoyed.

"Shut up!" I shouted at her. "I literally saw some guy with a knife in the conference room!"

"You're just going crazy!" she shouted at me.

Before I could say anything else to her, I heard a familiar voice from inside the classroom.

"What's the password to Fort Aza?" I heard someone say.

"Cute cat 127," I answered.

"What on earth?" Morgan asked.

Right at that moment, Ezra opened the door and pulled Morgan and me inside.

"What is Fort Aza?" Alex asked Ezra.

"A fort me and Aaron made when we were kids. I didn't know if he was at the door or not, but I knew if it was him, he would know that password," Ezra explained.

"I'm glad you thought of that. I was not in the mood to die," I said.

"Glad you're okay. Now let's go sit in the corner and act like we are prepared for a lockdown," Alex said to us.

"Sounds good," Ezra said as she sat down in the corner.

I sat down beside her.

"Thanks for letting me in," I whispered.

"No problem, King Awesome," Ezra said.

"Queen Diamond has everything under control," I joked.

We started laughing quietly with each other.

Everyone stayed quiet after a while, just wondering what

would happen next.

Thankfully, we no longer heard any screams, which I considered to be a good sign.

After a few hours of sitting in anticipation, the intercom turned on.

STUDENTS, PLEASE REPORT TO THE OFFICE TO BE PICKED UP OR SIGNED OUT. EVERYONE IS DISMISSED FOR THE DAY

Everyone quickly got up, collected their things and left the classroom. The halls were full again. It was nice. I just hoped that everyone was okay.

"Am I still coming over?" Ezra asked.

"Of course," I said as we started to walk towards the office.

Honestly, I had completely forgotten about Ezra and the plan until that moment.

We quickly signed out at the office and met Jaelyn at her car.

"So, do you know what happened?" I asked Jaelyn as we got in the car.

"I'm not a hundred percent sure, but I overheard someone saying that Jessica Robinson got attacked by someone," Jaelyn said.

"Are you serious?" Ezra asked, surprised. "Racist Jessica Robinson was attacked?"

"That's what I heard," Jaelyn said as she drove the car out of the parking lot.

"Is she okay?" I asked Jaelyn.

"I don't know," Jaelyn said. "I did hear the attacker wasn't caught, though, and they escaped the school."

"That's just great," Ezra said sarcastically.

"Well, we'll have fun and forget about this whole crazy day," I said, trying to lighten the mood.

We all arrived at the house shortly after.

No one would admit it, but we were all still in shock from the events of that morning.

It was hard to get those screams out of my head. I felt so bad for Jessica, even though she was a horrible person. No one deserves to go through something like that, not even her.

"Let's go inside," Jaelyn said as she turned the car off.

"Okay," Ezra said as she got out. "You coming?"

"Yeah, I'm just thinking," I said as I hopped out of the car.

"You know everything's okay, right?" Ezra asked.

"Yeah, today was just wild," I answered her. "Now, let's get inside; you need to help Jaelyn and me with a mini-project."

"That doesn't scare me at all," Ezra said jokingly.

We all walked into the house to find no one else there. Only this time, it wasn't a surprise. It was only noon, so we weren't expecting anyone to be home.

"So, what am I helping you guys with?" Ezra asked as she set her stuff down.

"Aaron, you explain. I gotta call Mom. She's in a panic," Jaelyn said as she walked away.

"Okay, tell her we're fine," I said.

"Will do," Jaelyn said as she dialed Mom's number.

"So is it explanation time?" Ezra asked.

"Sure is," I answered her. "So you know how I texted Emma Grace the night she went missing?"

"No, but keep going," Ezra said.

"Well, the message was marked as seen," I said.

"Okay?" Ezra said, confused. "What does that mean?"

"It means that either Emma Grace or her kidnappers have her phone," I explained.

"Okay, that's probably true, but what does that have to do with anything?" Ezra asked, still confused.

"Ezra, the phone is probably with Emma," I said, trying to get Ezra to realize what I was getting at.

"I'm still lost," she said.

"Ezra, we know how to track phones," I said.

Right at that moment, Ezra's eyes lit up. She realized what I was trying to get at.

"Aaron, you're a genius!" Ezra shouted. "Wait, does this mean we could save Emma Grace?"

"Possibly," I said.

"Well, what are we waiting for? Let's go," Ezra said as she dragged me to the computer in my room.

"Okay, do you remember how to do this?" I asked as we sat down.

"Yeah, I just need the phone number, I think," she said.

"Okay, it's 314-159-2653," I said.

"Perfect," Ezra said as she began to get all the tabs she needed opened.

"Well, Mom's an emotional mess," Jaelyn said as she walked into my room.

"Why?" I asked.

"Because her so-called babies were in danger," Jaelyn explained.

"Makes sense," I said as I looked over at the computer screen. "Wow, you're going fast."

"Yeah, I work faster under pressure," Ezra said.

"You're not under pressure, though?" Jaelyn said, puzzled.

"Yes, I am. Emma Grace has been kidnapped, and for all

79

we know, she could be hurt or worse. So we need answers ASAP," Ezra quickly explained.

"Guess you're right," I said. "Do you guys think this is dangerous?"

"Yeah," Ezra and Jaelyn said, nearly in sync.

"That's reassuring," I said while looking back at the computer.

"What did you expect? We're practically doing police work," Ezra said.

"Yeah, and if we do something wrong, these guys could easily track us down and kill us," Jaelyn said.

"You guys aren't helping!" I shouted at them.

"Okay, enough, Aaron. Do you know Emma Grace's password?" Ezra asked.

"No, I have no clue," I said.

"Well, I need it," Ezra explained.

"Try her birthday," Jaelyn said to us.

"And what's that?" Ezra asked.

"She was born May 3rd, 1996," I answered.

"Okay, may I ask how you know that?" Jaelyn asked.

"I have my ways," I answered her with a smirk.

"Of course you do," Jaelyn said with a slight chuckle.

"Okay, the password was 31996," Ezra said to us.

"That was quick," I said.

"All right, let's figure out where Emma is," Ezra said as she hit enter.

We all sat there for a minute, waiting for the location to pop up, but nothing happened.

"Try hitting enter again," Jaelyn said.

"Okay," Ezra said as she pushed the enter key one more time.

In a matter of seconds, the computer started acting weird. It started flashing and distributing hundreds of what seemed to be pop-up ads.

"What the hell?" I heard Jaelyn say under her breath.

Right at that moment, my phone's ringer started going off.

I looked to see one of the most disturbing messages ever.

My eyes instantly grew.

Before anyone else could read it, I threw my phone across the room.

Ezra and Jaelyn just looked at me weirdly.

"Aaron, what's wrong?" Jaelyn asked.

I couldn't answer. I started to shake.

"Aaron, it's fine; we're here," Ezra said while trying to calm me down.

Jaelyn walked across the room and picked up my phone. I looked up at her and saw her eyes widen. She didn't say a word and started to panic, just like me.

"Will you guys tell me what's happening?" Ezra shouted.

"Aaron got a message," Jaelyn said, trying not to panic.

"What does it say?" Ezra asked, still not understanding the situation.

"It's bad," Jaelyn said.

"Read it!" Ezra shouted.

"The message is from Emma's number," Jaelyn said. "And it says, *If you ever try to contact or find this number again, we will kill you and everyone you love.*"

"What?" Ezra shouted.

We all looked at each other and just sat there. This was unreal. We were just some dumb high school kids. We could've never seen this coming.

"It's my fault," I heard Jaelyn whisper to herself.

"No, it's not," I said.

"Yes, it is! This was my idea, and now we could all be in danger because of me!" Jaelyn shouted.

"Jaelyn, stop. If we just take turns blaming someone, we'll never get anywhere!" I shouted back at her.

They both just sat in silence. They knew I was right.

I knew we had to do something, but I didn't know what.

"Aaron, Jaelyn!" I heard my mom shout as she walked into the house.

"Great," I heard Ezra say sarcastically under her breath.

"Everyone pretend like everything's okay," Jaelyn whispered to us. "We're in here, Mom!"

I hoped Mom wouldn't realize something was wrong. It always seemed impossible to hide stuff from her. She can read Jaelyn and me like a book in a matter of seconds.

I just hoped Mom didn't ask me anything. I was a terrible liar.

"Hey, how are you guys?" Mom asked us as she walked in. "Hey Ezra, didn't know you were coming over."

"Yeah, sorry, I just came to chill," Ezra said nervously.

"You're fine, sweetie. So are you guys okay?" Mom asked all of us.

"Yeah, we're all fine," Jaelyn said, surprisingly calm.

"Yep," Ezra said in agreement with Jaelyn.

"Aaron?" Mom said.

"Perfectly fine," I said quickly.

Mom just gave me her look. She knew I was lying.

Jaelyn and Ezra were both amazing liars, unlike me.

"You sure?" Mom asked me while she walked up to me.

"Yeah," I said while looking over at Jaelyn.

"Hey! I'm talking to you, not Jaelyn," Mom said sternly.

"Sorry," I said while looking over at my mom.

"Jaelyn, Ezra, can you girls leave for a second? I need to have a word with Aaron," Mom said while looking over at me.

Jaelyn and Ezra walked out of the room while giving me the look of don't screw this up.

"You sure you're okay, sweetie?" Mom asked. "You look tense."

"I said I was fine. I wouldn't lie to you," I said, trying to sound as truthful as possible.

Mom sighed and looked over at me.

"Okay, well, don't hesitate to come talk to me," Mom said as she walked out.

Jaelyn and Ezra came back into the room the second my mom walked out.

Ezra shut the door behind them quietly while Jaelyn walked over to me.

"Please tell me you didn't tell her," Jaelyn said.

"I didn't. I think she knows I'm lying, though," I said while looking down.

"Well that's just a given. You're a horrible liar," Ezra said while coming over to us.

"Guess you're right," I said with a slight smile.

"Now, what do we do?" Jaelyn asked us.

"I have no clue; I'm still freaking out," I said while standing up.

"They're not gonna kill us," Ezra said, trying to calm me.

"You're right; they're not going to kill us. They're going to kill me. They have my phone number and my location, not yours!" I shouted in a stressed tone.

"Aaron, stop. You're gonna be fine," Jaelyn said. "We're a

team. Ezra and I won't let anything happen to you."

"I hope you're right," I said while looking over at my computer.

"What if we close all those pop-up ads?" Ezra asked us.

"Are you insane?" Jaelyn said. "They threatened to kill us, no."

"Okay," Ezra said while stepping away from the computer.

"I'm gonna go start on my essay now. It's due Monday. You guys don't do anything stupid," Jaelyn said as she walked out.

Right as Jaelyn left, Ezra sat down at the computer and started to move the mouse.

"What are you doing??" I asked.

"What Jaelyn told me not to do," Ezra said while continuing to move the mouse.

"Ezra, no, we don't need any more death threats," I said while trying to pull her away from the computer. "How are you so strong?"

"Aaron, if we find Emma's location, we can save her before they have a chance to kill any of us," Ezra explained.

"This is a bad idea," I said while pacing around the room.

Ezra was determined. She wanted to figure this out so bad.

I looked over at the computer to see Ezra starting to close the pop-ups one by one.

"See, this isn't so bad," Ezra said while continuing to press the little red X's.

"I guess," I said while looking at my phone.

All of a sudden, my phone started ringing. I looked at it to see I was getting a call from Emma Grace's number.

"Ezra, it's Emma's number. What do I do?" I asked frantically.

"Answer," she said while closing more pop-ups.

"What, no!" I shouted.

"If you answer, we can possibly get a voice which can help the police identify the kidnapper," Ezra explained.

"Fine," I said while hesitantly picking up the phone.

I didn't want to answer, but Ezra brought up such a good point; it'd be selfish for me not to answer.

"Hello," I said as I answered the phone.

"You seem young," a deep voice said on the other side.

"What do you want?" I asked them.

"You know why I called," the person said.

"Do I, though?" I said, trying to play dumb.

I looked over at Ezra to see her still closing the pop-up ads. There were so many....

"Kid, don't play dumb," the voice said sternly.

"I don't know what you're talking about," I said, obviously frustrating the person on the other side.

"Kid, we will kill you. Stop what you're doing. Now!" the person shouted.

"Well, technically, I'm not doing anything except talking to you," I said while trying to buy Ezra more time.

"I don't care who it is! Make them stop now, or else!" the person shouted angrily.

"Or else what," I said boldly.

The person didn't respond. They were mad.

I looked back over at Ezra to see her closing the ads even faster.

"I'll give you one last chance," I heard the person say.

"Last chance for what?" I said, still playing dumb.

"You know what. I know you know!" the person shouted, frustrated.

"But I'm bad at remembering. I'm a kid, remember?" I

said, still acting like an idiot.

"Then this will hurt even worse, kid," the person said while breaking up.

"Wait, what does that mean? You're not here. You can't do anything," I said, starting to panic.

The person was silent. I looked up at Ezra to see that she had made a lot of progress.

"Hurry," I whispered.

"I'm trying," she whispered back.

"You still there, kid?" the person asked.

"Yeah?" I said, confused.

"Good," he said while laughing to himself.

I waited for him to say something, but all I heard was movement on the other side.

"What is he doing?" I whispered to myself.

Right at that moment, I started to hear a slight ringing from the other side. I was so confused I didn't know what he was doing.

The ringing gradually started to grow louder and louder. It seemed like we were breaking up.

"Hello?" I said into the phone.

"Have fun," I heard the person whisper.

Before I was able to react, the ringing became so loud, it was all I could hear.

It caused a sharp pain to run through my body.

I quickly threw the phone away from me, but it didn't help. I put my hands over my ears to try and block any sound, but it wasn't working. The ringing was stuck in my head, and I couldn't do anything. It caused my body to ache, and after a while, I couldn't even stand. My legs went limp, and I fell to the floor.

"Aaron!" Ezra shouted as she ran over to me. "Are you okay?"

"No," I whispered. "Everything hurts."

"What happened?" Ezra asked me in a panicked tone.

"Ringing," I said while still holding my head.

"Ringing? What? Aaron, sit up," Ezra said while pulling me up.

I was fine for about two seconds, then the pain doubled.

"Ow!" I screamed as I fell back down.

"Aaron, what is happening?" Ezra shouted at me in a worried tone.

"I don't know!" I shouted in pain. "Make it stop!"

"Aaron, I don't know what to do," Ezra said, panicking.

"Mom!" I screamed.

I knew getting my mom probably wasn't the best idea, but I didn't know what else to do, and neither did Ezra.

Ezra looked down at me and realized that we needed an adult.

"Amanda!" Ezra shouted. "I'm gonna go get her. I'll be back."

Ezra ran out of my room while I lay there. I didn't know what was happening to me. All I knew was that I was in pain.

I looked over at my phone to see the call still going. I picked up my phone to see if he was still there.

"What did you do?" I whispered into the phone.

"That's a secret, Aaron," the person said evilly.

"What?" I whispered.

I had no idea how he knew my name. I never said who I was.

"Aaron and Ezra, I heard. You too aren't very quiet," the person said. "Now have a good night. I'll see you soon."

"No," I whispered.

"Oh yes," the person said while they hung up.

We were screwed.

Why didn't I listen to my gut?

I wanted to be angry or sad, but I couldn't. I was in so much pain.

"Ezra, Mom!" I shouted, hoping I'd get someone's attention.

In a matter of seconds, my mom and Ezra walked through the door.

My mom squatted down to me and started feeling my forehead, making sure I wasn't running a fever.

"Honey, what's wrong?" Mom asked.

"It all hurts," I said weakly.

"Do you want water, or a shower, or bed?" Mom asked frantically.

"Bed," I said quietly.

I didn't know what I wanted. I just wanted the pain to stop.

"Okay, sweetie," Mom said while helping me to my feet.

The second I stood up, I nearly collapsed, but my mom caught me.

My mom helped me to my bed and laid me down; it felt nice.

"You need a ride home?" Mom asked Ezra.

"That'd be great. I'm gonna say bye to Aaron first, though" Ezra said.

"Okay, meet me outside," Mom said as she walked out.

Ezra walked over to me and sat down beside me.

"Aaron, I don't know what happened, but I'm sorry, I shouldn't have made you answer the phone," Ezra said, obviously feeling bad.

"It's okay. Turn the computer off on your way out," I said while beginning to doze off.

Ezra didn't say anything else. She knew I needed rest.

She got up, turned the computer off and walked out.

The second I heard the door shut, I was sound asleep.

"Aaron," I heard my mom whisper as she came into my room.

"What?" I moaned while opening my eyes.

"Are you feeling better?" she asked me while walking over to me.

"Yeah," I said, still half asleep.

Honestly, I was feeling better. I wasn't in pain any more, which was nice, but there was still a slight ringing in my ears, which was annoying.

"Well, I'm glad. You think you'll be up for dinner tonight?" she asked.

"Yeah, what are we having?" I asked while finally sitting up.

"Pizza," Mom said with a smile.

"If it's cheese, count me in," I joked.

"Don't worry, half of it's cheese. You're not the only picky person in this house," Mom laughed.

I knew she was talking about Effie and me. We were both extremely picky; we always were. It's a blessing and a curse, if I do say so myself.

"Well, I have to go pick up Effie from her friend's house. You should try to get up and enjoy the rest of your Saturday," Mom said as she began to walk away.

"Saturday?" I said, surprised.

"Yep, you slept for close to twenty-four hours," Mom said while looking at my surprised face.

"That's a lot," I said while getting up.

"Sure is," Mom said while smiling at me. "I'll see you in a little bit. I love you."

"Love you too," I said as she walked out.

I couldn't believe I had slept for so long, and I felt fine, mostly.

I walked over to the mirror to see if I looked different, but, no surprise, I looked the exact same. It was like nothing ever happened to me.

If it wasn't for Mom coming into my room to check on me and the slight ringing, I would've been convinced that I had dreamt the whole thing.

"Aaron!" Jaelyn shouted as she came into my room.

"Yeah?" I asked while still looking in the mirror.

"Sit down. We need to talk, now," Jaelyn said sternly.

"Okay, why do you sound like you're about to kill me?" I asked while I sat down.

"You know why," she said, annoyed.

"Why does everyone say that? I just woke up like five minutes ago. I can't recall much," I said, already annoyed.

"Do you recall completely ignoring what I said and getting yourself hurt?" she said while using her baby voice.

"Is that what this is about?" I asked, annoyed.

"Well, no, duh!" Jaelyn shouted at me.

"Are you just mad? Or did you actually wanna talk to me?" I asked while trying to wrap up our little conversation.

"I want to know what happened that made you feel like you were about to die," Jaelyn said while getting close to my face.

"I was on the phone with a creepy guy, and he played this weird ringing thing, and it sent pain throughout my body that made me think I was going to die," I explained.

"Why didn't you just pull the phone away?" she asked.

"It happened too fast. I didn't have time to properly react," I explained.

"Okay, guess that somehow makes sense," she said while preparing to ask me another question.

Jaelyn was so worried. I didn't know why I was fine now. There was no need for her to worry.

"Did they ever get a name?" she asked.

"Name?" I said, confused.

"Did they find out your name?" she asked me slowly.

"Maybe," I said quietly.

"What!" Jaelyn shouted. "How?"

"While I was dying, the guy was still listening to us, and he heard us say our names," I explained.

"You guys are idiots!" Jaelyn shouted.

"We didn't mean to do anything!" I shouted back.

"Well, you did, and now your lives are in danger!" Jaelyn shouted.

"Okay, what am I supposed to say?" I shouted angrily.

"Maybe how I was right, and you should've listened to me!" Jaelyn shouted, completely done with me.

"Oh, I see you just want a pat on the back for being the smart one!" I shouted.

"You're really gonna act like this?" Jaelyn shouted. "You know, you're gonna get hurt again if you keep doing stupid crap like this!"

"You can leave now," I said while walking to my closet.

"Don't give me lip. This could kill you!" Jaelyn shouted at me.

"Do you want an invite to my funeral? Is that what you're waiting for?" I shouted while walking back over to her.

"You know what, at this point I wouldn't even go to your funeral. I'd be outside saying I told you so!" Jaelyn shouted right at me.

"I see how it is. You just avoid funerals," I said.

"Don't you dare go there!" Jaelyn shouted at me.

"I will if you don't leave me alone," I said angrily.

"That's a sore topic, and you know that," Jaelyn said to my face.

"I'm aware," I said while glancing at the door.

"It wasn't my fault," Jaelyn said while beginning to walk out.

"I don't know that," I said while looking up at her.

"What's that supposed to mean?" Jaelyn shouted as she whipped her head back around.

"You could've just skipped the funeral for all I know. I was only six," I said.

"You know I didn't!" Jaelyn shouted, clearly getting upset.

"I mean, it's not hard to believe that you couldn't stomach seeing the body. I was always the braver kid, after all," I said while trying to get under her skin.

"You can shut up! Of course I would've come. He was our father!" Jaelyn shouted at me.

I stood there for a little bit. I didn't think it was a bad idea to talk about the funeral incident at the time, but it clearly was.

The truth was, I knew Jaelyn was sick and wanted to be at that funeral more than anything. I just made it sound like I didn't know that.

"Sorry," I whispered.

Jaelyn just looked at me and shook her head.

"You're a horrible person," she whispered as she stormed out of my room.

Usually, I'd get mad at Jaelyn for saying that, but this time I wasn't. I knew I deserved it.

The rest of the day was fairly quiet. No one came and talked to me, and I didn't go talk to anyone.

Dinner that night was very strange. Usually, Jaelyn and I would be the ones starting up a conversation, but instead, we both sat there in silence. Jaelyn was still mad at me, and I just felt bad about the whole incident.

"How's the pizza?" Mom asked us, trying to break the silence.

"It's really good, Mom!" Effie shouted in excitement.

"Well, I'm glad. What do the rest of you think?" Mom asked all of us.

"It's splendid, darling," Carl said in response.

Mom looked over at Jaelyn and me, surprised neither of us was answering.

"Aaron?" Mom said, thinking I had fallen asleep.

"Mhm," I answered with a bite of pizza in my mouth.

"Can I assume you like it?" Mom asked while staring at me.

"Of course," I said once I finished swallowing.

"I'm gonna go to my room; thanks for dinner," Jaelyn said as she stood up and walked away.

Everyone just sat there and watched Jaelyn leave. It was unlike her to just walk out during dinner.

The second Jaelyn was in her room, everyone looked over at me.

"What did you do to her?" Carl shouted at me.

"Nothing," I said quickly.

"Are you guys okay?" Mom asked.

"Yes!" I shouted. "I'm gonna go to my room now."

I stood up and walked out of the kitchen. I looked in Jaelyn's room to see her reading. She looked up and made eye contact with me.

"You can leave!" she shouted at me.

"Sorry," I said as I walked into my room.

I sat down on my bed and looked at my phone. There were no new messages or anything, but I still decided to open up the messaging app. I scrolled down until I saw the messages between Emma Grace and me. I paused for a split second before I opened them up.

I read through them a few times to see if I saw anything, but I didn't. Honestly, this whole thing with Emma Grace had made me feel like I was in a movie, which was kind of crazy to me.

"Aaron?" Mom said as she walked into my room.

"Yeah," I said as I looked up at her.

"What is going on with you and your sister?" she asked.

"We're just mad at each other," I said while looking back down at my phone.

"Why are you guys mad at each other?" she asked. "You two usually get along great."

"We got into a fight," I said while wanting my mom to stop asking me questions.

"Okay, well, just try to make up. You guys still have to ride together Monday," she said as she began to walk out.

"Will do," I said as I shut my phone off.

The rest of the night, I just watched TV and tried not to think of Emma Grace or Jaelyn. I wanted to avoid conflict as much as possible.

Sunday was a drag. Usually, on weekends Jaelyn and I would entertain each other, but that obviously didn't happen.

Before I knew it, it was Monday, and Jaelyn and I were riding to school together.

We still hadn't said anything to each other since the argument, which wasn't ideal.

"Jaelyn, I'm sorry, I know you hate me, but you can't be mad at me forever," I said, finally breaking the silence.

Jaelyn just looked at me and rolled her eyes.

"Come on, Jaelyn, I'm sorry," I said, still trying to get a response from her.

Jaelyn kept quiet. She was obviously still mad at me.

We pulled up to the school quickly after my attempt at making peace.

I went to get out of the car when Jaelyn suddenly locked the doors. I looked over at her with a confused look on my face.

"I'll forgive you when I want to. So stop with this. I'm sorry, bullshit, it means nothing to me. If you truly cared about the situation, it would've never happened in the first place," Jaelyn said to me while looking out the window. "Now get out."

Jaelyn unlocked the car door and looked at me. I looked up at her, but she didn't say anything.

I got out of the car and walked into the school.

The halls were crowded like normal, but Ezra still managed to find me.

"Glad someone's here in one piece," Ezra said while she walked over to me.

"Me too," I said with a smile.

We walked over to my locker while I started to get my stuff out of my backpack.

"Guess who's back?" Ezra said while standing next to me.

"Who?" I asked while opening up my locker.

"Mrs. Jones," Ezra said.

"That's good," I said while setting my stuff down. "I like having a teacher."

"Me too," Ezra said jokingly.

Once I got all my stuff, we walked over to Mrs. Jones's classroom.

It was nice to see an adult in the room.

"Morning, Mrs. Jones," I said as I set my stuff down.

"Morning, Aaron," Mrs. Jones said while getting ready for class.

Everyone continued to talk to each other until the bell rang. After that, we all made our way to our seats and sat down.

"Good morning, class. Sorry I wasn't here Friday. I heard you guys had a pretty intense day," Mrs. Jones said while passing out papers.

"Where were you?" Alex King asked.

"That's for me to know, sir," Mrs. Jones said as she gave Alex a paper. "Darn it; I'm a few papers short."

"I can make some copies if you need," I said, trying to help out.

"That'd be very helpful, thank you, Aaron," Mrs. Jones said while handing me the last paper she had in her hand. "Make seven for me, please."

"Okay," I said while walking out of class.

I walked down the hallway to the copy machine. I was thankful to see no one else there. I wasn't in the mood to wait in a line.

I quickly made the seven copies and started to walk back to class when I all of a sudden heard my name. I looked in the teacher's lounge to see Mr. Smith on a phone call.

Why would he be talking about me?

I decided to stay and listen for a minute. I knew I could

easily come up with a reason for my absence if it was brought up. I was good at that kind of thing.

"I know it sounds crazy, but I'm almost a hundred percent sure it was him," I heard Mr. Smith say to the phone.

What did I do?

I still didn't know why I was being talked about.

"He's the only Aaron I know that has a friend named Ezra and screams like a twelve-year-old girl. I don't care if he's fifteen!" Mr. Smith shouted while obviously getting frustrated with the person on the other side of the phone.

"What on Earth?" I whispered to myself.

"I'm not crazy. It's him!" Mr. Smith shouted. "I'll prove it. I have my ways."

I was starting to panic. What on Earth was Mr. Smith talking about?

"The ring thing doesn't just go away. Anyone who's affected by it doesn't fully lose effects for at least a few months. I'll use that against him," Mr. Smith explained.

I started to think of what the ring thing could possibly be when it all of a sudden hit me.

"Crap," I said loudly.

"Who's there?" I heard Mr. Smith shout.

I didn't answer. I was thinking of what to do when all of a sudden, I realized how much danger I was in.

I decided to run back to Mrs. Jones's room as quickly as possible. I ran and ran, hoping Mr. Smith wouldn't see me.

The second I got to Mrs. Jones's room, I ran in, not caring if I disrupted her lesson.

"Sorry I'm late," I said out of breath.

"You're fine," Mrs. Jones said as she took the copies. "Next time, don't feel like you have to run."

"Okay," I said as I went back to my desk.

Mrs. Jones started passing out the papers when all of a sudden, she realized she was one short.

"Aaron, I thought you printed seven," Mrs. Jones said, confused.

"Me too," I said, also confused.

At that moment, someone knocked on the door.

"Come in!" Mrs. Jones shouted.

Everyone looked at the door to see Mr. Smith walk in. I froze; I didn't know why he was here. He had a first hour to get back to.

"I found this copy in the hallway," Mr. Smith said as he held up the copy we were missing.

"That's where it went," Mrs. Jones said with a slight chuckle. "Guess you did print seven, Aaron."

"I knew it," I said, knowing my cover was blown.

"Maybe don't run so fast next time," Mr. Smith said while looking right at me.

"Will do," I said nervously.

Mr. Smith looked at the class and waved goodbye.

"Thank you, Mr. Smith," Mrs. Jones said. " Guess you get to do work now, Morgan."

The whole class started laughing while I sat there in silence.

I couldn't believe Mr. Smith was behind all of this, and now he was going to kill me.

So many questions started running through my head. How did he kidnap Emma Grace? Was he responsible for Jessica's attack? Was he going to hurt Ezra? I knew I couldn't answer those questions. I didn't know a lot. All I knew was that I needed to find out more before it was too late...

Chapter 6

"Aaron, can we go already?" Ezra asked while waiting for me by the cafeteria doors.

Ezra was always starving by the time lunch came around.

She did have gym right before, though, so I was able to see why. That class eats your energy away like it's a freshly baked brownie.

"I'm actually skipping lunch today; you go without me," I said while shutting my locker.

"Why?" she asked me, confused.

"I have other things I need to do," I explained.

"Like what?" she said, still confused.

"Just stuff," I said while wanting her to leave me alone. "Just go before you get stuck with the half-cooked fish."

"Fine," she said while beginning to walk away. "This better not become a normal thing!"

"It won't!" I shouted.

The truth was I was starving, but I had better things I needed to do.

I needed to try and figure more things out about Emma Grace's disappearance.

I knew for a fact that most of the teachers, including Mr. Smith, ate their lunch in the teacher's lounge. So Mr. Smith's classroom would be empty, so I could do a little snooping without getting caught.

I walked down the hallway to see his classroom door wide

open.

"Yes," I said to myself quietly.

I walked into the classroom and over to his desk. Honestly, I didn't expect to find anything. So when I saw a paper with a bunch of information on it about the whole situation, I was shocked.

The paper was front and back with information on both sides. On the front side, it said the letters VK in bold, along with a bunch of addresses with street names I didn't even recognize. On the back, it had a bunch of people's names and ages. One of those people was Emma Grace; she appeared to be one of the older people on the list.

The ages of the people on the list seemed to vary, with a mix of both boys and girls.

I couldn't believe what I was looking at. All these people had disappeared, just like Emma Grace.

I recognized a few of the names from glances at Carl's newspapers in the mornings.

"I gotta give this to someone," I whispered to myself.

Right as I was about to walk out, Mr. Smith walked into the classroom.

"Shouldn't you be at lunch?" he asked me, confused.

"I need to do work," I answered him nervously.

"What are you doing at my desk?" he asked me while walking over to me.

"Nothing," I answered nervously.

"What's in your hand?" he asked me, getting closer.

"Nothing," I said, starting to back up.

"Give it," he said sternly.

"No," I said quickly.

"Hand it over," he said a little louder.

"I said no," I said sternly.

He walked closer to me and tried to rip the paper out of my hands but failed.

Mr. Smith may be stronger than me, but I was quicker.

"You don't wanna see me angry, Aaron, just hand over the paper," he said while starting to get sick of me.

"I'm not going to!" I shouted.

He looked at me and walked over until we were nearly face to face. I was terrified, but I stood my ground.

"I know you were the kid on the phone. I know you listened to my phone call, and I know what paper you have. Now hand over the paper and forget everything you know, and I might consider sparing you," Mr. Smith said right in my face.

"How could you do this?" I asked. "Emma Grace was your student."

"I don't care about my students. I just come here to make money. So if I have to hurt or kill one of them, it doesn't phase me," he explained.

"You've killed a student?" I asked with a shaky voice.

"Not yet, but I won't hesitate to make you my first," he said while trying to scare me. "Now, this is the last time I'm going to ask nicely. Hand over the paper."

"I can't. You can't get away with this," I said.

"Aaron, are you stupid?" he asked. "You're fifteen years old, and there's nothing you can do with a little piece of paper."

"I know you're lying," I said. "I can easily take this to a police station and have you thrown in jail, and you know it."

"I'm out of patience, Aaron. Hand it over!" He shouted at me.

"No," I said again.

His face was full of rage. I knew that if I didn't get out of there now, I wasn't ever going to make it out. I tried to get away when all of a sudden, Mr. Smith grabbed me and threw me against the wall. It felt like being thrown on the lunch floor all over again.

"Don't make me do this the hard way, kid," Mr. Smith said as he walked up to me.

I stood up and looked directly at him as he walked closer.

"Mr. Smith, just admit this is wrong and let me end it for you," I said, trying to reason with him.

"I don't do this because I think it's right, Aaron. I do it for justice. If you were in my shoes, you would understand," Mr. Smith explained while continuing to walk up to me.

"This isn't justice!" I shouted. "This is awful. You've kidnapped thirty-seven people, including a four-year-old; that's not okay!"

"It's not just me," he said.

"I don't care," I said. "All I know is you're one of them, and that's not okay. You're a horrible person!"

"I'm horrible?" he said, confused. "You wanna see horrible?"

Mr. Smith took both his hands and put them around my throat and lifted me up from the ground.

"Is this horrible?" he asked while happily watching the color drain from my face.

I couldn't respond. I had been in this situation before, but he was holding me tighter than anyone else ever had.

He had the goal of killing me, which automatically changed his grip from people like Teagan.

I knew I had to try and escape his grip quickly.

I had an idea, but I didn't know if it would work. It had failed me once before with Teagan, but maybe it would work now.

I looked at Mr. Smith and kicked him right where I knew it would hurt.

"Shit!" he screamed.

He released me and fell down to the ground in pain.

I put the paper in my pocket and started to run out when all of a sudden I heard a ringing like I did over the phone call. I looked back to see Mr. Smith holding what appeared to be a pen.

"This'll be fun," he said while pressing the pen thing.

The second he pressed it, a pain came through me just like it did the night of the phone call. I held my head and fell down to the ground in pain.

"Stop!" I screamed.

He walked over while still pressing the pen and looked down at me.

"Does that hurt?" he asked, knowing I would say yes if I could respond.

He bent down and pulled the paper out of my pocket. I wanted to stop him, but I couldn't.

"It sucks to fail so miserably, doesn't it?" he asked me while still pressing the pen.

My vision was beginning to blur. I tried to take deep breaths, but the pain just increased. I saw Mr. Smith walk over to the door and lock it shut.

"I'm sorry I have to do this, Aaron," he said as he started to walk over. "You were a good kid, just a little lazy."

I looked up at him, trying to make out if he was being sarcastic or not, but I couldn't tell.

Mr. Smith looked down at me with a strange look. I couldn't tell if he felt bad or just pitied me, but either way, he stopped pressing the pen.

The pain quickly faded away, and my vision returned.

"Why'd you stop?" I asked while looking up at him.

"'Cause that's not how I want you to go," he answered me as he walked to the closet.

"What's that supposed to mean?" I asked while slowly getting up.

"Brain explosions aren't fun to clean up. I want to kill you in a way there will be no mess," he explained while walking into the closet.

I took this opportunity to run over to the classroom door and try and open it, but he had locked it with a key.

"Help!" I screamed while banging on the door.

"Shut up!" Mr. Smith screamed at me.

"He's gonna kill me!" I screamed while still pounding on the door.

"Don't make me press the pen!" he screamed at me.

I listened to him and stopped pounding on the door.

This must be what defeat feels like, I thought to myself.

"Perfect," I heard Mr. Smith whisper to himself.

I started to panic. I knew I didn't care about my life too much, but I still had things to live for. I had my family and friends and many things I still needed to accomplish. I hadn't even had my first kiss.

At that moment, I realized I wasn't going down without a fight.

"Hello!" I screamed, banging on the door once again. "I'm in here! I'm trapped!"

Right at that moment, I felt Mr. Smith grab me from behind.

"Let me go!" I screamed.

"Not till I'm done," he said as he stabbed something into my arm.

I looked down to see what appeared to be a taser in my arm.

Right as I went to look at Mr. Smith, he activated the taser thing.

I thought the pen was bad, but this was a million times worse.

I screamed at the top of my lungs. I was in so much pain.

"Help!" I screamed.

I slowly started to lose strength. I couldn't even kick any more. I didn't know what to do.

"Don't worry, Aaron. I won't torture Ezra or Emma Grace as bad," he whispered in my ear.

"Don't lay a hand on them," I said with the little strength I had left.

"Or what?" he asked. "You gonna come back from the dead?"

I wanted to say one of my sarcastic comments, but I was in too much pain.

My vision started to blur once again, and I started to lose feeling in my limbs.

This must be what dying feels like, I thought to myself.

In the next few moments, I faded away. At least, I thought I did.

I woke up in a bright room. I sat up and noticed I was in a hospital room. How did I get here? I asked myself.

"Hello?" I said to see if anyone was around.

I looked over out the window and saw a mini flower garden. It was beautiful.

"At least they gave me a nice view," I whispered to myself.

Right at that moment, I heard the door to my room open. I looked over to see a nurse looking at me.

"He's awake!" she shouted out the door.

I looked over at her waiting for her to come over. I had questions that needed answering.

"Hi, Aaron, I'm nurse Carol. How are you feeling?" she asked me while walking over.

"I'm okay," I said, still trying to comprehend everything. "What time is it?"

"It's about two," she answered me.

"Still Monday, right?" I asked, hoping she'd say yes.

"Yeah, don't worry, you weren't in a coma," she said jokingly.

I laughed quietly.

"I'm gonna go get the doctor; you stay here," she said as she walked out.

That wasn't an issue, I thought to myself.

I tried remembering everything that had happened. None of it was forgotten. I just couldn't believe I was alive. I thought I had died. Mr. Smith sounded so sure that he was going to kill me.

"I need to stop thinking about this," I whispered to myself.

I looked out the window to try and distract myself. The scenery was really pretty. I didn't usually pay attention to scenery, but I did now, apparently.

Maybe it was because I never thought I'd see anything like it again.

"Hi, squirrel," I whispered to a squirrel outside the window.

The squirrel looked at me. It was like he heard me.

I waved at it; it looked so friendly.

After I waved, it looked me dead in the eyes and slammed into the window.

"Jeez!" I shouted as I jumped back.

Right at that moment, I heard chuckling behind me. I turned

around to see a doctor.

"I see you've met Nutty," he laughed as he walked over to me.

"That squirrel's crazy," I laughed.

"That's why he's called Nutty," the doctor laughed. "I'm Dr. Pain."

"What?" I said, confused.

"I know, it's a weird name. I get looks all the time," he said while smiling to himself.

"So, is there anything wrong with me?" I asked, not really knowing if I wanted an answer or not.

"Besides it looking like a snake bit your arm, no," he answered me.

"Good," I said, relieved.

"You're just here cause a lot of folks thought you weren't okay," he explained.

"Makes sense," I said while trying to find my glasses.

"Glasses?" the doctor asked.

"Yeah," I answered him.

"To your left," he told me

I looked over, and there were my glasses. I grabbed them and put them on my face.

"You up for visitors?" the doctor asked.

"Depends," I answered.

"It's your family and your girlfriend," he said.

"Girlfriend?" I said, confused.

"Maybe she's just a friend, I don't know," he said, laughing.

"You can let them in. Just tell them no screaming," I said.

"Will do," Dr. Pain said as he walked out.

I sat there nervously waiting. I wanted to see my family, but I was scared of their reaction.

I knew Carl would think this was just a waste of money, and Mom would be so panicked, which I didn't like.

The first person I saw walk in was Effie. I don't think she waited for my parents to tell her she could come in.

"Aaron!" Effie shouted as she ran over.

"Effie," I said as she jumped on the bed.

"I'm glad you're okay. I love you," she said.

"Love you too," I said.

I looked up and saw Mom, Jaelyn, Ezra, and Carl walk in.

"Effie, I told you to wait," Carl said.

"I wanted to see Aaron. I love him," Effie explained.

"We all do," Mom said as she walked over. "Do you feel okay?"

"Yeah," I answered her.

"You gave us all quite a scare," Carl said while walking over to us.

"I know, I'm sorry," I said while looking down.

"You don't need to apologize," Mom said. "We're just glad you're okay."

"Let's go fill out the paperwork, hun," Carl whispered to my mom.

"We'll be right back," Mom said.

"Take your time," I said.

"I'm going too," Effie said as she followed them.

"Okay, sweetie," Mom said as she followed her out of the room.

The second Mom, Carl, and Effie walked away, Ezra walked over.

"I'm never letting you skip lunch again," Ezra said.

"Noted," I said as I laughed to myself.

"What even happened?" Ezra asked.

"Not lunch," I answered her.

"Aaron, I'm serious. Jaelyn and I heard your screams. It sounded like you were being murdered," Ezra said.

"You heard them?" I said, confused.

"They were loud," Ezra said. "Now, what happened?"

"I did something I shouldn't have, and let's just say it ended with me being tortured," I explained.

"At school?" she said, confused.

"Yep," I said.

"Wow, I didn't think you could get involved with bad things at school," Ezra said.

"Me neither," I said.

"Well, I gotta get going. I'm glad you're alive," Ezra said as she left.

"Okay," I said as she walked out.

Now it was only me and Jaelyn left in the room.

She was avoiding eye contact with me, which made things a million times more awkward.

"Do you still hate me?" I asked.

"No," she said while walking over to me. "I forgive you, just no more dying."

"No promises," I said jokingly.

"Seriously though, I'm glad you're okay. I was scared. I thought I'd lost you," she said.

"It's okay, I'm here," I said.

"We gotta promise each other we're not dying until we're at least fifty," Jaelyn said jokingly.

"All right, pinky swear," I said.

"Seriously?" she asked.

"Seriously," I said.

She walked over and looked at me.

"Pinky swear," she said while holding up her pinky.

We shook our pinkies together. I knew it was childish, but it just felt right.

"Now, you're not allowed to die until you're at least fifty," Jaelyn said joyfully.

"That's the promise," I said.

She smiled and walked towards the door.

"I'm gonna go see when we're leaving," Jaelyn said.

"Okay," I said back.

Jaelyn walked out of the room, and it once again became quiet.

I looked out the window once again. This time I didn't see Nutty, and I didn't know if that made me relieved or scared.

"Aaron," I heard Jaelyn say.

"What?" I said back.

"You're allowed to leave," Jaelyn said joyfully.

"Yes," I whispered to myself.

In the next few moments, nurse Carol came in and gave me one last final checkup. She gave me my clothes back and wished me farewell.

I walked out into the hospital hallway feeling like the king of the world.

"Someone's in a good mood," Mom said as I walked over to them.

"Just glad I'm not dead," I said jokingly.

My mom slightly laughed. I could tell she didn't find my joke funny. Everyone was actually really worried about me. I didn't expect that.

"Let's go," Mom said after she finished talking to the front desk lady.

We all walked out into the parking lot and got into the car.

It felt good to be in there with everyone.

I was glad Mr. Smith's plan didn't work and that I was still able to be here with my family.

"Do you feel normal?" Carl asked me out of nowhere.

"Yeah," I said quickly.

"Good," he said while looking back at me with a smile.

I smiled back.

That was the first time Carl had smiled at me in years. It made me feel especially happy to be alive.

Chapter 7

Most people say that the first night of sleep after a hospital stay feels like the best night of sleep in your life. Honestly, I hoped that would be true, but it wasn't.

I wasn't up in pain or anything; I felt fine. The thing that kept me up was the flashbacks. Every time I went to shut my eyes, I got teleported back to Mr. Smith's classroom. It was awful. All I wanted to do was sleep.

I hoped the flashbacks would stop after the first night, but they didn't. The second night was even worse. The flashbacks became even more realistic. I was stuck between real life and the past, and it sucked. I just wanted everything to return to normal, but until I could make these flashbacks fade away, I was stuck here in my own traumatic world.

"Aaron, are you up for school?" Mom asked me while knocking on my door.

"I can't, Mom," I answered her.

Mom walked into my room and sat down on the bed next to me.

"Did you sleep last night?" she asked me in a worried tone.

"No," I said while looking up at her.

"Flashbacks still?" she asked.

"Yeah," I answered her in a tired voice.

"We need to get rid of these, Aaron. You were supposed to be back in school today," she said.

"I know," I said.

"I'll go tell Jaelyn you're not riding with her again," she said as she walked out.

The second I heard my door click shut, I sat up and started to look around my room.

Most people say their room is their safe place.

If that was the case, why did mine feel like a prison?

"Are you seriously staying home another day?" I heard Jaelyn ask me as she walked into my room.

"I have no choice," I said.

"Okay," Jaelyn said. "Take it easy today. I want you to come to school with me tomorrow."

"I'll try," I said.

Jaelyn smiled and walked out. She wouldn't admit it, but I could tell she missed me riding with her.

Once Jaelyn was out the door, I decided to get up and at least eat something. Maybe a full stomach will help me, I thought to myself.

I walked into the kitchen to see Carl looking for something in the cupboards.

"What are you doing?" I asked.

"Looking for something to maybe help you," he answered me.

"Help me?" I said confused

"Kid, you haven't slept in two days; that's not good," he said.

"True," I said as I walked over to the fridge.

I opened up the fridge and pulled out an apple. It was small and simple, but it would fill me up just fine.

"Found it," I heard Carl say.

"Found what?" I asked while biting into my apple.

"These pills can make you fall asleep in a matter of

113

minutes," he answered me.

"That sounds sketchy," I said.

"I used to use them when I had back problems, they work great," he said while tossing me the bottle. "Just try taking one after you finish your apple."

"Okay," I said. "These better not kill me."

"They won't," he said. "I gotta go to the store, be careful."

"I will," I said.

Carl left a few minutes later.

The second he was out of the house, I sat down on the couch and read over the bottle. Carl was a bigger person than me, so I wanted to make sure it was safe for me to take one of these pills.

"It's barely safe," I laughed to myself.

I was a small person. I was only five feet four inches, weighing about a hundred fifteen pounds. Everyone always laughed at how small I was, but I learned to accept it. It's kinda funny having a girl best friend that's taller than you. Ezra was about five feet six inches and always made short jokes about me. It used to annoy me, but now I just make jokes about her being tall.

After I finished my apple, I did as Carl said and took a pill.

Once I was done in the kitchen, I went to my room and laid down on my bed.

After a few moments, I started to get extra sleepy.

I was about to fall asleep when I suddenly saw another flashback, except I didn't recognize this one. I was no longer in Mr. Smith's classroom. I was standing in an area with a bunch of rocky mountains. I knew it wasn't real, but I was still able to walk around.

I walked around until I came across a huge hole. It appeared to be at least a hundred feet deep. I froze there until something pushed me.

I quickly shot awake.

"What just happened?" I asked myself.

I looked at my phone to see it read 7.35 p.m. I had slept through the whole day. It felt good, but that flashback dream thing was so weird. It felt real.

I decided to walk out into the kitchen and reread the bottle. I needed to see if weird dreams were a side effect.

"Hey, Aaron, you slept for a while," Carl said as I walked out.

"Yeah, where's the bottle?" I asked.

"Aaron, no!" Carl shouted.

"What did I do?" I asked.

"You aren't taking any more!" he shouted.

"I wasn't going to," I said. "I just need to read the label."

"I know you're lying. Go back to your room before your mother finds out," Carl said sternly.

"What do you mean before Mom finds out?" I asked.

"Find out what?" I heard my mom ask from behind me.

"Nothing, sweetie," Carl said, acting innocent.

"Bullshit, what are you two hiding from me?" Mom asked us.

"Honestly, I don't know," I said.

"Carl?" she said in an annoyed tone.

"Okay, honey, before I say anything, just know it helped him," Carl said.

"Are you talking about the sleeping pill?" I asked.

"The what?" Mom shouted.

"Honey, he needed to sleep," Carl said.

"So you gave him a pill!" she shouted.

"Yes, I did, and it's not my fault he wanted another," Carl said.

"He what?" Mom screamed again.

"Carl, that is not true!" I shouted. "I wanted to read the label."

"That's a horrible lie," Mom said.

"It's not a lie, though," I said to both of them.

"Go to your room, Aaron," Carl said.

"But I'm not lying!" I shouted at them.

"Now!" Carl shouted.

I listened and walked back to my room.

I couldn't believe that they would think I was addicted to sleeping pills. They could never see the simple truth, they always had to create stories to make their lives more interesting, and people wondered why I didn't tell them much.

I knew Mom still got flashbacks of the night Dad died, and I knew she hated pills because of that. She was scared we would turn out like him. Laying on the bedroom floor, found by his kids.

I was glad I didn't remember much of the night Dad died.

Jaelyn and I had both mainly forgotten about that night. We were too young to remember. I was only six, while Jaelyn was only seven.

The rest of that night was fairly quiet. Mom and Carl didn't bother to come to my room. They didn't care if they knew the truth or not; they just always wanted to be right.

Surprisingly that night, I was able to fall asleep normally. I guess the sleeping pill did help me a little bit. It helped my brain calm down and stop producing real-life nightmares.

Morning came quickly, but this time I was ready for it.

Mom and Carl still weren't talking to me, but I think they

were still glad to see me going to school.

I knew for a fact I would gossip about the whole sleeping pill situation to Jaelyn on the way to school. It was just too bizarre not to share.

I walked out to the car to see Jaelyn waiting for me. It felt like nothing had ever happened. It felt normal.

"Took you long enough," Jaelyn said as I got into the car.

"Sorry, I decided to be alive today," I said jokingly as I put my seatbelt on.

Jaelyn looked over at me and smiled. I could tell she was happy to have her passenger back in the car with her.

"These last few days have been weird," Jaelyn said as she began to drive. "I didn't have to wait on anyone."

"Must've been nice," I said.

"Not really," she replied. "I missed my little brother."

I smiled at her. I knew she missed me. I just didn't think she'd admit it.

"So, wanna explain to me why Mom and Carl think you're gonna be a drug addict," Jaelyn said jokingly.

"Carl gave me a sleeping pill, and I slept, and then I wanted to read the bottle, but they thought I wanted a second pill," I explained.

"Why would you want to read the bottle?" Jaelyn asked me, confused.

"'Cause I had a very weird dream, and I wanted to see if it was a side effect," I explained.

"Makes sense," she said. "Well, if Mom and Carl start to talk about you being a drug addict, I'll explain to them why you're not."

"Thanks," I said.

"You're gonna have a lot of homework over the weekend,"

Jaelyn said.

"Crap, I forgot about that," I said.

I had truly forgotten that I had been out of school for three and a half days. Monday just seemed like it was only yesterday.

"Okay, we're here. Good luck," Jaelyn said as she put the car into park.

"See you later," I said as I got out of the car.

"See you," Jaelyn said as she pulled away.

Once Jaelyn was gone, I began to make my way up to the main doors.

I walked in the door to see nearly everyone staring at me. I just kept my head low and tried to get to my locker.

"Aaron!" I heard someone shout.

I looked up to see Ezra running up to me.

"Morning, Ezra," I said as she wrapped her arms around me.

"I'm so glad you're back," she said. "I felt like such a loser without you."

"Aren't we usually losers, though?" I asked jokingly.

"Yeah, but I felt like even more of a loser," she said while letting go of me.

"Well, let's go to my locker," I said as I started walking through the hallway.

Ezra followed behind me through all the crowds, and before I knew it, I was opening my locker just like old times.

"Hurry up!" Ezra said, getting impatient.

I looked at her and purposely started moving slower than a sloth.

Ezra looked at me, grabbed my Algebra book, and ran away.

"Ezra!" I shouted as I shut my locker.

I ran up to her and tried to grab my book.

"You're annoying," I said.

"And you're slow," she replied.

"Let's go to class," I said.

She smiled and started to skip through the halls.

"Walk, Ezra Gray!" I heard someone shout from behind me.

I turned around to see Mr. Smith looking at me.

"Morning, Aaron," he said.

"Morning," I said nervously.

"Come on, Aaron," Ezra said, getting restless.

I looked at Mr. Smith and started to walk away.

I quickly caught up to Ezra, and before I knew it we were in Mrs. Jones's classroom.

"I can't believe teachers yell at me for skipping in the halls but won't yell at you for sprinting at full speed," Ezra said as she set my book down on my desk.

"I'm just lucky," I said jokingly.

"Aaron's not dead," I heard Morgan say from behind me.

"Morning to you too, Morgan," I said, knowing that wouldn't be the last death joke I got that day.

Morgan smiled and walked back to her desk.

"Did people actually miss me?" I whispered to Ezra.

"Yes, Aaron, I'm not the only one who cares for you," Ezra whispered back.

I smiled and sat down at my desk.

Ezra waved and went to sit at hers.

Mrs. Jones walked in shortly after with a handful of papers ready for class.

"Glad to see a full class," Mrs. Jones said while looking over at me.

"Aaron's alive!" Alex King shouted from behind me.

"Sure am," I said while looking back at him.

"What happened?" Alex asked. Why were you screaming? Did you think you were gonna die?

"Enough, Alex," Mrs. Jones said. "If Aaron wants to say what happened, he will. No need to bombard him with questions."

"Sorry," Alex said quietly.

Class started, and I caught on pretty quickly. I was still a little confused, but nothing too terrible.

Before I knew it, class was over, and I had to go collect my work from the last few days.

"So, what did I miss?" I asked while walking over to Mrs. Jones's desk.

"Some notes and an assignment, nothing too big," she said.

"Okay, I can copy the notes and get the assignment done," I said.

"You don't have to," she said. "You seemed like you were doing fine, and I don't mind exempting you from an assignment. I know you'll have a lot of work to catch up on."

"Well, thank you," I said, surprised.

"No problem," she said. "If you don't mind me asking, how are you feeling?"

"I feel fine, about eighty percent," I told her.

"Well, I'm glad to hear that. A lot of staff members were worried about you," she said.

I looked up at her and smiled.

"I gotta get going now; see you around," I said as I picked up my stuff.

"Okay, be careful," she said.

"Will do," I said as I walked out.

I did not want to go to my second hour at all. The last time I was in that room, I was nearly killed, but I knew if I didn't go, I would get in so much trouble. So even though every bone in my body was telling me not to go, I still did.

I walked quickly down the hall to Mr. Smith's class. I didn't want to be late; I already had enough stress, I didn't need a tardy to top it all off.

When I got to Mr. Smith's door, I froze. My head started filling with flashbacks all over again. My brain knew it was a bad idea to go in there, but what it didn't know was that I had no choice.

I opened the door and walked in at the same time the bell rang.

"Nice tardy dodge," Mr. Smith said as I walked in.

"Yeah," I said nervously.

I walked over to my seat and sat down. All I wanted was for the class to be over, but I knew I couldn't just time travel fifty minutes into the future.

"Class, pull out your textbooks and turn to page thirty-four," Mr. Smith said while shutting the door.

I took some deep breaths and tried to calm myself down.

Deep down, I knew Mr. Smith wouldn't do anything to me with a classroom full of possible witnesses, but I still had fear in the back of my mind.

Once I was a little calmer, I went to grab my textbook when all of a sudden, I realized it wasn't there. I forgot to grab it this morning; I was so distracted by Ezra it just left my brain.

"Mr. Cripple, I don't see a textbook on your desk," Mr. Smith said while looking over at me.

"I forgot it," I said hesitantly.

"Aaron, you can't slack off, or bad things will happen," Mr.

121

Smith said sternly.

I froze and started to panic.

Maybe I was wrong; maybe Mr. Smith didn't care if he had witnesses watching him.

"I'm sorry," I said quietly.

"Aaron's scared of Mr. Smith!" Alex shouted, trying to sound cool.

Usually, I would say a rude come back to him, but this time I didn't. I didn't care about Alex and his attempts at being cool, all I cared about right now was avoiding the wrath Mr. Smith had planned for me.

"Aaron, come talk to me in the hallway," Mr. Smith said while pointing at the door.

"I'm good," I said quietly to myself.

"You're what?" Mr. Smith shouted. "I wasn't asking you to come in the hallway. I was telling you!"

I didn't move. I knew if I went alone in the hallway with him, I'd be dead.

"Aaron?" Mr. Smith said, tired of me. "Don't make me send you to the office. You don't need to miss any more school."

"Fine," I said hesitantly.

I stood up and walked towards the door.

My legs began to tremble beneath me. I felt like I was walking to the gateway of Hell. This was horrible.

Mr. Smith held the door open for me as I walked out of the classroom.

He shut the door behind him as he followed me out.

"You're really bad at pretending to be fearless," Mr. Smith said while looking at me.

"It's not my fault my Chemistry teacher is a psychopath!" I shouted as I turned around.

"It's not my fault you're still alive!" Mr. Smith shouted. "If you would've just been quiet, all your fear and pain would've ended Monday."

"You're sick," I said.

"Think what you want but just know if you tell anyone about me or the VK, I will kill you and everyone you love," he said, trying to threaten me.

I stood there trying not to show him how panicked I was, but it wasn't working.

"I know where you live, and I know who you care about. Don't play with me. Do you understand?" he asked. "Do you understand?"

"Yes," I said, feeling defeated.

"Good," he said, knowing I was terrified.

I knew I physically couldn't go back into the classroom, so I decided to run.

"Get back here!" Mr. Smith shouted.

I continued to run. I didn't care about getting in trouble at this point. I just wanted to stay alive, and I knew Mr. Smith wanted me dead.

I ran and ran until I spotted a janitor's closet opened a crack.

I knew I had to hide, and this seemed like the perfect spot.

Once I made my way over to the door, I slowly opened it and walked in.

I shut the door behind me and slowly backed up. I just hoped that no one had heard or seen me go into the closet; that was the last thing I wanted.

I truly thought I was in the clear until I felt someone's ice-cold hand wrap around my shoulder...

Chapter 8

I instantly turned around and, without hesitation, threw my fist at the person behind me.

"Oww!" they shouted in pain. "What was that for?"

At that moment, I recognized who I had just punched in the face.

"Teagan?" I said, confused.

"Aaron?" he said, also confused.

"I'm so sorry," I said, hoping he wouldn't punch me back. "I didn't know it was you, and if I did, I wouldn't have punched you, I swear."

"You went into full attack mode," Teagan said while turning on the light. "Is my face bleeding?"

"No," I said while looking over his face. "Sorry, I feel bad."

"Don't feel bad; it's not really normal to grab someone's shoulder to get their attention," he said jokingly.

"Well, I'm glad you're not mad," I said, relieved.

"Yeah, I honestly deserved it," he said while laughing to himself.

"Why'd you deserve it?" I asked, trying to sound like a friend.

"I kicked you in the face not that long ago. It only seems fair," he said while looking at me. "Glad I didn't break your nose."

"Me too," I said while smiling at him.

"I felt so bad about that," he said. "I've always known you

had a thing with blood, and I didn't mean to hit you that hard."

"It's fine," I said. "It's in the past."

"You forgive people quickly," he said.

"Might as well," I said. "You never know when it'll be someone's last day."

"Damn, that's deep," Teagan said while sitting on a bucket. "So why'd you come in here?"

"To avoid chemistry, what about you?" I asked while sitting on the ground.

"I just came here to calm myself down," he explained.

"Do you want me to go?" I asked.

"No, you're fine," he said while looking over at the mops.

"Does someone like me now?" I said jokingly.

"Shut up," he said while laughing to himself.

"You know you're pretty chill when you're not trying to kill me," I said.

"Good to know," he said jokingly.

We continued having small talk for what felt like only an hour before we heard sirens outside the school.

"What's going on?" I asked Teagan while standing up.

"I don't know," he said.

I went to leave when all of a sudden, Teagan grabbed my arm.

"What are you doing?" he asked me, alarmed.

"Going to check it out?" I said, confused.

"That's a terrible idea," he said.

"I don't care. I have nothing to lose," I said while walking out.

"Wait," he said.

"What?" I said, annoyed.

"Don't tell anyone about this closet. This is my safe place,"

125

he told me.

"I won't," I said as I walked out.

Once I was out of the closet, I started to walk down the halls. I honestly had no idea where to go.

I had no idea what time it was either, so I didn't even know what class to go to if we were in lockdown again.

Thankfully nothing really happened until I heard someone shout my name.

"Aaron!" I heard Jaelyn shout.

"Jaelyn?" I said as I walked over to her.

"Where the hell have you been?" she shouted at me.

"Around," I answered her. "Why are you so worried?"

"Do you hear those sirens?" she asked.

"Yeah?" I answered her, confused.

"They're here for you," she said.

"They're what?" I shouted, so confused. "What did I do?"

"You disappeared," she said. "Last time you disappeared, you almost died. I don't think the school was taking any chances."

"Well, tell them it was a false alarm," I said. "I'm clearly fine."

"Aaron, I'm sixteen. I don't think I have the power to dismiss police officers," she said jokingly.

"True," I said. "Guess I'm gonna have to make it clear I'm alive."

"That sounds like a good idea," Jaelyn said. "I'll walk with you to the police."

"Okay," I said nervously.

Jaelyn and I walked down the hall until we saw an officer talking to Mrs. Wilson.

"He's alive!" Jaelyn shouted to them.

"Good," the officer said to us. "Guess my work here is done."

The officer waved at all of us and walked out.

"Jaelyn, I told you to stay in class," Mrs. Wilson said, frustrated.

"Yeah, but he's my brother, so I had no choice," Jaelyn said boldly.

Mrs. Wilson rolled her eyes and looked over at me.

"You okay?" she asked.

"Yeah, sorry I took off," I said.

"It's okay, just don't do it again," she said.

"I won't," I said. "Now, what time is it?"

"It's time for you to go to fifth hour," Mrs. Wilson answered me.

"Okay, will do," I said as I started to walk away.

As I began to walk down the hall, I saw Jaelyn run towards her fifth-hour class in the other hall. She always would run to places just like me.

I wouldn't be surprised if this school knew the Cripples as the kids who run in the halls freely, with no consequences.

I walked to Mr. Coleman's classroom and opened the door. Everyone looked at me like I had birds flying out of my head. I ignored the looks and just sat down, hoping I didn't disrupt class too much.

"Nice of you to finally join us, Aaron," Mr. Coleman said while giving me a death stare. "Do you have a pass?"

"I do not, sir," I answered nervously.

"Well, then, you can see me after school in detention," he said, annoyed with me.

I was gonna plead with him, but I decided not to. Everyone was already fed up with me today, and I didn't need to make

127

things any worse.

After school, I made my way back to Mr. Coleman's room for my detention.

I walked in to see him getting ready to leave.

"Mr. Coleman?" I said, confused.

"What?" he said, annoyed.

"Do I still have detention?" I asked.

"Yes?" he said, confused.

"Then why are you leaving?" I asked.

"You have your detention with Mrs. Jones like I told you," he said in a frustrated tone.

"You never said that," I said, confused.

"Yes, I did! You're just an idiot!" he shouted at me. "Now go to your detention!"

"Okay," I said as I walked out.

I knew for a fact that Mr. Coleman never told me that. He just wanted to seem more mature than me. Which shouldn't be that hard, but for him, it was.

I walked to Mrs. Jones's room and knocked on the door.

"Come in," she said from the inside.

I walked in and looked over at her.

"Are you Mr. Coleman's detention kid?" she asked me, confused.

"Yeah," I answered her while avoiding eye contact.

"Well, have a seat. I won't keep you here for long," she said while starting to do work on her computer.

"Okay," I said as I went and sat down.

I looked out the window to try and pass some time, but there wasn't anything exciting. There were no crazy squirrels or pretty gardens, just green grass with a single flower.

After a while, I looked away from the window and turned

my attention to Mrs. Jones. She looked like she wanted to say something, but I didn't know what.

"Is everything okay?" I asked hesitantly.

She paused for a minute, probably deciding what to say to me.

"Aaron, do you mind if I ask you a few questions about what happened to you Monday?" she asked hesitantly.

I didn't really wanna talk about it, but I knew she wouldn't ask something like that unless it was important to her.

"I don't mind," I answered while looking over at her.

She was about to ask me something but then stopped herself.

"You know what; this is a bad idea. Sorry I asked," she said while looking away from me.

"You're fine," I said.

I was relieved, but at the same time, I wanted her to ask me about Monday. I wanted to see what she wanted to know.

She was one of the smartest teachers at this school; she wouldn't have asked me about Monday unless she had a valid reason.

"Mrs. Jones, please feel free to ask me questions. I truly don't mind answering," I said in a reassuring tone.

Mrs. Jones just looked at me. She took a deep breath before asking her first question.

"Do you remember who attacked you?" she asked me hesitantly.

I froze for a second. I did remember who it was, but I didn't know if I should say anything or not.

"No," I answered quietly.

"That's a shame," she said. "Neither does Jessica."

"You talked to Jessica?" I asked, confused.

Jessica was stuck in basic math classes. I didn't know how Mrs. Jones would've gotten a chance to talk to her.

"She actually talked to me," Mrs. Jones said. "The situation messed her up, and I guess she wanted to hear advice from her favorite aunt."

"Aunt?" I said, confused. "Jessica is your niece?"

"Yep," she said. "She's my brother's little girl."

"That's cool," I said. "Do you have any other questions you want to ask me?"

"No," she said. "I was just hoping you'd remember who attacked you guys. Both of you deserve justice."

I looked up at her and smiled. The guilt was eating me alive, but I knew I couldn't do anything about it. I couldn't risk telling her about Mr. Smith. I didn't want my family to get hurt. I loved them.

After a few minutes of awkward silence, I looked up at the clock.

"Can I leave yet?" I asked.

"Why not? Just tell Mr. Coleman you were here for an hour," she said while looking over at me.

I stood up and started to walk out when I all of a sudden stopped in my tracks.

"Jessica is lucky to have someone to talk to," I said.

She looked up at me and smiled.

"You have a good night, Aaron. I'll see you Monday."

"See you," I said as I walked out of her classroom.

I walked out of the school to meet Carl in the car.

I could tell by the way he was looking at me he was pissed.

The whole car ride was silent, which was weird for Carl. Usually, he would just yell at me, not keep silent.

We got home fairly quickly, which was nice. I was glad to

get out of the car; Carl was acting weird.

I walked in to see my mom. I waved at her, but she didn't respond.

Why was everyone so mad at me? I thought to myself. I just got detention. It doesn't mean much.

I went to my room and set my stuff down.

"Aaron?" I heard Jaelyn whisper from her room.

"What?" I whispered back.

"Come here," she whispered.

I did as she asked and quickly ran across the hall to her room.

Once I was in her room, Jaelyn stuck her head out the door and made sure Mom and Carl weren't around.

She shut the door behind me and locked it.

"What's going on?" I asked.

"I did you a favor," she said.

"And what is that?" I asked.

"I got you this," she said while holding up the sleeping pill bottle.

"How'd you get that?" I asked, surprised.

"I have my ways," she said while tossing it to me. "You better not be taking any."

"I won't," I said as I caught the bottle.

I turned it over and started reading the side effects. Seeing if any kind of dream side effect was listed, but there was nothing.

"Darn it," I said to myself.

"What's wrong?" Jaelyn asked.

"There is no kind of dream side effect," I said.

"You probably just had a weird dream," Jaelyn said.

"Jaelyn, you don't understand. It wasn't like a normal

dream. It felt so real, too real," I explained.

"Dreams can be like that, Aaron," Jaelyn said. "Your mind's just playing tricks on you."

"Okay," I sighed. "Well, thanks anyway."

"No problem, now let me put that back," she said, grabbing the bottle. "Mom and Carl would freak out less if they saw it in my hands."

"That's true," I said, laughing to myself.

Jaelyn laughed and went to unlock the door before I stopped her.

"Before you go, do you know why Mom and Carl are extremely mad at me?"

"Detention?" Jaelyn said, confused.

"I know that's part of it, but they wouldn't be this mad over a regular detention," I said.

"Maybe they're mad that the cops were called," Jaelyn said.

"That's probably it," I said nervously. "What do I do?"

"I guess just go out there and apologize," Jaelyn said while pointing to the door. "While you do that, I'll put the pill bottle away. Your sap speech will be the perfect distraction."

"Okay," I said nervously.

I walked out of the room first to hopefully draw attention to myself.

"Hey, Mom," I said nervously.

She didn't respond.

"I'm sorry about today," I said. "I didn't mean to skip class. I was just trying to take a mini-break."

She still didn't respond. I looked over to see Jaelyn sneaking over to the cupboard. I knew I needed to be a better distraction.

"Mom, can you at least respond to me?" I asked.

Right as Mom was about to answer, Carl came down the stairs.

"What on earth are you doing, Jaelyn!" Carl screamed.

Jaelyn jumped back and looked over at him.

"Nothing," she said quickly.

"Well, that's a lie! Why did you have those pills!" Carl screamed while walking over to her.

"I didn't take any!" she shouted.

"Don't give me lip!" Carl shouted at her.

"Okay," she said as she began to walk away.

"Not so fast!" Carl shouted as he grabbed Jaelyn's arm.

"Let go of me," Jaelyn sternly said .

"Then tell me the truth," he said.

"I did," she said.

Carl looked so mad. He usually would get this mad at me but never Jaelyn.

"Don't make me smack you across the face!" Carl shouted at her.

"Do it!" Jaelyn shouted. "Show Mom and Effie how you truly act."

Jaelyn was scared, I could tell.

Her eyes started to water, and I felt bad.

I couldn't tell what Carl was going to do, but I knew I had to stop him.

"Leave her alone!" I shouted.

Carl and Jaelyn both looked at me like I was crazy.

"I said leave her alone!" I shouted again.

Carl let go of Jaelyn's arm and walked over to me.

"This was your doing, wasn't it?" Carl asked me, frustrated.

"Jaelyn got them for me," I said. "I needed to read the label, and she was the only one who believed me."

"You just fool her easily!" he shouted at me.

"You just don't want to admit I'm not the horrible person you think I am!" I shouted back.

Carl's face was so red. I knew he wanted to kill me, but I didn't know if he would or not.

"Say that again. I dare you!" Carl shouted.

"Honey, enough," Mom said.

"Shut up, Amanda!" Carl shouted.

"Leave Mom out of this!" I shouted as I pushed him back.

"Stop making me the bad guy!" Carl shouted at me.

"You're the only one making yourself the bad guy!" I shouted back at him. "It's always you! You're the only one who crowns yourself as the bad guy!"

Carl looked me in the eye and smacked me across the face.

A loud smack echoed through the kitchen.

I put my hand on my face and looked up at him.

"I never want to hear you say that again! Do you understand me?" Carl screamed.

I nodded my head.

"Piece of shit," Carl whispered as he walked past me.

I turned around to see Mom walking Carl upstairs. She was treating him like I had just punched him in the gut. It was ridiculous.

"Sorry," I said to Jaelyn.

"Why are you sorry?" she asked. "I didn't get smacked because of you."

"Yeah," I said while trying not to cry.

"You okay?" she asked.

"Yeah," I answered her. "Are you okay?"

"Besides a red arm, I'm fine," she said. "Let's go to my room."

"Okay," I said while beginning to follow her.

We walked into her room and sat down.

"You sure you're okay?" Jaelyn asked.

"It's just not fair, Jaelyn," I said. "Carl treats everyone like shit, and when someone finally treats him like shit in return, they're seen as the bad guy."

"I'm sorry Carl smacked you," she said while putting her hand on my shoulder. "It should've been me."

"It should've been neither of us," I told her.

"I know," she said.

After a little while, we both laid back on Jaelyn's bed and just relaxed.

"How different do you think things would be if Dad was still here?" I asked Jaelyn.

"They would be better," she said while starting to zone out.

"Agreed," I said while starting to close my eyes.

Before I knew it, Jaelyn and I were both asleep.

I woke up the next morning to see that we had both managed to fall off the bed in our sleep.

"This is why we don't sleep on beds horizontally," Jaelyn said jokingly.

"No kidding," I said while laughing to myself.

I got up a few minutes later and decided I was gonna make myself some toast.

I walked into the kitchen to see my mom looking through the mail.

"Someone wrote you a letter, Aaron," Mom said while holding out a piece of paper.

I grabbed the paper and read it.

Dear Aaron,

I've known you for quite some time and have liked you for a while. You're always so brave, smart, and charming. I'm surprised you've never had a girlfriend. I know that will change very soon, though, so that's why I decided to write this. I want to be yours before any other girl has a chance. Meet me at the pizzeria at three p.m. today. Can't wait to see you <3

−MJ

This letter was very strange.

I had no idea who MJ was. Was MJ her name? Or just her initials?

I guess I would have to go there to find out.

"Aaron has a date!" Jaelyn shouted from behind me.

"Jaelyn!" I shouted. "Mind your own business!"

"Are you gonna go?" she asked.

"I don't know," I said. "I don't even know who this is."

"Go and find out," she said. "You only live once."

"You know what, you're right," I said.

"Yay!" she shouted.

I couldn't believe I was about to go on a date. It felt wrong because my heart truly belonged to Emma Grace, but I couldn't live my life surrounding her.

I didn't want to admit it, but I had to move on for the safety of me and everyone I love.

Chapter 9

My mystery date came quicker than I expected. It seemed like my whole day had just zoomed by to get me to this point.

I honestly was pretty nervous. I had no idea what to expect from this mysterious person. For all I knew, they could be setting me up to kill me, but until I was able to explain that to Jaelyn and make her understand why, I think she would force me to do things like this, even if I was terrified.

Jaelyn loves me and wants the best for me, but she can become quite pushy at times.

"Are you really wearing that?" Jaelyn asked me as I walked out into the kitchen.

"Yeah?" I answered her, confused. "I wear this kind of stuff almost every single day."

"Exactly," she stated. "For a date, you need to be better dressed."

"Jaelyn, stop," I said, annoyed. "I'll dress better when I figure out who this person is."

"Fine," she said, annoyed. "Do you need a ride?"

"I'm good; the pizzeria isn't that far away," I said.

"Have fun," she said as I walked out.

"I'll try," I said as I shut the door behind me.

I walked down towards the sidewalk and started making my way to the pizzeria.

This whole mystery girl thing seemed weird. I had never had someone confess their love to me before, but I knew this wasn't how it was usually done.

Even though my anxiety was through the roof, I eventually made it to the pizzeria.

I looked down at my watch to see it read 3.02 p.m.

"Perfect timing," I whispered to myself. "Let's just hope for the best."

I walked in and tried to see if I could find this mystery girl.

I looked around, but I didn't see anyone familiar.

I was about to give up and go home when suddenly I felt someone put their hand on my shoulder.

"Glad you came," a voice whispered.

"Who's glad I came?" I asked, trying to get a name.

"A very lucky girl," she said. "Now go sit down. I'll be back in a minute."

The girl let go of my shoulder and walked away. I tried to see her face, but all I saw was the back of her head, which wasn't much help.

I decided to listen to her and go sit down.

After a few minutes of waiting, she came back and stood behind me.

"Do I ever get to figure out who you are?" I asked, hoping she'd say yes.

"I guess," she said with a slight chuckle.

The girl moved around and sat in the chair in front of me. She lifted her head, and I instantly knew who she was.

"Morgan?" I said, surprised.

"The one and only," she said jokingly.

"I did not expect to see you," I said.

"I could tell," she said with a smile.

"So why'd you sign your letter as MJ?" I asked.

"Morgan Jay, MJ is my initials," she explained.

"I had no idea your last name was Jay. I thought it started with a B," I said.

"A Lot of people don't know my last name," she said. "Honestly, I'm lucky if they know my first."

I didn't respond. It was sad how a lot of people didn't know Morgan. She's always seemed nice, but I guess to most people, she's just a background character.

"You wanna split a cheese pizza?" Morgan asked.

"Sure," I said with a smile.

She smiled back and went to order the pizza. I just sat and waited.

Part of me felt guilty about this whole thing. Morgan was about to buy me food for a date that I didn't even want to be on.

She's nice, but I don't love her. I love Emma Grace.

"It's gonna be a while," Morgan said as she walked back over to me. "Do you care if I get some groceries for my Dad real quick?"

"I don't mind," I said. "I'll wait for the pizza."

"Thanks, Aaron, you're a lifesaver," she said as she ran out.

I sat there and just waited.

My phone was only able to entertain me for about half an hour before it died.

After my phone died, I just sat there and waited some more.

I waited for so long that I ended up falling asleep.

When I woke up, I found myself on the floor in what appeared to be a school hallway.

I quickly stood up and started to walk around.

After a while, I realized I was in my school's hallway.

This was so weird. How did I get here?

I walked into the bathroom to see if I looked normal.

When I looked in the mirror, I noticed I was in a different

set of clothes.

"When did I put these on?" I asked myself.

I still had no idea what was going on.

I decided to walk out of the bathroom and see if I could find anyone, even though I really didn't want to.

After a few minutes, I started to hear talking, which meant I wasn't alone.

"Hello?" I said, trying to get a response.

I walked down the hall to see Mr. Smith standing there with a bunch of buff-looking guys.

"Perfect timing," Mr. Smith said.

"What?" I said, confused.

"Get him, boys; he's delusional," Mr. Smith said while pointing at me.

Right at that moment, four guys started charging at me.

I may have had no idea what was going on, but I knew I had to get out of there.

I started running down the hallways looking for the exits, but they all seemed to be moved.

After a while, I realized no one was chasing me any more.

I stopped myself and tried to catch my breath.

Once my breath was back to normal, I hesitantly continued to walk along the halls, still trying to find a way out.

After what felt like ages, I finally saw a door. A sigh of relief fell over me. I walked over to the door and was about to open it when all of a sudden, I heard a gunshot.

As the gunshot echoed through my ears, I felt a sharp pain run through my body, and I fell to the ground.

I woke up in a panic. I looked down at my chest to see nothing there.

I was back at the pizzeria.

"Were you asleep?" Morgan asked me as she sat down.

"I think so," I said, confused.

"You okay?" she asked. "You look pale."

"I'm fine," I said.

"Sorry I had to leave," she said. "If you need to go, that's perfectly fine with me."

"I'm just gonna step outside for a minute," I said.

I stood up and quickly made my way outside the pizzeria.

Soon after I went outside, my head started pounding. It felt like someone was punching my head from the inside of my skull.

I decided to just sit in the alley for a minute and wait for the pain to ease, even if it felt endless.

After a few minutes, I saw Morgan walk outside.

"Aaron, you're scaring me. Are you sure you're okay?" she asked me worriedly.

Morgan came over and sat next to me. She placed her hand on my face, probably deciding if I had a fever or not.

"Aaron, do you need me to walk you home?" she asked.

"No, I'm fine," I said.

"Aaron, stop lying," she said. "I know you're not fine. You're pale, covered in sweat, and look like you're about to start crying. Please just tell me the truth."

"I don't know what's wrong with me," I said while holding my head.

"Look at me," she said.

"Okay," I said while looking up at her.

She paused for a moment and took a deep breath.

She slowly raised her hand and put it on my forehead.

It stung for a second, but then all my pain just disappeared.

I looked up at her as she pulled her hand away.

As she placed her hand back down, I noticed it was glowing a vibrant orange color.

"Holy shit!" I shouted. "What's wrong with your hand?"

"Aaron, calm down," she said.

"Your hand is glowing!" I shouted at her. "Did you drug me?"

"Aaron, don't be silly. I did not drug you," she said.

"Then tell me why your hand is glowing!" I demanded.

"You wouldn't understand," she said as she stood up.

"Tell me!" I said, and I stood up. "I'm not stupid enough to believe that's normal."

"I know you're not," she said. "Just don't tell anyone."

"What did your glowy hand do to me!" I shouted at her.

"It helped you!" she said, frustrated. "Now stop screaming about it so loudly!"

"I'll shut up when you explain better!" I screamed at her.

"No!" she shouted. "You'll shut up now! Or else!"

"What are you gonna do? Smack me?" I shouted at her.

"No," she said calmly. "I'll make sure your little Emma Grace never sees the light of day again."

"What?" I shouted at her.

"You heard me," she said.

I grabbed Morgan and pushed her against the wall.

"Where is she?" I shouted.

"That's none of your concern," Morgan said.

"Yes, it is!" I screamed back at her.

"Just leave before I make you cry out to your daddy," she said. "Oh, I forgot, you don't have one, sorry."

"You're a horrible person," I said.

"That's what they all say," she said. "Now I gotta go."

Morgan looked up at me and punched me in the stomach. I

142

grabbed my stomach and fell back.

"Sorry it had to go this way, Aaron," Morgan said. "And for the record, just know I did love you, but I knew from the second you walked in that you didn't love me."

Morgan walked away and just left me.

I lay there for a few minutes before deciding to get up.

I couldn't believe what had just happened.

Morgan was one of them, too, and she could easily hurt Emma.

At that moment, I knew that I couldn't stop my search for Emma – especially now.

Once that thought had made its way through my head, I stood up and walked home.

On my way home, more thoughts were running through my head.

I had a mission now that I had to complete.

It no longer mattered if I was going to make it out alive or not. That sounds horrible to say, but it's true.

People in this world are born for a purpose, and I believe this is mine. To be a savior and protect those important to me, no matter the cost.

I arrived back home a few minutes later to see my aunt's car parked outside the house.

"Are you kidding me?" I said to myself.

I loved my aunt, but she could honestly get on my nerves.

She tries to keep a good relationship with Jaelyn and me just by buying us things.

That may not sound bad, but trust me, it is. A relationship that is built by money is not a relationship you want to have.

Once I was done dreading my aunt's arrival, I walked over to the front door and walked in.

The second I walked in, all heads turned to me.

"How'd it go?" Jaelyn asked excitedly.

"Fine," I said, not wanting to bring anything up.

"I can't believe my little Aaron went on his first date," my aunt said while looking right at me.

"I wouldn't count it as a date," I said.

"Aaron, stop," Jaelyn said. "Just admit you went on a date."

"Okay," I said, annoyed with her. "I'm going to my room."

"Aaron, we have company. Come sit down," Mom said sternly.

"Fine," I said with an eye roll.

I went and sat down on the couch a good six feet away from everyone else. I did not want to deal with anyone right now.

A few minutes later, Jaelyn managed to escape the conversation and walk over to me.

"So, are you and this mystery girl going on a second date?" She asked me, still in an excited tone.

"No," I said, annoyed. "Can you please stop asking about it now?"

"Can I ask one more question?" Jaelyn asked me, hoping I'd say yes.

"Fine," I said, just wanting her to leave me alone.

"Who was the girl?" she asked.

"Morgan Jay," I answered her.

"Morgan?" Jaelyn said, surprised. "Why didn't that work out? She's so sweet."

"Trust me, Morgan has a dark side," I said.

"Did you two get into a fight?" Jaelyn asked.

"Kind of," I said, confused.

I didn't want to give Jaelyn too many details about my date disaster. I didn't want to accidentally spill the fact that it made me realize I was still trying to find Emma.

"Are we done?" I asked.

"Fine," Jaelyn said, annoyed.

Jaelyn went around the couch and sat by me.

I knew that she was hating our aunt's visit just as much as I was. She was just better at hiding it.

"Wow, Amanda, we've been talking for so long!" my aunt said, obviously trying to get our attention.

"I know!" Mom said while giving Jaelyn and me a death look. "Why don't you talk to the kids? I gotta go start dinner."

Mom smiled at Jaelyn and me and walked to the kitchen.

Jaelyn just turned and looked at me. I could tell by her face she was just about ready to run to her room.

"How's school going?" our aunt asked us.

"Good," we both said, nearly in sync.

"That was so in sync!" our aunt said loudly. "You two are practically twins!"

"No," Jaelyn said awkwardly.

"Oh, take a joke, dear," our aunt said while coming to sit closer. "Have you kids heard about the disappearances?"

"Yeah," Jaelyn said quietly.

"What about you, Aaron?" our aunt asked loudly.

"Yeah, it's kinda a sore topic, though, so let's not talk about it," I said.

"Why's it a sore topic?" our aunt asked.

"'Cause we know one of the girls who disappeared," I explained.

"Don't we all?" our aunt said, trying to be relatable.

I didn't answer. I just looked over at Mom. She looked back at me and pointed at our aunt, hinting that she wanted me to continue talking to her.

I could tell she was about ready to kill me, so I just looked back at our aunt.

"So Aaron, I heard you got into some fights at school. What's that about?" our aunt asked.

"I don't know," I said, confused.

"What makes you get into them?" she asked.

"I don't know," I answered again.

"Well, Jaelyn here doesn't get into fights. What are you doing differently than her?" she asked me, trying to get an answer out of me.

"I don't know," I said in an annoyed tone.

"You gotta answer something besides I don't know, or else we won't get anywhere," she said while looking over at me.

"You gotta find better conversation topics, or else we won't get anywhere," I said while looking right back at her.

She didn't answer me. I could tell by her face I hurt her feelings.

I felt bad, but there was nothing I could do about it now.

"Aaron, can you come here?" Mom asked in a stern tone.

"Yeah," I said as I got up.

I walked into the kitchen and over to Mom. She grabbed my arm and pulled me outside.

"What the hell are you doing?" she asked.

"I don't know," I said.

"You gotta be nice to her; she's your aunt!" Mom shouted at me.

"I know that!" I shouted back. "She just talks about the worst things!"

"I know," Mom said with a sigh. "But she's Carl's sister; you gotta respect her."

"Okay," I said. "Can I go to my room?"

"Fine," Mom said. "But first, I want you to go apologize."

"Okay," I said with a sigh.

Mom and I walked back inside.

She walked over to the kitchen while I went to the living room.

I found my aunt looking at old family pictures while Jaelyn was sitting on the couch.

I walked over to my aunt and noticed she was looking at a young photo of Jaelyn and me.

"We used to be so small," I said, trying to lighten the mood.

"Yeah," she said while looking over at me. "Now, you guys are just mouthy teenagers."

"Sorry about that," I said.

"It's okay," she said. "I know I can be hard to talk to sometimes. My conversation ideas aren't the best. I know that, but I love you kids. So even though I know you guys hate talking to me, I still try to build somewhat of a connection."

"We don't hate talking to you," I said.

She looked over at me with one of her famous looks. She knew I was lying.

"There's no need to lie," she said. "It won't hurt me. All I care about is that I'm trying. That's all anyone can ever do."

"You can be quite inspirational," I said jokingly.

She smiled and put her hand on my shoulder.

"You have a bright future," she said. "Please don't waste it."

"I'll try," I said.

She took her hand off my shoulder and walked to the kitchen.

I went over to Jaelyn and pointed to our rooms. She looked up at me and stood up. We both went to our rooms as quickly as possible.

Jaelyn and I both loved having our own space away from everyone else, but I think that's pretty normal.

The second I got into my room, I lay down on my bed. It felt so nice.

I began to drift off to sleep when all of a sudden, an idea hit me.

I knew Mr. Smith kept the papers with Emma Grace and the other kids in his classroom, and since it was Saturday, he wouldn't even be in the building.

This was my chance, I thought to myself.

I quickly set an alarm on my phone for midnight and then lived out my evening normally. I ate dinner with my family, walked my aunt out, and then went to bed.

Quickly after I drifted off, my alarm went off, which meant it was time to take action.

Before I left, I decided to look through my clothes and picked out a black outfit so I could easily blend in with the night.

I went to put on my black outfit when all of a sudden, my brain started to recognize it like I had worn it before.

I didn't know why. I just shook it off as a feeling of nervousness and got dressed.

Once I was dressed, I snuck over to the front door and quietly walked out.

I was officially on my way to possibly save Emma Grace. That feeling made all the fear in my body temporarily disappear. I felt like I was invincible, like nothing could stop me. This kind of feeling is rare. It's like confidence times ten. With this feeling, I could do anything!

Before I knew it, I was standing outside the school. One step closer to success.

The feeling of immortality still hadn't left me, which I guess could be considered both good and bad.

I walked around the school until I was standing right outside Mr. Smith's windows. I looked at all three windows and tried to figure out which one would be the easiest to get in through smoothly.

After I looked for a while, I noticed a detail on the middle window that I had missed the first hundred times. It was open a crack. I couldn't believe I had missed that; I felt so stupid.

Once I was over my stupidity, I started trying to open up the window, but it wouldn't budge.

It was open only a few inches, and it was just enough to properly taunt me.

After a while of struggling, the window shot open.

"Woah!" I shouted as I jumped back.

I walked back to the window to realize one of the hinges had snapped.

My plan of going one hundred percent undercover wasn't currently working in my favor.

I decided to just go into the classroom and deal with the aftermath later.

I mean, if I was successful and saved thirty-something kids, I don't think anyone would care about a broken window.

I hopped into the classroom and began to look around. It was dark and very quiet.

The feeling of immortality had officially left me and had been replaced by a combination of fear and anxiety. I knew I had to do this, though, and that's why I chose not to turn around and run. I had to be brave for Emma.

I decided to walk over to Mr. Smith's desk and grab the sheet of paper I had seen before and possibly find others.

The first paper was easy to get. It was in the same spot I had previously found it in.

As I looked down at it, flashbacks started coming to me.

I placed my hand on my arm to try and tell my brain nothing was there; the taser thing was gone, and I was in no danger.

After I calmed myself, I went to find more papers when suddenly I noticed a stack of black and white pictures placed at the bottom of the desk drawer.

I instantly started looking through them to see if I recognized any of the people in them.

After about twenty photos, I finally saw a face I recognized, Emma Grace. She looked skinnier, her face was dirty, she had bags under her eyes, and her clothes were ripped all over. She looked awful...

I decided to count the photos and then count the names, and sure enough, they lined up. These photos were photos of all of Mr. Smith's victims.

I was in disbelief.

I still couldn't comprehend how a person I used to look at for guidance could be this awful.

"This is all I need," I said to myself. "I'm done."

I started to walk to the window when all of a sudden, I heard a voice echo from the hallway.

"Well, well, well," the voice said as it got closer.

I quickly started to head to the window when all of a sudden, I saw a bunch of cars pulling up to the school.

I instantly backed away from the window.

My gut screamed at me that those cars were bad news. A normal staff member wouldn't be coming to the school at nearly one a.m. With that logic, I decided to hide. I ran to the closet and shut the door behind me.

"Are we gonna play hide and seek?" the voice asked me as they made their way into the classroom.

I didn't answer. I'd be a true idiot if I did that. Instead, I listened closely to see if I recognized the voice, but I didn't. I thought it was Mr. Smith at first, but the voice sounded too deep.

"Don't make this hard," the voice said as they continued to walk around the classroom.

I just tried to stay calm. It was all I could do anyway. I was stuck in a closet, and the mysterious voice was outside of it.

I was about to start thinking of a plan when all of a sudden, I saw the doorknob start to move. I instantly put all my weight on the door so the person couldn't open it.

"I know you're in there!" the voice shouted at me.

I just kept holding the door. I knew I was screwed, but I didn't just want to give up. If I did that, I would automatically have a zero chance of winning.

I kept pushing on the door with all my strength, but I was soon outmuscled, and the door flew open and sent me flying to the ground.

The person grabbed me by my feet and threw me out of the closet.

The second I stood back up, I tried to run away, but I wasn't fast enough. The person wrapped their arms around me and held me back.

"Got you," the person whispered in my ear.

"What do you want?" I asked in a panicked tone.

"You're messing with the wrong things," he whispered.

"Where are you guys!" I heard a voice shout.

That voice I recognized, it was Mr. Smith.

Everything was officially going so wrong, and I felt helpless.

"Your room, moron!" The guy shouted back.

"Please don't do anything stupid," I said out of desperation.

The guy started laughing hysterically. It was sick how some people in this world found the torture of others amusing.

"Can I have some fun!" The guy shouted to Mr. Smith.

"I don't care!" Mr. Smith shouted back. "Just try to limit the bloodstains."

I started to panic. I kicked and squirmed in the hope of escaping this guy's grip, but it was no use.

"I can't believe a fifteen-year-old kid was about to stop the VK," the guy said. "I'm glad to know that's over."

"It's not!" I shouted. "If you want it over, you're gonna have to kill me!"

"Easy enough," he said with a smirk.

"What?" I said, alarmed.

The guy lifted me up and threw me across the classroom.

I landed on a bunch of desks and smacked my head on the solid ground.

I quickly reopened my eyes to see that everything had become blurry.

My head throbbed.

I attempted to stand up, but I tumbled down onto a desk.

I couldn't see clearly, but I could still hear fairly well.

I was able to hear the guy coming closer to me, but I couldn't tell which direction he was coming from. I needed proper eyesight for that.

Before I could figure out any kind of direction, I felt a cord wrap around my throat. I instantly got pulled backward with my airway being cut off.

I tried to pull it off, but it was no use.

This guy obviously wanted to prove to me how easy it was

to kill a fifteen-year-old.

I started to lose even more of my vision, and I was blacking out. This was it, I thought to myself. My decisions used to seem smart, but now they were going to be what finally kills me.

Chapter 10

July 13th, 2008, was one of the worst days of my childhood.

This day had haunted me for years. It gave me many nightmares until I was about thirteen.

What made this day so terrible wasn't necessarily the day itself but the night that followed.

That day was actually pretty good.

Back then, Carl used to actually try to form a relationship with me, which was nice.

On this day, he decided to take me to see the newest Batman movie. It made eleven-year-old me the happiest kid in the world.

My day seemed perfect until the walk home.

Carl and I used to always walk around town together, no matter the time. So when the movie ended later than we thought it would, we didn't think it'd be a problem to walk in the dark.

Little did we know what that decision would cause us.

While we were walking home, we decided to cut through an alley to save some time.

It seemed like a good idea at the time, but it really wasn't.

I remember I didn't want to go through the alley, but Carl made me.

He told me to stop being a baby and just do as he said.

I really didn't want to listen to him, but he was my guardian. I had to.

As we started walking through the alley, we started to hear

a bunch of rustling.

I remember Carl just told me it was a raccoon, but I was able to tell he didn't even believe himself.

A few moments after the rustling began, chaos struck.

Multiple guys jumped out from behind trash cans and held out knives and guns.

I remember how Carl and I just froze while the guys gave us crazy looks.

After a while, the guys started getting closer to us, and that's when Carl took action. He grabbed me and moved me behind him.

He started yelling at the guys, telling them to leave us alone; this sadly only aggravated them more.

I remember feeling someone grab me and pull me back.

I screamed and cried; I was only a kid, and I was terrified.

Carl quickly turned around and tried to grab me, but that ended up being a bad decision on his part. The second he did that, one of the guys threw a rope around his neck and pulled him back.

I remember just standing there in horror.

Watching a person you care about getting hurt is awful, especially when you know you can't do anything to help them.

Luckily Carl's brain was more advanced than eleven-year-old me, and he was able to get out of the situation in a matter of seconds.

Carl swung his head back as hard as he could and knocked the guy down to the ground.

I remember briefly looking down at the guy covered in blood. It was crazy how much damage Carl did to that guy's face.

Before eleven-year-old me could fully comprehend the

situation, Carl grabbed me, and we ran out of the alley.

Thankfully, we were okay.

I remember Mom was an emotional mess when we got home.

She didn't want to lose us, and she still doesn't, and that's why I'm glad I have this memory.

Thanks to Carl, I knew how to not get murdered.

I repeated his actions and swung my head back as hard as I possibly could. I hit the guy right in the face.

He fell down to the floor and held his face in pain.

I took this moment to run out of that classroom and try to find an exit.

I was running through the halls when suddenly a feeling of familiarity fell over me again. I ignored it and just kept running. I didn't have the time to figure out what was causing this feeling.

After what felt like hours of running, I finally saw an exit.

I went to open the door when all of a sudden, I knew why this was all so familiar.

"My dream," I whispered to myself.

Before I could comprehend how crazy this was, I remembered what happened at the end of my dream.

I didn't think twice before I jumped out of the way, and I'm glad I did. The second I moved, I heard the gunshot, but this time instead of me falling to the floor, it was the glass from the door.

"Are you kidding me!" I heard Mr. Smith scream.

I would've loved to respond to him with one of my sarcastic comments, but I chose my life over one of my famous comments. I knew I had to get out of there before he tried to kill me again.

I ran and ran, trying desperately to find another exit.

It was weird how the school seemed completely unknown to me.

I thought maybe it could've been because of my throbbing head, but I had no idea what was going on, so I didn't have the room to make assumptions like that.

After a little while, I finally made it to the front doors. It seemed like I was going to make it out until I heard the sound of a gun being loaded behind me.

"Don't move!" I heard Mr. Smith scream from behind me.

I turned around slowly with my hands in the air, hoping he wouldn't shoot me.

"Mr. Smith, please put the gun down," I said with a shaky voice.

"Why?" he asked. "With this, you actually listen to me."

As I was about to respond to Mr. Smith, three more guys walked up towards him, one of them being the guy I smacked in the face earlier.

"This is the high schooler that almost blew our cover?" One of the guys said, surprised.

"He looks ten years old," another one of them added.

"Please let me leave," I said to them. "I won't say a word about this"

"Bullshit!" Mr. Smith shouted. "Rex, go get that paper out of his pocket."

"Okay," Rex said as he came over to me.

Rex was the biggest guy out of all of them. A single limb of his was about the size of my whole body. This made him seem extremely scary to someone like me.

He walked over to me and just stared at me weirdly.

"Must suck to be an idiot, kid," he said while taking the

157

paper and photos out of my pocket. "He found the photos too!"

"Good," Mr. Smith said. "He can die knowing that none of these kids are safe."

"You're a monster!" I screamed. "You kidnapped one of your own students and a bunch of other kids. That's not okay!"

"I'm not the monster," Mr. Smith said. "I'm just getting justice."

"What kind of justice is this!" I shouted.

"You're too young to understand," he said.

"Understand what?" I shouted back. "Understand that all of you are idiots and are going to jail."

They all looked at me like I was crazy.

Mr. Smith looked over at Rex and the guy with a bloody nose and then pointed at me.

"Grab him," Mr. Smith said to them.

They started walking towards me.

I slowly started backing away when all of a sudden, Mr. Smith shot at the ceiling.

I screamed and covered my head.

"Don't forget about this, Mr. Cripple!" Mr. Smith shouted. "Cooperate, or one of these bullets will find its way through your skull!"

I didn't answer. I just nodded my head.

Tears started to fill my eyes. Right as I thought I had escaped death, it came knocking on my door once again.

While trying to hold back tears, Rex and the other guy came behind me and grabbed one arm each.

Mr. Smith looked over at the last guy and handed him the gun.

He started walking over to me while pulling out a sharp pocket knife.

"Before we get rid of you, I need a few answers," Mr. Smith said while moving the knife toward my face.

"Okay," I said with a shaky voice.

"How did you know I was behind you with the gun?" He asked.

"What?" I said, confused.

I knew he was talking about the first time he tried to shoot me, but I was playing dumb. I did not want to answer him.

"Answer the question!" he shouted while pressing the knife into my face.

"I don't know!" I shouted back.

I hoped he couldn't tell that I was lying, but I think he knew from the start that I was.

"Wrong answer!" he shouted while slicing my cheek.

"Ow!" I screamed in pain.

He grabbed my head and held it up.

"Answer the question," he said. "The next slice will be fatal."

I just looked up at him with tears in my eyes. I felt so small, so helpless.

Mr. Smith moved his knife down to my throat.

"Last chance," he said.

I stood there trying to think of a way to avoid this when all of a sudden, Mr. Smith started counting down.

"Three... two ..." he said while slowly pushing the knife into my throat.

"It was a dream!" I shouted.

"What do you mean?" he asked while still pressing the knife into my throat.

"I had a dream earlier today that told me I was gonna get shot," I explained.

"Weird," he said.

"Do you think he's like Morgan and Tyler?" Rex asked.

"What?" I said in confusion.

"Shut up, moron!" Mr. Smith screamed. "We will discuss that after this idiot is no longer in existence."

"What are you guys talking about?" I asked, confused.

"Nothing you'll have to worry about," Mr. Smith said while pushing the knife slowly into my neck. "Should've stayed out of my way."

As Mr. Smith was about to finish me off, he got lifted in the air by something weird.

It appeared to be a yellow mist.

I turned my head to see all the guys panicking.

"Put me down," Mr. Smith said while struggling for air.

I stared in disbelief. I had no idea what was going on.

I caught a glimpse of a weird figure below Mr. Smith before it started talking to us.

"Leave the boy alone, or I'm gonna snap all of your necks," the figure said while throwing Mr. Smith across the hallway.

The guys did what he said and threw me forward. I looked back to see them all running away.

"Cowards," I said to myself.

I quickly stood up and found myself face to face with the figure.

The figure moved his hand and put it on my shoulder.

"Thank you," I said.

"You're welcome," the figure said. "Now, you're gonna be in your yard. You're gonna walk up to your house and walk in. Your family is worried about you."

Before I could question anything, I was blinded by a flash.

When I opened my eyes again, I was in my front yard.

I looked around to see if everything was real.

I even pinched myself to make sure I wasn't dreaming.

"What the hell just happened?" I asked myself.

As I was about to walk up to my house, I felt something drip down my face. I whipped my hand across my face to see it covered in blood.

I had completely forgotten about the slice in my face.

I instantly moved my hand out of sight and ran up to the front door.

I started pounding on the door, hoping someone would let me in.

I felt like I was dying.

I was lightheaded from the blood, my head was still pounding from hitting it on the floor, and my neck stung from being strangled and nearly sliced open.

Right as I was about to pass out, I saw the doorknob turn.

"Hello?" I said in a worried voice.

The door slowly opened. I backed up and just stood there in anticipation.

The second the door was fully open, I saw Jaelyn standing there with a worried face.

Before she could say anything, I fell into her arms and started to break down. She held me close and helped me inside.

When we got into the kitchen, Jaelyn sat me down at the counter and turned on the lights.

She looked at me in disbelief.

"What happened to you?" she asked as her eyes began to fill up with tears.

I just looked down at the floor.

I didn't want to see Jaelyn cry.

She was strong. Seeing her cry always broke me.

"Mom and Carl are out looking for you," Jaelyn said.

I still didn't answer. I couldn't bring myself to look at Jaelyn.

"I'm gonna let them know you're home," she said as she walked away.

"Tell them I'm okay," I said in a shaky voice.

"Aaron, I'm telling them the truth," she said while beginning to cry. "You look like you were almost killed!"

I didn't respond to her. I knew Jaelyn wasn't stupid. I hadn't looked in a mirror, but I knew I looked awful.

Honestly, I didn't know if I was okay. I just hated to worry my family.

I heard Jaelyn get on the phone with Mom and start breaking down herself.

Hearing Jaelyn this sad put me at an all-time low.

I got up and tried to sneak into my room to avoid all of this madness, but Jaelyn stopped me.

"Where are you going?" she shouted.

"My room," I said while avoiding eye contact.

"No, you're not!" she shouted. "You're waiting in the kitchen for Mom and Carl!"

"Why?" I asked, annoyed. "I'm tired, and I've already had a long enough night."

"They need to make sure you're okay," she explained. "You're the one who decided to just disappear."

I looked up at her and sighed.

"Fine," I said as I walked back into the kitchen.

I had no idea the reaction I was going to get from Mom and Carl, and that worried me more than anything.

Jaelyn seemed to have calmed down, which helped, but I was still panicking.

I sat at the counter with my head in my hands.

I was dreading Mom and Carl's arrival.

Before I knew it, though, I saw the front door fly open.

Mom was the first one to run inside, followed by Carl. They walked over to me and tried to look at my face, but I wouldn't let them.

"Honey, are you okay?" Mom asked in a worried voice.

"Yeah," I said quietly.

"Can you look at us?" Carl said, annoyed at me.

I didn't answer. I just kept my head down. I wanted them to just walk away, but I knew they wouldn't do that.

"Honey, answer us," Mom said with a worried voice.

"Mom, I'm fine," I said, annoyed.

"If you're fine, then look at us!" Carl shouted.

"Can you just leave me alone?" I asked, still annoyed.

"No!" he shouted at me. "You're the one who disappeared and sent us all into a panic. We all thought you were dead!"

"I'm sorry," I said quietly.

Carl sighed and took a deep breath.

"You're fine," he said. "Can you please just let us see your face?"

"Fine," I said hesitantly.

I lifted my head up and looked up at Mom and Carl. Both of their eyes widened.

"Holy shit," Carl said. "What happened?"

"Stuff," I said in a worried tone.

I couldn't tell them what had happened. If I did, they could get hurt. I loved my family. I didn't want them to get hurt because of me.

"Stuff?" Carl said, frustrated. "Tell us what happened right now!"

"No!" I screamed. "That's none of your business!"

I stood up and started to walk away when all of a sudden, Jaelyn stopped me.

"Aaron, we're your family," she said. "We have the right to know what happened to you."

"I know you're my family," I said. "I just can't tell you guys."

"Why can't you?" Carl shouted at me.

"Reasons!" I shouted back.

"Aaron, you're either telling us or the police!" he shouted. "I won't hesitate to call them!"

"Carl, don't," I said, aggravated.

"I will!" he shouted back. "Stop being an idiot!"

"Can you just leave me alone?" I shouted. "I want to go to bed."

"No," Carl said sternly.

I just stood there while my head began to spin. It honestly felt like I was gonna die.

"I gotta go," I said quietly.

I started to walk away when all of a sudden, my vision blurred.

I walked right into the wall and fell backward.

Everyone quickly walked over to me and looked at me with concerned looks.

"You okay?" Jaelyn asked me in a panicked tone.

"Yeah," I said while standing up. "I just need to lay down."

I started to rub my eyes, but I still couldn't see.

This was great, my vision was nearly gone, and my head was still throbbing.

Everything just got worse and worse until I finally blacked out.

I woke up to see Carl and a random lady looking down at me.

"You okay?" Carl asked.

"My head hurts," I answered quietly.

"I'd figure that," he said. "You passed out and hit your head on the ground."

"Did you hit your head previously?" The random lady asked.

"I think so," I answered her.

Everything in my head was currently a blur. I couldn't recall many details. All I could recall was that Mr. Smith almost killed me, and then I was teleported away by a weird figure.

"Aaron, I know you're keeping things secret, but for your own health, I suggest you tell Dr. Lily what happened," Carl said.

"I don't know," I said weakly.

"What happened to your face?" Dr. Lily asked me, trying to narrow things down.

"A knife sliced it," I said quietly.

"Who's knife was it?" Carl asked.

"Can't say," I said while sitting up.

"Fair enough," Dr. Lily said. "What happened to your neck?"

"A rope tried strangling me, and a knife was slightly involved," I answered her.

"Okay," she said. "None of your injuries seem fatal. Just take it easy with your head and keep an eye on your cuts and see a doctor if you suspect an infection."

"Okay," I said while standing up.

"Be careful," she said while walking away.

I looked around to see Mom talking to a familiar man.

I walked over to her to try and see who it was.

"Hey, sweetie," Mom said while looking over at me.

"Hi," I said. "Who's that?"

"I'm Officer Miller. I believe we've met before," he said.

"Yeah," I said, confused. "Why are you here?"

"I'm here because your parents here believe someone tried to kill you," he said.

"I've already stated I'm not talking," I said.

"Well, it's either you talk, or I make an assumption you're not gonna want to hear," he said.

"Is that a threat?" I asked.

"Of course not," he said in a jovial tone. "It's just a fact."

"What's this assumption then?" I asked, annoyed.

"That you're more involved in the disappearance of Emma Grace than we thought," he said.

"What?" I said, surprised.

"That's ridiculous," Mom said.

"Well, what else could it be?" he asked us.

"It's none of your business!" I shouted.

"Fine," he said. "I'll play this game with you. I've played it with so many Cripples before. You won't be the first or the last."

"Fine by me!" I shouted. "Go ahead and think I'm a criminal. That'll be great for your job."

He looked at me with rage in his eyes. He moved his face closer to mine and looked at me.

"I'm watching you," he whispered.

He stood back up and walked out of the house.

Everyone was looking at me, but I didn't care. I had bigger things to worry about than my family's opinions.

Chapter 11

The rest of the night was fairly quiet. No one said a word to each other. That would usually worry me, but with the current circumstances, I didn't care.

After officer Miller left, I got in the shower.

I wasn't in there for long, but it felt nice to at least get some of the night off me.

Looking in the mirror was hard for me. The red on my face and neck just sent chills down my spine.

I still couldn't comprehend much of the danger I had just faced, and honestly, I don't think I ever will. It was pretty crazy.

After my shower, I was looking forward to finally being able to rest, but my brain was far from shutting down.

While I lay in bed, thoughts were running through my head all over again.

How did they know I was there? How did my dream predict the future? Do they know about Morgan's glowing hands? Who is Tyler? Was I supposed to die? Do I have powers?

All these questions refused to leave my mind. No matter how hard I tried, my brain wouldn't rest, even though it needed to.

I looked at my phone to see it flash the time 4.06 a.m. I couldn't believe how late it was. I guess the night just got away from me.

Right as I was starting to doze off, I heard a knock at my door.

"What?" I shouted.

"Can I come in?" Effie asked in a whimpering voice.

"Yeah?" I said, confused.

I had no idea why Effie would be at my door this late. I checked my phone to see it flashing the time 4.47 a.m.

"It's so late," I whispered to myself.

I sat up in my bed, and Effie walked in.

Her eyes looked red. She looked horrible.

"You okay?" I asked.

"I love you," she said in a whimpering voice.

"I love you too," I said. "Come sit down."

"Okay," she said as she walked over.

Effie sat down next to me and hugged her stuffed animal.

I put my arm around her and tried to comfort her.

"What's wrong?" I asked.

"Mommy and Daddy were arguing earlier," she said. "And it was about you."

"What?" I said, confused.

"You left, and Mommy and Daddy couldn't decide if you were dead or not," she explained. "Mommy was crying and screaming at Daddy. She was saying how she couldn't lose anyone else. I didn't know what she meant by that, but she made me sad because she was sad."

"Effie, it's okay, I'm here, and I'm clearly not dead," I said, still trying to comfort her.

"Well, that's good," she said. "It's good 'cause I don't want to be like Mommy and lose anybody. Losing somebody sounds sad."

"It is very sad," I said.

"Have you ever lost anyone?" she asked.

"I have," I said. "It was a while ago, though."

168

"Does that mean it's not important any more?" Effie asked.

"No, death never loses its meaning," I explained.

"So are you still sad about your loss?" she asked.

"Of course I am," I said. "When you lose somebody, they leave a hole in your heart, and that spot can never be refilled."

"That sounds really sad," she said. "I'm sorry you lost someone."

"It's okay," I said. "Do you want me to go tuck you back in?"

"Sure," she said while standing up. "Thanks for the advice."

"You're welcome," I said as I walked Effie out.

We walked upstairs to her room.

I quickly tucked her back into bed and then walked back downstairs.

As I walked into my room, I noticed someone sitting on my bed.

"You should listen to your own advice," Jaelyn said.

"Why the hell are you in my room?" I asked.

"Aaron, you gave a great lesson to Effie," Jaelyn said.

"Were you listening to us?" I asked, frustrated.

"When you lose someone, there's a hole in your heart that can never be refilled," she said.

"Are you just quoting me?" I asked, annoyed.

"You don't get it," she said.

"Get what?" I asked about ready to lose my cool.

"You're an idiot!" she shouted at me.

"I'm so lost," I said. "Why am I an idiot?"

"You just perfectly described what it's like to lose someone!" she shouted at me. "So that means you know what it feels like."

169

"Jaelyn, it's too early for this. I have no idea what you are getting at!" I shouted back at her.

"You're careless and selfish!" she shouted.

"Why are you attacking me!" I screamed at her.

"You almost died!" she screamed back at me. "We almost lost you! You almost left a hole in all of our hearts!"

"Jaelyn, I'm sorry," I said quietly.

"Are you, though?" she shouted. "'Cause last time I checked, you just left us! You can't do that. I need you. We need you. A world without you is not a world I want to live in. Aaron, you promised me you'd be careful. You are not listening to that promise, and that breaks me more than anything. When we were kids, we were taught that a pinky promise meant the world. It was the one thing that held meaning to us. I don't know why that changed for you. I don't know why you're changing. I just want my little brother to be normal, to be happy. Not almost dying twice a week. Aaron, you're gonna start to be careful, or you're gonna get the hell out of my life! I don't need this right now. I've already suffered enough, and you know that! So please spare me my voice and listen to me right now! 'Cause I'm not repeating myself! Do you understand me? Do you hear the words that are coming out of my mouth?"

"Jaelyn, I'm sorry," I said. "I know I've been horrible, and I know it sucks that you just have to accept that. You don't deserve this. You're an amazing sister; I couldn't ask for better. The one thing I need to ask, though, is that you don't question me. I'm a mystery that is supposed to be left unsolved. I'm going through things just like you, and I need you to understand that."

"So I'm supposed to just let you die?" Jaelyn asked me in an annoyed tone.

"That's not what I'm saying," I said.

"Then what are you saying?" she shouted at me. "You're a mystery? What the hell is that supposed to mean? You're not some movie star, Aaron! You're my brother. We tell each other things. Why is now so different?"

"You don't tell me everything!" I shouted at her.

"'Cause you never ask!" she shouted back at me. "If you were to check on me every once in a while, I'd tell you all the shit that's going on in my life, but you never do! So I don't bother talking about it! I'm asking you, though, so please talk to me."

"I'm sorry, Jaelyn, but that's not an option," I said. "I can't, and I can't tell you why I can't. You just have to trust me, like we always have."

"Just like how we always tell each other things!" Jaelyn shouted.

"Jaelyn, you need to stop!" I screamed at her. "It's five a.m.! Go to bed!"

"Do you remember the rules Dad taught us?" Jaelyn asked.

"Don't bring Dad into this!" I shouted at her.

"You've left me no choice," she said. "Dad always said to never hide anything and to always keep promises, and you're breaking both those rules."

"I don't care," I said.

"So you don't care about Dad or the way he raised us?" Jaelyn shouted in anger.

"Jaelyn, Dad was in my life for six years!" I shouted back at her. "He's dead! I don't need to listen to the rules I was taught in kindergarten! I'm in tenth grade! I've changed, and I'm sad to see you haven't."

"Well, Aaron, you got one thing right," she said. "You've

changed."

Jaelyn stormed out of my room and into her own. I looked in the hall to see her giving me a death look.

"Have fun meeting your demise, mystery man!" she shouted as she slammed her door shut.

"Thanks for the love and support!" I screamed sarcastically back at her as I slammed my door shut.

I was livid. I couldn't recall a time I had ever been this angry.

I looked in the mirror to see that my face was bright red. It was so red I couldn't even tell where my cut was.

I slammed my fist onto my desk as hard as possible. I was so angry it didn't even hurt.

"She's so inconsiderate," I said to myself. "She's the selfish one. She's the one who should be sorry. She's in my business."

As I was about to lay back down, I heard Jaelyn's door swing open. I opened my door to see her fully dressed, grabbing her keys.

"Where are you going?" I asked.

"None of your business!" she shouted at me.

"You're such a hypocrite," I said. "You yell at me for running off, and then you go ahead and run off yourself."

"At least I'll come back unharmed!" she shouted.

Jaelyn walked out the front door and slammed it shut behind her.

I walked up to the window and watched her car drive away.

I was mad at her, but I was also kinda worried.

Where was she going at five in the morning?

I stood in the kitchen for a few more minutes before I decided to try and get some sleep.

I went back to my room, lay in my bed and closed my eyes.

I expected thoughts to keep me up, but they finally decided to let me rest.

I slept for a few hours before I was woken up by the sound of people arguing.

I sat up and walked out to the kitchen to figure out who it was.

As I looked into the kitchen, I saw Jaelyn, Carl, and officer Miller.

I had no idea what they were arguing about, so I decided to listen in.

"This is stupid!" Jaelyn screamed. "I did nothing wrong!"

"Kid, you were trespassing on private property!" Officer Miller screamed back at her.

"That's bullshit!" Jaelyn screamed. "It's never been illegal before! Why is it now?"

"Jaelyn, you were at a construction site!" Carl screamed.

"It was never a construction site before!" She shouted back.

"Kid, that warehouse got torn down," Officer Miller explained. "We are building something better now."

"In the middle of nowhere!" Jaelyn screamed. "That makes perfect sense!"

"Jaelyn, you are being an idiot!" Carl shouted.

"No, I'm not!" she screamed back. "It's in the middle of nowhere. That's why the warehouse was abandoned."

"You're not wrong," Officer Miller said. "We're trying to bring life back into that area, and people like you aren't helping. Things need to be fixed. Places need to be built. The population is growing, and we need to be prepared for it."

"So you're saying a small town in Tennessee is going to be the difference between the world running out of room or not?" Jaelyn said, annoyed.

173

"You need to chill," Officer Miller said. "Why do you even care?"

"That's none of your business," Jaelyn said sternly.

"Jaelyn, stop being a bitch and go to your room!" Carl screamed.

"This is so unfair," Jaelyn said as she walked away.

Jaelyn stormed past me to her room. She didn't even look at me.

I started to feel bad about what I had said to her earlier. She seemed to be going through enough. She didn't need my smartass to top it all off.

Even though it seemed like she wanted to be alone, I decided to talk to her.

I walked up to her door and just walked in.

I shut the door behind me and walked over to her.

She looked at me like I had bugs crawling out of my head.

"What the hell do you want?" she asked.

"I just want to talk," I said.

"About what?" she said.

"Last night and the weird argument I just witnessed," I answered her. "I'll let you decide what I rant about first."

"I'd prefer if you did neither," she said, annoyed.

"Come on, Jaelyn," I said. "I feel horrible about our current relationship."

"Fine, talk about last night and then get out," she said.

"I'm sorry about what I said," I said. "I should've just agreed with you. You were right, and I'm sorry I didn't see that. Last night I was selfish and careless. I don't think about others as much as I should. I'm honestly a terrible person. I can sit here and rant about that all day, but I won't. I just want you to know I take back everything I said about you and Dad. I hope you can at least tolerate me now."

Jaelyn looked up at me and sighed.

"I'm sorry too," she said. "You had already been through enough, and I just made it worse. I wasn't lying about what I said, but I could've at least been a little less harsh, and I definitely shouldn't have used Dad's words against you. He would not have liked the way I used him."

"I forgive you," I said. "Can you forgive me?"

"Sure," she said. "You just have to promise me to not die in the next year."

"Deal," I said with a smile. "So am I still not allowed to ask about the weird argument?"

"You can have three questions," she said.

"That's fair enough," I said. "So, where did you go last night?"

"I went to a place that used to be special to me," she answered me.

"A construction site was special to you?" I said, confused.

"It used to be a warehouse," she explained.

"So why was it special?" I asked.

"When I was younger, I had some hard times," she explained. "I would get so sad or mad that I would just need to cool off. The first time was a month after Dad passed away. I ran to cool off, and I found the warehouse. Its pastel colors caught my eye. I walked inside to find nothing. It was empty, which was perfect. I was able to scream as loud as I wanted, and no one could yell at me. I went back a year later and then the year after that, but I never went back again after the third time. I had a pretty good life, I had you and Emma, and all my bullies were gone. I had no reason to go back until last night. You scared me, and our little fight just threw me over the edge. I needed to calm down, but sadly the warehouse no longer existed. I stupidly still walked outside, though, and I got my anger out. That was a bad idea, though. It got the police called on me, and then I got escorted home."

"Well, that answers all the remaining questions I had," I said.

"Good," she said. "That was my version of a rant."

"Well, I'm sorry about the warehouse," I said. "That place sounded important."

"It was," she said. "I'm sad it's gone, but there's nothing I could do."

I nodded my head at her.

As I was about to say something else, I heard Carl scream from the kitchen.

"Jaelyn and Aaron, get out here now!" he screamed.

I looked at Jaelyn with a nervous glance.

She quickly stood up and walked out. I followed quickly behind her.

I noticed that officer Miller was gone, but that didn't ease me at all. Carl's bright red face was very unsettling.

"Sit your asses down now!" Carl shouted. "We need to talk."

"Okay," I said as I sat down.

"You both have been complete idiots lately," Carl said. "I don't tolerate idiots. So until you two get your acts together, you're both grounded."

"What?" I said. "That's ridiculous."

"Is it, though?" he asked. "You almost died. You destroyed your mother. You can't do that. Amanda has been through enough, and she doesn't need you adding anything else. I don't know what she sees in you, but it makes her care about you. So

176

be careful before you lose that with her 'cause you've already lost that with me."

"I'm sorry," I said as my eyes began to water.

"Don't cry, you idiot," Carl said. "Don't act like you're six years old again."

"Shut up!" Jaelyn shouted. "You're being a dick."

"I'm being a dick?" Carl shouted.

"Yeah," Jaelyn said.

"How?" Carl shouted.

"You just told my little brother you didn't care about him, and then you got mad when he got upset!" Jaelyn screamed. "I don't know who you think you are, but you better stop treating us like shit!"

"Fine," Carl said. "Make me out to be the villain. That's perfect!"

Carl stormed upstairs. He was mad at us, but I didn't care. I was tired of him, and Jaelyn obviously was too.

"You okay?" Jaelyn asked.

"Yeah," I said. "I just need to stop letting him get to me."

"It's harder than it looks," she said, trying to comfort me. "Are you feeling better today?"

"I guess," I said. "My head still hurts."

"That makes sense," she said. "Concussions are brutal."

"No kidding," I said. "Wanna watch some TV?"

"Aren't we grounded?" she said.

"I'm not considering myself grounded until Mom says I am," I said.

"Makes sense," she agreed. "Let's watch TV now."

We quickly walked over to the couch and sat down.

She grabbed the remote and turned on the TV.

"Looks like Carl left the news channel on," I said. "Change

it before I die of boredom."

"Wait a second," Jaelyn said. "Is that our school?"

I looked up at the TV to see a photo of our school with yellow smoke behind the windows.

"Was the school on fire?" Jaelyn asked.

"I don't know," I said.

"I'm gonna listen to this for a minute," Jaelyn said.

I internally panicked.

I knew the school didn't catch on fire, but if I said that, I'd look suspicious. So I just had to sit there and watch the news talk about the place I almost died at.

Last night the school was broken into by unknown people. From what we've concluded, there were signs of an attack. There were bullet shells found around the school, along with a broken window and door. Security footage wasn't able to identify any faces but was able to spot some paranormal activity. This figure seemed to have been the source of the yellow smoke. No more details have been released to the public, but we will keep you updated, and as of now, South Ray High plans to stay open for classes tomorrow. Have a great day, ladies and gentlemen. Now back to your regular news program.

Once the news lady was done talking, Jaelyn looked over at me.

"Aaron?" Jaelyn said.

"Yeah?" I replied.

"Were you at the school last night?" she asked.

I froze. I didn't know what to say. She could tell if I was lying, which wasn't good for me.

I had to pick my next words carefully, and if I didn't, I could be putting Jaelyns life in danger...

Chapter 12

"Aaron?" Jaelyn said again. "Can you answer me?"

"What?" I said, trying to act clueless.

"Were you at the school last night?" She asked me again.

"Why would you think I'd be at the school?" I asked, trying to avoid answering the question.

"There was an attack at the school last night, and given the way you look, it wouldn't be that crazy of me to assume you were there," she said.

"I admit I don't look charming, but that still doesn't explain why you would think I'd be there," I said. "Besides, those people in the security footage look like grown men, and I'm obviously not a grown man."

"Fair point," she said. "So you weren't at the school?"

Before I was able to answer, Jaelyn turned her head and looked right at me, so we were face to face.

I knew what she was doing. She was gonna see if I was lying from my facial expression. She had picked up on that skill throughout our childhood.

I sat there frozen for what felt like an eternity.

I hesitated to answer her. I didn't want her to know the truth, but I knew I had to answer her eventually.

Thankfully I was spared a few minutes by a familiar nagging voice.

"What the hell are you two doing!" Carl shouted as he came downstairs. "You're grounded, remember, and what are you

179

even watching?"

"The news," Jaelyn answered. "Our school was attacked last night."

"Really?" Carl said while he looked closer at the TV. "Did they cancel school tomorrow?"

"No," Jaelyn answered. "I think they're just going to clean it up today the best they can and keep classes rolling tomorrow."

"Well, they're definitely rushing themselves," Carl said while looking at me. "Aaron, did you see any of this last night on your little outing?"

"No," I answered him quickly.

"I don't think Aaron is telling the truth," Jaelyn said to Carl.

"What's that supposed to mean?" Carl asked.

"I think he was at the school," Jaelyn answered him.

"I wasn't," I said to them quickly.

They both looked at me like I was crazy.

I knew I was gonna regret answering that question, but I didn't think it would be that soon.

"What?" I said to them, annoyed.

"You're lying," Jaelyn said.

"I'm not!" I shouted at her.

"Sure," she said, annoyed.

"You're so annoying!" I shouted while standing up. "I'm going back to my room."

"Aaron, I'm not done talking to you!" Carl shouted.

"I'm done talking to you!" I shouted back while walking to my room.

I walked into my room and locked the door behind me.

I knew I had just blown my cover, which sucked.

"Aaron Leon Cripple, open this door right now!" Carl screamed from outside.

180

I could tell by the use of my full name that Carl was extremely pissed.

He began to pound on my door and continued to scream.

I sat still, hoping he would just go away, but I knew he wouldn't.

"Aaron, I'm about to break this door down! Do you understand me?" Carl screamed. "Now, open this door!"

I didn't want to open the door with Carl this mad. He was about ready to kill me.

"Carl, please calm down," I said in an annoyed voice.

"Calm down. Calm down!" He screamed. "I'm far from calm!"

"Carl, you're being hysterical. Please just go cool off, and then we can talk," I said nervously.

I sat waiting for a response, but I heard nothing.

I walked closer to the door to hear Carl walk away. I was relieved until I heard him come back.

When Carl came back, I heard him start to mess with the doorknob until the lock started to turn. My soul completely left my body. I was terrified. I ran to the door and held it shut with all the strength I had.

Carl started to try and push the door, but he couldn't.

"Aaron, move," Carl said sternly.

"No," I said with a shaky voice.

"Have it your way then," Carl said as he stopped pushing.

I sat in front of the door in complete terror. Carl would never just let me have it my way.

As I was about to move away, I heard Carl come back. He started pushing on the door again, only this time he was using all his strength, which was obviously greater than mine. I quickly started to lose. The door slowly opened even though I was pushing it shut, and before I knew it, the door flew open, and I fell to the floor.

"Happy now?" Carl screamed.

I stood up as quickly as possible and looked at Carl. His face was redder than a tomato.

"You're gonna start talking right now!" Carl screamed. "I'm not playing your game any more!"

I didn't answer; I just slowly backed up. Carl's anger was unpredictable. I had no idea what he was about to do.

"Aaron, come back over here," Carl said in a stern voice.

"No," I said.

"No?" he said. "I don't take no as an answer!"

Carl started coming closer to me. I was mortified. I tried to quickly run around him, but it was useless. Carl grabbed me and threw me down on my bed.

"Let go of me!" I screamed.

"Answer me!" he screamed.

"Answer what?" I shouted back.

"Were you at the school?" he screamed at me.

I froze once again. I could tell he knew I was, but I didn't want to admit it.

I squirmed and tried to get out of his grip, but it was no use. He had both my arms pinned down. I wasn't going to be able to outrun him.

"Aaron, answer me!" Carl screamed while tightening his grip on my arms.

"Please leave me alone," I cried.

"Aaron, I just want you to answer me," he said.

"I can't!" I shouted as tears filled my eyes.

"Why?" Carl screamed.

"I just can't!" I screamed back.

Tears began to run down my face. If I weren't dealing with such threatening things right now, I would gladly tell Carl, but I couldn't.

"Give me a better answer than I can't!" Carl shouted.

"I would if I could!" I shouted back

"What is that supposed to mean? Is someone gonna kill you if you do?" Carl shouted.

I didn't answer. I just looked up at Carl as tears continued to run down my face.

"Aaron, what is going on with you?" Carl asked me in a worried voice.

"I don't know any more," I said in a teary voice.

Carl looked at me and let go of my arms. I sat up and looked at him.

"I didn't mean to scare you, Aaron," Carl said. "I just wanted to see what was going on. I care about you deep down. I just say stupid shit when I'm mad. I'll leave you alone, though. Just promise me to try and stay out of trouble."

I nodded my head.

Carl looked at me and then walked out.

I just sat on my bed, trying to calm myself down. I was an emotional mess.

After a few hours, I heard Mom and Effie come home from the store. I would usually go greet them, but I was not in the mood. Instead, I sat at my desk and played games on my computer until I heard Effie walk in.

"Aaron, guess what?" Effie asked excitedly.

"What?" I said as I spun my chair around.

"Mommy got me a rainbow loom set!" Effie said excitedly.

"That's awesome," I said.

"I get to join the rainbow loom circle now!" Effie shouted

joyfully.

"That's cool," I said.

"I would invite you, but it's only for cool second-graders like me," Effie said.

"Darn," I said. "Would've loved to join."

"Maybe they'll have one for big tenth-graders soon," Effie said, trying to sound positive.

"I bet they will," I said.

"I'm gonna go show Jaelyn now, bye," Effie said as she ran out.

"Bye!" I shouted back.

I turned around and started to play my game again when suddenly I felt a tap on my shoulder. I looked up to see my mom standing over me.

"Can we talk?" she asked.

"Sure," I said as I paused my game.

"So I heard what happened to the school last night," she said.

"Yeah, the word spread around quickly," I replied.

"I also heard a little rumor that you may have been there," she said.

"I wasn't, Mom," I said.

"I didn't say you were," she said. "I just needed a confirmation if the rumor was true or not."

"It's not," I said.

"Sweetie, you're a horrible liar," Mom said.

"If you're just gonna accuse me of lying, then you can leave," I said while turning my chair.

"Aaron, knock it off," Mom said while turning my chair back towards her. "I just want to know the truth. I promise you I'm not gonna pin you down like Carl did."

"You know about that?" I said.

"Yes, he told me. He feels bad about it," she explained.

"Well, he should," I said.

"Aaron, don't be like that," Mom said. "It was an honest mistake."

"I don't care what it was, Mom. It was wrong," I said.

"I know it was sweetie," she said.

"Great, end of discussion," I said while turning my chair.

"You definitely got your father's stubbornness," Mom said while messing up my hair. "We'll finish this later."

Mom walked out of my room and shut the door behind her.

I unpaused my game and continued playing until Jaelyn walked in.

"Look what Effie made me," she said while walking over.

"I really need a do not disturb sign," I said while pausing my game again.

"Very funny," she said. "What are you even playing?"

"BioShock Infinite," I answered her.

"Cool," she said. "Real quick, I just wanna say sorry about earlier."

"Why?" I asked.

"I was the reason Carl was about ready to kill you," she said.

"True," I said. "I'll accept your apology."

"That was quick," she said.

"I just wanna play my game, and accepting your apology will make you go away faster," I said.

"I'm not even surprised," she said.

As Jaelyn was about to walk out, we heard Carl scream.

"Holy shit!" he yelled.

Jaelyn and I looked at each other and ran out.

"What's going on?" Jaelyn asked.

"Two people died in that school attack last night," he said.

"What?" I said, surprised.

"Darn, Aaron, I told you to stop killing people," Jaelyn said jokingly.

"Very funny," I said while giving her a light punch on the arm.

"Stop joking around, you two. This is serious," Carl said to us. "Aaron, were you actually there last night?"

"I thought we were done with this," I said.

"Aaron, people died. I need you to answer me honestly," he said sternly.

"I wasn't," I said.

"Aaron, tell him the truth!" Jaelyn shouted.

"I did," I said.

"No, you didn't!" she shouted back. "I know you're lying."

"You are so annoying!" I shouted. "Leave me alone!"

"No!" she screamed back at me. "People died, and if you know anything, you should say something!"

"Jaelyn, they deserved it!" I screamed.

Everyone froze and looked at me.

"You were there," Carl said.

"Fine, I was. Happy now!" I screamed.

"Aaron, what happened at the school?" Jaelyn asked.

"Stuff," I said.

"Aaron, give us an actual answer!" Carl shouted.

"You guys don't need to know what happened!" I shouted back. "Just know the people who died weren't good."

"How do you know?" Jaelyn shouted at me.

"'Cause I was the only good one there!" I screamed. "Everyone else was a psycho!"

"The attack was on you?" Carl said, surprised.

"Who else would it be?" I asked. "I'm not strong enough to attack anyone, and you know that."

"The clip," Jaelyn said to herself.

"What?' I asked.

"Give me the remote," Jaelyn said to Carl.

Carl handed Jaelyn the remote and stepped back. Jaelyn went back to the beginning of the news and paused on the security video that was released.

"Which one's you?" she asked.

"Do I really have to answer?" I asked.

"Yes," Carl said. "Go point it out on the TV, now."

"Fine," I said as I walked up.

I looked at the TV and tried to find myself. The footage was dark, so it was hard to tell.

After a few minutes, I realized I was the one being held back.

"I'm that one," I said while pointing to myself.

Jaelyn and Carl looked up and tried to see my face for themselves.

"Play the clip," Carl said.

"Okay," Jaelyn said as she pushed play.

The clip played. It showed Mr. Smith about to kill me before the figure somehow lifted him in the air, and then it ended.

"You were about to die," Carl said.

"Yeah," I said as I began to walk away.

"Wait," Carl said. "I know this is hard, but you have to answer me one more thing."

"Fine," I said while turning around.

"Who are these people?" he asked.

"I can't say," I said.

"Why?" Jaelyn asked.

"If I do, they'll try to kill me again, and then they'll kill all of you," I explained.

Carl and Jaelyn froze. Their faces turned pale. I could tell they were scared for themselves and me.

"Can you at least say who the freaky guy is?" Carl asked while pointing to the figure.

"Honestly, I don't even know who that is," I answered him. "All I know is if he hadn't been there, I would've died."

"So the figure guy is good?" Jaelyn said, confused.

"I'm assuming so," I said.

"Kid, you need to talk to the police," Carl said.

"I can't," I said. "These guys will gladly kill me, and the police think I'm a criminal."

"Fine," Carl said. "Just please avoid these guys. I don't wanna lose you."

"I'll try," I said.

I walked back to my room feeling awful. I couldn't believe that I had just spilled almost everything to Carl and Jaelyn.

I'm such an idiot. I just hope this doesn't end up hurting anyone.

I sat back down at my desk and played BioShock Infinite until dinner. During dinner, I could tell Jaelyn and Carl were out of it.

They were still in denial, and that made me feel awful. I was glad, though, that they were both obviously avoiding telling Mom.

I think they both knew that telling her would do more harm than good.

Dinner ended, and I went back to my room.

I played BioShock Infinite until about eleven p.m., and then I went to bed.

I was nervous about school tomorrow, but thankfully that didn't keep me up for too long, and I was able to fall asleep fairly quickly.

The next morning Jaelyn and I got up and got ready.

Mondays were always the slowest, so we made sure to not fall behind schedule.

Once we were done getting ready, we quickly ran out the door and got into the car. Jaelyn put the car in drive, and we were off.

"Are you ready for today?" she asked.

"Sure," I said.

"Hopefully, they did a good job of cleaning up the school," she said.

"Yeah," I said back.

"Wonder what kind of rumors are gonna start about Saturday night," Jaelyn said.

"Yeah, they'll be funny to hear," I replied.

"They'll be funny 'cause you'll know if they're true or not," she said.

"Fair point," I said. "Please promise me you won't say anything about me and Saturday?"

"I won't," Jaelyn said. "I value our lives more than shutting down a rumor."

"Well, that's a good order of values," I said jokingly.

"Sure is," Jaelyn said with a smile.

We arrived at the school quickly after our conversation.

Jaelyn pulled up to the school and unlocked the doors.

"Have a good day," she said as I got out.

"I'll try," I said as I shut the door.

I walked up to the front doors and walked in.

My body instantly started to panic. Being at the place you almost died once does not do the body good.

As I walked down the halls, all eyes seemed to fall on me. It was so weird.

I walked until I saw Ezra waiting at my locker.

"Hey," I said.

"Hey?" she said while looking at me weirdly.

"What?" I said, confused.

"What happened to your face?" she asked.

"I fell," I said.

Honestly, I had completely forgotten about my face, so my response was off the top of my head, which made it not the best.

"Sure," she said.

I rolled my eyes and opened my locker. I quickly grabbed my things and shut the locker door.

"Let's go," I said to Ezra.

"Okay," she said while beginning to follow me.

We walked down the hall until we made it to Mrs. Jones's classroom.

We walked in and made our way to our desks.

I set my stuff down and walked back over to Ezra.

"Did you have a nice weekend?" I asked.

"It was okay," she answered me. "I'm gonna assume you didn't."

"Why would you say that?" I said.

"Two words, neck and face," she said.

"You can see my neck?" I asked quietly.

"Yes, what the hell even happened?" she asked.

"I'll explain later," I said.

"Okay." she said while sitting down.

"Why are you sitting?" I asked.

Ezra didn't respond; she just pointed behind me.

I quickly turned around to see Mrs. Jones standing there, waiting for me to sit down.

"Sorry," I said as I rushed over to my seat.

As I sat down, Mrs. Jones looked at me weirdly.

I knew what she was looking at, but I didn't want to acknowledge it.

School played out normally until the end of first hour.

As I walked down the halls, I saw Morgan standing at her locker, which instantly gave me an idea.

I quickly grabbed her and dragged her into a janitor's closet. I needed some answers, and I was gonna get them, even if that meant I would be skipping a few classes.

Chapter 13

"What the hell are you doing?" Morgan shouted at me, annoyed.

"Getting answers," I said.

"What is that supposed to mean?" she asked.

"You know a lot about the VK, and I need to know more," I explained.

"Why would I tell you anything?" she asked. "Last time I checked, we weren't friends."

"Morgan, please," I said. "I almost died because of them."

"I know," she said. "Many people like to get in their way and risk their own lives."

"Who else has gotten in their way?" I asked.

"Jessica Roberts?" she said, confused. "I thought you knew that."

"I knew she got attacked, but I didn't think it was the VK's doing," I said.

"So you thought some random person just attacked her for no reason?" she asked me, confused.

"Well, everyone at this school kinda hates her except a few people. She's not the best person," I explained.

"You're not wrong," she said. "I guess your hate level goes up when you're homophobic, racist and think everything good has only come from white people."

I turned my head and chuckled to myself.

"Guess she's trying to be a hero?" I said, confused.

"She tried to stop the VK for the same reason you did,"

Morgan explained.

"What?" I said, confused.

"What's wrong? You don't like being compared with a person like her?" she asked me jokingly.

"I mean, of course not. I just have no idea what we could possibly have in common," I explained.

"Emma Grace?" she said, confused. "Jessica was good friends with her, just like you. Just because you're not a disgrace to society doesn't mean you have nothing in common with her."

I rolled my eyes and looked back at her.

"Why is Emma friends with so many assholes?" I asked.

"She's a rare kind of person," Morgan explained. "She sees everyone for their best features, while most people see others for their worst."

"And that's why I've idolized Emma for the longest time," I said.

"Is idolized your way of saying you've had a crush on her?" Morgan asked me with a smirk.

"Maybe," I said while my face turned red.

Morgan laughed to herself and looked back up at me.

"I don't care if you have a crush. I already concluded you don't love me," she said.

I took a sigh and looked back up at her.

"Well, for the sake of my so-called crush, the VK needs to be stopped before anyone gets killed."

"Well, it's too late for that," she said.

"What?" I said, confused.

"The VK has already killed so many people," she said. "They've been at this for a while."

I stood there in disbelief. I thought the VK was a newer group, but I guess they weren't.

"How long has the VK been around?" I asked.

"They've been around longer than us," she answered me. "That's why they've killed so many. They aren't a new group that just started this year. They're a real threat, and if you value your life, you'll stay away from them."

"Why are you giving me a warning? Don't you hate me?" I asked, confused.

"I've known you for a while," she said. "We may currently hate each other, but that doesn't mean I want you dead. If the VK kills you, it won't be pretty."

"I don't hate you, Morgan," I said. "You were just being a real bitch Saturday."

"I know," she said. "I'm sorry I punched you and threatened Emma Grace. I would never actually hurt anyone unless I had to."

"It's okay," I said. "Do you know where Emma and all the other kids are?"

"I don't," she said. "Tyler and I aren't allowed to know their location."

"Tyler?" I said, confused. "Who's that?"

"My brother?" she said, confused.

"Does he have the weird glowy hands?" I asked.

"No," she said. "He has a weird mind, though."

"What does that mean?" I asked.

"He has a weird version of telekinesis," she explained. "His mind produces a yellow fog that'll lift whatever he wants."

"He was at the school Saturday," I said, stunned. "He saved me."

"Yeah, he does that," she said. "Don't tell anyone."

"I won't," I said. "I just can't believe he saved my life."

"Yeah, he was in the school while I was outside," she said.

194

"Why were you outside?" I asked.

"I was there just in case I needed to heal a gunshot or something severe," she explained.

"So you would've helped me?" I said, confused.

"I guess," she said with a smirk.

"Wait, are you and Tyler enemies of the VK?" I asked.

"Not really," she said. "Well, I'm not. They have no idea I hate them. Tyler, on the other hand, is clearly an enemy to them. They hate him. That's why he's in hiding most of the time. He can't even live at home."

"Does the VK know where you live?" I asked.

"Yes," she said. "One of them even lives with us."

"What? Who?" I said, surprised.

"My dad's one of the leaders," she explained.

"That must suck," I said.

"It does," she said. "He's a horrible father and an awful human being."

"Has he ever done anything to you or Tyler?" I asked.

Morgan looked at me like I was crazy.

"How do you think we got powers?" she asked. "It wasn't just a crazy accident or birth defect."

"Your dad gave those to you?" I said, confused.

"Sadly, yes," she said. "When Tyler and I were younger, my dad performed experiments on us. He didn't care what happened; he hated us. He always said we were the reason my mom died, which is not true. She died from cancer when I was one and Tyler was four, but my dad couldn't understand that. So he performed experiments every day on us. He hoped we'd either die, or he would get a crazy result. Thankfully we didn't die, but we were pretty darn close."

"So what kind of experiments did he do?" I asked.

"I don't remember exactly," she said. "The only thing me and Tyler know is that radiation traveled throughout our bodies and somehow mutated our DNA."

"That's insane," I said. "It doesn't even sound real."

"I know," she said. "It sounds like I'm a movie character."

"It really does," I laughed.

Morgan looked down at her watch and then looked back up at me.

"Well, I'm not going back to class in the middle of second hour," she said. "Any more questions I should answer?"

"Can you just give me a few quick facts about the VK?" I asked.

"Sure," she said. "The VK is a dangerous organization that has been around for at least twenty years. Their goal is to get revenge on those who have wronged them. VK stands for vengeful kidnappers. When someone does something the VK considers wrong, they'll wait until they have a kid and then kidnap them. The kid isn't killed until they turn eighteen. Until they are eighteen, the VK will send weekly videos to the parents of the kid being tortured. This usually is done with high-tech equipment that is untraceable. Most police officers don't even know they exist."

"That's a lot," I said.

"Sure is," she said. "Want me to go over anything in detail?"

"Yeah, what exactly happens to the kids who were kidnapped?" I asked.

"Well, as I said, they get tortured once a week on a video sent to their parents. The VK tortures them with these crazy weapons they created. I can tell by the screams I've heard that they are very painful. Other than the torture videos, the kids get one meal a day and never get to shower or even brush their teeth," she explained.

"That sounds awful," I said. "Why haven't you stopped them?"

"I would if I could," she said.

"Why can't you?" I asked.

"I don't have enough evidence, and the police hate me," she explained.

"Same," I laughed.

"Anything else?" she asked.

"Yeah," I said. "Why'd you answer my questions even though you said you wouldn't?"

"Well, I realized I would enjoy answering you more than gym, so it worked out," she said. "Is that all? The bell's about to ring."

I stood there for a second, trying to recall any other questions I had, when all of a sudden I remembered a big question I had, my dream.

"So, how do you know if you have a weird power?" I asked.

"Your hands glow, or you make things float?" she said, confused. "Why do you ask?"

"Something weird happened," I said. "When we were on that weird date thing, I had a dream that I got shot in the school, and then later that night I was in the same situation, but this time I knew what to do to not get shot."

"That's weird, but I don't think it's anything crazy," she said. "I think you just had a case of precognitive dreaming."

"A case of what?" I said, confused.

"Precognitive dreaming," she said. "It's when you have dreams about the future."

"Morgan, I don't think it was just any normal future

197

dream," I said. "It felt so real. It was like a warning. My dream didn't happen one hundred percent."

"Aaron, I think you're going nuts," she said. "Just take a nap after school and do yourself a favor and stay away from the VK. I can't attend a funeral of someone my dad kills."

"Fine," I said, annoyed. "Thanks for answering me."

"You're welcome," she said. "Just promise not to tell anyone where you got this information from."

"I won't," I said. "Let's leave now; it's passing period."

"Sounds good," she said while opening the door.

We slowly walked out and hopped into the crowd. I started walking towards my third hour when all of a sudden I heard a familiar voice behind me.

"Where have you been?" the voice asked.

I turned around to see Jaelyn standing there.

"Class?" I said, confused.

"Aaron, cut the bullshit!" She shouted. "Where were you?"

"I was talking to a friend," I said.

"Why?" she said, confused.

"I wanted to," I said.

"Aaron, it's not like you to skip class," she said.

"I know, I'm sorry," I said. "Now I'm gonna go to my third hour, so I don't miss another class."

"Fine," she said. "Just don't do anything stupid."

"I'll try," I said as I walked into my class.

I sat down at my desk and looked at my phone. There were so many messages from Jaelyn. She was so overprotective, always has been.

I put my phone back in my pocket and got ready for class.

After third hour the rest of the day was pretty boring. It was just lecture after lecture. The only interesting part was when

Ezra accidentally threw a grape at Alex King during lunch. She got detention, but it was so worth it.

After school, I met Jaelyn at her car like usual.

I got in, and we drove off.

The car ride was pretty quiet until I started talking.

"So, how did you know I wasn't in class today?" I asked.

"A teacher pulled me out of class and asked me where you were," Jaelyn answered.

"That's weird," I said.

"Not really," she said. "The first time you disappeared, you were almost killed, so I think it's completely normal if people get worried when you vanish."

"Guess that makes sense," I said. "I'm sorry I skipped class and sent everyone into a panic, again."

"It's fine," she said. "I'm just glad you didn't get yourself into anything serious."

"Me too," I joked.

Jaelyn looked at me and rolled her eyes. She seemed pretty chill until we turned onto our street.

"What the hell?" I heard her say under her breath.

I looked out the window to see a cop car parked outside our house.

"What is going on?" I asked.

"I have no idea," she said.

"Should we still go in the house?" I asked.

"Probably," she said. "We just need to make sure everyone's okay."

"Makes sense," I said.

We pulled up to the driveway and quickly got out.

Jaelyn ran ahead of me and went inside.

I think she was more concerned about the situation than I

was.

I went inside quickly after her to see Carl and Officer Miller standing in the living room.

"What's going on?" Jaelyn asked them.

"Nothing that has to do with you, little lady," Officer Miller answered her.

Jaelyn looked at him weirdly. People didn't usually talk to her like that. Sure she didn't have the best life, but she was at least respected.

"Why are you here?" I asked him, hoping I'd get a better response than Jaelyn.

"I'm here for you," he answered me.

"What?" I said, confused.

"I heard a rumor from your daddy that you were at the attack in South Ray High," he said.

"Okay, first of all, he's not my dad, he's my stepdad, and second I was not at the school during that attack," I said.

"Aaron, stop lying!" Carl shouted.

"Carl, I know you love me, but you gotta accept none of my genes came from you," I said jokingly

Carl gave me a stern look. He was done with me already, and I hadn't even been home for five minutes.

"Aaron, step outside with me for a second," Carl said while walking over to the door.

"Okay," I said while following him outside.

We walked outside, and Carl shut the door behind us.

"You need to tell Officer Miller the truth," Carl said.

"Why?" I asked.

"You were almost killed, Aaron," Carl said. "Those guys need to be put behind bars."

"I agree," I said. "But you need to trust me when I say we

can't tell anyone anything. Not even the police."

"Aaron, stop being childish," Carl said. "Nothing's going to happen if you tell Officer Miller."

"Carl, I'm not being childish," I said. "These guys are involved in stuff much bigger than me and you. Even if some of them get thrown behind bars, more will come to kill us."

"Aaron, I promise you they are not in a big killer organization," he said. "They're just a couple of idiots."

At that moment, I wish I could've told Carl everything.

If I could, I would've told him about the VK and what they do, but I couldn't.

I looked up at Carl and apologized.

Before he could answer, I ran back inside and ran to my room. As I sat on my bed, I heard Officer Miller and Carl talking. They both sounded frustrated, but I didn't care. There was nothing I could do that wouldn't end in someone getting hurt.

After a half-hour, Carl knocked on my door.

"He's gone, Aaron," Carl said. "I hope you're happy. You could've helped get these idiots in jail, but no. Instead, you wanted to act like a child and stay quiet. Now, thanks to you, criminals are still running around this town. People are gonna get hurt, and it'll be your fault!"

After Carl's rant, he just walked away. He never even stepped into my room.

I sat there for a while thinking about what Carl had said.

Should I have talked? Am I making this bigger than it actually is? Am I becoming the villain?

I had my own opinion on all those questions, but as the days continued to move on, I started to lose trust in my opinions more and more. Just a few days ago, my opinions seemed as good as facts, but now they seem like lines out of a fairytale.

For the rest of that night, I stayed in my room. I didn't even come out for dinner.

I didn't dare to look Carl in the eyes after what he said.

I was not in the state of mind to be able to determine the difference between lies and the truth, especially with Carl.

Throughout the night, no one bothered me, and I was grateful for that.

I was actually able to get some school work done, which was nice. I felt productive, and slowly my mind started to calm down, and before I knew it, I had forgotten about the whole night.

That night I was able to sleep so soundly. I felt like I was at peace with the world. I wished that feeling would've lasted forever, but I knew it couldn't. I was gonna get reconnected with the world and all of its problems and have to start this process all over again, but I knew that. Without connection in the world, life would be empty.

Emptiness can be a good break, but if it lasts for too long, the mind will lose its touch and slowly go crazy.

I always thought maybe that's what happened with Dad.

I may have been young, but I knew he didn't leave this world because of us. So maybe he just lost his touch with the world. Maybe that loss drove him to the point where he couldn't take it any more.

He had to leave and find a new place to connect to.

Chapter 14

The next morning Jaelyn and I woke up to an empty house, which was very unusual for us.

Mom had warned us that she would be working earlier shifts, but Carl didn't say anything about not being here. He didn't even have a job to go to, and it was too early for him to have taken Effie to school.

"Is Effie still here?" I asked Jaelyn while walking into the kitchen.

"I'll go check," Jaelyn answered me.

While Jaelyn was upstairs looking for Effie, I decided to make a bowl of cereal. I usually wasn't a breakfast person but my stomach said otherwise. I figured I was hungry because of my productivity last night, that was the only thing that would make sense to me at the time.

I sat down and started eating when Jaelyn came down the stairs holding Effie.

I looked up at them in confusion.

Why was Effie not with Carl?

"Effie's here?" I said, confused.

"Yep," Jaelyn said. "I found her asleep in her bed."

"Why would she still be sleeping?" I asked Jaelyn.

"I don't know," Jaelyn said. "She doesn't seem to be sick."

"This is weird," I said while continuing to eat my cereal.

"This morning's just weird," she said. "Carl's gone, Effie's still here, and you're eating."

"Guess I just worked hard last night," I joked.

"It's either that or the fact you skipped dinner," she said.

"Forgot about that," I said.

"I can tell," she said. "I'm gonna call Mom. You watch Effie."

"Okay," I said while Jaelyn walked away.

I ate a few more bites of cereal before walking over to Effie.

"Do you know where Carl went?" I asked.

Effie just shook her head. She was too tired to actually answer me.

I smiled and walked back over to the kitchen.

"Do you want anything to eat?" I asked while rinsing my bowl out.

She once again just shook her head.

It was weird for Effie to decline breakfast; unlike me, Effie was a breakfast person.

"You sure?" I asked. "I got a nice bowl of Cheerios."

"Aaron, stop," Effie said quietly.

I looked over at her in confusion. Something was definitely wrong.

I walked over to her and squatted down to her level.

"What's going on?" I asked.

"Nothing," she said.

"Effie, talk to me," I said. "I'm your big brother. We have to trust each other."

"Daddy's just a meanie," she said.

"What did he do?" I asked.

"He yelled at me," she answered.

"When?" I asked.

"Last night," she said in a pouty voice.

"Why'd he yell?" I asked.

204

"He was mad that I wanted to make a rainbow loom before bed," she said.

"I'm sorry he yelled," I said. "He can be a butt."

"He can be," she laughed.

I laughed with her and then stood up. I looked at the clock to see it flash 7.35 a.m.

"Shit, we have to leave in fifteen minutes," I whispered to myself.

"What does shit mean?" Effie asked.

"It means bad things. Never say it again," I said.

"Why'd you say it?" she asked.

"'Cause I'm bad," I said. "I'm so bad, I'm gonna get my rainbow looms taken away."

"That's awful," she said. "You can use mine."

"Thanks, Effie," I said. "I'm gonna go check on Jaelyn."

"Okay, can I watch TV?" she asked.

"Sure," I said as I walked to Jaelyn's room.

I walked into Jaelyn's room to see her still on the phone.

"What's going on?" I asked.

"Shut up," she whispered.

"Sorry," I whispered back.

I sat down at Jaelyn's desk and waited for her to hang up the phone, which didn't take very long.

"Was that Mom?" I asked.

"Yeah," Jaelyn said. "She's flipping out."

"At us?" I said, confused.

"Not us," she said. "She's flipping out at Carl. He just left us here."

"What are we gonna do?" I asked.

"Mom said we're gonna hurry and take Effie to school and then rush to our school," she answered.

"We're gonna be so late," I said. "We usually leave in like ten minutes."

"I know," she said. "Mom said she's gonna call the school and tell them what's going on, so don't worry."

"Okay," I said. "We better get dressed."

"Yeah, no kidding," she said. "Tell Effie to get ready as much as she can without our help."

"Okay," I said as I walked out.

I went to the living room and got Effie off the couch, and took her upstairs.

She was annoyed she didn't get to skip school and watch TV all day, but there was nothing I could do about that.

I rushed to the bathroom and brushed my teeth. After that, I ran to my room and got changed.

By the time I was ready to go, Jaelyn was already getting Effie into the car. I ran outside and threw my bag in the back, and got in the car.

Jaelyn finished getting Effie situated and hopped in herself.

"How did you get out here so fast?" I asked.

"I have my ways," she said.

I looked at her and smiled. She laughed to herself and began to drive us to Effie's school.

The car ride seemed longer than it usually was that morning.

I've ridden to Effie's school before, but this morning just felt different. Everything had been feeling different.

After we dropped Effie off, we rushed to our school.

Jaelyn didn't usually speed, but she sure did that morning. She went so fast that the car ride was nearly cut in half, and before I knew it, Jaelyn was dropping me off at the front doors.

"Don't forget to grab a pass before you head to class," she

said as I got out.

"I won't," I said as I shut the door.

I walked into the school to see an empty hallway. It felt weird, but given the fact I was thirty minutes late, I had to accept it.

I walked to the office and grabbed my pass before heading to my locker. As I walked to my locker, I saw Mrs. Wilson emptying Morgan's locker.

"What are you doing?" I asked.

"Locker cleaning," she answered.

"Why are you cleaning out Morgan's locker?" I asked eagerly.

"Her dad unenrolled her last night," she answered.

"Why?" I asked, confused.

"I don't know," she answered. "All I know is you need to get to class."

"That's true," I said.

As I was about to walk away, I noticed a photo laying on the ground right by Mrs. Wilson's feet.

I pretended to drop something to get a closer look at it.

Once I was closer, I saw it was Morgan with a guy that looked like her long-lost twin. That must be Tyler, I thought to myself.

I decided to grab the photo and quickly head to class.

Thankfully, Mrs. Wilson was too busy to notice me grab the photo, so I had nothing to worry about.

I quickly went to my locker, got my things for algebra II and headed to class.

The second I opened the door, all eyes turned to me.

"Nice of you to join us, Aaron," Mrs. Jones said while giving me a look.

"Sorry I'm late," I said while handing her my pass.

She grabbed my pass and looked at it.

"Go sit down and try to catch up. If you have any questions, ask me after class," she said while walking back to the whiteboard.

I nodded my head and went to sit down at my desk.

I looked at the whiteboard and realized they had started a new lesson.

"Of course," I whispered to myself.

I pulled out my notebook and started writing down as much as I could, even though I didn't understand a single thing I was writing.

After a few minutes, Mrs. Jones paused to let everyone write down anything they had missed, which was a blessing.

Thankfully I was able to write everything down before the bell rang. My hand was cramping so much, but it was worth it.

After class, I got a little bit more of an explanation from Mrs. Jones, which helped.

As I walked out, I turned to see Morgan's desk just sitting so empty. It looked like it was collecting dust, but I knew it was just my imagination.

I hoped Morgan was okay. We may have a love-hate relationship, but I didn't want anything bad to happen to her.

I was scared that her dad would hurt her again. He was part of a murderous group and didn't care for Morgan, which terrified me. She didn't have her father's love to protect her. She could die, and he wouldn't even attend the funeral if there was one. He was an awful person that I don't think anyone would want to mess with. I may have never met him, but I could just tell he was bad news.

The rest of the day, Morgan's face just kept haunting me. It was like my brain was trying to tell me something.

Maybe it was telling me to save her, or maybe it was telling me to find Tyler. Either way, I think my brain was trying to tell me I couldn't move on in finding Emma Grace until I located one of the Jays.

Throughout the day, Ezra was able to tell something was off with me. She kept asking me what was bothering me, but I just told her it was nothing. Ezra was like family to me. If she were to get hurt because she found out something from me, I would never forgive myself.

I already regretted telling Jaelyn and Carl as much as I did. I didn't need any more regrets to pile on top of that.

By the end of the day, I could tell Ezra was done with me, but I didn't care. I just wanted to go home and figure out how to locate one of the Jays.

When Jaelyn and I got home, we saw Mom and Carl arguing while Effie just stood there crying. She kept screaming at them to stop, but they didn't listen.

They usually didn't argue, so this was a very weird coincidence.

"Effie, come here," Jaelyn whispered.

Effie looked up at us and smiled. She ran over and jumped into Jaelyn's arms.

We all walked towards Jaelyn's room when all of a sudden, Carl noticed we were home.

"Where are you going?" he screamed at us.

"My room," Jaelyn answered.

"No, you're not!" he screamed. "This is your fault!"

"How is this our fault?" I asked, confused.

"You're all idiots!" he screamed.

At that moment, I realized Carl was a little drunk. He

209

must've been at the bar. I didn't know why he decided to go there, but I didn't care.

"Let's go," I whispered to Jaelyn.

"Okay," she whispered back.

We slowly started to walk away when all of a sudden, Carl realized we were leaving.

"Stay here!" he screamed.

Jaelyn and Effie kept walking while I stood there and gave him an ice-cold stare.

"Mom, can you calm him down?" I asked. "This is stupid."

"I know," she said. "Just go to your room."

"No! Stay here!" Carl screamed.

I ignored Carl and started walking when all of a sudden I heard a loud crash. I turned to see a shattered plate a few inches away from me.

"Carl, go lay down!" Mom screamed.

"Not until that brat pays!" he screamed.

At that moment, I realized drunk Carl was after me.

I quickly ran to my room and locked the door.

I heard Mom screaming at him from outside, but he just made his way over to my door. He started pounding and kicking at it. I just stood by my bed, mortified. Why was Carl so mad?

"Open the door!" Carl screamed.

"Don't make me call the cops!" I heard my mom scream. "Leave my boy alone!"

"He's the reason I'm wasted!" Carl screamed.

"What?" I said to myself, confused.

"He made me the bad guy, and now everyone hates me!" he shouted.

"Carl, what are you talking about?" I shouted.

"You made me mad, and then I yelled at my baby girl!" he

210

shouted.

I guess Carl was still pretty mad about me not talking to the police, which kind of made sense.

"I'm breaking this door down!" Carl screamed.

"No, you're not!" Mom screamed back. "Leave Aaron alone! I don't know what he did, but it probably doesn't deserve his door being kicked down."

"Yes, it does," Carl said quietly.

For a few seconds, everything was quiet until I heard a loud cracking sound. I looked over to see Carl's foot through my door.

"Aaron, come to the door!" Carl shouted.

"No! You're drunk!" I screamed.

"You're drunk!" he screamed back.

He continued to make holes in my door until he was about able to fit through.

"Mom! Do something!" I screamed.

"I called the police, honey!" she shouted. "Carl, stop! They won't arrest you, but they will not go easy on you."

"That's fine by me!" he shouted.

Mom made a huge mistake by telling Carl he wouldn't get arrested. Now nothing was left to hold him back.

He crawled through the hole in my door and stood up in my room.

"Stay away!" I screamed.

"You need to be punished!" he screamed back.

"I do not!" I screamed. "Carl, go lay down! You're acting crazy!"

"I'm good," he said as he walked over.

I quickly ran around him and ran out of my room.

The only good thing about Carl being drunk is that his

reaction time was slowed down drastically.

I ran out into the kitchen and stood there trying to catch my breath. Jaelyn came out of her room and ran over to me.

"You okay?" she asked.

"Yeah," I said while still trying to catch my breath. "He's insane."

"I know," she said. "Let's get Effie and run to the neighbors. Mom is out trying to find help."

"Okay," I said.

She walked over to her room and went to grab Effie, when all of a sudden Carl ran out and locked them in her room.

"Jaelyn!" I screamed.

Carl looked at me with a twisted smile on his face.

"They're fine," he said as he walked over.

"Leave everyone alone," I said.

He didn't answer. He just made eye contact as he ran over to me.

We ran around the house until he tackled me down over the couch. I tried to get up, but he had pinned me down.

"Let me go!" I screamed.

"After your punishment," he said.

"What are you going to do?" I asked, worried.

"Punishment," he said.

"Carl, stop. This isn't funny!" I screamed.

"It's not funny," he said. "It's punishment."

Carl quickly moved one of his hands around my throat and started to squeeze. I kicked and squirmed, but it was no use.

I slowly started to lose my breath. I just laid there helplessly.

I heard Jaelyn trying to break her door down along with police sirens in the distance.

I moved my eyes to align with Carl's. His stare appeared blank. It was like he didn't know what he was doing.

"Aaron, are you okay?" I heard Jaelyn scream.

I couldn't answer her, which made me feel horrible. I wanted to answer her so badly, but I couldn't

After a few moments of silence, I heard the sound of glass shattering.

I had no idea what was going on. All I knew was that my time was running out.

My vision began to blur, and I started to feel extremely lightheaded again.

Thankfully, right as I was about to blackout, I was saved.

"Get off my brother!" Jaelyn screamed as she tackled Carl off me.

I lay there and started to breathe heavily.

I still couldn't believe what had just happened.

I looked over at Jaelyn to see her slowly getting off Carl. She looked at me and ran over.

"Are you okay?" she asked me, worried.

"I think so," I said with a shaky voice.

Jaelyn looked over at me and hugged me tightly. I hugged her back. She did save me after all.

"Did you break a window?" I asked.

"Had to save you somehow," she said while letting go of me.

"Thank you," I said.

"Anytime," she said while helping me up.

We stood up and looked to see Mom and police officers running through the door.

"We'll save you, kids, don't worry!" One of the officers shouted.

"No need," Jaelyn said. "He's knocked out right over here. Take him to the slammer, and we'll call it good."

"He's not going to jail," Mom said.

"Yes, he is," I said.

"Why?" she asked. "You look fine."

"He tried to kill me," I said.

"Honey, him breaking down your door is not him trying to kill you," she said.

"He tackled me and had his hand on my throat," I told her.

"Mom, he was about to kill Aaron," Jaelyn said.

"You kids are just scared, and he's intoxicated. He didn't mean any harm," Mom said to us. "Can you fellas help me get him upstairs?"

"Sure thing," the police officer answered her.

"So he gets away with attempted murder?" I screamed.

"Aaron, calm down," Mom said. "You obviously drove Carl crazy."

"That's no excuse for what he did!" I shouted.

"Aaron, stop!" Mom screamed. "We'll get you a new door."

"He needs to be arrested!" I screamed back. "I don't feel safe with him!"

At this point, everyone was ignoring me.

I just watched in disbelief as they carried Carl upstairs.

"You kids didn't need to knock him out," one of the officers said.

"Yes, we did!" I shouted. "He was about to kill me!"

"Don't yell at me!" the officer screamed. "I won't hesitate to tase you."

"Fine," I said. "I'll just accept the fact there's no justice in this world!"

I stormed off to my room and shut what was remaining of my door.

I just laid there and broke down. This really made me question things. Even if I did successfully report the VK, would the police do anything? Has all this work to gather evidence been for nothing?

Chapter 15

The next morning everyone was quiet. No one even said good morning. I think everyone was internally pissed about the events that happened yesterday.

I felt bad for Effie. She was too young to understand what had happened. So while everyone was staying quiet, she just stood there, confused.

I felt really bad, but I wasn't going to say a word. That would be a risky move

Jaelyn and I got in the car quicker than usual that morning. I think we just wanted out of that house so badly we were willing to sacrifice a few minutes of our regular morning schedule.

"I do not want to do school today," Jaelyn said while starting the car.

"Me neither," I said back. "Yesterday was exhausting."

"No kidding," she said while pulling out of the driveway. "If I was a bad kid, I'd just make you skip school with me."

"That'd be nice," I laughed.

Jaelyn looked at me and smiled. It was nice to see a smile on her face, but I could still tell she had something on her mind.

"You okay?" I asked.

"I'm fine," she said. "I'm just thinking about yesterday."

"Makes sense," I said. "Yesterday was pretty crazy."

"I'm just glad it didn't end in tragedy," she said while looking at me.

"Me too," I said.

The rest of the car ride we were pretty quiet. We had no other topics to talk about really, and staying on the topic of yesterday would've just put us in a terrible mood.

Before I knew it, Jaelyn was dropping me off at the front doors and I was heading to class.

I stopped at my locker like normal and then went to Mrs. Jones's class. It was weird though, Ezra wasn't waiting for me like usual.

I walked into class to find Ezra sitting at her desk, just looking out the window. I set my stuff down and decided to walk up to her.

"Hey," I said while walking over.

"Hi," she said in an annoyed tone.

"You good?" I asked.

"I'm fine," she said, still sounding annoyed.

"Are you mad at me?" I asked.

She didn't respond. She just kept looking out the window.

"Ezra?" I said. "Talk to me."

"I'll talk to you later," she said, annoyed. "Now, please leave me alone."

"Okay," I said while walking away.

Ezra was acting weird and I didn't know why. I didn't think I did anything, but I was unsure at this point.

Class started, and everything started to feel normal again. For a few classes, I had completely forgotten about yesterday and Ezra. It all left my mind until lunch.

I didn't directly remember anything until I sat down at a cafeteria table across from Ezra.

"So, how's your day been?" I asked while sitting down.

"Fine," she answered me.

"So you wanna tell me what's bugging you?" I asked.

"I will after you answer my question," she said.

"Okay," I said, confused. "What's your question?"

"What happened yesterday?" she asked.

"What?" I said, confused.

That was the moment I remembered yesterday even happened.

"Why do you ask?" I asked.

"Well, I heard Jaelyn telling one of her friends yesterday was crazy, and I heard a rumor there were police cars outside your house," she said.

"Nothing happened," I said.

"Really?" she said, sounding frustrated.

"Really," I said, just wanting to end this conversation.

"I'm done," she said while storming off.

"Ezra, come back!" I shouted. "What is wrong with you?"

"You!" she shouted. "You're what's wrong!"

"What is that supposed to mean!" I shouted back at her.

"You don't tell anyone shit!" she screamed. "You act like you're the main character. You act like no one else's problems matter, and no one will say anything because they think you're going through hell, but honestly, no one knows. You don't say a word, so no one says a word to you!"

"Ezra, what is that supposed to mean?" I asked, confused.

"It means you're isolating yourself," she said.

"Why does that affect you?" I asked, still confused.

"Aaron, you're my best friend," she said. "We used to tell each other everything. I even told you about my period. You told me about all the crazy shit that happened to you, and all of a sudden, you stopped. You slowly stopped inviting me over. We used to cry if I couldn't come over every day after school. What

218

happened to that? What happened to us?"

"Do you really think we're drifting apart?" I asked.

"You're drifting from everyone," she said.

"Why do you say that?" I asked, confused.

"You don't tell Jaelyn things any more either," she said. "We're worried about you."

"Why are you talking to my sister?" I asked.

"Really?" she shouted. "Aaron, you're not the only Cripple I've known since I was five years old. I'm as close to Jaelyn as I am to you. It's sad; lately, I've been feeling like I know her better than I know you, and I think she tells me more than she does you."

"That's bullshit," I said. "Jaelyn is my sister. I obviously know more about her than you do."

"Okay," she said. "Did you know Jaelyn had a boyfriend?"

"What?" I shouted.

"I'll take that as a no," she said.

"Ezra, I'm sorry," I said. "I admit it, I have been more distant, but that doesn't mean I want to drift away from you. I have had a bunch of crazy shit going on in my life, and just because I can't tell you doesn't mean I care about you any less. How about we go get pizza after school? I'll pay."

Ezra looked up at me and smiled.

"I guess that could be fun," she said. "I'll see you later."

Ezra walked out of the lunchroom to the bathroom. I felt bad, but at the same time, I was relieved. She has had some crazy things happen at her house, so I was just glad nothing alarming happened to her.

I walked back over to the lunch table and cleaned up for both of us. It was the least I could do.

I didn't like Ezra getting mad at me, but I was glad she did.

I now realized what I was doing.

I may not be able to change my hiding things, but at least I could become more aware of it.

After school, I told Jaelyn to drive home on her own and that I was going to hang with Ezra. She did not like the idea of going home alone, but she was glad to hear that Ezra and I were finally hanging out after school again.

Once I was done telling Jaelyn about my evening, I met Ezra by the doors, and we walked out.

"So, what kind of pizza are we getting?" I asked.

"How about pineapple?" she said.

My face changed from happy to absolutely disgusted in a matter of seconds. Ezra knew I hated pineapple on pizza, so I hoped she was just playing a joke on me.

"Are you serious?" I asked.

"Sadly no," she said. "I'd love a pineapple pizza, but I won't torture you that much."

"That's a relief," I said. "You pineapple pizza people scare me."

"Good," Ezra said while laughing.

I couldn't help but laugh along with her. I loved her sense of humor, and I was glad to see it slowly coming back.

"So, what kind of pizza are we actually getting?" I asked.

"Wanna just do a classic cheese pizza?" she asked.

"Sure," I said.

During the rest of our walk to the pizza place, we just talked about random crap. It was pretty nice. Ezra and I hadn't had a chill conversation like this in a while.

When we finally got there, the line was so long. It was going outside the building.

"Why are so many people getting pizza on a cloudy

Wednesday afternoon?" I said, annoyed.

"I think they're having some kind of sale," Ezra said.

"That would make sense," I said.

"Guess you'll just have to be stuck with me longer," Ezra joked.

"Oh no," I said jokingly. "Whatever will I do."

Ezra just looked at me and rolled her eyes.

We had a long wait ahead of us.

I hadn't been in a line this long since I went to Disney World in 2008.

We stood there for a while in silence.

I guess even the closest of friends run out of things to talk about eventually.

After a while, I found myself looking down the streets of this small town in Tennessee. It was honestly kind of peaceful.

I was just doing it to pass the time, but quickly I became glad I was looking down the street.

I saw a familiar figure making its way down the street.

I knew if my hunches were correct, I had to take action now, even if that meant I had to leave Ezra.

"Ezra, I have to go," I said.

"What? Why?" she said, confused. "We're so close."

"I just have to go," I said. "We can do this again another day."

"You're a piece of shit," she said. "I'm getting pineapple pizza next time."

"Fine," I said as I started to walk away. "I'm so sorry."

"Whatever," she said, annoyed. "I'll see you tomorrow."

"See you," I said as I quickly ran down the street towards the figure.

I felt bad for leaving Ezra, but honestly, I had no choice. I knew she was gonna hate me, but I knew she'd forgive me eventually.

To be more sneaky, I decided to quickly circle around a building to where I was walking behind the figure.

Now, it was time for the true test, I thought to myself.

"Tyler?" I said to the figure.

The figure turned and looked at me.

"Where'd you learn that name?" he asked angrily while approaching me.

"Wait, so are you Tyler?" I asked.

He didn't answer; instead, he walked up to me and grabbed my arm.

He pulled me into an alley and looked me in the eyes.

"I'm not gonna ask again," he said. "Where'd you hear that name."

"The name Tyler?" I said, confused.

"Don't play dumb with me!" he screamed while using his powers to throw me through an old building.

I quickly flew through the old wooden planks and hit the concrete ground. It made everything in my body ache

"You work for them, don't you?" he screamed.

"Work for who?" I said, confused while managing to stand up.

"You know who!" he screamed.

He used his powers and pulled my legs out from under me. I instantly fell flat on my back.

This was starting to seem more and more like a bad idea each time I hit the ground.

He walked over and looked down at me with anger in his eyes.

"One last chance before I kill you!" he shouted.

"I'm not a bad guy, Tyler," I said in despair. "I found you by luck. No one sent me."

"That's the worst lie I've ever heard!" he screamed.

He lifted me in the air and threw me back on the ground as hard as he could.

"Any last words?" he asked.

I lay there in pain as my body ached.

What was I supposed to do to make him realize I'm not the bad guy he thinks I am?

As I was about to lose hope, I came up with the perfect thing to save my life.

"Your sister's name is Morgan," I said. "Your name is Tyler. You saved my life. I was at the school"

"Wait, you're the idiot kid that tried to fight the VK?" he asked me, confused.

Yes," I said. "And now I'm the idiot kid trying to get help from a person who could kill me in two seconds."

"What do you want me to help you with?" he asked me, still confused.

"I need your help to find Morgan and to overall just stop the VK," I said.

"Wait, Morgan's gone?" he said, alarmed.

"Your dad unenrolled her from school, and no one's heard from her since," I explained. "And I've heard about your dad, so I don't think this is a good thing."

"Shit!" he screamed. "How long has she been gone?"

"Since yesterday," I said.

"Okay, not too long," he said to himself. "That's good."

"So, will you help me?" I asked.

"I'm gonna help save my sister, but I'm not helping with the VK," he said. "I've tried to stop them before, and it almost killed me."

"You're so powerful, though," I said.

"I'm not the only powerful one when it comes to the VK," he said. "Two members of the VK replicated the experiments done on my sister and me to gain powers for themselves."

"That's alarming," I said.

"Sure is," he said. "I suggest if you want to live past graduation you leave the VK alone. Trust me, they're too strong for you."

"I know I should, but I don't think I can," I said. "I've already come too far."

"Whatever you say," he said. "Meet me here tomorrow at eight, so we can check out my old house and see if Morgan's there.

"Eight p.m, right?" I asked.

"Yes," he said. "You never investigate in the light."

"Makes sense," I said. "I'll see you tomorrow."

"See you, idiot kid," he said while walking away.

I stood there for a minute, trying to comprehend what I was getting myself into. Was I doing the right thing? Would this help me get closer to stopping the VK? I didn't know, but I did know this was the only way to figure those things out. I just had to start taking risks; that was the only way to get anywhere.

Quickly after Tyler left, I started to make my way back home. Everything in my body ached, but the evening scenery was so peaceful I almost couldn't feel any pain.

The streets were slowly emptying. Everything was becoming darker. It kinda freaked me out, but at the same time, it was quite nice. There were no crazy people yelling or crying babies, it was almost silent, and I liked that.

Before I knew it, my peaceful walk was over, though, and

I had made it back home.

I walked into the house to see Mom making dinner.

"Did you have fun with Ezra?" she asked me as I took my shoes off.

"Yeah," I said quickly.

"You still have room for dinner?" she asked.

"Of course," I said. "What are we having?"

"Mashed potatoes and green beans," she answered.

"Well, that makes me glad I didn't fill up on pizza," I said.

"Me too," she said. "You need to eat something healthy at least once a day, and I don't expect the school to fulfill that."

"Me neither," I said while laughing.

Mom looked up at me and smiled. I think she had let yesterday go and realized that I didn't need to take the blame.

"Can you do me a favor after you put your bag down?" she asked.

"Sure," I said, not knowing what she was going to ask me.

"Can you go check on Carl?" she asked me hesitantly.

"Mom, I can't," I said. "I need a few days before I even look at him again."

"Aaron, please," she said. "He didn't mean any harm."

"He tried to kill me," I said. "That doesn't sound friendly to me."

"Aaron, he did not try to kill you," she said. "He was just mad at you and lost control."

"Him putting his hand around my throat and locking Jaelyn and Effie away is more than just losing control!" I shouted.

"He was intoxicated," she said. "He didn't know what he was doing."

"I don't see that as an excuse!" I shouted as I stormed out.

I loved my mom, but she always took Carl's side, no matter

225

what.

I swear he could murder someone, and my mom still wouldn't care. She was blinded by her love for him, and that was annoying.

I sat in my room just playing candy crush until Jaelyn walked in.

"So, how was the pizza?" she asked.

"Good," I said while still looking at my phone.

"Really?" she said. "Because last time I checked, non-existent pizza doesn't taste that good."

"What?" I said, confused.

"I know you left Ezra," she said. "And just so you're aware, she's pissed."

"I'm sorry," I said. "Something came up."

"What could've possibly come up?" she asked, confused.

"Stuff," I said.

"Give me a better answer, or I'm telling Mom!" she shouted at me.

"If you tell Mom, I'll tell her about your boyfriend," I said.

"Shut up!" she shouted. "How did you even figure that out?"

"Ezra told me," I said.

"Are you kidding me?" she said, annoyed.

"Don't freak out," I said. "I won't tell Mom unless you make me."

"So you're going to blackmail me?" she asked.

"When you say it like that, it sounds bad," I said jokingly.

Jaelyn smiled and rolled her eyes. She came down and sat next to me.

"Please let me have this," she whispered.

"Please don't get me grounded for life," I whispered back.

"Deal," she said. "You stay quiet about my boyfriend, and I'll be quiet about whatever it is you do."

"Sounds like a deal," I said. "Pinky swear?"

"Pinky swear," she said.

We locked pinkies and shook our hands.

"So, who is this mysterious man?" I asked.

"Dave," she said.

"The Junior jock?" I said, confused. "Really?"

"Dave's more than just a jock," she said. "He's been a friend for a while, and lately we started hitting it off."

"Well, good for you," I said. "I'm gonna finish this level, and then I'll meet you at the table for dinner."

"Sounds good," she said while walking out. "What level are you even on?"

"Thirty-two," I said. "What level are you on?"

"Thirty-six," she answered. "I'm superior."

"The annoying superior," I said.

"I'll take any superior title I can get," she jokingly said.

I rolled my eyes and turned my attention back to my phone. After a few minutes, I finally got past the level and was able to put my phone away.

I walked out into the kitchen and sat down at the table in the seat across from Jaelyn. She looked at me and mouthed the word superior.

I rolled my eyes and flipped her off.

"Aaron!" Mom shouted from across the kitchen.

"Sorry," I said.

Jaelyn looked at me and laughed. I knew she didn't care when I flipped her off. I think she just enjoyed the reaction our parents had.

Before I knew it, dinner was served, and everyone was

eating.

I was glad Carl didn't come down to join us, but I still felt off. I found myself avoiding eye contact with my mom, which rarely happened. It was definitely weird.

After dinner, I went to my room and almost instantly fell asleep.

I guess I was just exhausted from everything that had happened earlier that day.

It felt like I was about to have the best night of sleep in my life, but sadly that wasn't the case. Instead of sleeping like a baby, I slept in absolute chaos. This wasn't because of my mind racing or the temperature. It was because of the dream I had.

In this dream, I was with Tyler, and we were walking around this place that looked slightly abandoned. We were trying to find Morgan in this building, and we ended up walking into a library when chaos struck. Out of nowhere, there was a huge green explosion that sent us both flying across the room. I flew into a bookshelf and then shot awake.

I hated these dreams with a passion, and now I hated them even more. I no longer could tell if they were just dreams or pieces of the future.

I couldn't tell if they were a warning or just a figment of my imagination. These dreams made me question my sanity, and honestly, at this point, I wouldn't be surprised if I woke up in an insane asylum one morning.

I was officially losing my mind.

Chapter 16

The next day was dreaded. I dreaded seeing Ezra and going to find Morgan with Tyler. I dreaded both of these for different reasons, though.

Ezra was mad at me, and I couldn't handle seeing her upset. That was more of a dread with emotion, while the other dread was more fearful. This mission with Tyler scared me.

If my dream comes true, we probably won't make it out of there alive.

I knew I had told myself that I needed to devote my life to stopping the VK, but I still had to remember I'm just a kid, and deep down, I'm scared to die.

Even though the morning was dreadful, it seemed to fly by.

At school, Ezra full on ignored me. It hurt, but it seemed to be the best way to handle things right now.

After I got over Ezra, the school day flew by.

Every minute was officially leading up to the mission with Tyler.

At home, I couldn't bring myself to eat or drink anything; my nerves wouldn't allow me to.

Multiple times I considered quitting on the mission and just bailing on Tyler, but deep down, I knew I couldn't do that. I had committed to this, and now I needed to stay with it.

Before I knew it, it was almost eight. Which meant I had to sneak out now.

I grabbed my phone and slowly walked over to the door.

Everyone was upstairs, so this seemed to be a pretty easy getaway.

I slowly opened the door and walked out.

I was officially on my way to Tyler.

As I walked down the street, my heart started to race. My nerves were starting to get to me, but I didn't let that stop me. I continued to walk down the street until I saw Tyler standing in the alley waiting for me.

"Took you long enough," he said as I walked into the alley.

"Sorry," I said. "I'm just a little nervous."

"Why?" he asked.

"I don't know. I just am," I said. "Should we go?"

"It's better now than later," he said. "Wanna run or teleport?"

"I don't care," I said.

"Okay then," he said. "I'm gonna choose the quicker one."

He placed his hand on my shoulder and looked at me.

"Close your eyes," he said. "That'll make this painless."

"Okay," I said nervously while tightly closing my eyes shut.

Tyler put his other hand on my other shoulder and teleported us to his old house. I opened my eyes and looked around. It was weird to be in a different place after just closing my eyes.

As I looked closer, I noticed that the house looked abandoned even though Morgan still lived there. It was weird.

"Let's go," he said. "We don't have much time."

"We're on a time limit?" I said, confused.

"If we wanna see Morgan alive, then yes we are," he said.

"Okay," I said. "Let's do this."

"Alrighty then," he said.

We ran up to the front door and looked through the windows. Inside it looked so old and disgusting; it really did look abandoned.

"Are you sure your dad still lives here?" I asked Tyler.

"Positive," he answered. "This house is his baby; he would never leave it."

"Okay," I said. "How do we get in?"

"The door," he said. "It's never locked."

"Then why are we still standing here?" I asked.

"Because you keep asking dumb questions," he answered.

"Very funny," I said. "Let's go in."

"Whatever you say," he said as he opened the door.

The second the door opened, my nose filled with a horrific smell.

"What happened here?" I asked Tyler.

"Honestly, I don't know what made the smell," he said. "It's been here for as long as I can remember."

"You lived in this?" I asked, surprised.

"Yeah," he said. "It used to be worse."

"How could it get any worse?" I asked.

"You don't want to know," he said. "Now come on in. The smell will grow on you."

Tyler walked in and started to look around. I followed behind him.

As I looked around, I was disgusted. This place looked and smelled awful. I couldn't imagine how anyone lived here.

Tyler looked back at me and saw my disgusted look.

"It's not that bad," he said.

"For you," I replied.

"I can continue alone if you're too much of a baby to go on," he said, annoyed.

"No," I said. "I'm gonna keep going."

"Alrighty then," he said.

We continued to walk around the house, trying to find something, anything.

Occasionally in the filth, I would see an old family photo of the Jays. I felt bad about how much their family had fallen apart.

Sometimes I would think my family fell apart, but now I started to realize I didn't have it nearly as bad as some people.

"Can you stop looking at the stupid photos?" Tyler shouted at me, annoyed. "We're on a mission, remember?"

"Sorry," I said while setting the photo down. "You guys just looked so happy."

"Yeah," he said. "But happy things don't last. They never do."

Tyler stormed off into another room.

I felt bad. We were on a mission, and here I was distracting him about how happy he used to be.

I quickly followed Tyler into the room and froze.

"What's wrong?" he asked. "Are you sad there are no more family photos in the library?"

I didn't answer. As I looked across the library, I realized it was the same one that was in my dream.

"Tyler, can we go to another room?" I asked.

"Why?" he said, confused. "This room has a bunch of good places clues could be hiding."

"Tyler, please just trust me," I pleaded with him. "This isn't safe."

"Didn't we already agree this mission wasn't safe?" he said, confused. "Stop being a baby."

"Tyler, I had a dream we were in an explosion in this

room!" I shouted. "It was green, huge, and sent us both flying."

"It was a dream," he said. "Stop pretending you're special and come help me."

"Tyler, I had a dream like this come true before. I'm not crazy!" I shouted.

"Okay then," he said, annoyed. "You can either feed into your weird dream and quit or help me find my sister."

"Tyler, please," I said. "I don't want you to get hurt."

"If you cared about me, you wouldn't have brought me back to my dad's house!" he shouted at me.

"I didn't bring you here!" I shouted as I walked into the library.

"This was your idea!" he shouted.

"No, it was not!" I shouted back. "I told you about your sister! That's all I did!"

Tyler looked at me with rage in his eyes. I could tell he knew I was right. He just didn't want to admit that this bad idea was his own.

"You can leave, idiot kid," he said. "I don't need your help anyway."

"I never said you did," I said.

"Okay, we've agreed. Now you can go," he said while pointing to the door.

"Fine," I said.

As I turned to walk away, I saw a figure standing in the doorway with its hand glowing green.

I was about to turn to Tyler when suddenly the figure threw a ray of green energy in the center of Tyler and me.

Just like in my dream, we both flew back and smacked into the bookshelves behind us.

I fell to the floor and lay there for a second before deciding

I needed to see what was happening. As I lifted my head up from the ground, I saw the figure walking over to Tyler. Tyler tried to stand, but he couldn't. The figure looked down at him and just laughed.

"Why the hell did you come back here?" the figure asked Tyler.

"Where's my sister?" Tyler screamed at the figure.

"That's not important," the figure said.

The figure moved his hand around Tyler's throat and lifted him off the ground.

I heard Tyler start struggling to breathe.

At that moment, I knew I had to do something. I looked around and saw a metal rod that had broken off the bookshelf. I leaned over and grabbed it.

I looked over to see Tyler still struggling. I stood up and slowly went behind the figure. Tyler saw me and smiled.

"I hope you rot in hell, Dad," Tyler said to the figure.

"I'll meet you there," Tyler's dad said.

"I don't think so," Tyler said.

Right at that moment, I swung the metal rod across the back of Tyler's dad's head. He instantly fell to the ground releasing Tyler.

Tyler landed on his feet and looked up at me.

"Are you glad I stayed?" I asked.

"I guess so," he said jokingly. "Thanks for the save."

"No problem," I said. "I owed you one."

Tyler looked at me and smiled.

"I'm gonna go look in my dad's secret rooms that I somehow know the combination to," he said. "You continue looking around the library."

"You're leaving me with your psycho dad?" I said,

alarmed.

"You'll be fine," Tyler said. "He's out cold, and you have that metal rod if anything happens."

"You're really putting a lot of faith in me," I said.

"I'll be in the other room," he said. "Just scream if you need me."

"Fine," I said. "Be careful."

"I will," he said as he walked out.

As soon as Tyler walked out, I looked over at his dad's unconscious body. I couldn't believe that I had done that.

After a solid minute of staring at Tyler's dad's body, I walked over to the desk and started looking through the papers on it.

Nothing was really popping out to me; it all just seemed like old letters from the 90s.

I was about to go look somewhere when all of a sudden I froze. As I turned away from the desk, I saw Tyler's dad standing right behind me, looking at me with a sick smile.

I tried to scream for Tyler, but I couldn't.

As I was about to reach for the metal rod, he placed his glowing hand on my forehead.

I wanted to scream so bad, but I still couldn't bring myself to.

The feeling of some kind of power running through my brain felt so weird.

"What's your name, son?" Tyler's dad asked.

Without even thinking, I answered him.

"My name is Aaron Leon Cripple."

"Good to know," he said. "When were you born?"

Once again, the answer just came out of my mouth.

"I was born July 10th, 1997."

"You're younger than I thought," he said. "Why are you here?"

During this answer, I tried to fight back the weird urge I had to answer him, but I couldn't.

"I'm here to save Morgan from her crazy dad."

"I'm crazy?" he said, confused. "You haven't seen crazy, kid."

All of a sudden, Tyler's dad removed his hand from my head.

It instantly sent a sharp pain throughout my head, and I fell back onto the desk.

"Did that hurt?" he asked.

I just looked up at him like he was crazy. He gave me a crazy look in return.

Right at that moment, I reached and grabbed my metal rod and tried to knock him out again, but he stopped me.

He ripped the rod out of my hand and smacked me across the head with it.

I instantly fell to the ground. I was surprised I was still awake.

"That doesn't feel good, does it?" he said.

"What do you want?" I said quietly.

"I want idiots like you and my son to leave me alone and let me do my own thing," he answered me.

"You won't be left alone if you're hurting people!" I shouted.

"Who am I hurting?" he asked.

"Your kids and all the kids you idiots from the VK have kidnapped!" I shouted.

"You know about that?" he said, confused.

I froze. I realized I shouldn't have said that. Now I was in

236

even more danger than I already was.

"You're that kid the VK's so worried about, aren't you?" he asked.

I didn't answer. Instead, I started to try and stand up, but he kicked me back down.

"Answer me," he said sternly.

He looked at me and kicked me in the side again. It sent a sharp pain through my body.

I tried to hold in my tears, but my eyes started to fill with water.

"You gonna cry, little kid?" he asked. "Just answer my question, and I won't need to hurt you any more."

"No," I said. "You've already heard enough from me!"

"Didn't want to have to do this," he said. "But you've left me no choice."

Tyler's dad moved down and flipped me onto my back.

He used his powers and pinned me down so I couldn't move.

I tried to free myself, but just like the previous experiences, I couldn't. Instead, I was stuck there as I watched Tyler's dad pull out a gun from his jacket.

At that moment, I gained the ability to scream again.

"Tyler!" I screamed loudly. "Help!"

"He's not gonna save you," Tyler's dad said. "No one will; you have no one!"

Right after he said that, he pointed the gun at my head and pulled the trigger. I closed my eyes in fear, but I never felt anything hit my head. After a while, I hesitantly opened my eyes to see a bullet being held above my head by a yellow-looking bubble. I turned my head to see Tyler standing in the doorway.

"That's enough, Dad!" Tyler screamed.

Before Tyler's dad could say anything, Tyler flipped the bullet around and sent it right into his dad's eye. Tyler's dad fell off of me and screamed in pain.

I quickly shot up and ran to Tyler.

"We need to go," I said quickly.

"No shit," he said while grabbing my arm. "Close your eyes."

I listened to Tyler and closed my eyes.

Before I knew it, I was standing in a cheap-looking apartment.

"Is this your place?" I asked.

"Yeah," he said. "It's dad-free."

I started to laugh when suddenly the sharp pain in my side returned. I grabbed my side as I moaned in pain.

"What's wrong?" Tyler asked.

"My side," I said while falling back onto the floor.

Tyler ran over to me and looked at my face.

"What happened?" he asked, alarmed.

I tried to answer him, but I was choked back by tears.

My breathing began to speed up, and I started to panic.

"What happened?" Tyler screamed.

"He kicked me in the side, hard," I answered while breathing heavily.

"Okay," Tyler said in a panicking voice. "You probably have some broken ribs."

"No shit!" I screamed back.

"I'm gonna get some pain killers; I'll be back," Tyler said as he ran off.

I lay there holding my side, just waiting for him to come back. This pain felt unreal. I didn't realize how much a broken bone hurt.

Tyler returned quickly and sat down by me.

"Let me help you to the couch," he said. "That'll feel better than a hardwood floor."

I shook my head and grabbed his hand as he pulled me up. Standing up hurt like hell, but I knew I had to do it.

Tyler quickly helped me over to his couch and laid me down.

He handed me some pills and a glass of water.

"Those'll help," he said.

I looked at the pills hesitantly. I knew Mom would kill me if she ever found out I was doing this, but I didn't care. This pain needed to go away. I took the pills and laid my head back.

"Thank you," I said weakly.

"You're welcome," he said. "Try and get some rest now; you need to heal."

I closed my eyes and slowly began to doze off when all of a sudden, I remembered I had school the next day. I sat up and looked over at Tyler, who was sitting at the counter looking at his phone.

"I need to go," I said.

"Why?" he asked. "You are in no condition to travel."

"I have school tomorrow," I said. "I have to be home, or my mom will kill me."

"You need to rest," he said. "School can wait."

Even though I wanted to argue with him, I knew he was right. I needed rest so I could walk around without being dragged down by pain.

I laid back down and shut my eyes, only this time, I let myself fall asleep.

Chapter 17

The next morning I woke up to find Tyler sitting at the counter looking through my phone.

"What on earth are you doing?" I asked as I sat up from the couch. "That's my phone."

"I know," he said. "I was just seeing who the hundreds of calls and text messages were from."

"I have hundreds of messages?" I shouted, alarmed. "Who are they from?"

"They're from contacts labeled Mom, Carl, and Jaelyn," he answered me. "Is Jaelyn your girlfriend?"

"No! She's my sister!" I shouted. "What time is it?"

"About ten thirty," he answered.

"Shit!" I shouted.

"What's wrong with you?" he asked.

"I had school today, and my family doesn't know where I am," I answered him.

"You didn't tell your family where you were going?" he said, confused.

"Of course not!" I shouted. "We went on a deadly mission!"

"Did you even tell your parents you were leaving the house?" he asked.

"No," I said.

"Well, that was a stupid move," he said.

"I have strict parents, Tyler. They wouldn't have let me leave," I said.

"Then why'd you come?" he asked.

"To find Morgan!" I shouted. "Are you stupid?"

"Sorry," he said. "You want your phone?"

"Yes, please," I said.

Tyler walked over to the couch and handed me my phone. I looked at the notifications to see 439 missed calls and 231 text messages.

"I'm so dead," I said to myself.

"Why would you say that?" Tyler asked.

"My family thinks I'm dead, and I haven't answered them," I said.

"Fair point," he replied.

At that moment, my phone started to ring. My mom was calling me.

"Time to face your mother's wrath," Tyler said jokingly.

I took a deep breath and answered the phone. As I moved it to my ear, I was able to hear Carl yelling at my mom. He was saying how she should stop wasting their time calling me.

I heard my mom's cries as she yelled back at him. Her tears broke me. I couldn't bring myself to even say anything.

"Is she there?" Tyler asked.

I just shook my head. Tears started to fill my eyes. I hated hearing my family upset; it always broke me.

After a while of listening to Mom and Carl's screams, I decided to finally say something.

"Mom?" I said softly into the phone.

Mom and Carl's bickering quickly came to a halt once they heard my voice. My mom picked up the phone and quickly put it to her ear.

"Aaron?" she said anxiously. "Are you okay, honey?"

"I'm fine, Mom," I said.

"Honey, where are you?" she asked me nervously. "Do you need us to come pick you up?"

"I don't know exactly," I answered. "I'm gonna ask my friend real quick."

"You're with a friend?" she said, confused.

"Yeah," I said. "I'm gonna put the phone down for a sec; I'll be right back."

"Okay, sweetie," she said.

I set the phone down and looked up at Tyler.

"So what should I say to her?" I asked.

"About what?" he said, confused.

"My location," I said. "Were you not listening to my conversation?"

"I'm not an eavesdropper," he said. "I respect people's privacy."

"Fair enough," I said. "So should I tell my mom I'm here?"

"No," he said. "That's dangerous."

"Why's it dangerous?" I asked.

"It just is," he said. "Tell her I'll give you a ride home."

"Am I actually getting a ride, or are we doing the teleportation game?" I asked.

"An actual ride," he said. "I do have a car."

"That's very nice," I said. "I'll tell her that"

I picked up the phone and put it back to my ear.

"Mom?" I said into the phone.

"I'm here, sweetie," she said. "What's happening?"

"I'm getting a ride home from my friend," I answered her. "I'll be back soon."

"Okay," she said. "I love you."

"Love you too," I said.

"Be careful, sweetie," she said.

"I will," I said back.

Quickly after I answered her, I hung up the phone.

"When do we leave?" I asked Tyler.

"In a few minutes," he said. "Take some painkillers so you can walk to the car."

"Okay," I said.

He handed me the bottle and a glass of water.

"Take as many as you need," he said.

"Okay," I said as he walked out of the room.

I looked down at the bottle and started to panic. The bottle felt different than just having a few pills in my hand. I had no idea how many to take. I didn't know how much was too much or how much was too little.

Tyler walked back in and saw me sitting there awkwardly.

"Have you never opened a pill bottle?" he asked me, confused.

"I have," I said quickly.

"Then why are you not taking any?" he asked.

"I don't know how many to take," I said.

"It's not rocket science, kid," he said. "Just take a few so we can go."

"How many is a few?" I asked, nervously.

"Like two or three?" he said, confused. "Why are you freaking out so much?"

"No reason," I said.

I opened up the bottle and took two pills out. Before my brain could think about how much of a disappointment I was, I swallowed the pills and set the bottle down.

"Are you ready to go?" he asked.

"Yeah," I said.

I stood up and walked towards the door. My side still hurt

pretty bad, which sucked for me, but I knew the painkillers would kick in soon enough.

"You want some painkillers to go?" Tyler asked.

"No!" I answered quickly.

"Okay?" he said, confused.

I felt bad that Tyler didn't know why I was panicking, but it's kind of hard to just casually say a bottle of pills is the reason you don't have a dad any more.

Tyler and I walked out of his apartment to a crappy-looking car.

"Is this yours?" I asked.

"Yeah," he said. "Get in."

I did as Tyler said and got into the car.

Tyler started the engine and we were off.

"Do you know where I live?" I asked.

"Yeah," he said. "I teleported you home once, remember?"

"Forgot about that," I said. "How long is the drive?"

"Only like twenty minutes," he said. "That's the perfect amount of time for me to ask you some questions."

"Questions?" I said, confused.

"Yeah," he said. "I need to know why you had a dream that perfectly predicted the future in a place you've never been before."

"I'd love to answer that, but I can't," I said.

"Why?" he said, confused.

"Because I don't even know the answer myself," I said. "These dreams just started happening, and I don't know why."

"Well, they must be pretty handy," he said.

"They are when people listen to me about them," I said.

"Yeah, sorry about that," he said.

"You're fine," I said. "I just wanted to ruffle your feathers about it."

"Well, you're a little asshole," he said.

"Hey, you had the chance for me to die," I said. "Don't blame me for anything I do."

"I should've watched that bullet go through your skull," he said jokingly.

I rolled my eyes and laughed.

"You would've missed me," I said.

"For a small period," he said.

"I think it'd be for the rest of your life," I said.

"Really?" he said.

"Yeah," I said. "You'd be fighting your weird magic friends, and you would miss the weird kid with the metal rod."

"You were pretty good with that thing," he said.

"Thanks for the compliment," I said.

"No problem," he said. "Now get out of my car."

"What?" I said, confused.

"We're at your house," he said.

"That was quick," I said.

"Very," he said. "You try and stay alive now."

"I will," I said as I got out of the car.

I walked up to my driveway and looked at my house. I had a hesitation fall over me when I walked up to the front door. I was glad to be home, but I was scared of the wrath I would get once I went inside.

I was just grateful the painkillers had kicked in, and I could barely feel my side. It would've looked even worse if I walked in holding my side. I eventually built up the courage and walked into the house. I walked in to see no one in the kitchen. I was relieved.

After seeing no one was around, I decided to sneak to my

245

room. I tiptoed through the kitchen and was almost through my door when suddenly I heard a familiar voice shout at me.

"Where the hell have you been?" Jaelyn shouted at me.

"Out," I said.

"We've been worried sick about you!" she shouted.

"Sorry," I said.

I turned around to walk into my room when all of a sudden, I felt a hand grab my wrist.

"Sorry won't cut it, Aaron!" Jaelyn screamed at me. "Tell me where you were!"

"I was with a friend," I said.

"Did that friend smack you across the head?" she shouted.

"No," I said. "I just hit my head."

"Really?" she said. "I know you're lying!"

"Okay," I said. "You're being crazy."

"Am I, though?" she shouted. "You disappeared, again! And now you are just acting like everything's okay when it's clearly not!"

"It is though," I said.

Jaelyn looked at me with an ice-cold stare; she was pissed.

I was about to say something when all of a sudden, I felt the pain in my side start to come back.

"I need to lay down," I said. "Please, let go of my arm."

"Why?" she asked me, annoyed.

"I just do!" I shouted.

"That's not a good enough answer!" she said. "Tell me why!"

"I don't have to!" I screamed.

She looked at me and tightened her grip around my wrist.

"Yes, you do!" She shouted at me.

I didn't answer her. Instead, I tried to focus on my breathing so the pain would lessen.

"You okay?" she asked me, confused.

"Yes!" I shouted at her. "Please just let me lay down."

"Aaron, I'm worried about you," she said.

"Don't be!" I shouted at her.

I ripped my wrist out of her grip and started to walk to my room when all of a sudden, the pain in my side intensified. It felt like I was just stabbed.

I quickly fell onto my desk chair and grabbed my side.

Jaelyn instantly ran over to me and helped me stand up.

"Aaron, please tell me what's going on," she said worriedly.

"I can't," I said quietly.

I grabbed my side even tighter and tried to walk to my bed when all of a sudden, I fell back down to the floor.

"Aaron!" Jaelyn shouted. "Are you okay?"

"No," I said. "It hurts."

"Let me see," she said. "I took a summer of nursing classes with Mom. I know what I'm doing."

"It's my side," I said.

"Okay," she said. "Just try and breathe."

Jaelyn lifted my shirt and looked at my side.

"What does it look like?" I asked.

"It's all red and swollen with a few darker bruises," she said. "What happened?"

"Can I answer that later?" I asked. "This hurts a lot."

"Yeah," she said. "I have to get Mom; this looks bad."

"Okay," I said in pain.

Jaelyn quickly ran out of my room while I lay there on the floor in pain. I tried to focus on my breathing, but it didn't help. It hurt too much.

Jaelyn quickly came back with Mom a few minutes later. My mom ran over to me and looked at my side in horror.

"It hurts," I whispered.

"I know," she said. "It's gonna be okay."

My mom felt my side. She was trying to feel for broken ribs.

I knew she was trying to help but touching it made it hurt a million times more.

"Stop!" I screamed.

"Sorry, sweetie," she said worriedly. "I think you have some broken ribs."

"I guessed that," I said while breathing heavily. "What do we do?"

"I don't know," she said. "The hospital can't do much for a broken rib."

"Give him some painkillers," Carl said from my doorway.

"No!" Mom shouted.

"Mom," I said as I grabbed her hand. "One won't kill anyone."

"Aaron, no!" she shouted at me.

"Mom, he's got a point," Jaelyn said.

"Honey, he can take one pill and be fine," Carl said.

"I know that!" Mom screamed. "One pill won't do anything, but before you know it, one pill becomes a whole bottle, and you find them on the bathroom floor!"

"Mom," I said while re-grabbing her hand. "I would never do that to you."

My mom looked at me and didn't say anything. She pushed my hand away and walked out of my room.

"Fuck you," she said to Carl as she walked by him.

Carl just shook his head and walked out with her.

Jaelyn walked over to me and helped me up. She helped me lay down on my bed and plugged my phone in for me.

"I'm gonna get some ice," she said. "I'll be back."

Jaelyn walked out of my room, and Carl walked back in. Carl walked over to my bed and handed me a bottle.

"Take those and don't tell your mother," he said.

I was about to listen to him when all of a sudden I froze. I remembered how last time I was with Carl, he tried to kill me, so why wouldn't he now? I was in the perfect state for being murdered. I was injured and not thinking clearly.

I looked up at Carl and handed him the bottle back.

"I'm good," I said.

"Aaron, ignore your mother; she's crazy," he said. "These will help you."

"I said I was good," I said.

"You are acting weird," he said.

"Just leave me alone," I said.

"Fine, drama queen," Carl said, annoyed.

He turned away and stormed out of my room.

Quickly after Carl stormed out, Jaelyn walked in with an ice pack.

"Why was he in here?" she me.

"He was trying to give me some painkillers," I told her.

"Why didn't you take them?" she asked me, confused.

"I don't trust him," I said.

"Aaron, I don't think he has a huge plot to kill you," she said.

"You forgave him?" I said, confused.

"I never said that," she said. "I'm just saying I think he was generally trying to be helpful."

I looked at her with a disgusted look. I couldn't believe

what she was saying.

"Set the ice pack down and leave," I said.

"Are you mad at me now?" she asked, confused.

"No, I'm just annoyed," I said.

"Why are you annoyed?" she asked.

"You used to always take my side, and now you're taking Carl's," I said. "It's just weird."

"You're being overdramatic," she said. "I'm not taking anyone's side."

"Whatever," I said.

Jaelyn walked over and set the ice pack on my side. She looked at me and smiled.

"Try and get some rest," she said as she walked out.

"Will do," I said.

After Jaelyn left, I shut my eyes. I tried to drift off, but I couldn't. Instead, I found myself listening to the things around me. I heard the birds chirping along with the leaves rustling against my window. It was honestly kind of peaceful.

If I wasn't in so much pain, I could've easily mistaken that moment for a spot in paradise.

After a few hours of relaxation, I decided to check my phone.

I opened it to see a message from Ezra, which was very odd.

Aaron, I don't know what's going on with you, but I just want you to know I'm worried for you. You're keeping to yourself more, and it scares me. I'm sorry if I distance myself. I just don't like to see the people I love slowly fall apart. I'm sorry.

Why would Ezra be sending me this message now? This

was very weird for her. She rarely texted me; she was always busy watching her little brother. I didn't know why she would take time out of her day to write this. It was odd, and because of that, I didn't respond. I decided to just talk to her at school Monday.

The rest of my weekend was very boring. I was informed I was grounded for the weekend, but that didn't make a difference. I was in so much pain that even if I weren't grounded, I wouldn't have left my room.

Mom decided to ground me in hopes that I would never sneak out again, but I think we both knew that this wouldn't be the last time I left the house without her knowing.

I didn't hear from Ezra any more over the weekend. I guess that message was just really out of the blue.

Since I couldn't move much, I was left alone with my thoughts most of the time. I mainly reflected on the failed mission with Tyler.

I thought about how things could've gone differently. I thought of how they could've gone better or worse. I also realized how close to death we both actually were. Tyler would've died if I wasn't there, and I would've died if he wasn't there. I guess we both owed each other some gratitude.

I wondered to myself if Tyler would ever want or need to work with me again. Sure we almost died, but the adrenaline rush was kind of worth it. Most people say don't live your life like it's a movie, but I think those people live too safely. People in movies have exciting lives, so why shouldn't we?

Chapter 18

Monday morning filled me with both dread and excitement.

I was excited to finally get out of the house and no longer feel like a prisoner, but I was also dreading going to school.

I knew I had to talk to Ezra, which honestly scared me.

I love her, but she is not a person you want to have problems with.

When we were younger, some classmates used to try and pick on her, but that ended quickly after she gave some kid a black eye.

Ezra was strong and wasn't afraid to show her true colors. It's a good trait for a friend, unless they're mad at you, of course. In that case, you want to avoid them as much as possible. Sadly for me, though, avoiding her wasn't an option.

I got to school a few minutes earlier that morning. I told Jaelyn about Ezra and how I needed to talk to her, and she insisted that I get there earlier, and since she was the driver, I couldn't say anything about it.

After I put my things in Mrs. Jones's classroom, I went to find Ezra. I looked for a solid five minutes before I saw her standing in the hallway talking to some freshman girl.

"Hey, Ezra," I said while walking up to them.

She looked at me like I was crazy and then looked back at the freshman.

"Ezra?" I said, trying to get her to look back over at me.

Ezra stayed turned around and whispered something to the

freshman girl. The girl looked up at me and moved between Ezra and me.

"She obviously doesn't want to talk to you!" the girl shouted at me.

I stood there for a second, completely dumbfounded, before I decided to respond to the freshman.

"She doesn't have to talk to me, but I have to talk to her," I said sternly back to the girl.

The freshman girl was about to start attacking me when all of a sudden, Ezra turned around and pulled her back.

"Go to class, Amy, I'll be fine," Ezra said.

"Fine," she said to Ezra. "But if he does anything, just tell me and I will kick his ass."

"Noted," Ezra said. "Now go."

Amy started to walk away when all of a sudden, she turned around and flipped me off. I just stood there and rolled my eyes.

"So, what do you want?" Ezra asked me, annoyed.

"I need to talk to you," I said.

"About what?" she said, pretending to play dumb.

"Your message," I said.

"What's wrong with it?" she asked.

"Nothing's wrong with it," I said. "You just talked about distancing, and I don't understand why."

"You don't?" she said, confused.

"I mean, I kinda do," I said. "I just don't want you to distance. You're my best friend. I can't lose you."

"Wish you would've thought about that sooner," she said angrily.

"Please give me another chance," I said. "We've been friends for the longest time. Please don't let my stupid actions ruin that."

"Aaron, I can't be friends with people who don't tell me anything," she said.

"I've only been secretive a few times," I said.

"A few!" she shouted angrily. "You don't tell me anything any more. You keep getting hurt and changing, and I don't know why. I don't even know you any more!"

"Ezra, you're being overdramatic," I said. "I got a few scratches and didn't feel like sharing my story. So what? It doesn't matter."

"It matters to me!" she shouted while her eyes began to water. "Maybe I'd forgive you if this was coming to an end, but it's obviously not. You have a massive bruise on your head, and Jaelyn told me how you mysteriously came home with broken ribs. This isn't okay!"

"Ezra, chill," I said, annoyed. "This is my life, and I'm going to decide what people know about it and what people don't. I don't care how close you are to me; you don't have to know everything!"

"I love how you still consider us close!" Ezra screamed at me. "You can't consider yourself close with anyone any more! You hide things and then tell people it's for the best. That makes no sense."

"It may make no sense, but it's true," I said.

"Fine!" she screamed at me. "I'm done. You're a mess, and I hate to say this, but you're a mess that's impossible to clean up."

"That's fine by me," I said. "So you gonna go hang out with your feisty freshman now?"

"Yeah," Ezra said. "At least I can talk to her."

"You can talk to me too, but you won't," I said.

"I only talk to people who share their side of the story too," she said. "And you don't fit that any more."

"Fine," I said. "Just walk away and end a friendship you've had since you were five years old."

"That's what I'm doing," she said with a cold stare.

Ezra turned around and stormed off.

I instantly looked around and realized everyone was staring.

"This isn't a movie, people!" I screamed. "Move along!"

I stormed through the hallway, furious. I hadn't been this mad in a while. Ezra was so stupid; why would she just leave me. She doesn't know what I'm going through, and her solution is to leave me. This kind of thing is what turns people to do unthinkable things. Luckily I wasn't heading down that road, but if I was, this would've definitely sent me over the edge.

I got into Mrs. Jones's classroom and just sat at my desk with my head down, waiting for class to start.

I was about to fall asleep when I finally heard the bell. As I lifted my head, Ezra walked in. We exchanged a glance but didn't say a word.

During class, it felt like everyone was watching us. It was like Ezra and I was the new hit movie across the school.

Everyone gets into fights. I didn't know what made mine and Ezra's so interesting.

I thought the stares would stop after a while, but they only got worse. By the time lunch came around, we were officially the number one gossip topic around the school.

When I got to lunch, I kinda froze. I had never had it before when I had no one to sit with. Ezra and I were kinda losers, but we were losers together, and now I was a loser alone, which wasn't a good thing.

I went and sat down at the table where Ezra and I normally

shared and tried to convince myself to eat, but I couldn't. Today was so messed up. I had no appetite.

I was just sitting at the table staring at my food until I felt a tap on my shoulder.

"You might wanna eat if you want those ribs to heal," Jaelyn said as she sat next to me.

"I can't," I said.

"It's not that bad," she said jokingly. "School food is only ninety-eight percent trash."

I couldn't help but laugh a little bit.

"Stop making me laugh," I said. "My ribs don't like it."

"Sorry, ribs," she said jokingly while looking at my side.

"I'm gonna punch you," I said.

She laughed and looked at me.

"I'm sorry," she said seriously.

"About what?" I said, confused. "The ribs are gonna be fine."

"I heard about you and Ezra," she said.

"I think everyone has," I sighed.

"I'm not taking sides, but from what I heard, I don't think I'm against Ezra," she said. "All she wants is the truth."

"I know," I said. "I wish I could tell you and her, but it's not safe."

"Then make it safe," she said. "I may be stuck with you, but Ezra's not. She can easily leave you, and I don't want that for you. You guys make a good pair, and I'd hate to see your friendship end because of a stupid decision you made."

"I don't know how to make it safe, though," I explained.

"Try to end whatever it is you're doing," she said. "Get the ending and complete this before you lose her forever."

"That's not a bad idea," I said. "I might try it."

"Well, good," she said. "And when you do end it, be sure to fill me in too. I'm just as curious as Ezra."

"Will do," I said.

Jaelyn looked at me and smiled.

"I gotta go," she said. "Do whatever you need to do."

"I will," I said.

Jaelyn patted me on the back and walked away.

As I watched her walk away, I figured out exactly what I had to do to possibly end this madness.

All I had to do to stop the VK and end this all was to get evidence to the police station proving their guilt, and I knew exactly where I was going to get it, Mr. Smith's classroom.

Mr. Smith may be part of the VK, but he's not the brightest. He keeps those papers filled with the evidence in the same spot even though I've tried to take them several times.

So to end this, I will take them again, only this time I will be successful. I will go into his classroom at the end of school and quickly grab the papers before he even notices I'm in there. After that, I will run out to the car and tell Jaelyn to drive to the police station. I'll give the papers to the police and explain what they are and finally end the VK's wrath. Emma Grace and all those kids will be saved, and it will be thanks to me. I'll be able to tell Ezra and Jaelyn what's been going on without them getting hurt, and everything will work out perfectly.

The rest of the school day was kind of a blur to me. I didn't pay attention at all. I was just thinking about my plan for the rest of the day. I was so excited to finally end this that my brain didn't even comprehend how badly my plan could go wrong.

After school, I waited by the lockers outside Mr. Smith's classroom, pretending to be getting my stuff when in reality, I was just waiting for him to walk out.

It only took a few minutes before I saw him finally leave his classroom.

I didn't wait a single second. As soon as he turned the corner, I bolted into his classroom. I ran behind the desk and instantly opened the drawer with the papers. As soon as I opened it I saw all the papers and pictures just sitting there. I instantly grabbed them and went to walk out when all of a sudden, I ran into Mr. Smith.

"What are you doing?" he asked me while pushing me back into the classroom.

"Getting my work," I said.

"What assignment?" he asked me, knowing I was full of it.

"The one we got today," I said.

"That's weird," he said. "I didn't give an assignment today, and even if I did, you wouldn't know given the fact you haven't attended my class for quite a while."

"I wonder why," I said sarcastically.

"Hand them over," he said sternly.

"I'm good," I said jokingly.

"You still don't understand the seriousness of what you're trying to do," he said.

"I think I do," I said. "I've gotten my ass kicked plenty of times because of this. I think I know it's important."

"Then stop trying to stop us," he said. "'Cause this will only end badly for you. Winning isn't an option when you're a fifteen-year-old against a bunch of grown adults."

"It is," I said. "And that's what I'm going to do."

While Mr. Smith was comprehending what I had just said, I attempted to bolt out of the classroom, but it was no use. He tackled me down and grabbed my legs. He dragged me back away from the door and shut it.

"Let me out!" I screamed.

"Give me the papers!" he screamed back at me.

"Let me end this!" I screamed. "This is ruining my life!"

"I gave you many opportunities to end this, Aaron," he said. "You're just an idiot and wouldn't take any of them."

"None of those opportunities offered justice for the kids you've kidnapped and tortured!" I screamed.

"Those kids won't get justice, just like you," he said sternly.

Before I could respond, Mr. Smith grabbed me by the shoulders and threw me into the whiteboard.

"You could've lived through this, Aaron," Mr. Smith said. "You just chose not to."

Mr. Smith slowly started walking over to me. I quickly stood up and looked around to see if there was anything I could use to defend myself. To my luck, I saw a trophy sitting on his desk that was not one of the cheap ones. I grabbed it and looked to see it labeled #1 teacher, which was very ironic.

I quickly swung it at his head, but it didn't help.

I looked up at him to see a gash on his head dripping blood, but he didn't seem phased at all.

"Nice try, Cripple," he said.

Mr. Smith quickly yanked the trophy out of my hand and smacked me with it. I instantly fell back down to the ground.

I quickly turned around to see what he was doing.

"I'll enjoy this," he said as he pulled out a huge pocket knife.

"Don't do anything stupid," I said in a stern voice.

He just looked at me and smiled.

With the blood dripping down his face and his knife in hand, he officially looked like a villain you'd see in the movies.

Mr. Smith moved closer to my face and stabbed the knife

right through the floor next to my head. I couldn't help but let out a scream.

Mr. Smith quickly covered my mouth and leaned closer to me.

"Be quiet, and maybe I won't make your death that painful," he whispered.

He moved his hand off my mouth and down to my throat. He ripped the knife out of the floor and held it above my face.

I looked at it in horror. I didn't know what to do.

"Please," I said in a quiet voice. "I'm fifteen and I haven't lived long enough. I have a family with two sisters and a mother that's already lost enough. Please don't make her plan her son's funeral."

"I know all of this," he said. "So telling me it won't spare your life."

Mr. Smith moved his hand back over my mouth and lowered the knife to my throat.

"Bye, Aaron," he said with a grin.

As Mr. Smith was about to slit my throat and end it all, I heard a familiar voice yell from behind him.

"Leave him alone!" the voice screamed.

At that moment, someone from behind smacked Mr. Smith over the head with a fire extinguisher.

He instantly fell back and revealed my hero, Jaelyn.

"What are you doing here?" I asked while slowly standing up.

"Saving your life apparently," she answered me.

"Thanks," I said while trying to catch my breath. "We have to go now."

"Okay," she said. "I need some explanation, though. Like why was our science teacher literally about to murder you?"

"I'll answer everything in the car," I said while running down the halls.

We quickly made it outside and into the car.

Jaelyn started the car and looked at me.

"So, where are we going?" she asked.

"The police station," I said. "I gotta give them these."

"What are those?" she asked me while beginning to drive out of the parking lot.

"They're papers that'll hopefully save a lot of people," I said.

"Okay," she said, confused. "While I speed to the police station, give me a quick explanation as to what's happening."

I did as Jaelyn asked and quickly told her everything. I told her about the VK and how they have so many people held hostage, including Emma Grace. I told her how I've been trying to stop them for the longest time.

I also told her how I was scared she'd get hurt if I had told her sooner.

Once I was done telling her, she froze for a second; she was in disbelief.

"This is so dangerous," she said.

"I'm aware," I said. "I just felt responsible for saving those kids."

"Well, I hope this works and you're crowned a hero," she said.

I smiled and looked away. I couldn't believe how close I was to ending all of this. Everything seemed to be going great until we had to drive through a neighborhood.

"Are you kidding me?" Jaelyn screamed out of the blue.

"What?" I said, alarmed.

"This idiot behind me is riding my ass," she said, annoyed.

"Just speed up," I said. "We're in a hurry anyway."

"It's twenty miles per hour for a reason," she said. "Kids play in the streets."

"I see no kids, Jaelyn. Step on it!" I shouted at her.

"Fine," she said, annoyed.

Jaelyn stepped on the gas and quickly started speeding. Her speed was doubling by the second, but I was in such a hurry that I didn't care.

"What the hell?" Jaelyn said, confused.

"What?" I said.

"I'm doing nearly fifty through this neighborhood, and this guy is still on my ass," she said.

I turned around to see the truck driver giving us a cold stare.

"Is he flipping us off?" she asked.

"No," I said. "He just looks pissed,"

"I'm flipping him off," she said.

"Jaelyn," I said.

"Let me have this," she said, annoyed.

"Fine," I said.

Jaelyn turned around and flipped the driver off. I laughed to myself and turned to look back at the road to see the last thing I expected.

"Kids!" I screamed at the top of my lungs.

Jaelyn quickly turned around and slammed on the brakes.

We sat there for a second, comprehending what had just happened.

"That was too close," she said with a shaky voice.

"It's okay," I said. "You didn't hit anyone."

"I almost did, though," Jaelyn said while still freaking out.

"Jaelyn, calm down. It's okay," I said while patting her shoulder.

I looked out Jaelyns window to see the truck driver speeding around us.

"At least that idiot's gone," I said, relieved.

"Yeah," she said while pulling herself together. "Now let's go finish your mission."

Jaelyn was about to start driving again when all of a sudden she froze.

"Is that truck coming at us in reverse, or am I just crazy?" she asked.

I looked out the window to see exactly what Jaelyn was talking about.

"Shit," I said to myself. "He is. Reverse back. We cannot get hit!"

"Okay," Jaelyn said worriedly. "Watch out the front window and tell me if he gets too close."

"Okay," I said.

Jaelyn quickly started reversing back through the neighborhood. I wanted to be able to tell her that she could stop reversing, but I couldn't. This guy was insane. It was like he was trying to kill us.

After a few moments, a thought crept into my mind.

"Jaelyn, this guy might be part of the VK," I said.

"Why do you say that?" she asked me while still reversing through the neighborhood.

"He's obviously out to get us," I said. "I'm sorry, Jaelyn, I'm gonna be the reason we die."

"Aaron, stop worrying yourself," she said. "This guy is just probably having a weird episode of road rage."

"I hope you're right," I said.

We had to reverse until we were completely out of the neighborhood. This idiot was literally making us go backwards.

Once we got out of the neighborhood, Jaelyn quickly pulled over to the side of the road and let the guy drive by.

I watched the guy look back at us and smile before he started going forward again.

"Asshole," Jaelyn said to herself.

As Jaelyn was about to start going again, I looked out my window to see a horrifying image.

A truck was coming directly at us with no signs of slowing down or stopping…

Chapter 19

"Jaelyn, drive!" I shouted as I looked back at her.

"I'm trying to!" she shouted back at me while trying to start the car. "It's not working!"

I looked back out the window to see the truck getting closer, still with no signs of slowing down or stopping.

"We're gonna die," I said to myself.

Then Jaelyn looked up out my window and saw exactly what I saw.

She quickly turned back and tried to start the car again, but it wasn't working.

"Start, you piece of junk!" Jaelyn screamed at the car.

"We have to get out," I said.

I went to open my door, but it wouldn't budge.

"Jaelyn, unlock the door!" I shouted at her.

"It is unlocked!" she shouted back at me. "Why is everything going wrong!"

"I'm sorry, Jaelyn," I said. "This is all my fault."

"It's okay," she said. "I love you, Aaron. Now cover your head. This isn't going to feel good."

I shook my head at Jaelyn. I knew she was right. I just hoped that we'd make it out of this.

I looked out the window one final time before covering my head.

The truck quickly slammed into us. Everything happened so fast, but at the same time, it seemed to play out in slow motion.

The door on my side caved in from the impact, and then the car flew through the air spinning out of control.

While in the air, I briefly looked over at Jaelyn and saw how she was scared for her life. I looked out my window and felt like I was a hundred feet in the air; this felt unreal.

It was my side of the car that hit the ground first.

The window on my door shattered instantly and sent glass everywhere. Once we were on the ground, the car continued to roll for a solid minute before it landed up on its wheels.

Once the car was still, I looked over at Jaelyn.

"Jaelyn?" I said with a shaking voice. "Are you okay?"

"I think so," she said quietly. "Are you okay?"

"I think I am," I said.

We quickly looked at each other and just took a sigh of relief. I was glad Jaelyn was okay, and I think she was glad I was too.

"Avoid a mirror for a couple of days," Jaelyn said jokingly.

"Is it that bad?" I said while laughing to myself.

"You got one scratch," Jaelyn said while pretending to sound worried.

"Oh no! I'm probably gonna die," I said jokingly.

Even though we almost died, Jaelyn and I couldn't help but laugh a little bit. We always made horrible situations funny. It was how we dealt with trauma, which could be seen as weird.

"I better look at the car," Jaelyn said. "You call Mom and Carl."

"Why me?" I said as she got out.

"'Cause this is my car," she said.

"Fair enough," I said. "Where's your phone?"

"Use yours," she said while starting to look at the car.

"Mine's at the school," I said. "I was intending to grab it

after my easy mission."

"Of course," she said. "My phone's in the middle console."

"Okay," I replied.

I opened up the middle console and found her phone. I pulled it out and tried to unlock it, but I quickly realized she had changed the password.

"Jaelyn! What's the password?" I shouted at her.

Jaelyn stuck her head back in the car and looked at me.

"Just give me the phone," she said.

"We almost died, and you can't tell your brother the password?" I said.

"Give me my phone," she said, annoyed.

"Fine," I said as I rolled my eyes.

As I was about to give Jaelyn her phone, I noticed someone's hand trying to grab her shoulder.

"Jaelyn!" I shouted at her.

Jaelyn quickly turned her head and saw a tall man standing next to her. She instantly screamed and stumbled backward.

"Sorry," the guy said. "I didn't mean to scare you."

The guy put his hand out and helped Jaelyn up.

"I'm Steve. I saw what happened up there. Are you kids okay?" he asked Jaelyn calmly.

"I think so," she said. "We're just trying to get hold of our parents."

"Okay," he said. "If you need any help, I'd be more than happy to do my part."

"Thank you, but I think we're okay," Jaelyn said.

"Okay then, have a nice day," Steve said as he walked away.

Jaelyn quickly looked back at me and gave me a hand signal to hand her the phone.

"You don't love me," I said jokingly.

"You are dramatic," she said. "Now give me my phone."

I went to hand her the phone when suddenly we heard a loud gunshot echo through the air.

"What was that?" I said, alarmed.

"I don't know," Jaelyn said while looking around.

While Jaelyn was looking around, she quickly noticed where the gunshot came from.

"Steve!" Jaelyn shouted as she ran away from the car.

Jaelyn!" I shouted and got out of the car.

I ran around the car and up the hill, following Jaelyn.

Eventually, I saw her bend down over Steve's lifeless body.

I ran up behind her and looked down at him.

"I'm gonna go get help," Jaelyn said with a shaking voice. "You see if he's alive."

Jaelyn quickly ran farther up the hill and left me with Steve. I looked down at him and felt sick. His chest was covered in blood, and his eyes were glistening in the sunlight.

I squatted down next to him and tried to feel a pulse, but there was nothing. He was gone.

I sat next to him, waiting for Jaelyn, until I heard another gunshot. Instantly I feared that Jaelyn was hurt.

I quickly stood up and bolted the way Jaelyn went only moments ago.

I ran so fast I couldn't even comprehend what I was running past.

I ran and ran until I saw my worst fear laying only inches away from me.

"Jaelyn!" I screamed as I ran over to her.

I bent down next to her and looked into her eyes.

"Jaelyn. Please talk to me," I said as I grabbed her hand.

"Don't leave me."

Jaelyn squeezed my hand and looked at me.

"You're gonna be okay," I said as tears filled my eyes.

She looked at me as her eyes began to fill with tears. She shook her head and moved her hand to my face.

"It's okay," she said quietly. "I'll get to see Dad again."

"Jaelyn, you're gonna be fine," I said with a shaking voice. "You're gonna get help, and you'll be okay."

I moved my hand to her chest and tried to stop the bleeding, but it was no use.

She used her hand on my face to wipe away some of my tears. She looked at me and smiled.

"Thank you for being an amazing brother," she said while she began to cry. "I'm sorry I won't get to grow up with you."

"Jaelyn, stop," I said while continuing to cry. "You're gonna be okay. I'll get to meet your kids, and you'll meet mine. We'll both graduate and become adults. I'll start driving you places. It'll be great."

Jaelyn looked at me with tears running down her face. She knew she wasn't going to make it.

"We will in our next lives," she said. "I'm sorry."

Jaelyn's eyes slowly began to close, and her hand fell down to the ground.

"No!" I screamed. "We were supposed to live till we were fifty, together. You can't leave me! You pinky promised!"

I looked down at her and went to feel her pulse.

She was gone, and there was nothing I could do.

My head fell on top of her. I couldn't help but cry even harder.

I thought losing my dad was hard, but this was even worse.

I lay on top of her, crying until I heard someone speak

behind me.

"I warned you, Aaron," the voice said from behind me. "I told you what would happen if you kept messing with us, but you didn't listen, and now here we are."

I turned around to see Mr. Smith standing behind me with a gun in his hand.

"You monster!" I screamed. "She was your student! And you killed her! What kind of teacher are you!"

I stood up and stormed over to him, getting ready to kill him, when suddenly he pointed his gun at me.

"I'm the kind of teacher that doesn't like high school kids snooping through my stuff!" he shouted at me. "This wasn't how everything was supposed to play out."

"What went wrong?" I shouted. "'Cause if I were you, this would be perfect! You killed a kid, and you're getting ready to kill another! Congrats!"

"You were both supposed to die in the car," he said. "We kept the car engine off and doors shut for a reason."

"You did that?" I said in denial.

"Your death was supposed to be quick and painless," he said. "But now it has to be slow and painful."

Mr. Smith slowly started walking closer to me with his gun still pointed at me.

I started walking backward, but it didn't seem to help.

"For the record, Aaron, your sister was the first student of mine that I actually killed. So I'm not that bad," he said.

"You're right," I said angrily. "It's not bad. It's terrible! You're a monster!"

"I have to do my job, Aaron," he said. "It doesn't matter who I hurt. Kid or not, and you can't do anything about it. I'm the adult here, and you're just a worthless kid who no one will miss."

I just stood there, not able to respond. He was right in some ways. I was the kid; what could I possibly do now? My sister was dead, and I was about to join her.

Mr. Smith kept walking toward me while I kept backing away. He looked at me and laughed.

"You can't run from a bullet, Aaron," he said. "Your sister tried, and look at her now. She's dead, and you could've prevented this. I just want you to know that."

"I didn't shoot her!" I shouted. "I'm not the murderer! I didn't have control of the gun!"

"That is true," he said. "But you provoked the murderer into doing this crime, so technically it all falls back on you!"

I stood there for a second, comprehending what he said. I didn't want to agree with him, but he was right. This was my fault.

Jaelyn had so much to live for, and because of my stupid actions, her life was over. She's gonna be in a coffin underground when she's supposed to be graduating high school and dominating the world.

"Now that you feel worthless, maybe this won't be as hard on me," Mr. Smith said with a slight chuckle. "I'll just be putting you out of your misery."

I looked down to the ground as tears began to fill my eyes.

I guess it was my turn to pay for my actions. I deserved this fate.

I looked up at Mr. Smith to see him pull the trigger. I closed my eyes tightly and prepared myself for the worst. I stood there for a second, waiting to feel a sharp pain, but nothing happened. I looked up to see a bullet being levitated right in front of me again.

"Tyler?" I said, confused.

"Wrong, Jay kid!" I heard someone shout from behind me. I turned around to see Tyler's dad standing right behind me.

"Why'd you save me?" I asked, confused.

"I saved you because Donald over there forgot the half of the plan that comes before your death!" Tyler's dad shouted.

"I didn't forget. I just ignored it, Antonio!" Mr. Smith screamed at Tyler's dad.

"Well, that's selfish!" Antonio screamed at Mr. Smith.

While Antonio and Mr. Smith were arguing, I decided to try and make a run for it. I bolted back towards the car.

I knew if I was going to make it out of this, I needed to get help from the authorities.

I ran and ran until I made it to the car. I quickly opened the door and grabbed Jaelyn's phone.

Since I didn't know the password, I switched over to an emergency call on her phone and dialed 911.

I quickly moved the phone to my ear and waited until I heard someone on the other end.

"Hello, this is 911 operator Mariam. How may I help you?"

"Hi, Mariam, I'm Aaron, and these guys are insane. They killed my sister and are trying to kill me. Please help."

"Okay, Aaron, where are you?"

"At the bottom of some hill. I'm not sure."

"That's okay; I'm getting your location now. Just stay on the line."

"Okay."

I stood there frantically waiting for Mariam to say the police were on their way, but it seemed like it was taking ages.

"Mariam, are they coming?"

"Aaron, you need to calm down. Everything's going to be okay."

I wanted to yell at her so bad, but I knew she was just doing her job.

I would sound like a real asshole if I just started yelling at her.

I stood there waiting for her when all of a sudden I saw Mr. Smith running at me.

"Mariam, hurry! I'm gonna die!"

Before Mariam could respond, Mr. Smith tried to shoot me again. Luckily it hit the car instead of me, but it made me drop the phone and run away.

I hid behind the other side of the car, waiting for either Mr. Smith or the police to find me.

"Nice try calling 911 Aaron," Mr. Smith said while slowly walking over to me. "I don't think they'll be able to save you, though."

"He's right," I heard Antonio say from the other side of me.

That was the moment I realized I was trapped. I stood there frozen while they both walked around the car towards me.

"How should we handle this?" Mr. Smith asked Antonio.

"I'll get him," Antonio said to Mr. Smith. "You bring the van over here. I have a feeling this will be a little bit of a challenge."

I watched as Mr. Smith walked away and Antonio walked towards me. I went to run away, but I was quickly stopped by an energy blast to the back. I flew down to the ground quickly.

As I lay on the ground, I heard Antonio walk toward me.

"I'll make you a deal," he said. "If you cooperate, I'll tell the VK to let the rest of your family live."

I slowly lifted my head and looked back at him.

"You don't even know who my family is," I said weakly.

"I do, actually," he said. "It's been a while, but I know them."

"How?" I said while standing up.

"I had a daughter who grew up in your class," he said. "I was at every stupid class party you ever had. I saw your mom with your stepdad, and of course, I saw little Effie."

"You wouldn't dare hurt them!" I shouted.

"I watched Jaelyn die," he said. "Why wouldn't I watch any more of your family members die?"

At that moment, Mr. Smith drove a van up to us and honked the horn.

"Hurry up!" he shouted at us. "I heard sirens a few blocks back."

Antonio looked at me and smiled.

"This is the time where you choose your family member's fates," he said.

I looked up at him with fear in my eyes.

Right now, I had two choices. I could run and hope the police got here in time, or I could cooperate with them and hope that my family would be safe.

It was a tough choice, but it was one I knew I had to make.

Before I had the chance to make my choice, though, I felt a sharp pain in the back of my head. I fell backward and looked up to see Antonio and some random guy looking down at me.

"Nice job," Antonio said to the guy. "This'll be much easier if he's knocked out."

Antonio looked down at me and smiled.

"Nighty night Aaron," he said.

Before I was able to say anything back, I blacked out. Just like he wanted...

Chapter 20

I woke up with sharp pains all over my body. My head throbbed, and my side ached.

I tried to recall how I got here, but I couldn't.

As I looked around, I realized I was in some type of cell. It was dark and cold. The walls appeared to be made out of stone, while the floor was constructed of concrete.

I sat up and looked around a little more, but the only thing I was able to spot was a bucket. I knew why it was there, but I didn't want to admit that.

I quickly decided to stand up and walk around my little cell.

Standing up was harder than I thought it'd be, though. All my bones and muscles screamed at me to sit back down, but I had to ignore them.

Once I stood up and got balanced, I decided to walk over to the bars of my cell to see if I could see anyone.

The walk was painful but necessary.

Once I got over to the bars, I held onto them for support. I looked out of my cell to see a guy sleeping next to a TV.

"Hello!" I shouted. "Are you alive?"

The guy quickly jumped awake and looked at me.

"You're alive?" he said, confused.

"Last time I checked," I said. "Now tell me why I'm here."

"I honestly have no idea," the guy said. "They brought you in and just threw you in that little cell."

"Who brought me in?" I shouted.

"Donald and Antonio," he said.

"Why?" I shouted again.

"I said I didn't know!" He shouted.

"Well, if you don't know, then you can let me out," I said. "For all you know, I'm innocent."

"You saying that makes me think you murdered someone," he said. "You're staying in there until I say otherwise."

"Until you say otherwise?" I said, confused. "Last time I checked, you were very clueless. I'm guessing that maybe you work for Mr. Smith and Antonio. You need some kind of guidance, apparently."

"Ouch," he said.

"Am I wrong?" I asked.

"No," he said. "But I'm not taking shit from a twelve-year-old."

"I'm not twelve!" I shouted.

"Then why'd you call Donald, Mr. Smith?" he asked.

"Because that idiot used to be my science teacher," I said.

"He teaches high school science," he said. "Aren't you a middle schooler?"

"I'm a sophomore in high school," I said, annoyed.

"Well, you look like a child," he said.

"I know that," I said. "Now let the child out, and maybe you won't go to jail."

"No can do high school baby," he said.

"Don't you dare start calling me high school baby!" I shouted.

"I won't, cranky high school baby," he said.

"If I weren't stuck in here, I'd kick your ass!" I shouted.

He rolled his eyes and looked away from me.

"Don't look away!" I shouted.

Right at that moment, my ribs decided to remind me that they were broken. I grabbed my side and bent down, trying to control my breathing again.

The guy looked back at me and saw me struggling on the ground.

"You good high school baby?" he asked.

"Stop calling me that," I said quietly.

The guy walked over to my cell and bent down next to me.

"I would call you your name if I knew it," he said.

"Aaron," I said quietly.

"Well, Aaron, I'm Oliver," he said. "Now, why do you look and sound like you're dying?"

I looked up at Oliver and was about to answer when I suddenly saw Antonio walking in.

"Ask him," I said while pointing to Antonio.

Oliver quickly stood up and walked over to Antonio.

"So why do you have a high school kid held hostage?" Oliver asked Antonio.

"That's none of your concern," Antonio said to Oliver.

"I think it is," Oliver said to Antonio. "I have the power to release him, and I need to know why I shouldn't."

"Well, Aaron decided to get into our business," Antonio answered. "Don't let him convince you he deserves anything better than what he's getting."

"He's in pain, Antonio," Oliver said. "The least we can do is help him."

"I know he's in pain," Antonio said. "I'm the one who caused it."

"That's nothing to be proud of," Oliver said.

"You're an idiot!" Antonio shouted. "I got better things to do than to help a kid who's going to be killed in a few days."

Oliver stood there and looked at Antonio with a disgusted look on his face.

"I'm gonna go now," Antonio said to Oliver. "Don't you dare let that kid out!"

"Yes, sir," Oliver said to Antonio.

Antonio walked over to my cell and looked down at me.

"You deserve what's coming to you, and you know that," he said. "Now stop making my workers feel bad for you."

"Why am I even here?" I asked. "Why didn't you just let me die?"

"That would've been no fun," he said. "And I also need something from you."

"What could I possibly have that you want?" I asked, confused.

"You'll see," he said as he began to walk away.

I watched Antonio walk out of the room before turning my head back toward Oliver.

"Do you still think I'm guilty?" I asked.

"My opinion doesn't matter," he said. "I have to do what my boss says."

"No, you don't," I said. "You are an independent man. You can make your own decisions."

"I know that," he said. "And listening to my boss is the decision I'm making."

Oliver sat back down on his chair and turned the TV volume up.

"Oliver, please!" I shouted. "You were gonna help me. That doesn't have to change."

"Shut up!" he shouted. "You're not my problem to deal with!"

"I can be!" I shouted. "Pretend I'm your child for like five minutes, please."

"No!" he screamed. "Besides, my kids look nothing like you."

"So you have kids," I said. "Do you think they'd like it if their dad just let someone suffer?"

"Zip it!" he screamed. "My kids like to have food on their plate, and that's all that matters! So please stay quiet before I lose this job!"

I looked at him and shook my head. He turned back around and turned on the news channel. I ignored it until I heard my name. I quickly pulled myself up off the floor and watched the TV.

"Sad day here in Rayburn, Tennessee," said the news lady. "Tragedy struck here late afternoon yesterday. Two people were found dead, and one was reported missing. Officers arrived yesterday at the crime scene after getting a 911 call from a young teenage boy. In his call, the boy stated how mysterious men had murdered his sister and were now after him. The call was quickly ended when the boy was shot at. Officers couldn't figure out what happened to the boy, but they did figure out that his sister and another person were, in fact, killed. The families of the lost ones are left heartbroken, and we wish the best for them. As for the boy, we hope that he finds his way home. Back to you, Simion."

After the news lady finished, I looked down. Tears filled my eyes all over again. I knew Jaelyn was dead but hearing it officially announced just broke me.

"You were that boy, weren't you?" Oliver asked.

"Yeah," I said while trying not to cry.

"I'm sorry for your loss," he said.

"It doesn't matter," I said. "She was just my annoying

sister. Everyone dies."

"Don't pretend you don't care," he said. "That doesn't help anything."

"I know," I said. "I just can't believe she's gone."

Oliver walked over to me and sighed.

"Sorry I yelled at you," he said.

"It's fine," I said while wiping away my tears.

"If I had no family, I'd let you out in a heartbeat," he said. "But I gotta do this for them."

"I get it," I said. "My stepdad would do anything to get some money right now. It's hard to get a stable job with no cons."

"That is true," he said. "Your stepdad sounds nice."

"He used to be," I said. "Something changed about him, though. He's a completely different person."

"Why do you say that?" Oliver asked.

"He tried to kill me," I said.

"What?" Oliver said, confused. "Doesn't he love you?"

"I thought he did," I said. "I guess not, though."

The second I said that, Oliver froze and went into deep thought.

"What's your stepdad's name?" he asked.

"Carl," I said, confused.

"Carl what?" he asked quickly.

"Carl Davis," I said, still confused.

"Oh my god," he said quietly.

"What?" I said, alarmed.

"He didn't hurt you willingly," Oliver said.

"What?" I said confused. "How do you know that?"

"Well, not that long ago, I overheard Antonio saying how he tested this pill on a guy named Carl Davis," Oliver explained.

"He said the pill would make him lose it on the last person he was angry at, which I'm guessing was you. Antonio also said how the guy could be useful in getting rid of a nuisance, and since he seems to despise you, concluding you are the nuisance seems reasonable."

I looked at Oliver with shock in my eyes.

"At least you know your stepdad doesn't actually want you dead," Oliver said.

"Yeah," I said quietly.

Oliver looked at me and put his hand on my shoulder through the bars.

"I gotta go sit back down, Aaron," he said. "Antonio's probably gonna be back soon, and I gotta pretend I'm a heartless bastard."

I laughed to myself.

"Okay," I said. "Have fun."

Oliver started to walk away when all of a sudden, he stopped in his tracks.

"You good?" I asked.

Oliver didn't answer me; he just stared to the right.

I tried to see what he saw but I couldn't.

"I told you to stay away from him!" I heard someone shout.

"I'm sorry, boss," Oliver said anxiously.

At that moment, I realized Antonio had been watching us.

"You got one more chance before I send you up to help film the weekly videos!" Antonio shouted. "Now, go take your break so I can talk to that idiot."

Oliver just shook his head and walked away.

I stood there anxiously waiting for Antonio to walk over to me. I was able to hear his footsteps as he slowly approached me, which didn't help my nerves.

"You don't like to listen, do you?" he asked.

"We were just talking," I said. "That TV can only be entertainment for so long."

Antonio's eyes filled with rage. He used powers and lifted me slightly off the ground.

"You're here as a prisoner!" he screamed at me. "You're not supposed to be entertained!"

"I'm sorry," I said in a shaking voice.

Antonio looked at me and dropped me. I attempted to land on my feet but failed. Instead, I landed flat on my back.

"Next time, I won't be so nice," Antonio said.

He walked out of the room while I just lay there.

I sat up and took a deep breath.

I didn't exactly want to die, but at this point, I wished that I would've just died next to Jaelyn. That would've been much easier for everyone.

I sat in my cell, counting the stains on the wall for a good hour before hearing someone say my name.

"Aaron?" I heard someone call out my name.

I quickly stood up and walked over to the bars so I could see who was calling me.

I was very surprised when I saw Mr. Smith walking over to me with a smile on his face.

"What do you want?" I asked with an annoyed tone.

"I got some great news," he said.

"What is it?" I asked, confused.

"School was amazing," he said.

"Okay?" I said, confused.

"Do you wanna know what we did?" he asked.

"Sure?" I answered him, confused.

"We had an assembly," he said.

"Fun?" I said, still confused.

"Do you wanna know what we did in the assembly?" he asked.

"Sure," I said in an annoyed tone.

Honestly, at this point, I had no idea what he was getting at. All I knew was that it was probably something that I wouldn't like.

"We told the student body about the Cripple tragedy," he said.

"What's that?" I asked, confused.

"It's what we're calling your disappearance and your sister's death," he explained. "You should've seen all the tears. It would've made you feel cared about."

"You're sick!" I shouted.

"I had to pretend I cared about you guys," he said. "Little do they know I'm the one who did it."

"You're gonna get caught," I said.

"Sure," he said with a slight chuckle. "Just for fun, do you want to know who had my favorite reaction to the Cripple tragedy?"

"No," I said.

"Too bad," he said. "Your little friend Ezra had a great reaction."

"We're not friends any more," I said. "Thanks to you."

"She still seemed pretty upset," he said. "During the assembly, she fell to her knees and broke down crying. She was hysterical. Apparently, she likes your family, so this was hard for her."

"You're an asshole!" I screamed. "I didn't need to know that!"

"Well, now you do," he said. "You'll die knowing that your

disappearance ruined many people's lives."

"Many?" I said, confused.

"Did you forget about your family?" he asked. "They had to come clean out Jaelyn's locker. It was quite funny watching them break down. The principal even tried to make them clean out your locker, but your mom refused. She was a hysterical mess."

I stood there in silence. My brain was just picturing Ezra and my family breaking down. I started to tear up myself before I snapped at Mr. Smith.

"Go away!" I screamed.

"Why?" he asked. "Do you not like hearing the truth?"

"I said go away!" I screamed as I punched his face through the bars.

"Ow!" he screamed as he moved backward. "That's gonna give me a black eye!"

"Good!" I screamed. "Maybe now you'll learn to shut your mouth!"

"You're gonna pay for this, you brat!" He screamed.

He quickly stormed off and left me there again with the mysterious stains on the wall.

I sat in my quiet cell in peace for a while before I heard a bunch of people running and screaming upstairs.

I stood up and walked over to the bars to see if anyone was there that could tell me what was happening, but I couldn't see anyone.

"Hello?" I shouted. "What's going on?"

No one answered me. I just stood there confused.

I listened closer to the screams seeing if I recognized any of them.

I didn't expect to, but the closer I listened, the more the

284

scream sounded like Emma Grace.

"Emma?" I shouted.

Again, I didn't get a response.

"Hello?" I screamed again. "Can anyone hear me?"

"Will you shut up!" Someone shouted at me.

I looked over to see Antonio coming down the stairs.

"What is going on up there?" I shouted.

"The weekly videos," he said.

"Is Emma Grace up there?" I asked.

He looked at me, confused, and walked over to me.

"Did you say, Emma Grace?" he asked.

"Yeah?" I said confused.

"How do you know her?" he shouted.

"She's my friend," I said. "I thought I heard her."

"You did," he said.

"Leave her alone," I said. "She's one of the sweetest people alive. She doesn't deserve whatever this is!"

"I don't care whether she deserves it or not," he said. "No one is going to make me release one of my prisoners, especially a kid."

Antonio gave me one last look before walking back upstairs.

I just stood there in shock.

I was glad Emma Grace was alive but to hear her scream was horrible. I just couldn't believe that the girl I had been trying to find was right above me. I felt so close yet so far. That night it was very hard for me to fall asleep, but when I finally did, it was far from peaceful. I was haunted by nightmares all night.

I had a nightmare with Jaelyn yelling at me, saying how everything was my fault. I had another one with Ezra and my family, and how they didn't want me back because of all the damage I caused. My last nightmare was with Emma Grace.

The dream seemed good at first. I saved Emma, and we were heading home when suddenly she got killed right in front of me. That night made me think my brain was out to get me.

I was just glad these dreams felt normal, though. They didn't feel like a warning. They were just my brain taunting me.

In between each dream, I woke up in a cold sweat. Each time, I didn't want to fall back asleep, but I always did.

The next morning I was exhausted. I didn't want to get up, but my survival instincts told me to. I woke up and heard my stomach going crazy. That's when I realized that I hadn't eaten in quite a long time. I quickly stood up and walked over to the bars to see if anyone was out there. I looked to see Oliver passed out in his chair.

"Oliver?" I said hesitantly.

I didn't want to get either of us in trouble, but I was starving.

"Oliver?" I said a little bit louder.

He was still sound asleep. I wanted him to wake up, but I didn't want to yell.

"Oliver?" I said louder.

Thankfully for me, Oliver shot awake. He turned around and looked at me.

"What do you want?" he asked me while rubbing his eyes.

"Food," I said.

"What makes you think I have any?" he asked.

"I don't know," I said. "Isn't there a food stash around here?"

"It's not for you," he said.

"Come on, Oliver," I said. "I haven't eaten in nearly two

286

days."

"That's not my problem," he said.

"Why are you so cold all of a sudden?" I asked.

"I want to keep my job," he said. "And I don't want to have to help film those horrible videos upstairs."

"Fine," I said. "Do you think they're just gonna starve me?"

"I have no clue," he said.

"Can you find out?" I asked.

"Do you want me to lose my job?" he asked, annoyed.

"Just ask if you're allowed to give me food," I said. "You can say I'm being annoying and won't stop shouting at you."

"Won't that get you in trouble?" he asked.

"Probably," I said. "But I don't care about that. I just want food."

"Fine," he said.

Oliver stood up and walked upstairs.

I just stood there waiting impatiently. I was so hungry; I'd literally eat anything at this point.

Oliver soon came back downstairs, followed by Antonio. He walked over to me and mouthed the words sorry. I was instantly able to tell why he was sorry. I wasn't mad, though. I told him to throw me under the bus. All he did was listen to me.

"I told you to stop talking to Oliver!" Antonio screamed as he walked over.

"Sorry," I said. "I was just hungry, and no one else was around."

"I don't care!" he screamed. "You disobeyed me!"

"You're not my parent," I said. "I don't need to obey you! Why don't you make your own kid obey you? She's obviously somewhere around here!"

"Don't talk about Morgan! He screamed. "You don't know

287

anything about her!"

"I know that she was in school until you said otherwise!" I screamed.

He just stood there for a moment and took a deep breath. He looked at me and his eyes turned bright green.

"What the hell," I said under my breath.

I looked at Antonio as his hand slowly filled with energy. He looked down at it and smiled.

"I love when idiots make me angry," he said. "It allows me to use my powers to the fullest."

He moved his hand up and pointed it in my direction. A line of green energy slowly came into my cell.

I watched it in horror as it behaved like a snake, following his every command. It floated through the air and slowly wrapped around my throat. It slowly got tighter and tighter. I tried to pull it off, but to my hands it was nothing but thin air.

Oliver was watching in horror as my face turned blue. I looked over at him and mouthed the word help. I didn't think he'd do anything, but he did.

Oliver ran over to Antonio and grabbed his arm.

"Leave him alone!" he screamed. "You're gonna kill him!"

"Why do you care?" Antonio asked him with a crazy look in his eyes.

Oliver was about to answer him honestly when all of a sudden, he thought of an answer that'd get us both out of this.

"You said you needed something from him," Oliver said. "If you kill him, you won't get that."

All of a sudden, realization came over Antonio. He quickly let me go, and I fell to the ground. He walked closer to the bars and squatted down.

"You are lucky I need something from you," he said.

Antonio stood up and walked away. The second Antonio was out of sight, Oliver ran over to the cell and looked at me.

"Are you okay?" he asked, looking worried.

"Yeah," I said as I sat up. "Thanks for the save."

"It's the least I could do," he said. "Sorry I threw you under the bus."

"It's fine," I said. "I'm the one who told you to."

"That is true," he said. "I'll just remind myself not to take advice from children."

"That sounds like a good idea," I laughed.

Oliver smiled and stood up.

"You remind me of my son," he said. "You sound a lot alike."

"He sounds nice," I said.

"He was," Oliver said.

"Was? Is he gone?" I asked him while standing up.

"He passed a year ago today," Oliver said.

"I'm sorry," I said.

"It's okay," he said. "He's in a better place, with your sister."

"I hope so," I said.

Oliver smiled and walked away.

I looked up and thought about how Jaelyn was probably watching over me and laughing at my stupidity. I missed her but having the feeling that she was watching me just made things a little bit brighter.

Chapter 21

The next few days went by very slowly.

They were mainly filled with pain and boredom.

I still wasn't allowed to have any food, which didn't help anything. Oliver was able to sneak me a bottle of water, but that was all I got. I guess he just wanted to see me at least survive a week or two.

I still had no idea why they hadn't just killed me yet, but honestly, I didn't know if I wanted to know. I was curious but also scared. These people were evil; they seemed like the kind of people who would cut off my head and leave it on display somewhere just for fun.

Throughout the next few days, I didn't see much of anyone. I didn't see Oliver, Antonio, or even Mr. Smith. It was odd but also kind of a relief. I was honestly starting to think that they had forgotten about me. It seemed that way until I saw Antonio again a few days later.

He walked past my cell and just looked at me with a sick smile before walking away. I thought it was kinda weird for him not to say anything but that wasn't a major concern of mine.

That afternoon I just started to count the stains on the ceiling. I had already finished counting those on the wall; there were a hundred twenty-seven stains.

This would seem like a sad activity to do for someone who's at home with a normal life, but for me, it seemed fairly normal. It was one of the only things I could do.

I actually got pretty far in counting that afternoon, and

honestly, I probably would've finished if I wasn't interrupted halfway through.

As I was counting the stains on the ceiling, I heard the sound of my cell opening. I looked over to see Antonio, Mr. Smith, and a few other guys walking in. I quickly stood up and looked at them with a look of confusion.

"What's going on?" I asked them in a worried voice.

They didn't answer me; they just slowly walked closer. I quickly bent down and grabbed the bucket off the floor. It was empty, but they didn't know that.

I held it up and pretended I was about to splash them with something they wouldn't like.

"Stay away from me!" I shouted at them while holding the bucket.

Antonio looked at me with an annoyed look, while everyone else just looked disgusted.

The guy with the most disgusted look turned to Antonio and shouted, "If I get this kid's pee on my face, I'm quitting!"

"Calm down, Mike!" Antonio shouted. "Aaron won't do anything. He's an idiot."

"You wanna take that chance?" I shouted while moving the bucket.

"I'm not doing this," Mike said.

"Yes, you are!" Antonio screamed. "He's a kid. We can handle this."

"Are you sure about that?" I asked. "I heard from my mommy I'm a real handful."

"You shut up!" Antonio shouted at me.

"I'll grab him," Mr. Smith said to them. "I'm not afraid of some pee."

"That's a bad idea," I said.

"All of this is a bad idea," he said. "Now, please make my life easy."

Mr. Smith started to walk over to me when I decided to take action. I quickly swung the bucket right into his head. The combination between the metal bucket and my scaredy-cat force caused him to black out. I looked up and saw everyone looking at me with horrified looks on their faces.

"Anyone else?" I screamed at them. "I'll gladly knock you all out!"

I stood there still holding the bucket while waiting for a response.

"Cute move, Aaron," Antonio said, annoyed.

Antonio started to walk over to me when all of a sudden, Mike grabbed his arm.

"This kid's gonna kill us all," Mike said. "Let's just leave."

"He hasn't killed anyone," Antonio said, annoyed. "And he won't kill anyone. He's not strong enough."

Antonio ripped his arm out of Mike's grip and started to walk over to me.

"It's hard to win, Aaron, when you're against someone who can do things you couldn't even imagine," he said.

Antonio looked at me and lifted me with his powers. He moved me forward and then threw me against the wall. It felt like I just landed on water from a hundred feet in the air, back first.

The bucket flew out of my hand, and I fell to the ground. I looked up to see a smile appear on his face.

"I told you he was no threat," Antonio said to them.

"What do you even want from me?" I asked him while trying to sit up.

"I need your little power," he said.

"My what?" I asked, confused.

"You know what I mean," he said.

"No, I don't," I said. "I can't make things fly through the air or anything like that."

"I know that," he said. "But you can do something I can't."

"And what is that?" I asked, still confused.

"You can predict the future," he said. "And I want to be able to do that too."

I froze for a second. I didn't think that those dreams meant anything. Sure they predicted things, but I thought they were just coincidences. I thought they were some kind of power at first, but Morgan shut down that thought of mine real quick.

Was she wrong?

"Aaron, we can either do this the easy way or the hard way," Antonio said while looking down at me.

"I still don't understand what you're supposed to get from me," I said, annoyed.

Antonio looked at me with anger in his eyes.

"How'd you get this little trick of yours?" he demanded.

"I don't know!" I shouted. "Honestly, I think it's just a coincidence. I wasn't put under experiments like some people! I'm a normal high schooler who just had a few strange dreams."

"You know this isn't a coincidence," he said sternly. "Now tell me how you are able to do this!"

"I don't know!" I screamed. "You can leave now!"

I stood up and got right in Antonio's face.

"You're going crazy," I said. "There's nothing special about me."

"We'll see about that," he said. "Grab him, Mike! I need to see if he's lying."

Mike slowly started to walk over to me. I looked at him

293

with a crazy look in my eyes.

"Don't come any closer!" I screamed. "You don't want to mess with me!"

Mike stopped and looked over at Antonio. It was funny how I was able to scare a grown man. He truly thought I was insane.

"You are a moron, Mike!" Antonio screamed. "He's a child."

I stood there laughing internally at Antonio and Mike arguing. It seemed like everything would go my way until I felt someone grab me from behind. I forgot there was a third person.

"Let go of me!" I screamed.

Antonio looked over and smiled at us.

"Nice work, Rex," he said as he walked over to us. "You're a much better worker than Mike."

I looked over at Mike to see him walking out. If he weren't a member of the VK, I probably would've felt bad for him.

Antonio got closer and closer to me until his face was only a few inches away from mine.

"Let's try and make this easy, okay?" he said.

Antonio lifted his hand to my forehead as it began to glow green. I knew what he was doing. He was gonna force the answers out of my mouth like he did only a week ago. I knew he wouldn't find much information out, though. He could only learn what I knew, and I didn't know much. As his hand made contact with my forehead, I felt the weird feeling of magic running through it all over again.

"First question, Aaron," he said. "Do you have powers?"

I looked at him as the answer came out of my mouth.

"I'm not sure."

Antonio looked at me, confused, before asking the second

question.

"Can you predict the future?" he asked.

"I have in two dreams in the past," I answered him.

"Only two?" he said, confused. "Why are you having these dreams?"

I looked at him and said the answer that was true to my mind.

"I don't know."

"You don't know?" he shouted, confused.

Antonio ripped his hand off my forehead, leaving me with a sharp pain in my head.

"How do you not know?" He screamed.

"These dreams just started happening," I said. "I don't know the cause."

Antonio looked at me for a second before putting his hand back on my head.

"You know!" he screamed. "I'm gonna figure it out!"

"I don't know!" I shouted as magic started running through my head again.

"Why can you predict the future?" he screamed.

"I don't know," I replied.

"He knows," Rex said to Antonio. "Just take your power up a notch. Maybe his brain is blocking it out."

Antonio did as Rex said and pumped more magic through my head. It felt like I had animals running around in my brain. It wasn't exactly painful, but it was very uncomfortable.

"Why do you have these powers?" he screamed again.

"I don't know!" I screamed back.

Antonio clearly wasn't taking *I don't know* for an answer. He pumped even more magic through my head. At this point, it was starting to cause me pain. I just tried to focus on breathing even though I didn't have control of my own mind.

"How'd you get powers?" he screamed. "Answer me!"

"I don't know," I cried out.

Antonio ripped his hand from my head and stormed off. He finally realized I didn't know.

Rex dropped me and followed behind him. I lay on the floor for a few minutes with the worst migraine of my life before I blacked out.

I woke up a few hours later to notice that Mr. Smith was gone, and my cell door was locked again. I sat up and rubbed my eyes. I had never passed out from a headache, so that was weird for me. I stood up cautiously and prepared myself to faint again.

Once I knew I was fine, I walked over and picked up the bucket. I moved it back to its corner. It just felt right. After I was done with that, I lay on the floor and started counting the ceiling stains again. I got pretty far before my eyes decided they needed to rest. Thankfully I was actually able to listen to them and finally doze off peacefully.

The last few days had left me more and more tired. I couldn't tell if it was because of my sleeping arrangement or the fact that I hadn't eaten in a while. I just knew it wasn't from any kind of activity. Counting does not make people that tired.

The next day I woke up expecting my day to be full of counting weird stains. I was thinking that I'd maybe move to a different wall today. That was my goal, at least. It seemed achievable until I got company.

About halfway through the day, Antonio and Rex came back to my cell. When I saw them, I panicked. I was only there for my so-called powers, and since they couldn't get them, I served no use any more. I instantly thought they were gonna kill me, but I was wrong. When they walked into the cell, Antonio looked at me and smiled.

"Take two," he said. "Let's see if you'll crack."

"What?" I said, confused.

In my moment of confusion, Rex came from behind me and grabbed me all over again.

"What's going on?" I shouted at Antonio.

"I'm getting my answers," he said.

When Antonio started walking up to me with his green glowing hand, I realized what was happening. He was gonna do the same thing he did yesterday to me, again. I guess he truly still thought I knew.

To Antonio's disappointment, today played out just like yesterday. I kept saying I didn't know, and eventually, he stopped. I got dropped to the floor and blacked out all over again.

I would love to say that this was the last time Antonio and Rex did this to me, but that was sadly not the case. They came back into my cell every single day for an entire week, doing the same thing over and over again. They hoped they would get a different result, but they never did.

The only thing that changed was the amount of time I was out for. Each day I would blackout for longer and longer.

By the end of the week, I was rarely awake. I spent most of my time blacked out on the concrete floor, and because of this, Antonio and Rex stopped bothering me. They had finally realized that I didn't know what they thought I did. It just sucked that it took me becoming half-dead for them to realize that.

I thought over the next few days I would get better and not sleep for twenty hours a day, but that sadly never happened.

At this point, I had accepted that I was finally dying. The

starvation and injuries were finally catching up to me. All it took was a little bit of magic to my head to push me over the edge. The edge of life.

Once I realized I wasn't going to get any better, I stopped standing up. I stopped talking to Oliver. I stopped begging for food and water. I just stopped living. I didn't have anything to live for. So why would I keep going?

Before I started to fade away, I was able to tell how many days had passed. I would hear the VK members upstairs throwing the kids their meal for that day, and I would know it was a new morning. I would hear them lock a million doors upstairs, and then I would know the day was over. I didn't listen for that any more. I had no reason to.

As I looked back on everything, I realized how close I was to actually making a difference in this crummy little world.

I was so close to stopping the VK and saving the love of my life.

As I began to feel everything shut down, I just hoped that Emma Grace would find a way out of this mess. I hoped she would get to continue her beautiful life and make the difference in the world I never could. I hoped she would find someone to treat her right and who she could happily grow old with. I hoped her story would have a happy ending and that this experience for her was just a bad chapter in her life. I wished the best for her because I loved her. I loved her so much…

Chapter 22

"Hello?" I heard a voice say as my cell door swung open.

As soon as I heard the voice I began to listen very closely.

"Are you okay?" the voice asked.

I couldn't tell much but I could tell this person was a girl. I heard her start to slowly walk up to me. I decided to just pretend I was asleep so she would hopefully leave me alone. I was already dying, I didn't need any more shit to top off my final days.

"Can you hear me?" the girl asked while grabbing my shoulder.

She carefully turned me over onto my back. I felt one of her hands move to my wrist.

"At least you're alive," I heard her say.

She moved a finger under my nose. It was starting to get hard to stay still, but in my mind, I had no choice.

"Alive and breathing," she said to herself. "That's a good sign."

She moved her hand back down to my shoulder and started lightly shaking me. She was obviously trying to wake me up, but I couldn't let her see me awake. I couldn't trust a stranger.

Maybe if I stayed still long enough, she would think I was in a coma and leave me alone, I thought to myself.

She continued to shake me for a few more minutes before getting up and walking out of my cell. I stayed still just in case, but I was glad she was gone.

I laid there peacefully for a few minutes before being forcefully woken up by a bucket of cold water to the face.

I quickly shot up from the ground and looked to see a young girl holding an empty bucket. I flew up on my feet and grabbed her shoulders. I pinned her against the wall and gave her a dirty look.

"Who are you?" I shouted. "What do you want from me?"

She stood there with a horrified expression on her face. She took a deep breath and looked up at me.

"You don't need to be scared of me," she said in a surprisingly calm voice. "I'm Ivy, Ivy Brown, and I'm here to help you."

I quickly let go of her and took a step backward. As I looked closer at her, I realized I recognized her. She was one of the kids the VK had taken. I recognized her from one of the many photos I saw in Mr. Smith's desk.

"You're one of the kids the VK took," I said. "How'd you get down here?"

"A vent broke upstairs," she said. "I was the person who volunteered to climb out and get help."

"So why are you here?" I asked. "Shouldn't you be going to find a police station?"

"Well, me and the kids upstairs voted for me to check on the boy downstairs, you," she explained.

"Is that actually what I'm known as?" I asked while quietly laughing to myself.

"Yeah," she said. "I mean, we don't know your name, so the boy downstairs was the best we had."

"Well, I'm Aaron," I said. "Previously known as the boy downstairs."

Ivy laughed to herself and then looked back up at me.

"Well, Aaron, we should probably work on the part of this plan where we find a police station," she said.

"We?" I said, confused.

"Well, I assumed you'd rather leave this place than stay here any longer," she said.

"I would love to leave, Ivy, but I would only slow you down," I said. "I've been kinda fading away the last few days. I'm always asleep. My body is slowly shutting down, and there's nothing I could do about it."

"That's bullshit," she said. "Your body isn't shutting down. You're just giving up on life. You're not fighting back the urge your body has to die any more. Instead, you're letting it win. A person in our situation can't truly die until we give up. You're giving up, and once you give up fully, your body will too. That's how it works. That's how you die! Don't die yet! You look young. You have a lot to live for. Come with me and together we'll escape this mess and save everyone who can't follow along. We'll avenge the people who are victims of this shit! We may not be able to save the fallen, but at least we can save the living."

I looked at her with wide eyes. She looked like a middle schooler, but she had the maturity of an old lady who lived through a war. She had that personality to do what's right, no matter what. We need more people like her in this world.

"Are you coming?" she asked. "I'm leaving now with or without you."

I looked at her and smiled.

"Let's do this," I said. "Let's end these idiots once and for all."

She looked at me and smiled. We quickly ran over to the door and opened it. The second the light breeze touched our faces, Ivy and I stood frozen and shocked. This had been the first time we had seen the outside world in a while.

"It's beautiful," she said.

"Sure is," I said.

We started to walk down the driveway until we saw a car driving toward us. We both froze and looked at each other.

Ivy quickly looked forward again and realized we had time. She grabbed my arm and pulled me behind a tree. We sat behind it in horror as we watched the car drive by. I thought we were in the clear until the car stopped in front of us. The person in the car rolled down the window and looked at the trees.

"I know you're there!" the person shouted at us. "Come out now, and I won't tell any of the other VK members about this!"

Before we made a choice, I looked closer at the person in the car and realized it was Oliver.

"Let's go out there," I whispered to Ivy.

"Are you crazy?" she replied. "This guy will throw us right back in our cells."

"Trust me," I whispered.

"I hardly know you," she whispered back.

"Then get to know me," I whispered back. "When you do that, you'll realize I try to think before I act."

She looked at me and took a deep breath.

"Fine, Aaron," she whispered. "I'll trust you. Please don't make me regret this. The last time I trusted someone, I ended up here."

"You won't, Ivy," I whispered. "I pinky promise."

I held out my pinky, and she shook it.

"Hopefully, that means something to you," she whispered.

"Don't worry, it does," I whispered back.

I grabbed her hand and pulled her out from behind the tree.

We walked over to the car and stood in front of the window. Oliver looked at us and sighed.

"How'd you do it?" he asked us.

"That's not important," I answered him. "All you need to know is that we're leaving."

Oliver reached through the window and grabbed my arm.

"Don't make me hurt you," he said.

"You won't," I said. "I know you won't. You're a good guy just thrown in the wrong situation. Now please just go back up there, and when the other VK members come back, tell them we were gone when you came back. Please. I need to see my family again. What's left of it."

Oliver looked at me and let my arm go.

"Please don't make me regret this," he said. "Stop them, Aaron. I know you can."

"I will," I said.

Oliver shook his head and looked at Ivy.

"Be careful, you two," he said. "I wish you the best of luck."

Oliver drove away and left Ivy and me in the driveway.

"Let's hurry," I said. "We have no time to waste."

Ivy looked at me and smiled.

"All right," she said. "Follow my lead."

Ivy started running down the driveway, and I followed her. We felt so free. That feeling felt nice.

I felt like a kid running with Ezra again. I missed her. I missed my life before all of this. I just hoped everything would return to normal, and Ivy and I would succeed in this mission. I wanted to help create a safer world for everyone. That was the goal.

Once we had made our way down the driveway, Ivy quickly

turned left and kept running. I couldn't believe how much energy she had. I got tired halfway down the driveway. Even though I was exhausted, I kept running behind her.

I was a little bit of a distance back but I was still able to see her. After what felt like hours of running, Ivy finally stopped. I caught up to her and stood next to her while panting heavily.

"You seem out of breath," she said while beginning to look around.

"Yeah," I said while still trying to catch my breath. "How are you not out of breath?"

"I did cross country for a few years before all of this happened," she answered.

"Were you good?" I asked while finally catching my breath.

"Decent," she said. "I never medaled or anything, but I never got dead last. I guess that's an accomplishment."

"How on earth did you never medal?" I said surprised. "You just ran like a beast."

"Adrenaline probably helps my time," she said jokingly.

I smiled and shook my head.

"So, where are we going now?" I asked.

"Probably farther that way," she answered while pointing in front of us. "I just stopped to make sure you didn't drop dead."

"You could've kept going?" I asked, surprised.

"Yeah," she said. "We only ran a few miles."

"Miles?" I said surprised. "How athletic do you think I am?"

"You appeared to be somewhat in shape," she said. "I didn't think a few miles would hurt."

Ivy started to walk forward and look at all the plants and

scenery. I quickly caught up to her and walked next to her.

"What are you looking for?" I asked while watching her hands move through the tall grass.

"Nothing," she said. "I'm just taking everything in."

"So you're paying attention to our surroundings?" I asked, confused. "Is this so we can turn around if necessary?"

"We won't be turning around," she said. "I'm just looking at nature. I haven't seen it in quite some time."

"How long has it been?" I asked.

"Well, I don't know what day it is," she said. "So I have no idea. Do you know what day it is?"

"Maybe late March," I said. "I vanished early March, so that would make sense."

"That's later than I thought," she said.

"So, how long have you been with the VK?" I asked.

"About a year," she answered. "I was taken while walking home from an evening track practice in early April."

"That's a long time," I said. "How did you survive that long?"

"I don't know," she said. "I just did."

"Well, I'm glad you made it out," I said.

She looked at me and smiled.

"I'm glad we made it out," she said. "Are you ready to start running again?"

"Oh no," I said. "Do we have to run?"

"If we wanna save everyone quickly," she said.

I sighed and looked around. Ivy was right. The nature was pretty. Too bad I wouldn't get to admire it for long.

"I'm done waiting for you," Ivy said jokingly.

She grabbed my arm and started running forward.

Running right next to her made me feel like the flash. I felt like I was running a hundred miles per hour.

We continued to run for about a half-hour before Ivy finally stopped.

"It's harder to run when I'm pulling someone along," she said while looking at me.

"You grabbed my arm," I said while laughing to myself.

"Fair point," she said.

Ivy started to walk forward a little bit when all of a sudden, she stopped dead in her tracks. I quickly ran up to her to see why she stopped when all of a sudden, she grabbed my arm again.

"What's going on?" I asked.

She looked up at me and smiled.

"I have an idea," she said.

She pulled my arm and started running forward. I looked ahead of me to see a huge field of flowers. Ivy took me right through the field and kept running.

"Look how pretty!" she shouted with joy.

She grabbed my other arm and started to spin in circles until we both fell over.

We laid down for a second, just watching the birds fly through the bright blue sky. It was nice.

"Did you like my idea?" she asked me while sitting up.

"Yeah," I said while sitting up myself. "It was fun. It made me feel like a kid again."

She smiled and stood up.

"We should probably continue," she said while helping me up.

"Agreed," I said.

We started walking out of the field when all of a sudden, I felt a sharp pain in my stomach.

"Ow," I said while grabbing my stomach.

Ivy looked back at me with a worried look on her face.

"You okay?" she asked while walking towards me.

"Yeah," I said. "It's just a little stomach pain."

"Did you eat a weird plant?" she asked.

"No," I said. "I didn't eat anything."

"When was the last time you ate?" she asked me with a concerned tone in her voice.

"The day before I disappeared," I answered her.

"You haven't eaten in almost a month?" she shouted, concerned. "You need to eat!"

"It wasn't by choice!!" I shouted.

"I know," she said. "Sorry I yelled. You just seem so nice, and I don't want you to get hurt. You're my runaway buddy."

"Sorry I yelled too," I said. "I guess pain can make me cranky."

She looked at me and grabbed my hand.

"I have an idea that'll work well for both of us," she said while pulling me forward.

We walked for a while before we came to the top of a hill. Ivy looked down the hill and smiled.

"You see that small village down there?" she asked me while pointing down the hill.

I looked down the hill and saw what she was talking about.

"I see it," I said. "Are we gonna go down there?"

"You're gonna go down there," she said.

"What?" I said confused. "Why only me?"

"You need help. I don't," she said.

"I still don't see why we both can't go," I said. "We can call the police down there."

"No, we can't," she said. "That village can help with food,

but not calls. They're weird. They don't believe in phones or any kind of technology. The only connection they have with the outside world is the newspaper."

"Then why am I going alone?" I shouted at her. "We should both eat!"

"I can finish this journey without food," she said, annoyed. "You can't. You'll collapse. So go eat and rest while I continue and find the police."

"Ivy, you're being irrational!" I shouted. "I'm your runaway buddy. We can't just leave each other."

"We have to, Aaron," she said. "We can't risk us both taking a break. Kids could die because of our choices right now. So please just listen to me and get help while I go help the others."

I looked at her and sighed. I didn't want to leave her, but I knew she was right. We had to get help quickly, and I couldn't continue any more. So it would be best if she continued without me.

"Fine," I said. "Please be careful."

"I will," she said.

She looked at me and hugged me.

"Thanks for being the best runaway buddy I could've ever had," she said while squeezing me.

I hugged her back and pulled her close.

"I hope we see each other again," I said.

"We will if fate allows," she said while letting go of me. "I'll never forget you, Aaron, or should I say the boy downstairs."

I smiled and looked at her.

"Bye, Ivy," I said.

"Bye," she said while beginning to walk down the hill.

I stood there and watched as she walked away.

We hadn't known each other for long, but it was still sad to see her go. She was amazing, and I would never forget her and all she did for me.

Chapter 23

I turned around and started to walk towards the small village. I was honestly curious to see what it was like there. The way Ivy described it was interesting. I continued to walk down the hill until I made my way into the village.

It looked strange. The ground was just dirt, with no grass or road, and the layout of the village looked like a gigantic farmer's market. There were booths everywhere selling all different kinds of fruits and vegetables, and the people were either walking through the streets, selling goods, or riding horses.

It was weird, but at the same time it was quite peaceful. These people may have no technology, but they seemed overall happier than most people I met. The only grumpy people I was able to spot were some old guys working at a booth selling oranges, and I think they were just mad because they were being swarmed by fruit flies.

As I continued to walk down the street, I started to receive some stares from some of the adults at booths. I just thought they were looking at me cause I wasn't from here, but that was only a guess. After a while, I heard a kind young woman start calling me.

"Excuse me, son?" she said while looking over at me.

"Yeah?" I said. "What do you need?"

"Can you come here?" she asked.

"Sure," I said while walking over to her.

"You're not from here, are you?" she asked.

"What gave it away?" I joked.

She laughed and looked at my hand holding my stomach.

"You all right?" she asked me while pointing to my stomach.

"I'm fine," I said. "I just have a little bit of a stomach ache."

"That stinks," she said. "Want some medicine?"

As I was about to answer her, I was cut off by a guy behind me.

"This kid's skin and bones!" The guy shouted from behind me. "Do you eat?"

"It's been a while," I said with a nervous laugh.

"How long, sweetie?" the lady asked.

"Maybe a couple of weeks," I said nervously.

"Weeks?" she said, surprised. "Why so long?"

I was about to answer her when I was suddenly cut off again by an older man holding a newspaper.

"I think I know why," he said while walking over to me. "Is your name Aaron Cripple?"

"Yeah?" I said, alarmed. "How do you know my name?"

"You're on the front page of our local newspaper," The old man said while holding out the paper.

"What?" I said while snatching the paper out of his hand.

I looked over the paper, and sure enough, I was on the front page, there was a picture of me and everything. I skimmed through the article to see it talked about me and Jaelyn and how I was suspected to be dead, but no one was sure.

"This seems unreal," I said to them. "My sister and I are the hit story in a newspaper."

"So you were kidnapped?" the young guy said, confused.

"Yeah," I said. "It's been a rough couple of weeks."

"You poor thing," the lady said while walking out from behind her booth. "How about you eat supper with my family tonight."

"That'd be nice," I said. "What are you having?"

"Spaghetti," she said. "But I can make something else if you have an allergy."

"Spaghetti sounds perfect," I said. "Thank you."

"No problem," she said. "Would you like to come inside and get cleaned up?"

"That'd be nice," I said. "Thank you for being so sweet to me."

"It's my pleasure," she said. "I'll lead you to the house."

She gestured for me to follow her, so I did.

Her house wasn't that far. It was like a five-minute walk, if that.

"It's right over here," she said. "I'll come in with you and introduce you to the family, and then I'll leave you be."

"That sounds fine," I said.

I followed her up the stairs and to the front door. She pulled her key out and quickly opened the door. She held the door open and gestured for me to go in. I did as she wanted and walked into the house.

It was weird how different my house looked from this. This house was structured in an old-fashioned kinda way, with many walls and floors being made of natural wood. It felt like a cabin from the 90s.

"This is my house," she said. "Please make yourself feel at home."

"It's very nice," I said. "I like the decorations."

"Thank you," she said. "You're one of the only people to ever compliment me on my decor."

"That's surprising," I said.

She smiled and walked toward the bottom of her staircase.

"Family meeting!" she shouted up the stairs. "They'll be down shortly."

"Okay," I said.

In a matter of seconds, I saw four kids and a young man come running down the stairs. They all quickly ran to the large sofa and sat down in an order that appeared to be from oldest to youngest. They all looked up at me in confusion.

"No staring!" the lady shouted at them. "This is Aaron, and he's going to be having supper with us tonight. All of you be nice and treat him like he's part of the family."

"Yes, mam!" they all shouted in sync.

"Now, Alan, can you please show him where the washroom is?" The lady asked the man on the far side of the couch.

"Yes, darling," he said while standing up. "Follow me, son."

I followed behind him through a weird-looking hallway.

I knew I had complimented this lady on her decor earlier, but some of it was creepy.

As we were walking down the hall, Alan quickly noticed the way I was looking at all the decor.

"It's creepy," he said. "Just avoid eye contact with the statues."

"Okay," I said while continuing to follow behind him.

We stopped in front of a door that looked like it was older than my grandparents.

"This is the washroom," he said.

He opened the door and gestured for me to go in. I walked in and looked around.

"The shower won't work today, but you can use the wipes,"

he said while pointing to a pack of wipes on the counter.

"Okay," I said. "Thank you."

"You're welcome," he said while shutting the door.

The second he shut the door, I turned to look in the mirror to see myself. I couldn't believe what I was seeing. Sure it was me, but I didn't look the same. My hair was disgusting, and my skin was pale. I looked sick. I was so thin and tiny. It felt unreal.

I quickly pulled my eyes away from the mirror and moved them to the pack of wipes. They were the only things that looked normal in this house. I quickly pulled out a wipe and started to wipe my face, arms, and legs. Once I was done, I looked around the bathroom to see if they had deodorant of any kind, but they didn't. So I just wiped my armpits.

It was the best I could do in the circumstances.

After I was done cleaning myself, I walked out of the bathroom and back into the living room. I looked to see three of the four kids playing with trains on the floor. One of them noticed me staring and looked up at me.

"You wanna join?" the kid asked.

"I'm good," I said. "But thanks for asking."

I walked over and sat on one of the couches and laid back. It felt so nice to sit on a couch again.

The youngest kid now noticed me and looked up at me.

"Can I sit with you?" she asked.

"Sure," I said.

She looked up at me and smiled. She set her train down and ran over to the couch. She climbed up and sat next to me.

"No one ever lets me sit with them. This is nice," she said.

I smiled and looked at her.

"You remind me of my little sister," I said.

"What's her name?" she asked.

"Effie," I said.

"That's a pretty name," she said.

"What's your name?" I asked.

"I'm Luna," she said. "I wish my name was Effie, though."

"Why?" I said. "Luna is such a pretty name."

"Really?" she said, surprised. "I thought my name was stupid."

"It's not even close to stupid," I said. "I wish my name was as cool as yours."

"Your name is kinda boring," she said. "I feel like every white guy is named Aaron."

"You're not wrong," I said.

She laughed and lay on top of me.

"You're the best guest we've had," she said.

"That's sweet of you to say," I said.

"She's not lying," one of the other kids said. "All our guests are boring."

"Well, glad to know I'm superior," I joked.

They all laughed.

"Shouldn't you introduce yourselves?" Luna said to her brothers.

"Probably," the older one said. "I'm Louis, and that's Luke."

"Well, it's nice to meet you guys," I said to them.

After we were all properly introduced to each other, we started talking and getting to know each other better.

We talked about our favorite things and what we like to do for fun. I told them all about my life before I had been with the VK.

I avoided telling them stories with Jaelyn, though. I didn't want to inform them of someone they'd never get to meet.

Our conversation seemed to go quickly before we were interrupted by the call of food.

"Suppers ready!" their mom shouted.

We all quickly stood up and walked into the kitchen. I stood there while everyone ran to their assigned seats at the table.

"Can Aaron sit by me, Mommy?" Luna asked while pointing to an empty seat next to her.

"That's fine, sweetie," her mom said while finishing the spaghetti.

I walked over and sat next to Luna.

"Is milk okay, Aaron?" Their mom asked me while pouring all her kids a glass.

"That's fine," I said.

"Do you actually like milk?" Luna whispered.

"Yeah" I whispered back.

"How? It's so gross," she whispered.

"It helps you be big with strong bones," I whispered.

"Isn't that a myth?" she whispered.

"Absolutely not," I whispered. "The internet never lies."

"What's the internet?" she asked me out loud.

At that moment, I remembered what Ivy said, and I panicked.

"It's a weird shoe," I said.

"You don't have to lie to her, sweetie," their mom said while handing out glasses of milk.

"Oh," I said with a worried tone.

"I think they know you don't come from here," she said.

"So what's the internet if it's not a shoe?" Luna asked.

"It's a thing that has all the information in the world," I said.

"So it's full of facts?" she said. "Do you even need to be

316

schooled?"

"Not all facts," I said. "Some things aren't true."

"So, is milk a lie?" she asked.

"The milk thing is true," I said. "I learned that from my school."

"So you have all the information in the world, and you still have to go to school?" Luke shouted, confused.

"Yep," I said.

Just then, their mom came over and set plates of spaghetti in front of all of us.

"Eat up, kids," she said to us. "Seconds are available once you show me a clean plate."

Everyone started eating except me. I just stared at the spaghetti for a solid minute. It looked and smelled like heaven. My mouth quickly started to water. I grabbed a fork and wrapped spaghetti noodles around it.

I stared at the bite before shoving it in my mouth. The second it touched my taste buds, I felt like I was in paradise.

I swallowed and looked over at the mom of the house.

"This is really good," I said. "Thank you."

"You're welcome," she said. "Don't eat too fast."

"I won't," I said as I turned back to my plate.

I continued to eat with everyone.

Each bite kept taking me to a new place in paradise. This spaghetti was one of the best meals I had ever eaten.

After dinner, everyone got up and moved back to the living room. I sat on the couch with the kids' mom while all the kids played trains.

"Why wasn't your other daughter at dinner?" I asked.

"She is really scared of strangers," she answered me. "I'll make her come say hi if you want."

317

"That won't be necessary, mam," I said.

"Please call me Mrs. Parker," she said. "The word mam makes me feel too important."

"Okay, Mrs. Parker," I said.

We continued to sit in the living room for a few minutes before Alan walked into the room.

"So, when are we going to take this kid home?" he asked his wife.

"I don't know," she said. "Where do you live, sweetie?"

"In a small town close to Nashville, Tennessee," I answered her.

"Tennessee?" Alan said, alarmed.

"Where am I now?" I asked them.

"Kentucky," Alan answered.

"Kentucky?" I said, alarmed.

"We can still take him home," Mrs. Parker said to her husband.

"Nashville is like three hours away from here?" Alan said.

"This kid's been through enough," Mrs. Parker said. "The least we can do is reunite him with his family. Imagine if one of our kids disappeared. All you'd want is for them to come home safe and sound."

"You got a point," he said. "Well, if we're gonna go, let's leave as soon as possible."

"You guys are really gonna take me home?" I asked them, surprised.

"Of course," Mrs. Parker said. "What's your town's name?"

"Rayburn," I said.

"I know that town," she said. "It's the one that was named after a huge fire in the 1850s."

"That's the one," I said.

"Well, Alan and I are going to get ready. You just wait here," she said.

Mrs. Parker walked out and went towards Alan.

They quickly got everything they needed, including a babysitter for the kids.

Once they were done, they came into the living room and told everyone to say goodbye to me.

Everyone was sad to see me go, and I was sad to leave them, but I was so excited I'd get to see my family again.

Once I was done saying my goodbyes to everyone, I stood up and followed Mrs. and Mr. Parker out the back door.

Out the back door was a nice-looking car just sitting there.

"You own a car?" I said confused.

"We have some modern-day technology," Alan said as he walked to the driver's side door. "Now get in. I want to be home before the sun rises back up."

I quickly walked over to the side door of the car and opened it. I crawled in and shut the door behind me. Mrs. Parker got in shortly after me. Once everyone was in, we started to drive off. I was finally going to be able to see my family again. I was so excited.

For the first few minutes of the car ride, I just sat there, staring out the window. I looked at the stars as they glistened throughout the night. They were beautiful.

I thought I was just going to be staring out the window forever, but my mind had different plans.

I slowly started to sink in my seat, and my eyes started to close. I was starting to drift into a deep slumber, but I didn't mind. Being able to sleep somewhere that wasn't a hard concrete floor felt so nice. I felt like I was laying in a cloud.

I would have slept forever if I hadn't been woken up by Mrs. Parker.

"Aaron?" she said as she gently shook me awake.

I opened my eyes and looked up at her.

"What," I murmured while rubbing my eyes.

"We're in Rayburn," she said.

Those words instantly caught my attention. I instantly shot up from my seat.

"Already?" I said surprised.

"You were out for quite some time," she said. "What's your house number?"

"It's… Umm," I stuttered.

My house number just completely slipped my mind. I guess not seeing something for a while can easily cause you to forget about it.

"I can't remember," I said. "It's the gray house with no gnomes in front of it."

"Okay," she said.

Mrs. and Mr. Parker started looking out the window, trying to find my house. I would've helped them, but I couldn't see out my window. It was pouring, and the heavy rain took away my privilege of being able to see anything. After a few minutes of searching, Mr. Parker finally found it.

"Is that it?" he asked while pointing to the house to his left.

I leaned over the seat and looked out his window and sure enough, it was my house.

"That's it," I said in disbelief. "Don't go up the driveway, you'll never get out."

"I'll take your word for it," he said with a slight chuckle.

Alan put the car in park and unlocked the door. I quickly opened the handle and stepped out of the car. Before I walked away I turned back to look at Mrs. and Mr. Parker.

"Thank you," I said. "I owe you guys big time."

"You're welcome, sweetie," Mrs. Parker said.

"Be safe, Aaron," Mr. Parker said. "We'll gladly help you again but let's make it at least another year."

"Sounds good," I said while shutting the door. "Bye."

"Bye, Aaron," they both said while waving.

I shut the door behind me, and they quickly drove off.

I walked up my yard in disbelief. I couldn't believe I was home. I slowly began to make my way up to my front porch.

As I looked around the porch, I noticed a lot of flowers and notes from neighbors. I picked one up and read it. It was saying how sorry they were for my family's loss. I took a deep breath and put the note back down by its bouquet.

I quickly turned my attention to the front door.

"Here we go," I whispered to myself.

I went to turn the knob when all of a sudden I realized it was locked.

"Of course," I said to myself.

Right as I was about to ring the doorbell I remembered my mom telling me about a key she hid under the mat. I didn't remember if this key was for the door or not but it was worth a shot. I moved the mat and sure enough, there was a key. I picked it up and moved it to the doorknob.

"Here goes nothing," I whispered to myself.

I quickly put the key in and turned the knob, it worked.

I slowly pushed the door open and walked right in.

Chapter 24

Before I started to walk around the house, I just had to freeze for a second. I was so glad to be standing in my own home again. It felt unreal. I took off my wet shoes and started to walk across the house.

It felt like I was exploring a lost city. I looked over at the clock to see it flash 12.07. I couldn't believe how late it was. I continued to walk around until I made my way to the counter.

The counter was covered in way more papers than usual. They were mainly newspapers that didn't really catch my eye. There was only one thing that managed to grab my attention. It may have been dark, but it didn't take much light for me to recognize the face on the front of the pamphlet. It was Jaelyn.

The photo was captioned with the words "*A life ended too soon.*"

That statement made me sad because it was true. I opened up the pamphlet and started reading it some more. The more I read, the more sad I felt. It talked about all Jaelyn's accomplishments and all the dreams she had that she could never fulfill because of me.

Obviously, the pamphlet doesn't blame me, but I blamed myself. I quickly realized the pamphlet was used at Jaelyn's funeral. It kind of made me sad that I missed her funeral, but at least I got to say goodbye while she was still here.

After a while, I decided to finally put the pamphlet down and make my way to my room. I walked across the kitchen and to my door. I instantly noticed that my door had been replaced. It was nice that even though everyone thought I was dead, they still decided to go ahead and fulfill my wish of having a new door.

I went to turn the knob when all of a sudden I realized it was locked.

"That's weird," I said to myself.

I was about to go find the key when I heard the toilet flush from the bathroom behind me.

I stood there frozen, waiting to see who would come out.

It only took a few seconds for the door to swing open and reveal who was inside.

"Effie?" I said to the short figure walking out of the bathroom.

"What," she said while rubbing her eyes.

Effie was clearly half asleep. She had no idea what was going on.

"I missed you," I said.

She looked up at me in confusion for a second before realizing who I was.

"Aaron?" she said, surprised.

"Yeah," I said while squatting down to her level.

"You're alive?" she said, confused.

"Last time I checked," I said jokingly.

Effie smiled and ran over to me. She launched herself into my arms before starting to cry.

"I missed you," she said as she cried into my shoulder.

"I missed you too," I said while comforting her.

We sat on the floor, just hugging for a good few minutes.

She was hugging me tightly while I was hugging her back. I missed her.

"Where did you go?" she asked me while finally starting to let me go.

"I'll answer that later," I said. "In the meantime, how about I tuck you into bed."

"Okay," she said with a sigh. "Please don't leave me again."

"I won't," I said while standing up. "Now, let's go up to that fun room of yours."

"Okay," she said while starting to walk toward the stairs. I followed her until we made it to her bed. She crawled under the cover and looked at me with a huge smile.

"I'll make you a rainbow loom bracelet tomorrow," she said while closing her eyes.

"Sounds good," I said while moving her hair out of her face.

I stood there for only a few minutes before Effie was sound asleep. As I walked out, I decided it was time to visit Mom and Carl. I started to walk down the mini hallway leading to their room before I was stopped in my tracks.

I noticed that the mini table that was usually covered in family photos looked dull. Most of the photos were flipped over or covered up. As I began to pick a few of the photos up, I realized why they were covered; they were photos that contained Jaelyn and me.

I guess my mom couldn't stand looking at our faces, thinking she was never going to see either of us again.

It made me sad looking at everyone so happy in the photos and then thinking of them now.

Just like the pamphlet, I quickly stopped looking at the photos. It was just too hard for me.

I decided to continue walking down the hall until I was

finally in front of their door.

I was about to turn the knob when all of a sudden I heard a noise coming from the other side.

"Someone's in the house," I heard Carl say, alarmed. "I'm gonna go kill them."

I froze at the door. I knew Carl didn't think I was there, but he was still crazy. So I had no idea what he'd do to me.

I heard Carl get up from his bed and grab the metal bat.

I decided to just stay there and wait for him to open the door.

I didn't have the energy to run anyway.

I quickly saw the knob turn, and the door swung back. Carl jumped through the door and swung his bat at me. It missed, but I fell down to the ground like a coward.

He still didn't realize it was me, so he swung again, but this time I grabbed the tip of the bat.

"Carl!" I shouted.

I saw a look of confusion come over his face. He looked down at me, and his eyes widened. He instantly dropped the bat and helped me up.

As I stood up, he looked at me more closely. It was like he didn't believe I was really there.

"Aaron?" he said, confused.

"Yeah," I said.

Carl moved his hand to my shoulder. He still couldn't believe that I was there. Once he figured out that I wasn't a ghost, he pulled me into his arms and hugged me tightly.

I knew Carl and I had some bad history, but I really did miss him, so I hugged him back.

We stood there for a while before he finally let me go.

"I missed you, kid," he said. "We all missed you."

"I missed you guys too," I said. "Is Mom sleeping?"

"She won't be for long," he said with a smile. "Amanda!"

"What?" Mom said while hiding in her covers.

"Come here," he said.

"Why?" she asked.

Before Carl had a chance to answer her, I ran over and jumped on the bed next to her.

"Carl, I'm trying to sleep," she said, annoyed.

"I'm trying to see my mom," I said. "But she likes to sleep more than her own son, apparently."

My mom instantly shot up and turned on her lamp. She looked over at me with disbelief in her eyes.

"Aaron?" she said as tears began to fill her eyes.

Before I could say anything, she wrapped her arms around me and pulled me close. She squeezed me tightly while putting her hand on my head.

I heard her start to cry. I could tell she missed me.

After a few minutes, she finally let me go, and I was able to sit up.

As I looked into my mom's eyes, I could tell they were still in denial that I was there.

I wanted to say something, but all the words I was gonna say were taken right out of my mouth. I was speechless. I was just as surprised as my mom that I was there. It felt like only minutes ago, I was laying on a concrete floor just waiting to die. I never thought I'd be with my family again. It seemed like a dream that was out of reach.

After a few minutes of me and my mom staring at each other, I was finally able to get some words out.

"I missed you," I said.

"I missed you too, baby," she said while wiping her tears.

"I thought I'd never see you again."

"I thought I'd never be here again," I said while my eyes started to fill with tears.

"We both missed you very much," Carl said as he came over and sat on the bed with us.

I looked over at him and smiled.

"Do I get room access again?" I asked them.

"Of course," Carl said with a slight chuckle. "How about you get in the shower while I go unlock your door."

"That sounds good," I said. "I probably stink."

"You do," he said jokingly.

I laughed with him for a few seconds before standing up.

"I'll be back," I said to my mom while walking out of the room.

I walked through the hall and down the stairs. I was looking around, seeing if all the strange marks of my house were still there, and sure enough, they were.

I eventually made my way to the bathroom. I shut the door behind me and looked around. I was glad nothing had been messed up.

Everything looked about the same, just the way I liked it.

I quickly got undressed and hopped into the shower.

The warm water running down my face and through my hair felt so nice. I didn't realize how much I missed showering.

Showering is one of those things that many people take for granted, and to be honest, I did too.

Once I was done in the shower, I dried myself off and wrapped a towel around my waist. I quickly left the bathroom and went to my room.

As I walked into my room, I saw my mom dusting a bunch of things.

"Really?" I said as I walked in.

"Sorry," she said while looking over at me. "Your room had just been collecting dust for the past few weeks."

"You're fine," I said. "Can you just take a short break while I get dressed?"

"I guess," she said while beginning to walk out. "Did the shower feel nice?"

"Of course," I said.

"Well, I'm glad to hear that," she said. "Come out when you're done."

"Okay," I said to my mom as she shut my door.

I quickly got dressed into my comfiest pair of PJs.

It felt so nice to be wearing a different outfit than I had been for the past few weeks.

Before I walked out to the kitchen, I looked around my room. It sure was dusty, just like Mom said.

Besides the new dust bunnies though, my room seemed exactly the same.

It was just how I left it, except for the door, of course.

Once I was done looking around my room, I walked out into the kitchen to see Carl at the counter making a cup of coffee.

"Coffee in the middle of the night?" I said as I sat down at the counter.

"Well, I'm gonna be driving soon," he said. "I need to be awake."

"Driving?" I said confused. "Did you get a nighttime job?"

"Good guess, but no," he said. "We're going to the ER."

"ER?" I said confused. "Who's hurt?"

"Hopefully, no one," he said.

"Carl, why are we going to the ER?" I asked, annoyed.

"Your mom and I think you need to get checked out," he said. "And the ER is the only kind of medical place that's open at this time."

"Carl, we don't need to go to the ER," I said in a panicked tone.

I don't mind getting a checkup, but the ER has all the people who are literally dying. That means blood. I went to the ER once when I was eleven, and I nearly blacked out.

"Aaron, we need to make sure you're okay," he said. "You've been gone for so long. Anything could've happened."

"Carl, I didn't get stabbed or anything!" I shouted, annoyed. "I'm fine. Please don't waste your money."

"Aaron, I know you hate the ER, but we're going," he said sternly.

I rolled my eyes and laid my head down in my arms.

"This is stupid," I said, annoyed.

"You're just cranky that you might see someone's arm hanging off again," he said jokingly.

"Carl!" I heard my mom shout from the living room.

I looked up at Carl and laughed. Carl rolled his eyes and looked over at my mom.

"I was just messing with him," he said.

My mom rolled her eyes at him and walked over to me.

"You'll be fine," she said. "It'll be over before you know it."

I nodded my head as she walked to the kitchen to take a sip of Carl's coffee.

"Did you get the neighbor to answer?" my mom asked Carl.

"No," he said. "My sister did, though. She's gonna be over to watch Effie any minute now."

"Perfect," Mom said. "Are you ready to go, Aaron?"

"I just need shoes," I said. "But I'll put those on as we're leaving."

"Sounds good," she said.

She turned around and took another sip of Carl's coffee before walking back over to him.

I saw my mom lean toward Carl's ear and whisper something to him. The second my mom was done, Carl nodded his head, and my mom walked upstairs.

Carl walked over and sat at the counter next to me.

"So, Aaron, can you tell me anything about the last few weeks?" he asked.

"Is this supposed to be some kind of interrogation?" I asked.

"Maybe," he said jokingly.

I rolled my eyes and looked up at him.

"You get five questions," I said. "After that, I'm shutting up, so make them good."

"Okay," he said. "Where have you been these last few weeks?"

"In this weird house-looking place inside a cell," I answered him.

"Cell?" he said, confused. "Were you in jail or something?"

"Do you really wanna waste one of your questions with that?" I asked.

"No," he said. "Do you know who took you?"

"Yep," I said. "I know some of their names."

"What are the names you know?" he asked me in a concerned tone.

"There were guys named Mike and Rex," I said. "And the other guys were Antonio Jay and Donald Smith."

"I recognize the last two guys' names," he said. "Do I know

330

them?"

"The last two?" I asked.

"Yeah," he answered me.

"You do," I said.

"How do I know them?" He asked, confused.

"Well, Antonio Jay is one of my classmates' dads," I said. "I'm assuming you met him at one of my class parties in elementary school."

"And the other guy?" he asked.

"Donald Smith is Mr. Smith," I answered him.

"Okay?" he said, confused.

Carl didn't realize what Mr. Smith I was talking about. He just thought I was saying what I called him.

"Mr. Smith," I said again.

"Aaron, I don't know a Mr. Smith," he said.

"Yes, you do," I said, annoyed.

"No, I don't!" he shouted.

"Carl!" I shouted. "Mr. Smith! My chemistry teacher!"

"What?" he shouted. "Your teacher is one of the people that took you away?"

"Yep," I said. "He's the best."

"I'm gonna kill this guy!" Carl shouted.

"Carl, calm down," I said.

Just as Carl was about to shout more, my mom came down the stairs and looked at us.

"You all right?" Mom asked Carl.

"No," he said.

Before Mom could chime in, I cut them off.

"Let's go," I said to them. "I heard that four a.m. is their rush hour, so let's beat it."

"Carl, what's wrong?" My mom asked while walking over.

Before Carl could answer, I stepped in front of him and cut them off once again.

"Let's talk later," I said to them.

I grabbed my mom's hand and dragged her out the door. Carl looked at me with confusion. I just looked away and walked to the car.

"What is going on?" My mom asked, confused.

"We're gonna be stuck in rush hour," I said. "That's what's going on."

"Aaron, you're acting strange," she said.

"Sorry," I said. "I'm just a little sleep-deprived."

"Sorry, baby," she said. "I kinda forgot that you've been gone for so long. You'll sleep like a rock later tonight."

"I'm counting on it," I said while getting in the car.

My mom quickly got in the car after me.

We sat there in awkward silence while waiting for Carl to make his way outside.

It seemed like ten years before Carl came out, but he eventually did.

He got in the car with the same expression he had in the kitchen.

At this point, I couldn't tell if Carl was mad at me or the whole situation.

Quickly after Carl got in the car, he started to drive to the hospital. The car ride was pretty quiet until my mom decided to talk to Carl again.

"Sweetie, we have a long car ride ahead of us," she said. "We have time to talk about what's bothering you."

"I don't think we should talk about this right now," I said to them. "It's really late, and we're all probably tired."

"Aaron, do you know why Carl is upset?" she asked while

looking back at me.

Before I could answer her, Carl finally got his word in.

"He knows exactly why I'm not in the best mood," Carl said to my mom.

"Really?" she said, confused. "How does he know something about you that I don't?"

"I'm upset about something with him," Carl answered her. "So he obviously knows what it is."

"Carl!" my mom shouted. "He just came home, and you already found a reason to be mad at him?"

"I'm not mad at him!" Carl shouted back. "I'm mad about something he's involved with."

"And what is that?" my mom asked, annoyed.

"I'll let him tell you," Carl said while pointing back at me.

My mom turned around and looked at me.

"I'm not talking about this right now," I said quietly.

"Aaron, we have so much time," she said. "Feel free to talk to me."

"Mom, this has nothing to do with time," I said, annoyed. "I'm not talking about this."

"Sweetie, I need to know," she said.

"No, you don't!" I shouted back.

My mom looked at me with a surprised look. I could tell she was just trying to solve everything and find out what was wrong, but she gets so over-dramatic about everything. If I told her something that normal people would freak out about, she would be a nervous wreck.

"Aaron, it's not that hard," Carl said, annoyed. "How hard is it to say my chemistry teacher is a psycho?"

"What?" my mom shouted. "What is that supposed to mean?"

"Aaron's teacher is one of the people that caused him to disappear," Carl explained.

"Aaron, is that true?" my mom asked me with a worried tone in her voice.

I didn't answer. I just nodded my head.

My mom turned back around and looked out the window. I could tell this whole thing was messing with her, and I felt bad. She didn't deserve all of this stress.

"Sorry," I whispered to them.

My mom turned around and looked at me.

"It's okay," she whispered back. "It'll all be okay."

I looked up at her and smiled. That smile may have been the fakest smile I've ever done in my life, but it made my mom feel better, and that's all that mattered.

We all stayed quiet in the car for a little bit before Carl decided to start talking again.

"Aaron, can I ask you something?" he asked.

"Depends," I said.

"Do you remember most of what happened to you?" he asked.

"Yeah?" I said, confused.

"Do you remember what happened before you got taken?" he asked.

"Yeah?" I said, still confused.

At this point, my mom was looking at Carl with a weird look. She was just as confused as I was.

"Do you remember things that happened before Jaelyn passed?" he asked.

"Carl what are you getting at?" I asked, annoyed.

"Do you know who killed your sister?" he quickly asked.

I froze. Thankfully before Carl asked me again, my mom

334

cut in.

"This is not the time for that question!" My mom shouted.

"But he knows the answer!" Carl shouted back. "I can tell."

"I'm not talking about this right now," I said.

"Yes, you are!" he shouted at me.

"No, I'm not!" I shouted back.

Carl got frustrated and pulled the car over at a gas station.

"What are you doing?" my mom asked, confused.

"Taking a breather," Carl said. "My road rage is getting close to kicking in."

"That's fine," she said. "I have to pee anyway. I'll be back. Don't be stupid."

I watched from the window as my mom walked to the gas station.

The second she walked in, Carl opened my side door and looked at me.

"You didn't pull over for a breather, did you?" I asked.

"No," he said. "Now, please answer my question."

"I told you earlier I'm only answering five for now, and you already asked your five," I said.

"I don't care about that!" he shouted at me. "I need to know what happened to my daughter!"

"She wasn't your daughter!" I shouted back.

"She was more mine than she was your dumb father's!" He shouted back at me.

"Don't bring my dad into this," I said, frustrated. "He did nothing to you."

"I know," Carl said. "It just bothers me how you and your sister always compared me to him. To you two, I'm the worst person ever! Did you guys ever consider how I lived to see you two graduate elementary school! You were practically babies

335

when he left you! Who's been here longer? Who went to all those stupid class parties? Who was there for you for more than six years of your life? Me! It's always been me!"

I sat there frozen for a second. Carl was right to an extent, and I didn't like that.

"Please, Aaron," he said. "Tell me who hurt your sister."

I looked down, and my eyes filled with water.

"I can't right now, Carl," I said while trying not to cry.

"Aaron, I'm done!" he shouted at me. "Just tell me!"

"This isn't easy for me!" I shouted while unbuckling my seatbelt.

I got out of the car and quickly pushed past Carl.

"Don't walk away from me!" he shouted while walking over to me.

"You wanna know who was there for me longer than you or my dad?" I shouted.

"What?" he said, confused.

"Jaelyn!" I shouted. "She was my natural-born best friend. She was the person who knew me the best! You may be able to compare yourself to my dad, but don't think for a minute you can top Jaelyn. Don't think that you miss her more than me! She was my everything, and I had to watch her die! You know how hard that is?"

"Aaron," he said. "I'm sorry."

"Are you, though?" I shouted. "'Cause you were shouting at me only a few seconds ago because I couldn't bring myself to talk about my own sister's murder!"

"Aaron, calm down," he said. "You're making a scene."

"Who's here to see my scene?" I shouted. "The gas station squirrels?"

Carl didn't answer me; he just looked at me with sadness

in his eyes. As I stood there waiting for a response, I noticed my breathing starting to get heavier and quicker.

Carl started to walk toward me. I could tell he felt bad, but his sympathy quickly turned into panic when he noticed my breathing.

"Aaron," he said as he quickly ran over to me. "Are you okay?"

I looked up at him and tried to control my breathing, but I couldn't.

"Breathe, Aaron," he said. "I'm sorry. Please don't work yourself up."

I looked at him with panic in my eyes. Before he could say anything though I felt my head start to spin. Everything got blurry.

I felt like I was going insane until I blacked out into Carl's arms.

Chapter 25

"Aaron?" I heard someone say.

I quickly opened my eyes and looked around. Everything was black.

I could see my hands clearly, but everything else around me was dark. I couldn't even see anyone else.

"Hello?" I shouted. "Carl? Mom? Anyone?"

There was no response. I was alone.

I started to walk around to see if there was a place that wasn't full of darkness, but there was nothing. I was trapped in what appeared to be an endless black room.

I started running around. I was going insane. I was like a chicken with my head cut off.

I kept running and running until I heard a voice again.

"How does it feel?" the voice asked.

"What?" I said confused. "Who are you? Where are you?"

"Answer me, then I might answer you," the voice said.

"I don't understand what you're asking me!" I shouted to the voice.

"How does it feel, Aaron?" the voice shouted at me.

"I don't know what you mean!" I shouted back.

The voice stayed quiet. Without it talking, I felt isolated.

"Hello?" I screamed.

"She had such a bright future," I heard my own voice say.

"Who's talking?" I shouted. "I didn't say that!"

"You did," the voice said. "It was just in the past."

"Why am I hearing it again?" I shouted.

"She had a bright future," I heard my voice say again.

"Shut up!" I shouted.

"Why does that bother you?" the voice asked.

"'Cause it's annoying!" I shouted.

"Don't lie to yourself," the voice said.

I didn't answer for a second. Deep down, I knew why I hated hearing those words, but I wasn't going to say that out loud.

"Just tell me what you want," I said to the voice.

"I'll let her tell you," the voice said.

Before I could say anything else, I saw a light from the corner of my eye. I quickly turned around to see a familiar face standing in the light.

"Jaelyn?" I said, confused.

"Why'd you do this?" she asked.

"Do what?" I asked, confused.

"Why'd you cut my life short?" she asked. "You even believed I had a bright future. Why'd you take that away?"

"Jaelyn, I didn't mean to," I said. "I'm sorry."

"Sorry won't fix this," she said while moving her hand from her chest.

Under her hand was the bullet hole that killed her.

It was a horrifying sight.

I quickly turned around and looked away.

"You won't look 'cause you know I'm right!" she shouted.

"This isn't real," I said to myself.

"You just don't want it to be real!" Jaelyn shouted from behind me.

"Stop, make it stop!" I screamed out loud.

"It should've been you," she whispered in my ear.

"I know," I said. "I can't change anything. Please just know how sorry I am."

"My life is over because of you!" she shouted. "Sorry won't fix anything!"

I looked back at Jaelyn to see her eyes glistening. She looked dead.

"Jaelyn?" I said.

I moved my shaking hand up to her face like she once did to mine. It seemed like the right thing to do.

The second my hand made contact with her face, I was shot backward, at least a hundred feet. I flew through the air, screaming along the way.

I quickly hit the ground, hard. I stood back up and looked in front of me to see another familiar person.

"Antonio?" I said while slowly getting up.

"It could've just been her," he said. "Now I have to kill everyone you love."

"No," I said. "Don't you dare!"

"You left us," he said. "You were supposed to die. You could've just let that happen, but no. You were selfish, and now all your loved ones have to die."

"No!" I screamed as I fell to the floor.

"I'll see you again in the real world," he said as he got really close to my face.

The second Antonio was done talking. I shot awake. I looked around to realize I was in the hospital.

"Hello?" I said while continuing to look around.

As I looked around, I noticed I had an IV in my arm, and I was connected to a machine that was reading my heart rate.

"At least I know I'm not dead," I said to myself jokingly.

At that moment, a doctor walked into the room with a

smile.

"Glad to see you're awake," the doctor said. "You gave everyone quite a scare."

"I know," I said quietly while looking down.

"Everyone will just be glad to know you're awake," he said in a joyful tone.

I looked up at him and smiled.

"Before anyone comes in, can I ask you a question?" I asked the doctor.

"Sure," he said.

"Am I okay?" I asked.

"I'll discuss that when your folks are in here with you," he said. "Just know you aren't going to die."

"Okay," I said as he walked out.

While I waited for my parents, I just sat on my hospital bed with guilt eating me alive. I knew I couldn't help passing out, but it still made me feel bad. I scared everyone again, and it hurt me. I hated being a burden, and lately, that's all I've been feeling like.

A few minutes later, Mom and Carl burst through the door.

"Aaron," Mom said as she wrapped her arms around me.

I hugged her back and looked over at Carl. He was standing a few feet back. I kinda felt bad. I was almost positive he blamed himself for the incident.

After a few moments, my mom let go of me and looked over at Carl.

"You wanna say anything?" she asked.

Carl took a deep breath and looked at me.

"I'm sorry, Aaron," he said. "I wasn't thinking, and it caused you to, you know."

"Carl, this wasn't your fault," I said. "I probably don't have the best health right now, and it's showing in the worst ways possible."

Before Carl could respond to me, the doctor walked in with a clipboard and walked over to us.

"We all need to talk about the kid," he said.

My mom nodded her head and sat down on the bed next to me. Carl followed her lead and sat down.

"Before I start, I just want to say some stuff may sound bad, but he's not going to die," The doctor said.

I took a deep breath and sat up, preparing myself for the worst.

"Okay, I'm just gonna read down the clipboard," he said. "There are signs of a past rib fracture that's still trying to heal, does that sound right?"

My mom nodded at the doctor. He looked back down at the clipboard and continued to read.

"There were quite a few cuts and bruises," he said. "Thankfully, none of them are alarming. Some bruises on the head though may indicate some possible brain trauma; because of that, we will be doing an MRI scan after our discussion."

My mom nodded as her eyes began to fill with tears. I moved my hand on her shoulder and looked at her.

"It'll be okay," I whispered.

She looked at me and attempted to smile.

We turned our attention quickly back to the doctor as he read the last few things off the clipboard.

"I saved the worst for last," he said to us. "Aaron here has very high levels of dehydration and malnutrition. We guess he didn't eat or drink much for a few weeks. He can probably confirm our predictions, though."

Everyone's eyes looked over at me, burning with curiosity.

I looked at them and sighed.

"It's true," I said to them in a quiet voice.

I saw Mom and Carl's eyes quickly widen.

"What?" Carl said, confused.

"Well, I wasn't exactly held prisoner in a castle," I said. "They never fed me, and I only managed to get one bottle of water from this guy who felt bad for me."

"That bottle of water probably saved your life," the doctor said.

"Figured," I said. "So is that it?"

The doctor nodded at me and moved his comforting gaze to my parents.

"We'll prescribe a diet to get everything back on track," the doctor said to my mom and Carl. "He'll need fluids for a couple of days, but after that, he should be fine and ready for a normal life again. Now I'm gonna take him to get an MRI scan."

My mom nodded and looked at me. I could tell she was nervous. Her eyes were still teary, and her hands were shaking.

"It'll be okay," I said while the doctor temporarily pulled the IV out of my arm and disconnected me from the heart rate machine.

"Let's go, Mr. Cripple," he said. "We'll be back."

The doctor and I walked out of the room, and he led me to a room with a huge machine.

"Woah," I said to myself.

"Have you ever seen one of these?" he asked.

"No," I said. "I shouldn't be impressed, but I am."

"It's perfectly normal to be impressed," he said. "It's an amazing piece of technology that has saved many people's lives."

The doctor walked over to this other guy, and they started

whispering. Quickly after they were done, the doctor walked back over to me.

"Aaron, I'm gonna ask you to please lay down and remain as still as possible," the doctor said.

"Okay," I said while walking over to the machine.

I laid down as they asked and stayed still. I closed my eyes and felt the bed move back into the machine. I laid there as still as possible, still keeping my eyes closed tight.

I tried to just zone out until I heard a sound of panic coming from the outside. I wanted to shout and ask what was wrong, but I was scared to move. I didn't want to mess anything up. I was more scared of being a burden at that moment than actually dying.

Quickly after I heard the sound of panic though the bed moved out, and I was able to open my eyes. The second I went to sit up, I was yanked off the bed by the doctor.

"What is going on?" I asked, confused.

"The machine's glitching," he said. "And smoking."

"What?" I shouted, confused.

I looked back at the machine to see smoke coming from where my head had been only a few seconds ago.

"What do we do?" I asked.

"You're gonna go back to the room and tell your parents everything's fine. Your head is fine," he said.

"How do you know?" I asked. "You said the machine was glitching."

"I caught a slight glimpse of your head before it started to glitch," he said with a smile.

I could tell the doctor was lying, but I didn't care. At this point, it seemed like I was going to die with or without head trauma.

"Okay," I said as I walked down the hall to my room.

I walked in to see Mom and Carl talking to each other. The second my presence was noticed, they both moved their attention to me.

"So?" Carl said. "How'd it go?"

"Everything's good," I said to them.

"Well, I'm glad," he said. "Where's the doctor?"

"He's dealing with something right now," I said to them. "I'm sure he'll be back soon."

Carl nodded and looked back over at my mom.

While waiting for the doctor, I decided to walk over to the window and watch the rain run down. It was quite calming.

I stood there for what only felt like seconds before the doctor returned with a paper.

"All right, folks, I got everything you need," he said.

He handed a paper to my parents before explaining everything on it.

"Here's the diet we suggest," he said to them. "This should help his nutrition go back up. With the dehydration, he will stay here for a few days for the IV, but after that, he'll be allowed to go home."

"He can't go home?" Carl said, confused.

"It's for the best," the doctor said.

"I'll stay here with him," Mom said to Carl.

"Honey, you have work. I'll stay," Carl said.

"You have to take care of Effie, though. She's on spring break," Mom said.

"Both of you, go home," I said to them. "I'll be fine. Just live your lives like you have been for the last few weeks, without me."

Mom and Carl both looked up at me. They didn't want to

say it, but they knew I was right. I'd be fine.

"Okay," Carl said. "We'll be back to pick you up ASAP."

"Okay," I said. "Drive home safe."

"We will," Carl said while leading my mom out the door.

A few moments after Mom and Carl left, the doctor hooked me back up to the IV and made sure I was all right.

"You want the remote?" he asked.

"I'm good," I said. "I think I'm just gonna sleep. Thank you, though."

"Okay then," he said. "Be sure you don't roll on that IV."

"I won't," I said.

He smiled and walked out of the room. As soon as he walked out, I shut my eyes and drifted off. It was peaceful falling asleep to the rain on a nice soft bed.

My next few days at the hospital went by fairly quickly. I was greeted and given amazing food by the nice nurses. I watched my favorite shows, and overall just had a nice peaceful stay.

Even though my stay was nice, it was still great when I got to go home. By the time I was on my way home, I already felt a million times better than I previously did. I felt pretty good.

When I got home, I was instantly greeted by Effie. She was really happy to see me.

Once I got settled, I was informed by my mom and Carl what my life would look like for the next few weeks. They told me I was on a diet that involved me slowly consuming more food than I usually would.

They also told me that in order to be able to pass tenth grade, I would need to complete a month's worth of school work in two weeks. On top of all of this, though, I was also required to get at least eight hours of sleep every night, have regular doctor visits to make sure I was doing okay, and I would have to answer questions from the police about everything.

All of this seemed very chaotic, but I was ready to get my life back on track.

During the first week of my new lifestyle, I was very stressed. Everything was piled on top of me so quickly. The police questioning sessions always sent me into a panic, the school work was overwhelming, and the doctor visits just seemed like an unnecessary cherry on top of the sundae of chaos.

Thankfully, the second week was less stressful. I had learned to manage my new lifestyle, and the police questioning sessions happened less and less often. It was nice.

Even though those two weeks were crazy, they were quickly over, and before I knew it, I was heading back to school.

The morning before I left for school stressed me out so much. Almost no one knew I was even alive. My return wasn't well known yet.

I knew I'd get so many stares and questions, and that terrified me. I didn't want to be the school's top gossip topic. I just wanted to go back and instantly be the loser I've always been.

The only reason I ended up not convincing my parents to give me another day was because of Ezra. I knew this whole thing was messing with her badly. She didn't even know I was back. I had no way to tell her.

I kinda felt bad that she had to learn at the same time as everyone else, but there was nothing I could do.

It was weird that morning getting in the car with Carl instead of Jaelyn. I missed her more and more each day, and it didn't help that I was still haunted by that dream I had at the hospital.

I knew Jaelyn wasn't haunting me and didn't want me to die, but these dreams and thoughts sure made me feel that way. I felt responsible for her death no matter what anyone said to me. It was like a creature slowly eating me from the inside out.

I just hoped that no one would ask about her at school even though deep down I knew they would, but I still had hope. Hope that maybe my classmates would be able to put themselves in my shoes and think about what I was going through before they opened their mouths.

Chapter 26

The trip to school that morning seemed to drag. I couldn't tell if it was because of my nerves or the fact that I had no one to talk to. Either way, I still felt like I was in that car for twenty years.

The trip did soon come to an end, though, and we were right outside the school.

"You'll do great, kid," Carl said while handing me my bag from the back seat.

"Thanks," I said.

I took a deep breath and got out of the car.

The school looked like I had never left. It looked exactly the same.

"Have a good first day back," Carl said while driving off.

I turned my head and watched him drive away.

This was really it. I was gonna get my life back.

I didn't know if I was ready or not, but I did know that I had to do this to get my life properly back on track.

I slowly walked up to the front doors and walked in.

The second I stepped through the doors, I felt like thousands of eyes were watching me.

As I walked through the halls, whispers slowly started and looks only grew. I tried to keep my head down and avoid eye contact, but it didn't help.

I missed my life, but I did not miss people.

I kept walking through the halls with my head down until I managed to accidentally walk into someone.

"Watch it, shortie," the person said while stepping back.

I looked up at the person to see a familiar face.

"Teagan?" I said.

Teagan's face froze as he looked at me.

"Aaron?" he said, surprised. "When did you…?"

He froze. He was at a loss for words.

"Good to see you," I said. "But I gotta go to my locker, I don't want to be late."

I started walking towards my locker when Teagan suddenly snapped out of his trance.

"Wait up," he said while following me. "Since when were you alive?"

"I never died, Teagan," I said while starting to open my locker.

"Well, I figured that!" he said. "Why did everyone think you were dead, though? You seem fine."

"I disappeared," I said while opening my locker. "This thing looks like it hasn't been open in years."

Teagan looked over in my locker.

"That phone looks sadder than anything I've ever seen before," Teagan said while picking up my phone.

"Is it dead?" I asked.

"Dead as a doornail," he said while handing back my phone.

I set my phone back in my locker and got everything I needed for Algebra II.

"So, where were you?" Teagan asked while looking at me.

"Kentucky, apparently," I said.

"Sounds nice," he said sarcastically.

"It was a glorious vacation in hell," I said jokingly.

Teagan chuckled to himself before looking back at the

clock.

"This morning flew by," he said while looking back at me.

"Sure did," I said. "It was nice seeing you again."

"You too, shortie," he said.

I rolled my eyes and laughed to myself. Teagan smiled at me and walked away.

It was nice seeing him again. I missed his dumb insults.

I quickly started walking down the halls and heading to class when suddenly, I was stopped by another familiar voice.

"It's true!" The voice shouted while running over to me.

"Alex?" I said as he ran over to me.

"Wow," he said. "I heard a rumor you were alive, but I didn't think it was true."

"Well, it is," I said.

"That's good," he said. "A Lot of people missed you."

"Well, I'm glad to hear that," I said. "I gotta go to class."

"Wait!" he shouted at me. "Before you go, I think there's something you should know."

"And what is that?" I asked, confused.

"It's about Ezra," he said.

"Is she okay?" I asked.

"She's alive," he said.

"Alex, get to the point!" I shouted. "What's going on?"

"Okay," he said. "When you and your sister disappeared, Ezra couldn't handle it. You guys mean so much to her. It broke her. She blamed herself. I don't know why; she just did. She felt bad for the fight you two got in and felt she could've stopped this somehow. Aaron, she stopped eating. She's so skinny, and I think she's sick. I'm not sure, but she doesn't look good."

I froze and looked down.

"I need to talk to her," I said. "Is she still at school?"

351

"Yeah," he said. "She just sits at her desk with her hood up."

"Okay," I said. "Thanks for letting me know."

I quickly walked over to Mrs. Jones's room and walked in. Everyone looked at me in surprise, but I didn't care any more. I quickly set my stuff down and walked over to Ezra.

I sat at the empty desk next to her and tapped her shoulder.

"Morning, stranger," I said jokingly.

"Leave," she said, annoyed.

"Ezra, lift your head," I said while continuing to tap her shoulder.

I could tell she had no idea who I was. If she knew who I was, her head would've already been up.

"Do I need a password or something?" I asked jokingly.

Ezra didn't answer; she just moaned to herself and kept her head down.

"Cute Cat 127," I whispered.

The second she heard those words, her head shot up. She quickly whipped around and looked at me.

"Hey," I said.

She was frozen. Just like Teagan, she was in disbelief.

She lifted her hand up and touched my face.

"I'm real," I said. "I know it's been a hot minute."

She smiled as her eyes filled with tears.

"Sure has," she said while hugging me tightly.

I hugged her back.

I was glad to see her again.

After a few minutes, Ezra finally let go of me. She stood up and walked around her desk.

"I'm such a mess," she said while wiping her tears.

"You're not a mess," I said while standing up with her.

"You just missed little old me, apparently."

She laughed to herself while continuing to wipe her tears.

"I owe you an apology," she said while looking at me.

"What for?" I asked.

"I was a jerk," she said. "I unfriended you."

"Is that still in play?" I asked.

"Yeah, that's why I'm crying over your return," she said sarcastically. "Of course it's not in play any more. Once you were gone, I quickly realized no one could top you. You're the perfect combination of idiot and loser."

"Thanks?" I said with a slight chuckle. "That freshman girl didn't beat me?"

"No, I actually ended up kicking her ass a few days after you left," Ezra said while holding back her laughter.

"Why?" I asked, confused.

"She was saying how your disappearance was the best thing that could've happened to me," Ezra explained. "She was also telling me how I needed to stop being upset over my best friend's disappearance."

"That is just rude," I said.

"I know," Ezra said. "That's why I kicked her ass."

"Did you get in trouble?" I asked.

"Of course," she said. "I got three days of suspension."

"That's not that bad," I said.

"No," she said. "It was worth her broken nose."

"You broke her nose?" I asked, surprised.

"Yeah," she said. "Her family wanted to press charges, but my dad was too drunk to negotiate."

"At least your dad's dumb life choices helped you once," I said.

"I know, right," she said with a smile.

We stood there laughing for a minute before the bell rang.

"Dumb bell," I said.

"I know," she said. "You better sit down. You've missed a lot of school."

"I actually did it at home," I said while walking back.

"How?" she asked, confused. "How long have you been back?"

"Two weeks," I answered her.

"And I didn't know?" she said, surprised.

"I didn't have my phone," I said. "And my parents didn't want people to know I was back for some weird reason."

"They'll pay later," she said jokingly.

I walked over to my seat while laughing at Ezra.

I quickly sat down and waited for Mrs. Jones to walk in, which didn't take long.

"Sorry guys," Mrs. Jones said while walking in. "The printer was being a butt."

Mrs. Jones walked in and looked right over at me and smiled.

"Morning, Aaron," she said.

"Morning," I replied.

"Aaron's alive?" one kid shouted from the back of the classroom.

"Thankfully," Mrs. Jones said to the class. "Now, no one bombard him with questions; he's already been through enough."

"Yes, mam," Alex said from behind me.

Mrs. Jones smiled and walked over to her desk.

During class I made a great discovery. I was one day ahead of the rest of the kids, so everything was really easy.

I was always the first to answer and have it right.

Everyone was so surprised one kid even shouted, "How is he doing so well? He was dead for like a month!"

Mrs. Jones gave him a dirty look while I just laughed.

The rest of my morning was about the same. Everyone was surprised to see me, and then they were even more surprised to find out I knew what I was doing.

It was also a treat when I found out Mr. Smith was properly arrested.

He deserved life in prison, and I hoped he'd get it.

He was the definition of a teacher that was just in it for the money.

My day seemed to go by quickly. It didn't seem to slow down till lunch. During lunch, I got to chill and catch up with Ezra more.

"It's nice to have someone to sit with for once," Ezra said as I sat down with my lunch tray.

I looked over at her and smiled.

I quickly noticed that she had no lunch tray by her.

"Where's your food?" I asked.

"Oh, that," she said. "School lunch is gross, so I stopped getting it."

I looked at her with a weird look.

"You sure that's why?" I asked. "Feel free to talk to me. I know I just got back, but that doesn't mean I can't be there for you."

"It's nothing," she said.

"Ezra," I said. "I'm gonna throw this PB&J at your head."

"Please don't," she said, annoyed.

"You have a hood to protect your hair," I said.

"Yeah, but what's gonna protect my hood?" she asked.

"Fate," I said.

"You're weird," she said.

"You want a baby carrot?" I asked.

"I'm good," she said.

"Suit yourself," I said while beginning to stuff my face.

I couldn't believe that Alex was right. Ezra had stopped eating.

I hoped he just didn't pay attention to her, but I guess he did.

"So why do you wear a hood now?" I asked.

"I don't know," she said. "I just do."

"You should take it off," I said. "I missed seeing your beautiful poofy brown hair."

"Well, it doesn't look beautiful right now," she said.

"Come on," I said while still stuffing my face.

"You get ten seconds," she said.

"All right," I said.

She hesitantly pulled her hood down and revealed her messy hair. It looked strange. Some pieces didn't even look attached.

"Is your hair falling out?" I asked.

"Of course not," she said while quickly pulling her hood back up.

That move was a mistake on Ezra's part. The second the hood was over her head, a chunk of hair fell onto the table.

"Ezra," I said.

She quickly grabbed her hair clump and stood up.

"I gotta go," she said in a panicked tone.

She quickly rushed out of the lunch room. I followed her.

I needed her to tell me what was going on. There was only so much information I could get from Alex King.

Ezra was the only one who could give me the whole story.

"Ezra!" I shouted as I followed her into the hallway.

"Aaron, please go finish your food," she said while continuing to walk forward.

"Ezra, please come talk to me," I said. "Look, I know you haven't been eating. I learned it from Alex. He's worried about you. I'm worried about you."

"Aaron, he was lying!" she shouted at me while turning around.

"Was he, though?" I asked while walking over to her. "'Cause last time I checked, you had extremely healthy hair, and now it's falling out. Hair loss is a sign of malnutrition, Ezra. I'm not stupid."

"I never said you were," she said, annoyed.

"Okay, we've both agreed I'm not an idiot," I said. "Now, please tell me what's going on. I need to hear it from you."

"Why?" she shouted at me. "You already figured out what's happening."

"Why'd you stop eating?" I asked. "Alex had a guess, but I don't know if it was right or not."

"Stress," she said.

"What could've possibly stressed you out so much that you stopped eating?" I shouted.

Ezra took a deep breath before answering me.

"Thinking I caused my best friend to disappear forever," she said.

"Why would you think that?" I asked.

"I don't know," she said as tears filled her eyes. "I just missed you, and my brain made me feel guilty as a stupid way of comfort."

"I'm sorry that happened to you," I said. "I'm here now, though."

357

"Yeah," she said while looking up at me.

"Let me help you get your health back in order," I said.

"I'll go to the lunch line with you every day," I said. "I'll help you find treatments for your hair. I'll do whatever you need me to."

"The lunch line is not an option for me," Ezra said quietly. "My dad found out I wasn't eating and got excited. He thinks that having one less mouth to feed is a great way to save money."

"Your dad is the definition of a scumbag," I said. "I'll get you a lunch tomorrow."

"Really?" she said, surprised.

"Really," I said. "I want my best friend to feel a hundred percent again. Even if that means I have to eat some pineapple pizza."

Ezra laughed and smiled at me.

"I knew you were irreplaceable," she said.

I smiled at her and patted her on the shoulder.

"Let's get back into the cafeteria before a lunch lady throws a corndog," I said.

Ezra laughed and followed me back into the cafeteria.

The rest of that day flew by, and before I knew it, I was bringing Ezra lunch to school the next day. She couldn't eat the whole thing, but I was glad she was eating something. Seeing her finally eat again was the highlight of my day.

Throughout the week, her portions grew more and more. It filled me with joy to know I was helping someone I cared so much about.

That week flew by, and before I knew it, it was Friday, and Ezra had eaten her fourth meal of the week. She was already looking better, and that made me glad.

The week almost played out perfectly. It would've been a hundred percent perfect if Dave never showed up. He came out of nowhere and quickly ruined my whole week.

"Hey, Aaron!" he shouted.

I quickly turned around and looked at him.

"What do you want, Dave?" I asked while coming to a stop.

"Where's your sister?" he asked.

"Effie?" I said, confused.

"I'm not looking for a child!" he shouted. "Where's my girlfriend?"

Everyone's eyes quickly turned on me. They all wanted to know what I was going to say to him.

"Dave, she's gone," I said. "I'm sorry."

"You were gone too!" he shouted. "Why are you here, and she's not?"

"Dave, she passed away. I'm sorry," I said.

"Why is she dead, and you aren't?" he shouted.

"I don't know," I said.

"Well, that's just stupid!" he shouted. "It should've been you!"

I froze. I didn't know what to say.

"She was smarter than you!" Dave shouted. "She was prettier than you! She was a better person! Why did she die?"

"I don't know!" I shouted.

"She probably hates you!" he shouted. "She knows she deserves to be here more than you!"

My eyes started to water. I couldn't believe a person could be so cruel.

"Dave, please stop," I said as a tear rolled down my cheek.

"Why?" he asked. "Is it because you know I'm right?"

I stood there, not knowing what to say.

"Answer me, Aaron," he said as he got closer to me.

"You can shut up now," I said.

"Is it because I'm right?" he shouted again.

At that moment, I completely lost it.

"Yes!" I screamed. "I know it's my fault! It should've been me! I don't deserve to be here!"

Everyone froze. No one expected that reaction from me, not even Ezra. The silence wasn't broken until one of Dave's friends butted into the conversation.

"Why do you care so much about his sister?" he asked Dave. "You didn't even like her. It was a dare."

Dave froze. He clearly didn't want anyone to know that.

"What?" I screamed. "You dated my sister for a dare, and you have the audacity to make me feel like shit!"

"I loved her," he said. "I swear."

I walked closer to him while my eyes filled with anger.

"If you really loved her, you would've known that she loves family more than anything," I whispered to his face. "So she'd want me to do this."

Then I punched Dave in the face. He instantly fell to the ground in pain.

"What on earth!" he shouted while holding his face.

"Oops," I said. "Guess I forgot I can be an asshole too."

Dave stood up and looked at me.

"You'll pay for this," he said.

"Can't wait," I said while walking away.

As I walked down the halls, I felt like a king. Everyone was looking at me like I was an army soldier that just saved a country of puppies. It felt amazing.

Sadly my heroic walk was cut short when I heard my name over the intercom.

Aaron Cripple, please come to the principal's office.

"Shit," I said to myself.

I knew I was in deep trouble.

I made my way to the office to see a pissed-off principal sitting at her desk.

"In my defense, he deserved it," I said as I sat down.

"Aaron," she said. "No student deserves to be punched in the face."

"This one did," I said. "Trust me."

"You're not helping your case," she said.

"Sorry," I said.

"Aaron," she said. "I know you've been going through hard times. So I'm just going to make you leave early today. You'll be allowed back Monday. Please take this weekend to think about what you've done."

"Yes, mam," I said.

I sat in the office for another fifteen minutes before Carl showed up and took me to the car. He was so mad at me until I told him why I punched Dave across the face. After that, he decided to buy me an ice cream cone.

He wanted to reward me for honoring Jaelyn. He even admitted that she was probably rooting me on from the afterlife. I agreed with him a hundred percent.

Once we got home, I just chilled in my room and played on my computer. My night seemed like it would be pretty normal until I found something strange. It was an old note.

I picked it up and instantly received a face full of dust.

"How long has this been here?" I asked myself.

I opened up and read the first line. It was from Jaelyn...

361

Chapter 27

I held the note in my hand like it was gold. This was written before Jaelyn had passed. How did I just find this now?

I was shocked at what I was looking at. It felt like a jewel.

I knew I had to read it. I didn't care how much I started crying. I needed to know what Jaelyn wrote to me before meeting her fate.

So just like that, I started to read it to myself.

Hey, Aaron, it's Jaelyn; I hope you find this. Sorry if this seems to annoy you. I just needed to say some things that I can't bring myself to say to your face. I know you've been going through a lot. I know you're hurting physically and mentally. I can see it; I'm your sister, after all. I don't know what or who is doing this to you; all I know is I want you to be happy again. I don't know what it'll take to get you to that point, but I just want you to know I'm here for you, and if you need me to, I'll help you finish whatever it is you got yourself into. I know you don't quit things; you never have. We have distanced a little bit lately, but I doubt you've lost your determination. I don't want to take that trait away from you. I want to help you embrace it. Aaron, I love you. I want the best for you. I want you to embrace everything about yourself. You're perfect the way you are, and it makes me sad that not everyone sees that. I won't waste any more of your time. Just know I want to see you succeed. Complete what you started. It's who you are. Please don't lose that. The world may throw punches at you and break you down, but I want you to punch it back even harder. I know you can. I love you, my favorite brother. Don't hesitate to ask me for help. I'll always be there for you, I pinky promise.

P.S.– We need to go out sometime. I miss our days out.

Love, your favorite sister– Jaelyn

The second I finished reading the letter, I fell down to the floor in tears. I missed Jaelyn way more than I could've ever imagined.

She really was my natural-born best friend. We knew everything about each other.

All she wanted was to help me fix my messed-up life, but instead, my problems became hers, and she perished.

I sat on the floor for quite a while before finally pulling myself together. I stood up and sat the letter down on my desk.

I moved over to my bed and laid down. I just wanted to go to sleep and forget about this day, but that didn't happen. Instead of me dozing off, I lay there wide awake, thinking about the letter.

Jaelyn talked about the determination she thought I had. She thought I could do anything if I put my mind to it. I didn't think that was true, but the more I thought about it, the more I realized she was right and that only meant one thing. I had to complete what I had started. I wanted to be the person Jaelyn saw me as.

Once I realized that this mission was far from over, I knew I had to take the next step to complete it. I had to find out more, and I knew exactly how I would do that.

The first step in my plan took place Saturday morning. I went to visit an old friend. I hadn't known her for long, but I knew she was one of my best hopes in finding out more information about the VK and finally stopping them.

"Hey, stranger," I said while walking into her hospital room.

"Well, if it isn't the boy downstairs," she said as I walked over. "What brings you here?"

"I need your help," I said.

"With what?" she asked.

"Stopping the VK once and for all," I answered her.

She looked at me like I was crazy.

"You realize last time you tried to do that, you almost died, right?" she said.

"Ivy, please," I said.

"Fine," she said. "What do you need to know?"

"Did you guys move around places usually?" I asked.

"Are you talking about the other VK kids and me?" she asked.

"Yes," I said.

"We moved between five different locations," she answered me.

"Do you know where those places are?" I asked.

"No, but I know how you can find that out," she said.

"How?" I asked, intrigued.

"Donald kept a list of the locations at the school, in his classroom," she said. "He had a horrible memory, so he needed them. I know he was arrested, but if those locations are still there, you can probably figure out where the kids are being kept."

"Wow," I said. "That'll help a lot. Thank you."

"No problem," she said. "You're one of the few hopes those kids have. The police aren't doing shit."

"I know," I said. "That's one of the reasons I'm

continuing."

"Well, good for you," she said. "I gotta go to bingo night now. It's the highlight of my life."

"Have fun, you old lady," I said as I walked out.

"Aaron!" She shouted.

I quickly whipped my head around and looked at her.

"Good luck," she said.

"Thanks," I said while making my way down the hall.

I couldn't believe what I had just discovered. If I could narrow it down and find the proper location, I could actually save people.

I knew I probably didn't have the highest chance, but I had to pretend like I did. If I lived my life like every chance was low, I'd never get anywhere. In order to get somewhere, you must act like there is zero chance of failure. That is one of the only ways to succeed in life. Pretend success is the only option.

The rest of my weekend seemed to drag. All I could think about was going to school Monday and getting that list and figuring out where the VK was, and finally putting a stop to them.

Even though my weekend dragged on, Monday did eventually come. I was nervous but also excited.

I had decided that I would stay for morning classes, but the moment fourth hour was over, I would give Ezra her lunch and then run to Mr. Smith's old classroom and look for the paper. It seemed like a solid plan, so I did it.

I waited through my morning classes and then took action the moment the fourth-hour bell rang.

I failed to consider one thing, though, and that was Ezra. Sure, giving her lunch was in my plan, but I never considered how confused she'd be.

I didn't realize it'd be an issue until my plan started coming together.

"Here's your lunch," I said while handing her a grocery bag full of food. "Enjoy it."

I started to walk towards Mr. Smith's old room when Ezra suddenly stopped me.

"What are you doing?" she asked me while grabbing my arm. "The cafeteria's that way."

"I know," I said. "I got other things I have to do."

"Aaron," she said, annoyed. "Last time you skipped lunch, you almost died."

"I know," I said. "Just go eat. I'll be fine."

"No," she said. "It's either you're going to lunch with me, or I'm coming with you."

"Ezra, go to lunch," I said sternly. "You need to eat. Your health still isn't the best."

"Your health isn't that great either!" she shouted.

"I know!" I shouted back. "But it's better than yours!"

Ezra just stood there and looked at me with an ice-cold stare.

"I'm gonna go," I said. "Please go eat."

"Fine," she said, annoyed.

Ezra stormed off to the cafeteria while I made my way to Mr. Smith's old classroom.

The second I walked in, chills ran down my spine. I hated this room more than anything in the world, but I had to continue.

I quickly made my way over to his desk and started looking around. Most of the drawers had been cleaned out, which worried me.

After a few minutes, I started to lose hope when all of a sudden, I felt something. It was a piece of paper taped underneath the desk. I quickly ripped it off and looked at it.

The paper had a list of five locations just like Ivy said it would, but it also had something else which made that little piece of paper even more useful.

It had arrows going from each place. It was showing the order they moved in. So all I had to do was figure out where I was at, which wasn't hard to do. Only one of the five locations was in Kentucky, so I just figured out which one that was and then followed the arrow to a place called Snowballs Cabin.

The name instantly rang a bell, and then I remembered where it was. I pulled out my phone and looked it up just to be safe, and sure enough, it was exactly where I thought it was. It was about a mile away from school.

Once I figured out where I needed to go, I grabbed the paper and my phone and went to leave school. All of a sudden, I heard someone call my name.

"Aaron!" Ezra shouted from behind me.

"What?" I said, frustrated as I turned around.

"Where are you going?" she asked me while walking closer.

"A place," I said. "Now, if you don't mind, I'm gonna leave now."

"I do mind, actually," she said, annoyed.

"Ezra, I'm leaving whether you like it or not," I said, still annoyed.

Before I could start to walk away, Ezra snatched the paper from my hand and started reading it.

"What is this?" she asked me sternly.

"A piece of paper," I said. "Can I have it back?"

Before Ezra answered me, she inspected the paper more closely.

It didn't take her long to realize what it was from.

"This is from Mr. Smith's room, isn't it?" she said while holding the paper up. "Why are you going somewhere that involves a group that tried to kill you?"

"That's none of your concern!" I shouted.

"Yes, it is!" She shouted back. "You're my best friend! I can't lose you. Did you see how much it destroyed me the first time? Imagine how upset I'll be if you actually die."

"Ezra, please just trust me," I said. "This is for the best."

"Aaron, don't go!" she shouted. "You have so much to live for! Don't let this destroy your life."

"It already has!" I shouted. "It killed my sister. It gives me nightmares and panic attacks. I have major trust issues now, and thanks to this piece of shit, I feel like I deserve to die!"

Ezra just stood there frozen. She didn't know what to say.

"I'm gonna go now," I said.

"I'm coming," she said. "Let me help you, please."

At that moment, I realized I was gonna have to trick Ezra; it was the only way to get past her.

"Fine," I said. "I gotta get something from the janitor's closet before we go, though."

"Okay," she said while walking over to the janitor's closet.

I felt bad about what I was going to do, but I knew I had no choice.

I made my way over to the closet as Ezra opened the door.

"What do you need?" she asked me while looking in the closet.

I looked around the closet and randomly pointed to something in the back.

"That black thing right over there," I said.

"Okay," she said while walking into the closet.

Once Ezra had both feet in the closet, I quickly slammed the door shut and moved one of the hall chairs in front of it.

"Aaron!" Ezra shouted at me. "Let me out!"

"I'm sorry, Ezra," I said. "You'll understand why I had to do this later."

I quickly walked back to the front doors and made my way outside.

I ran over to the bike rack to see whose bike was free to take. Thankfully I found a blue bike my size that was not chained up.

I quickly hopped on it and started to pedal to Snowball's Cabin.

I was pedaling as fast as possible. I knew I had to get to Snowball's Cabin quickly. I just hoped everyone would be okay when I got there.

After what felt like years of peddling, I finally arrived. I quickly hopped off the bike and ran to the cabin.

Snowball's cabin was a place where people could isolate themselves and feel relaxed. It was only available in the colder months (October to February). So it made sense why the VK would be hiding out here. It was nearly April. The place was practically abandoned.

Once I made my way to the cabin, I looked through the window.

I had stayed in the cabin with my family once when I was younger, and let's just say the cabin looked exactly the same.

I couldn't see any signs of activity, so I decided to just go in.

I walked over to the door and pushed it open.

The second I opened the door, the smell of freshly cut wood filled my nose. It felt kinda soothing. I remembered the cabin smelling the same from when I was nine.

After a few seconds of just taking everything in, I fully entered the cabin. The floorboards creaked under me after every step I took. It made me feel like I was in some kind of movie. I just didn't know the genre it made me think of.

I continued to look around the cabin until I heard footsteps behind me. I quickly grabbed a pan from the kitchen and turned around.

I was filled with shock when I saw who was behind me.

"Morgan?" I said surprised. "Are you okay?"

"Why wouldn't I be?" she asked.

"You disappeared," I said. "You had a lot of people worried sick."

"My bad," she said. "I guess I didn't realize people would actually miss me."

I looked over at her and set the pan down.

"Well, I'm just glad you're okay," I said.

She looked at me and smiled.

"So why are you here?" she asked. "Snowball's Cabin isn't in service right now."

"I have reason to believe that the VK is keeping their prisoners here," I answered her. "Why are you here?"

"I have a part-time job here," she answered me. "I'm the lonely worker on cleaning duty today."

"Good for you," I said. "Have you seen anything weird?"

"Nope," she said.

"Okay," I said. "Sorry I intruded."

"It's fine," she said. "Have a good rest of your day."

"You too," I said as I began to walk out.

I walked all the way to the door before I stopped myself.

I didn't know why, but my brain was telling me that

Morgan was lying, and I had to keep looking around the cabin.

"Hey Morgan, I know you didn't see anything strange, but could I still look around?" I asked while walking over.

"Why do you need to look around?" she asked me anxiously.

"I had a really strong lead that something was here, and I can't just ignore that," I said.

"I'd prefer it if you left," she said. "I've got work to do, and I don't want you to get me fired when the other cleaner shows up."

As Morgan said that, I knew her whole story was a hoax.

"You're lying," I said sternly.

"What?" she said, confused. "Why would you think that?"

"You said you were the only worker on cleaning duty today," I said. "Now the second worker's gonna get you fired? It doesn't add up."

"You're annoying," she said.

"I already knew that," I said. "Now, Morgan, where are they?"

"I don't know what you're talking about," she said as she walked closer.

"Yes, you do!" I shouted.

"You're right," she said as her hands started to glow orange. "I wish you could see them. They'd like you."

At that moment, Morgan pointed her glowing hand to my feet.

I was stuck in place. I couldn't move.

"Morgan, what are you doing?" I asked while trying to walk away.

"Helping my daddy," she answered me. "He didn't upgrade my powers for nothing."

I just looked at Morgan with a confused look in my eyes.

"What happened to your dad being the villain?" I shouted.

"I realized that family came before friends," she answered. "So I gotta help him. Even if that means I hurt someone."

I looked her in the eyes and laughed to myself.

"You wouldn't hurt me," I said.

"That's why I'm not going to be hurting you," she said. "I'm just the distraction."

At that moment, I heard the sound of a gun being loaded from behind me.

"Sorry, it had to be this way, Aaron," she said while looking at me.

As soon as Morgan was done talking, I heard the sound of a gunshot. I waited for my death, but it never came. Instead of the bullet piercing through my skull, it hit the ceiling right above us.

Morgan and I both screamed out of fear.

Morgan quickly let go of me and ran back towards the kitchen. I followed in her footsteps and ran back towards the door to avoid the falling ceiling remains.

It thankfully only took a few seconds for everything to calm down.

Once everything was quiet, I looked over at Morgan to see her staring at the door with a surprised look. I turned my head to see what she was looking at. Let's just say our facial expressions quickly matched.

"Ezra?" I shouted in surprise.

"Hello, meanie," she said while helping me up.

"What on earth are you doing here?" I shouted at her.

"Saving your life apparently," she said. "Did you know some guy was trying to shoot you?"

"I figured that out fairly quickly," I said.

"I'm the reason you're not dead," Ezra said while trying to rub it in.

"Yeah," I said, annoyed. "Thanks for the save, but now you are going to leave."

"No," she said. "You need me."

"No, I don't!" I shouted at her.

"Do I need to remind you how you almost died a second ago!" she shouted back.

As I was about to shout back at Ezra, Morgan walked over to us.

"Ezra!" she said, pretending to sound excited. "Thanks for the save, you little hero."

"No problem," Ezra said. "At least you appreciate me."

I took a deep breath and looked over at Morgan.

"Stay the hell away from her, you monster!" I shouted at her.

"Aaron!" Ezra shouted. "Morgan was in the situation with you. She didn't shoot you. Calm down!"

I walked away from Ezra and towards the pile of rubble.

I grabbed a piece of wood and walked back over to them.

Without hesitation, I smacked Morgan over the head with the wood. She instantly fell to the ground as blood dripped from her scalp.

"Aaron!" Ezra screamed at me. "What the hell is wrong with you?"

"Ezra, let me explain," I said.

"This better be a great explanation!" she screamed.

"Morgan lied to me and was helping that guy kill me," I said. "You probably couldn't tell, but Morgan was keeping me still. Morgan was also keeping me from what I was getting to."

"What are you trying to get to?" Ezra asked.

"All the kidnapped kids of the VK." I answered her.

"What's the VK?" she asked.

"I'll answer that later," I said. "I'm gonna go downstairs and look for the kids. If I holler that I found them dial 911 immediately."

"This makes no sense," she said.

"I know," I said. "Just trust me, please."

"Okay, Aaron," she said. "I trust you."

I took a deep breath and quickly walked over to a set of stairs leading to the basement.

It looked dark and creepy, but I knew I had to go down there.

Quickly, before I went downstairs, I ran back over to the kitchen and grabbed the pan, just in case.

I walked back to the top of the staircase and started to make my way down.

The second I entered the basement, I noticed two things. It was dark, and there were a lot of doors.

"Hello?" I shouted, hoping I'd get a response.

No one answered me, but as I walked over to the door of this bigger room, I heard faint whispers.

They all sounded like younger voices, so I had hope.

"Hello?" I said while knocking on the door. "Is anyone in there?"

The whispers continued, but no one answered me. I pressed my ear against the door to hear them better.

"Shut up," I heard a girl whisper.

"Why don't we answer?" another girl asked in a whisper.

"We want to stay alive," a guy answered in an annoyed tone.

"I can hear you," I said to them. "I promise I'm not going to hurt you."

I stood there waiting for a response. It took forever, but someone finally spoke up.

"Why should we trust you?" a guy asked.

"I want to help," I said. "I know what it feels like to be tortured by the idiots of the VK. It's awful."

"Do you really, though?" the guy asked.

"Please," I said. "I escaped with a girl named Ivy Brown. She helped me get here. She wants me to save you guys. She cares about you, and so do I."

The kids froze. I could tell by their silence they knew exactly who Ivy was.

"Is Ivy okay?" another voice asked.

"Yeah," I said to them. "It was clever for you guys to get her out through a vent."

"Thanks," one of the voices said.

"So, how can I help you guys get out of here?" I asked them.

"You'll need a key," someone said. "It might be hanging somewhere."

"Okay," I said to them. "Give me a second."

I quickly ran over to the bottom of the stairs and shouted at Ezra.

"I found them!"

"Okay!" she shouted back.

I quickly ran back towards the door and started looking for a key. Honestly, I didn't think I'd find it. Thankfully for me, though, I found it fairly quickly. I instantly ran back over to the door and unlocked it. The second the door opened, I met the eyes of at least fifty terrified kids.

"Hi," I said to them. "You're all safe now, don't worry. I need all of you to go upstairs. Up there, you'll see my friend Ezra. She's really sweet. She'll make sure everything's okay. Now, is this everyone?"

"There're two kids in filming rooms," one of the older girls said.

"Who are they?" I asked.

"A boy named Chase and a girl named Emma," she answered me.

"All these little rooms are filming rooms, that key should be able to open them right up," another person added.

"The locked ones are the only ones in use," a third person added.

"Okay, thank you guys," I said to them. "Be careful."

"We will," one of them said.

I watched the kids start to walk upstairs before running over to the little rooms. It took me forever to find a locked door, and when I did, I was met with horror.

The second I opened the door, I saw a corpse laying on the floor. I instantly stumbled backward and held my mouth so I wouldn't scream. This kid had been mutilated. His throat was slit open along with his stomach. The floor was covered in blood and guts.

I quickly got out of there and shut the door behind me so I wouldn't pass out.

I stood against the now shut door, trying to calm myself. I was panicking. I knew this boy's death wasn't my fault, but I felt somewhat responsible. After a few minutes, I finally calmed myself down and went to find the other locked door.

It didn't take me long to find it, but it took me a while to work up the courage to open it.

Once I finally did, though, I was met with an empty room.

"Hello?" I said as I walked in.

Before I could fully get my feet in the room, I felt a metal chair smack into my side. I instantly fell to the ground.

I looked up to see a girl holding a chair looking down at me.

Before she had another chance to hit me, I managed to stand up and get a closer look at her.

"Emma?" I said.

She didn't care that I knew her name. She smacked me back down to the ground with her chair. I quickly turned back around to see the chair flying at me again. This time I was able to act quickly, and I grabbed it.

"Emma Grace!" I shouted. "It's me! I'm not going to hurt you."

She quickly looked down at me.

Her eyes widened, and she let go of the chair.

"Aaron?" she said with a shaky voice.

"Yeah," I said while standing up. "Are you okay?"

She looked at me and nodded while tears filled her eyes.

"Sorry," she said while wiping her tears. "I'm just happy to see someone I know."

"It's okay," I said. "Let's go upstairs quickly. Help should be here soon."

"Wait a minute," she said, surprised. "Help? I'm gonna get to go home?"

"Yeah," I said.

She smiled and just looked at me.

"Well, let's not wait any longer," she said while beginning to walk out.

I followed closely behind her.

We started to make our way towards the stairs when I suddenly heard a weird sound.

"Did you hear that?" I asked.

"Yeah," she said in a worried tone.

"I'm gonna go check it out," I said. "If anything goes wrong up there, just know there's a gun by a knocked-out guy in the front yard."

"Okay," she said. "Please be careful, Aaron."

"I will," I said.

Emma Grace quickly walked upstairs while I went towards the noise.

I didn't know what to expect. All I knew were the things I didn't want to see.

I walked over to the door from where the noise was coming from.

I opened it and looked inside to see a huge green blast coming at me.

It all happened so quickly. The blast hit me and sent me twenty feet backward. I smacked down on the hard concrete.

Once I knew I wasn't dead, I looked up to see someone walking toward me.

"I told you I'd see you again," the person said while walking over. "Whether you could predict it or not."

As the figure got closer, I recognized his evil grin.

"Antonio?" I said, surprised.

"Surprised?" he said with a grin. "You had no idea this was going to happen, did you?"

"Umm... No?" I said confused.

"Guess your power doesn't work with a magic block," he said. "I had a feeling my plan would work."

"Your what?" I said confused.

"My plan," he said. "I disguised it so perfectly you didn't even know it was taking place."

I just looked at him in shock. I was so confused.

"A magic block has great properties, you know?" he said. "It feels just like a truth spell, but it acts completely differently."

"So you were never trying to read my mind?" I said, surprised.

"The first time I was," he said. "But after I learned you didn't know anything about your little power, I decided to block it. So no one could use it."

"You jerk," I said.

"Jerk?" he said, confused. "I think mastermind."

"You're evil," I said. "Is this whole magic block thing why an MRI machine nearly exploded?"

"Probably," he said. "It must've been a nice treat for those doctors."

"I can't believe how messed up you are!" I shouted. "You really are a villain, and now thanks to you, Morgan is too!"

"Villains don't exist, kid," he said. "It's all based on point of view, and I did not change Morgan. I just pushed her towards the better direction for her life, a life without you interfering with it."

I just looked at him with rage in my eyes. I still couldn't believe what I was hearing.

"What do you actually want, Antonio?" I asked while standing up. "I'm assuming you didn't just want a conversation."

"I want to see you perish," he said. "You destroyed my whole operation, and now I'm gonna destroy your life."

I looked at him in disgust.

"Haven't you already done that enough?" I asked.

"I guess," he said. "I'll just use this precious time to remind you of it."

Before I had a chance to respond, Antonio disappeared.

"Hey!" I shouted. "I wasn't done with you!"

"Were you done with me?" I heard a young voice ask me.

I quickly whipped my head around to see Luna standing behind me.

"When did you get here?" I asked.

"I never got to come here," she said. "My life was cut short thanks to you."

"What?" I said confused.

"They killed me," she said. "Just like they should've done to you."

Before I could respond, Luna's eyes rolled to the back of her head, and she fell to the ground.

"Luna!" I shouted as I ran over.

I tried to help her, but the second my hand touched her, she turned to dust.

"No!" I shouted.

"Guess you care about her more than your own sisters," I heard a voice say behind me.

I turned around once again to see Jaelyn and Effie standing behind me.

"This isn't real," I said to them. "Jaelyn's dead!"

"So am I," Effie said.

"No," I said. "You're at school doing basic math and learning how to spell."

"I wish I was," she said while looking at Jaelyn. "We both wish we were still in school."

"Shut up!" I screamed at them. "None of you are real! Effie and Luna aren't dead!"

"How do you know?" I heard a deep voice ask from behind me.

I turned around to see a face I hadn't seen in years.

"Dad?" I said confused.

"You don't know if they're alive," he said. "You're stuck in this figment of imagination."

"Stop talking!" I shouted. "This definitely isn't real, especially with you here."

"Harsh," he said. "I should be sad right now, but I'm actually thrilled. Wanna know why?"

"Sure?" I said, confused.

"You get to finally see all the people's lives you've ruined!" he shouted.

As his voice began to echo, a blast of light appeared right in front of him. Behind the light stood many people that were close to me.

"Why?" my mom asked.

"Why can't we be happy?" Alex King asked.

"Why does it all revolve around you?" Carl asked.

"Why am I just the side character?" Teagan asked.

"Why am I the villain?" Morgan asked.

"Why don't you help me?" Ezra shouted.

"What are you doing?" Emma Grace asked me in a teary tone.

I was frozen. I knew this wasn't real but being surrounded by everyone I cared about while they guilt-tripped me made my anxiety hit new levels.

"Stop!" I screamed. "I'm sorry!"

"Are you, though?" Effie asked me while walking closer.

Before I could respond, I started to get surrounded. Everyone walked towards me until I was pinned against a wall.

"Leave me alone!" I screamed as everyone hovered above me.

I covered my ears, but I could still hear everyone clearly. This was unbearable.

Thankfully it all went quiet after a gunshot.

I opened my eyes to see Antonio's lifeless body lying in front of me with a gun in his hand.

"What the hell?" I asked myself.

I looked up from his body to see Emma Grace standing back with a gun in her hand.

"Emma?" I said confused.

She quickly put the gun down and ran over to me.

"Are you okay?" she asked me in a worried tone.

I nodded my head at her.

She grabbed my hands and helped me up to my feet.

"I guess you got a lot of girls who like to save you," she said jokingly.

I grinned at her.

She grabbed my hand once again and led me upstairs.

As Emma led me to the front door, I noticed that Morgan had left. That was the least of my worries, though.

As Emma Grace opened the door and pulled me outside, everyone cheered.

Ezra ran over to me and wrapped her arms around me.

"You idiot," she said. "I thought I lost you."

I hugged Ezra back for a second before pulling her off.

"This was worth almost dying for," I said.

"Why'd you do all of this?" she asked. "I mean, there has to be a reason."

I took a deep breath before answering her.

"Well, this was originally all for Emma," I said. "I love her so much, and I couldn't bear the thought of never seeing her again."

"Makes sense," Ezra said.

"Surprised you even had to ask," I said jokingly.

Ezra smiled at me for a second before her face changed to her idea face.

"You'll thank me later," she said. "Emma! Aaron needs to tell you something!"

Emma quickly walked over and looked at me.

"What's up?" she asked.

"Be honest with her," Ezra whispered in my ear before taking a few steps back.

I took a deep breath and looked at Emma.

"I like you," I said. "I have for a long time. When you went missing, I couldn't stand the thought of never seeing you again, so I made it my mission to save you. I know it sounds stupid, and I'm sorry."

Before I could finish my rant to Emma, she grabbed my face and kissed me.

"You kissed me?" I said confused.

Emma just looked at me and smiled.

"Yes!" Ezra shouted. "I've been shipping you guys since seventh grade!"

Emma and I just looked at each other and laughed.

"I love you," I said.

"I love you too," she said.

We slowly leaned toward each other and kissed again. This felt like a dream come true. All the kids started to cheer, but none of their cheering was louder than Ezra's.

This was it, I thought to myself. Everything I had been working for had led me to this moment. I was kissing the love of my life.

After a few moments, we heard police sirens followed by tons of cars. Everyone's families were there, along with at least twenty ambulances and police cars.

Emma and I pulled away from each other and looked back to see what we had all been waiting for.

"This is it," I said to Emma. "You get to go home and live your life."

"Thanks to you," she said while giving me a hug. "I owe you my life."

I hugged her back while officers came over. I quickly heard Emma's family calling her.

"I'll see you again soon," I said. "Go see them; they've missed you so much."

Emma smiled and gave me a quick goodbye kiss, then ran over to her family.

Watching her jump into their arms made me smile from ear to ear.

"This is amazing," Ezra said while walking over to me.

"I know," I said. "I feel like such a hero."

"You are one!" Ezra said. "You deserved to have the best first kiss in history."

"I guess," I said jokingly.

"And I deserve a pineapple pizza later," she said.

"Oh my gosh," I said while laughing.

"Come on!" she said. "We can eat it while rewatching your first kiss."

"You got it on video, didn't you?" I asked.

"Of course," she said. "It was Cripple history."

"I hate you," I said with a smile.

"I love you too," she said jokingly.

I couldn't help but laugh. This was what true happiness felt like. It felt like a perfect ending.

Chapter 28

Before everyone knew it, May had rolled around, and that meant senior graduation, which we knew we couldn't miss.

Throughout the last month, I was happy to see all the VK kids' lives go back to normal, especially Emma. It was nice to see her return to school and quickly brighten up the halls again.

To my surprise, Teagan remained friends with Emma and me, even though we were officially dating.

Teagan had become a good friend, which was why we had to see him cross that stage at graduation.

The day of graduation was set up to be perfect. The weather was beautiful, and I had a beautiful date.

Emma and I had gotten so close recently. It made me happy.

At the graduation, we got to see all the seniors for the last time.

It was weird seeing the kids I once saw as the big dogs of middle school crossing the stage. I knew every single one of them, and they knew me.

As the seniors crossed the stage, Emma and I cheered, but we saved our loudest cheer for Teagan.

He looked so happy to finally be crossing that stage. High school seemed endless to him, until now, of course.

After the seniors crossed the stage, we got to hear speeches from administrators and a few students, including Teagan, which was surprising.

I guess if your dad rigs the high school student council

election freshman year and you get elected president, you get a speech at graduation.

Emma and I found that hilarious.

Even though Teagan didn't earn this speech the right way, we still paid close attention and listened to every word as if he was talking to us.

We both knew Teagan wanted to leave this school on a great note, so we were excited to see what he came up with.

"Good morning, family and friends," Teagan said as he started giving his speech. *"If you didn't already know, this year has been crazy for many students, including me. It included loss and grief. This school year, we lost many amazing people. Some returned, but some moved on to a better place. Even though that sounds depressing, it can actually show some good. It shows the world how strong the individuals are at this school. Ninety-nine percent of students successfully passed their grade level, including some who disappeared. That says a lot about our community and who we are as people. To the class of 2013, I'm proud to be graduating beside you. I'm proud to call most of you my friends. And to the younger classmen watching, I will miss you guys. Some of you are pretty chill and fun to be around. I hope as we leave, the people of this school will only become stronger. I don't see any reason why they shouldn't. The new upperclassmen are strong people, and I don't question their ability to make a difference in this world at all. Before I wrap my speech up, I gotta do the sappy part where I thank people. Thank you to my family for pushing me to succeed. Thank you to my friends for teaching me the difference between right and wrong. And thank you to my teachers for putting up with me for all four years of high school. I love all of you guys, and I will miss everyone I met here at South Ray High. As I leave you guys*

today, please promise me you'll stay amazing. Keep striving and remember to always look out for each other. You never know what someone's going through. Be the better person. Strive to succeed. It'll pay off. I know it will. Thank you!"

The whole crowd instantly stood up and cheered. Teagan's speech was amazing.

Emma and I looked at each other with our mouths wide open. Tegan's speech was perfect. It showed everyone who we were at South Ray High, which was needed after the year we had.

After the graduation, Emma and I instantly walked over to Teagan.

"Amazing speech," I said.

"Thanks," he said. "It took me quite a while."

"I bet," I said.

"Congrats on graduating high school," Emma said.

"You never thought I'd get here," Teagan said.

"You're not totally wrong," Emma said jokingly.

We all started laughing so much. We could've talked for hours, but Teagan's family wanted to see him.

"I gotta go," he said to us. "I'll see you later."

"See you!" Emma and I shouted as Teagan walked away.

We held hands and walked over to my family, who had been playing with a frisbee the whole graduation.

"We're back!" I shouted.

"How was it?" Mom asked.

"It was good," I said. "You should've been there. Teagan gave an amazing speech."

"You can tell us about it later," Mom said while throwing the frisbee to Carl.

"They really didn't care about this graduation," Emma

whispered.

"I know," I whispered back.

Shortly after Emma and I stopped whispering, Effie ran over to us.

"Can we make matching rainbow loom bracelets later?" she asked us.

"Not tonight," I said.

"Aww," she said.

"We'll do it another night, I pinky promise," I said while holding out my pinky.

"What's a pinky promise?" Effie asked.

"It's a promise that I'll never break," I said. "You secure it with a pinky shake."

Effie looked at me with a smile and shook my pinky.

"I like pinky promises," she said with a smile.

"Good," I said. "I use them a lot."

Effie smiled and ran back to Mom and Carl.

"Teaching her the old family pinky promise?" Emma asked.

"Of course," I said. "Gotta teach them young."

Emma smiled and looked at me.

"Didn't Jaelyn teach you what a pinky promise was?" Emma asked me,

"Yeah," I said. "She pinky promised me we would build a couch fort."

"That's a good promise," she said.

"It was the best couch fort ever," I said while looking up.

Emma looked at me and then looked up at the sky with me.

"She's proud of you," Emma said.

"I hope so," I said. "I miss her."

"I miss her too," Emma said. "Just remember not to dread

her name. She would hate to be remembered as a feeling of sorrow or guilt."

"I know," I said.

As I stared up at the clouds, I felt at ease. I had nothing to fear.

I had my family, friends, and an amazing girlfriend. It was my perfect ending.

If I could've shared a message with the world at that moment, it would've been that great things take time. They take work. No one ever achieved anything great by sitting around.

I believe most people that have achieved greatness have been to hell and back. That's what achieving greatness looks like. It's not a trip to the park. It's a long hike through deserts and storms; it's getting smacked down by a wave enough times until you learn to push it back.

Life is the ultimate test, and to get the best results, you must work hard. I've learned that, and I hope others can too.

9 781800 747838